Under the Mistletoe

KATIE FLYNN

Under the Mistletoe

CENTURY

1 3 5 7 9 10 8 6 4 2

Century
20 Vauxhall Bridge Road
London SW1V 2SA

Century is part of the Penguin Random House group of companies
whose addresses can be found at global.penguinrandomhouse.com.

Penguin
Random House
UK

First published in Great Britain by Century in 2020

www.penguin.co.uk

A CIP catalogue record for this book is available from the British Library.

ISBN 9781529123883

Typeset in 13/16.5 pt Palatino LT Pro
by Integra Software Services Pvt. Ltd, Pondicherry

Printed and bound in Great Britain by Clays Ltd, Elcograf S.p.A.

Penguin Random House is committed to a sustainable future for
our business, our readers and our planet. This book is made from
Forest Stewardship Council® certified paper.

Acknowledgements

The Naafi girls.

Dad, the man who helped me carry on xx

Prologue

24 December 1923

Agnes McKinley pulled the large ring of keys from her skirt pocket and went through them until she found the correct one for the front door to the orphanage. As she slid it into the lock she paused momentarily. Was it her imagination or did she just hear movement coming from the other side of the door? She listened hard, then froze. There was no doubt about it, she definitely heard something that time! Someone was moving around outside, trying their best not to be heard. She pursed her lips. It'll be one of those nasty little brats, she thought bitterly, no doubt thinking that just because it's Christmas Eve, they can have themselves some fun, larking about in the snow, probably making themselves a snowman to scare one of us when we open the door. She nodded to herself. That's what she could hear, the sound of snow being rolled into a ball. She jutted her chin in a determined fashion; she was going to give someone a nasty surprise! She would catch them unawares and smash their snowman to smithereens before carting them off to see Mrs Ancrum. She grinned maliciously. Mrs Ancrum and her husband had managed Greystones Orphanage for over ten years, and in that time they had come up with a variety of punishments which would soon make a naughty child regret their decision to play in the snow on Christmas Eve.

Seizing the tarnished brass handle in her skinny white fingers, she whipped the door open shouting, 'Gotcha!' Much to her surprise, instead of looking into the upturned face of one of the girls, she found herself looking down at the balding head of an elderly man. He was leaning over something lying at the top of the snow-covered steps, whilst he retrieved his homburg hat which she assumed must have fallen off his head. He stood up hastily, glaring at Agnes, then brushed the snow off his hat and rammed it back onto his head.

Agnes, however, was more interested in the small bundle lying on the steps. Bending down she tweaked the blanket to one side. Eyes narrowing, her jaw tightened angrily.

She spoke through pursed lips. 'I don't know what you think you're doing, but you can ruddy well take it with you!' Standing up she thrust the bundle towards the man who backed away, his hands held up in a placating manner.

'You've got the wrong end of the stick,' he spluttered. 'This is nothing to do with me.'

Glaring at him, she indicated the thick undisturbed snow which carpeted the ground. 'Well, whoever dumped it must've flown away, 'cos yours are the only footprints in the snow!'

He glanced at the footprints which led to the front door, then his eyes darted wildly around before fixing Agnes with a steely glare. 'Whoever abandoned her must've done it before it started snowing!' He shook his head in disgust, adding 'stupid woman' as he did so.

'I'm stupid?' spat Agnes, furious that he had the audacity to call her stupid, when he'd made such a ridiculous statement. 'If they'd dumped her before it started snowing she'd be *under* the snow, not on *top* of it!' Muttering 'idiot' beneath her breath, she was about to carry on with her verbal attack when something he had said caused her to stop in her tracks. She re-ran his statement through her head, then pointed an accusing finger at his chest. 'You said "her". How do you know it's a girl?'

He gawped at her, a muscle twitching in his jaw as he groped for a response, but Agnes wasn't going to give him time to think of any more pathetic excuses. She moved the baby's blankets to one side and peered down before covering her back up. 'I *knew* you were lying!' she said, her eyes narrowing even further. 'Typical man! Thinking you can just dump your unwanted baby willy-nilly, like a sack of rubbish, assuming that we have to take her in just because we're an orphanage.'

He wore a thunderous expression as he struck the ground with the tip of his walking cane. 'She is *not* my ...'

Perhaps it was the fact that this man's attitude towards his daughter reminded her of her own baby's father, or perhaps she was just tired of listening to him; either way, Agnes had had enough. Stepping forward, she thrust the baby into his arms, causing him to drop his cane.

Shocked to find himself holding the baby, he stared at her in disbelief. 'I – I ...'

'I – I,' she mimicked with a sneer. 'Take your baby and bugger off else I'll call the police!'

The man's sharp blue eyes narrowed at the mention of the police and he stared at her with a look of pure venom, as flecks of white spittle became visible in the corners of his mouth. 'You dare to threaten me?' he bellowed, his face turning puce as anger swept through him. 'I ...' He stopped abruptly as the sound of his own voice reverberated around the empty streets. His eyes darted to the building behind her. The last thing he needed was to draw more attention to his current predicament. Taking a few deep breaths in an effort to calm himself, he stared down at the baby in his arms whilst he tried to think of a different approach. Looking up, he tried to reason with Agnes. 'Why are you making such a big deal out of it? This is an orphanage. That's what you do, take in unwanted children. What difference is one more going to make?'

She cast him a withering look. 'One more miserable mouth to feed? One more bed to provide? One more unwanted brat to clothe? Oh no,' she cried in mocking tones, 'one more won't make any difference!' She paused. Something had been bothering her about the man but she hadn't been able to put her finger on it until now. Folding her arms, she stared at him

4

accusingly. 'You're not even from around these parts yet here you are dumping your kid on our doorstep like it doesn't matter. What's wrong with orphanages where you come from? All full up, are they?'

Unnerved that the woman might have guessed his regional identity, he began to splutter a protest. 'I don't know what you're talking about . . .'

'I knew I recognised your accent!' Agnes interrupted. 'You're a Scouser! A posh one, I'll grant you, but a Scouser nonetheless.' Her eyes travelled from the homburg hat which adorned his head, down to the black woollen tailored coat and the gold wedding band, finishing with his highly polished Oxford shoes. She appeared to come to a decision. 'Doesn't look to me as though you can't afford a child, so I reckon you got some poor girl pregnant, then fetched her up here to Glasgow where no one knows either of you so she could give birth before your wife or your posh pals found out.' Seeing the look of utter fury which crossed his face, she nodded smugly. 'I'm right, aren't I?'

He strode past her without bothering to reply and placed the baby back on the top step. Ignoring her protests, he descended the steps and picked his cane up off the pavement.

Realising his intentions, Agnes moved to grab hold of his arm. 'Don't you dare!' she snapped. 'You take her with you, you dirty old . . .' She fell silent as he spun round and thrust the handle of the cane inches away from her nose.

Agnes went cross-eyed as she stared at the heavy-looking, elaborate silver handle which weaved back and forth in front of her eyes. It was in the shape of a cobra's head, with its fangs bared and neck frilled. She could not help but wonder how much damage such a solid, sharp-looking object could do if he were to strike her with it.

Leaning forward so that his nose was close to hers, he hissed through gritted teeth, 'You *ever* speak to me like that again and I'll crack your head like a walnut ...' Without moving his cane he pushed his hand into his pocket and pulled out a fistful of notes which he thrust against her with such force that it caused Agnes to stagger back. Staring at her with utter hatred, he took a step back, adjusted his hat and straightened his coat. Seeing some of the notes fall to the ground, he indicated them with the tip of his cane. 'Pick them up!' he snarled.

Her mouth dry, Agnes did as instructed, taking care to keep one eye on the hand that was holding the sinister-looking cane.

As she stood up, he took a step back and, much to her relief, brought his cane back by his side, although she noticed his fingers were still tightly curled around the stem. Agnes gripped the money tightly. She watched as his eyes travelled down her form, resting on her swollen belly for a second or so before going back to her fingers which were bare of rings. He snorted as he fixed her with a look of disapproval. 'You have the audacity to stand in judgement of me, when you're clearly with child, yet I see no wedding band?'

'Only I'm not giving my child away,' Agnes replied quietly.

He looked at her with condescension then muttered, 'Well, more bloody fool you!' and strode away before Agnes had a chance to respond.

She wiped the tears of frustration from her cheeks. She had half a mind to call him back, to forbid him from leaving, so that she might have a chance to set the record straight on her pregnancy, but what was the point? He would have no interest in listening to someone like her – his kind never did, they thought themselves above women like Agnes, and the fact that she was pregnant without the benefit of marriage would only further his belief that she was less of a human being than he. All he wanted to do was dump his child and disappear into the night without fear of consequence. Her bottom lip wobbled at the unfairness of it all. The detestable old goat actually believed he was better than her, purely because she wasn't married. What was worse, Agnes secretly agreed with him because deep down she was thoroughly ashamed of her sinful condition. If she could only turn back time, she would tell herself not to listen to the lustful yearnings of a man who had promised her the world. She recalled the fateful day when she had told him of her condition. She had worried that he might be angry, tell her she should have been more careful, instruct her to abort the unwanted baby, but she couldn't have been more wrong. He had held her in his arms, and assured her that they would get married as soon as he got back to port in three months' time.

'I told you the night we first made love,' he whispered softly, as he brushed the hair back from her tear-stained cheeks, 'that I loved you and wanted you to be my wife. None of that has changed because you're pregnant.'

Three months later, when her lover's ship, the *Duchess*, arrived in port, Agnes offered to run an errand for Mrs Ancrum so that she might quickly nip down to the docks and see her betrothed. Looking up at the deck of the ship, she had hailed a group of sailors who were chatting idly. Waving in acknowledgement, one of the sailors came down the gangplank to greet her.

Agnes's heart sank as she remembered the awkward look the man had given her when she had asked the whereabouts of Seaman Fitzpatrick.

'He left the *Duchess* as soon as we docked in the Americas.' He made the statement as though it were common knowledge. 'A lot of the crew did. Didn't he tell you of his plans?'

Agnes had scoffed with disbelief. 'You've got it wrong, you must have misunderstood him. He told me we would get married when he came back to Glasgow ...' She fell silent, seeing the look of embarrassment which settled on the seaman's face.

He stared wretchedly at his own feet. 'He told us as soon as we left dock.' He ran his fingers through his hair before casting her a look of sympathy. 'Sorry, love, but you know what they say ...'

Agnes had nodded briefly then turned away before the man could see her foolish tears. 'A woman in every port.' That's what the staff at Greystones had warned her, only Agnes hadn't wanted to believe them, convinced that they were only jealous.

Now, with the memories washing over her, Agnes stared down at the baby in her arms. 'You can't be more than a few hours old, yet look at the trouble you've already caused.' She glanced at the retreating old man. 'Good riddance to bad rubbish is all I can say. I dread to think what sort of child you'd turn out to be with *that* as your father.' Sighing heavily, she made her way back inside. 'I might not always approve of the Ancrums' ways, but at least they'll make sure you don't turn into a spoiled brat.' With the money and baby still tightly clutched to her chest she tried to shut the door, but it was no use, she simply had too many things in her arms. Placing the baby on the floor, she was pushing the money into her bodice when a sharp voice called out from behind, startling her.

'Agnes McKinley!' snapped the voice of Mrs Ancrum. 'What on *earth* do you think you're doing?'

Fearing she had been caught in what could be deemed a compromising situation, Agnes hastily pulled her hand out from her bodice, scattering notes onto the floor as she did so. Before she had a chance to explain herself, Mrs Ancrum had crossed the floor and was picking up the money. Her eyes flicking towards the baby, she stood upright and waved the money in front of Agnes's face. 'Well?' She glanced at Agnes's bosom, where several notes protruded from the top of her bodice, and held her other hand out. 'Hand it over!'

Shamefaced, Agnes began pulling the notes out. When she had handed the last one to her employer she bent down and scooped the baby into her arms, frantically gabbling her excuses. 'I wasn't nicking the money, only I couldn't hold the baby and lock the door at the same time, so I thought ...'

Mrs Ancrum looked at her with feigned surprise as she tucked the money into her skirt pocket. 'You thought the baby belonged on the floor and the money in your bodice?'

Agnes shook her head, her eyes wide with horror. 'No! That's not it at all!' she spluttered. 'The key was in my pocket, and my hands were too full ...'

'So?' said Mrs Ancrum, as she took the baby from Agnes's arms. 'Put the money on the floor and keep the baby in your arms. Just goes to show—' she stopped short. She had been so surprised to catch one of her employees trying to conceal a considerable amount of money down the front of her bodice, she hadn't questioned the presence of the newborn baby. She glanced at Agnes's belly. 'I can see it's not yours, so where did *this* come from?' she asked, raising the baby in her arms.

Relieved the conversation had taken a different route, Agnes began, 'Some old man dumped her outside ...' She explained what had happened, hoping that once Mrs Ancrum had heard her tale she would not only believe what she had to say but sympathise with her predicament. Unfortunately, Mrs Ancrum was regarding her with reproving disbelief.

'How convenient!' she snapped, eyeing Agnes with suspicion. 'No witnesses to back your little story, just a fistful of notes and a baby at your feet.' She glanced at Agnes's stomach again. 'I reckon this amount of money would prove pretty handy with a baby on the way.'

Agnes swallowed hard. Why couldn't Mrs Ancrum see that she was telling the truth? She tried seeing things from her employer's point of view then wished she hadn't, because the other woman was right – it was a lot of money – and if Ancrum hadn't caught her red-handed, when push came to shove, just what would she have done with that amount? Would she really have handed it over when no one else knew of its existence? After all, there was no fear of the old man returning. Placing a hand on her stomach, she lowered her gaze. 'I swear on my baby's life … ' she mumbled beneath her breath before being cut short by Mrs Ancrum who was shaking her head.

'May God forgive you, you wicked girl!' she snapped. 'The evidence speaks for itself. Someone left their baby, along with a considerable sum of money …' Her face remained impassive. 'Did they pay you to turn a blind eye?'

Agnes's mouth hung open. 'That wasn't it at all!'

Mrs Ancrum raised a disbelieving brow. 'Wasn't it? How am I meant to know what really happened? You're going to struggle for money when your baby's born, especially on your wages.' She patted the pocket of her skirt, which was now bulging with money. 'A tidy sum like this would tide you over for a considerable time.' She shook her head fervently as Agnes tried to protest. 'I can only go by the facts, and I saw you shoving the money down your bodice.' She looked at the baby who was sleeping peacefully in her arms. 'Stealing from a baby!' Wrinkling her nose in disgust, she fixed Agnes with an icy stare. 'I should give you your marching orders …'

Agnes burst into tears. 'P-please don't! I swear I wasn't taking the money! I'll do anything, but I can't bring up a baby on my own, especially with no job …'

11

She glanced around the walls of the hallway before fixing her employer with a beseeching look. 'And this is my home, I've got nowhere else to go!'

Mrs Ancrum drew a deep breath. 'As I was saying, I *should* give you your marching orders, but as I can't prove your intentions, I suppose I shall choose to be lenient under the circumstances.'

Sagging with relief, Agnes held a hand to her forehead. 'Thank you, Mrs Ancrum, I promise I won't let you down.'

'You'd better not!' snapped the older woman. She held the baby towards Agnes, who stepped forward to receive the child. 'You say it's a girl?'

Sniffing loudly, Agnes nodded.

'Then take her to the nursery. She shall be named Jessica Wilson after the founder of Greystones.'

Agnes nodded briefly before leaving the room. She glanced down at the baby, who was beginning to stir. 'Your old man nearly cost me my job as well as my home, and that's all thanks to you, Jessica Wilson.' A fluttering sensation in her tummy reminded her of her own unborn child. 'My baby's not going to be a Jessica Wilson, 'cos I'd never give her up, let alone dump her like she was a sack of rubbish ...' She hesitated. Whilst that might be true, what would she have done had Ancrum followed through with her threat? With no job and no home, she might have been forced to do exactly that. A hollow feeling began to rise in her throat as the enormity of her narrow escape sank in. She stared down at Jessica with angry disapproval. 'From now on it's just me and my baby. I'll not bother sticking my neck out for a kid that doesn't belong to me in future, 'cos my baby's going to be a Bonnie, or a Billy, and I'm going to make sure she or he has the very best in life as well as a stable home, and not end up in Brownhill.' She pushed the door to the nursery open with her foot. 'Welcome to Greystones, Jessica Wilson – your stepping stone to the poorhouse.'

Chapter One

3 September 1939

Hearing the church bells chime the hour, Jessica Wilson slipped off the top bunk, tiptoed over to the window and peered down onto the cobbled courtyard below. She looked at the clock on the rooftop opposite, which read six o'clock. Her tummy fluttered with nervous anticipation. In another five hours the country's Prime Minister, Neville Chamberlain, would be making an important announcement in which he would let them know the outcome of his ultimatum, that Germany should withdraw her troops from Poland or consider herself at war with Britain. She crossed her fingers. It wasn't that she wanted Britain to be at war with Germany, but if the rumours were true and war was declared, the children who lived near big cities would be evacuated to the country, and with Greystones Orphanage being within walking distance of Glasgow's city centre, she felt certain they would be evacuated. She didn't care where to, as long as it was far away from the abomination where she had spent the first fifteen years of her life.

'It could be our ticket out of here, Rubes,' Jess had assured her best pal Ruby Anderson as they'd made their way to church the previous Sunday. 'I overheard one of the cooks gossiping with the delivery boy that brings the tatties – she was telling him that Greystones would have no choice but to close if we go to war!'

Ruby gave her friend a cautious smile. 'Are you sure? It sounds almost too good to be true ...'

'Positive!' Jess said with certainty. "Cos the cook was moaning that she'd be out of a job. She even said she's already started looking for work just in case, and asked the delivery boy if he could keep an ear to the ground for anything suitable.'

'My daddy reckons we're bound to go to war,' Ruby said knowledgeably.

Jess smiled. Ruby's father was never wrong on such matters. The girls had put his extensive knowledge down to his travelling as a seaman aboard the *Moray*, a large vessel which sailed the world carrying goods far and wide. Jess had only met Mr Anderson a handful of times as he spent most of the year out at sea. She glanced sympathetically at her friend. According to Ruby's father, he and his wife had been madly in love, with dreams of starting a large family, and they had been thrilled when they discovered that Ruby was on the way, but their dream had turned into a nightmare when Ruby's mother had died during childbirth. With no other family able to look after his daughter whilst he earned a living, Stewart Anderson had had no choice other than to hand his daughter over to the orphanage within days of her birth.

16

She turned to Ruby. 'What'll your father do? Stay on the *Moray* or join the Navy?'

Ruby had shrugged. 'I should imagine he'll stay on the *Moray*. Life moves on, war or not.'

Now, standing by the window, Jess cast an eye over the beds in her dormitory, the occupants of which were still fast asleep. Stepping lightly across the floor, she climbed back onto the top bunk and pulled the thin blankets up around her chin. Envisaging the day ahead, she wondered whether they would still be attending church service as they did every Sunday. She heaved a sigh. Of course they'd be going to church, same as the boys from Nazareth Orphanage.

They'll want us all to pray for good news, thought Jess miserably. She nibbled her bottom lip guiltily. Depending on what your version of 'good news' was, of course. It wasn't that Jess didn't believe in God, she just didn't revel in the idea of sitting on hard wooden pews in the freezing cold church whilst the vicar droned on for hours about how they should be grateful for everything they had. She wasn't grateful for everything she had; in fact, she often wished she was not in Greystones, but far away in a cottage by the sea with a loving family. She knew she wasn't the only one who felt this way. Even the children like Ruby, who had either one or both of their parents, would rather be with their families than in the god-awful institution they called Greystones Orphanage. So, having to sit in a church surrounded by her like-minded peers, knowing full well they were only giving thanks because of the punishment that would follow if they did not show their gratitude, was a prospect she did not relish.

She did, however, enjoy the walk to the church which took them past a large, unoccupied semi-detached house which belonged to the Durnings and was rumoured to be haunted. Several of the younger orphans had even claimed that they had seen the curtains twitch as though someone was watching them in secret, whilst others said they had seen the ghostly shape of a woman dressed in white glide past the downstairs window, even claiming they had heard a howling and wailing noise. Having never been witness to anything unusual herself, Jess wasn't sure whether she believed the rumours of ghosts or not, although after hearing the wild stories of some of the children she could see why the rumours had started.

The butcher's boy had told some of the younger children that the house had been derelict for quite some time, because Mrs Durning, the woman who owned it, had gone, as he called it, 'funny in the head' before being carted off to a mental institution. However, his wasn't the only version of events. According to the telegram delivery boy, the tales were totally false, because the postman, a friend of a friend of his father's, had discovered old ma Durning's body at the bottom of the stairs with a pile of unopened mail on top of her.

Jess paid little attention to their wild imaginings. She had only one interest in the Durnings and that was the beautiful front garden which had been left to grow wild. Looking at the drab, colourless walls of the dormitory, she smiled as she envisaged how different the room would look if the walls were covered with the wild rambling roses and the beautiful wisteria which covered the front of the Durnings' house. Her smile broadened. It would look like a scene from her favourite book, *The Secret Garden* by Frances Hodgson Burnett.

This reminded her of the day she and Ruby had been walking to church when George Miller, one of the boys from Nazareth Orphanage, had told Jess that the Durnings had one of the largest back gardens in that particular row of houses.

'How do you know?' whispered Jess as they made their way into the church grounds. Talking to boys was strictly forbidden so she was careful to speak without moving her lips.

George spoke from the corner of his mouth. 'I seen it when I were running an errand for Father Blakely.'

'Oh?'

He gave a small nod. 'I was taking some candlesticks to Greystones ...'

Jess frowned. 'You don't need to cut down the back of the houses to get to Greystones ...'

George chuckled. 'You do when they got one of the tastiest apple trees in their back garden.'

Ruby, who was beside Jess, pursed her lips. 'That's stealing!' she said as quietly as she could.

He pulled a face. 'They were windfalls, you can't steal windfalls!'

'If they're not yours, then that's stealing,' Ruby said resolutely. She cast a careful eye round to see if anyone was paying them attention, but it seemed as though their little tête-à-tête had gone unnoticed.

He gave her a sidelong glance. 'Finders keepers?'

Hearing Ruby's disapproving 'hmmph', Jess intervened. 'You best make sure Father Blakely doesn't know what you've been doing else he'll give you the cane.'

'We don't have the cane,' said George. 'We have the rod – same thing only a lot harder.' He rubbed the palms of his hands as he spoke, something which hadn't gone unnoticed by Jess.

'You had the rod before, then?'

He pushed his hands into his pockets. 'We all have, not because we've done owt wrong ...' He shook his head as Ruby opened her mouth to remind him that stealing apples was wrong. 'I know taking the apples was wrong,' he admitted, 'but that wasn't why I got the rod. In Nazareth House they're firm believers of "spare the rod, ruin the child". Father Blakely gives you ten strokes across the palms of your hands at least once a fortnight, 'cos he reckons it teaches us to be grateful.'

Jess regarded him with a look of horror. 'Grateful for what?'

He shrugged. 'That we've got a roof over our heads.'

Jess might have detested living in Greystones, but at least they didn't get beaten for doing nothing. She decided to ask him about the errand with the candlesticks.

'That's the only good part of being in Nazareth House – they send us on messages all over the city. It's what they call earning our bread and butter.'

Jess eyed him enviously. 'I wish they'd send us on messages. We're only allowed out to go to church on Sundays.'

'And they make us earn our bread and butter by scrubbing dirty sheets,' Ruby added grumpily.

He grimaced. 'That's because you're women and you can't expect a feller to do ...' He got no further because Bonnie, the daughter of Agnes McKinley, had marched up to the three of them.

'That's enough of that! You know the rules, no talking.'

'Wind your neck in,' hissed George, eager not to draw the attention of Father Blakely. 'It's not like we was smoochin' …'

Bonnie's cheeks flushed scarlet. 'I'd not put anything past some of these girls …' She shot Jess and Ruby a withering glance.

'Steady on,' said George, 'I was only joking.'

'Maybe you were,' said Bonnie in scathing tones, 'but it's only a matter of time. From what I've heard some of these girls are—' she got no further.

'Don't judge others by your own standards!' hissed George angrily.

Bonnie's eyes bulged. 'I'm telling me mam,' she seethed, adding spitefully, ''cos I've got one to tell.'

George turned apologetically to Jess and Ruby. 'That's torn it. I hope you don't get into any trouble.' He jerked his head at Bonnie, who was strutting towards her mother. 'Naggy Knickers.'

'Naggy Knickers!' giggled Jess. 'Don't let her hear you callin' her that! Besides, it's not you she's angry at, it's me. She's always had a bee in her bonnet when it comes to me.'

'Oh?'

'Don't ask me why,' said Jess, ''cos I haven't a clue.'

'Watch out …' hissed Ruby as Bonnie made her way back.

'Me mam says you're not allowed to talk to the boys,' said Bonnie with some satisfaction. 'None of us are!'

'Difference being none of the boys would want to talk to you,' quipped George.

'Because they know I'm out of their league!' Bonnie gave a mirthless laugh. 'After all, why would I want someone else's cast-offs?'

George's face turned thunderous. 'You spiteful little ...'

Ruby placed a hand on his elbow. 'Careful, George, she's not worth getting into trouble over.'

He looked over to Father Blakely who was casting a keen eye around at the children as they gathered in the church. 'I'd best be off before her vicious tongue reaches the ears of old Blakely.' He smiled briefly at Jess and Ruby. 'Cheerio, girls.'

Seeing him hurry off towards his friends put Jess in mind of the first time she and Ruby had met George. She had been sitting next to Ruby in church when Ruby suddenly spun round, clapping her hand to the back of her head.

Jess looked at the accusing scowl on Ruby's face. 'What's up with you?'

Ruby was pulling a small ball of wet paper from her hair. Grimacing, she wiped it from her fingers onto the floor. Miss McKinley, who was sitting several rows ahead of the girls, had turned to see what was going on, so Ruby quickly lowered her head and continued with her prayers, only to snap her head back up a second or two later, and retrieve another ball from her hair.

Jess shot Ruby a sideways glance, warning her to ignore the hushed giggles coming from the boys who were sitting in the pew behind them. Keeping her head down, Jess placed her elbows on the pew in front of her and locked her hands in a prayer-like fashion so that she might peep at the boys from under her arm. As she had expected, she saw one of the boys removing a small ball of paper from his mouth then pushing it into a thin pipe which he placed to his lips. He was about to blow, when Jess's hand shot back and she snatched the pipe from his hand. Her plan would have been a success had the boy not started choking on the piece of paper which he had inadvertently inhaled.

Tears streaming down his face, the boy clutched his throat, whilst his friend slapped him heartily between his shoulder blades.

Worried that they would get into trouble, Jess slipped the pipe into her pocket. The vicar stopped speaking and several faces turned towards them. Keeping their heads down, the girls were careful not to make eye contact with anyone.

At the end of the service Jess and Ruby watched guiltily as the boy received a dressing-down from Father Blakely.

'I know he was being a mischievous sod,' Ruby whispered to Jess, 'but I wouldn't like to see him get into any trouble. He didn't mean any harm.'

Jess pulled the pipe a little way out of her dress pocket to show Ruby. 'Don't worry, I've still got this so they can't really accuse him of anything except choking, and they can hardly cane him for that.'

They had waited until Father Blakely walked away before approaching the boy. Keeping their backs turned to him, Jess pulled the pipe from her pocket and held it up. The boy took it from her fingers whispering, 'Thanks for not dobbing me in.'

As their eyes met, he winked at Ruby. 'Thanks for being a good sport.'

Ruby couldn't explain why, but far from being angry at him for spitting balls of paper at her, she felt a sudden fondness towards the boy. She supposed it was his mischievous grin and sparkling brown eyes.

From that day on, Ruby, Jess and George had become friends and they would often try to snatch a quick hello on their way to or from the church.

Now, as she lay in her bed, Jess wondered why they had not seen George since the day Bonnie had tattle-taled to her mother. Knowing that Father Blakely used the rod on the boys for the slightest thing, she found herself worrying that the horrible man might have done something so bad that George couldn't attend church.

She shuddered at the thought. She would never forgive herself if he had been punished because she wanted to hear more about the Durnings' back garden. She decided she would keep an eye out for George when they made their way to church later that morning.

She looked at the wall opposite her bed and wished it was covered with ivy so that she might find a hidden door which would lead her into a secret garden, just like the one in the book. Sighing happily, she envisaged an array of hollyhocks and foxgloves, as well as gypsophila and cornflowers. In the middle of the garden there would be a bird table, and off to one side she would find a pond with lily pads and a trickling waterfall. So far away was she in her thoughts that she never heard the door to the dorm open, and when someone struck the metal post of her bunk bed with a poker she nearly jumped out of her skin. 'What the—' she began before being rudely interrupted.

'Get up, you lazy beasts!'

Jess rolled her eyes and muttered, 'Bonnie bloomin' McKinley ...' under her breath. Much to the orphans' disapproval, Mrs Ancrum had charged Bonnie with the task of getting the girls up each Sunday morning. It was an undertaking which Bonnie very much enjoyed and she took the opportunity to be as bossy and obnoxious as possible.

Sitting up on one elbow, Jess frowned at Bonnie who had her arm held back ready to strike the bed for a second time. Not prepared to give Bonnie the satisfaction, Jess swung her legs out of bed, muttering, 'Go boil your head.' Loud enough for Bonnie to hear, but not loud enough to be overheard by any of the staff who might happen to be passing.

Pretending not to hear, Bonnie swung the poker back round, catching Jess across her shins.

Yelping with pain, Jess clutched her hands to her legs and fell back onto the bed. Tears coursing down her cheeks, she glared at Bonnie. 'You evil cow ...'

Bonnie's mother, Miss McKinley, hurried into the room and grabbed the poker from her daughter's hands. 'What on earth is going on?'

'It was an accident!' cried Bonnie, wide-eyed. 'I didn't realise she was awake.'

Tears still streaming down her cheeks, Jessica shook her head. 'You rotten liar, Bonnie McKinley! You knew

I was awake 'cos I told you to ...' Jess fell silent. Owning up that she had told Bonnie to 'go boil her head' would not be a good idea.

'Did you?' said Bonnie, her face a picture of innocence. 'I'm afraid I didn't hear you ...' She eyed Jess tauntingly. 'What did you say exactly?'

Jess shot Bonnie a withering look, knowing perfectly well that the other girl had heard her words. 'Can't remember,' she muttered as she rubbed her shins. 'My legs are killing me, I reckon you've broken them!'

Ruby, who slept in the bed below Jess's, glared at Bonnie. 'You did know she was awake, we all did, you—' she stopped short as she caught Miss McKinley's eye. The woman was daring Ruby to say something which didn't favour her daughter. 'Never mind,' Ruby mumbled lamely.

Agnes McKinley nodded. 'Just as I thought, Miss Anderson.' She turned to address the room. 'Stop gawping and get ready for church!' She stiffened as a grumbling moan swept the room. 'I'll have none of that! You all need to get on your knees and pray to God that this country doesn't go to war! Imagine where you'd be without Greystones to call home!' She shot Bonnie a warning glance. 'Come with me, Bonnie.'

Jess waited until the McKinleys had left the room before speaking her thoughts. 'A lot bleeding happier than we are now,' she mumbled beneath her breath.

'If the Germans do come, I hope they blow Greystones to smithereens,' said Ruby, 'and I hope that witch McKinley and beastly Bonnie end up in Brownhill like the rest of us. That'd wipe the smug smirk off their faces!' She eyed Jess's bruised legs sympatheti-cally. 'Poor Jess, you didn't deserve that.'

Jess gingerly slid off her bed and winced as her toes touched the floor. 'I'm not sure I want to spend the rest of my days in Brownhill with the McKinleys,' she said. 'We'd best pray for war so that we can get away from them and this god-awful hovel.'

Penny, one of the girls further down the dorm, gave a snort of contempt. 'Comes to something when war's seen as the better alternative.' She glanced at Jess. 'Are you okay?'

Jess nodded. 'They hurt like billy-o, but I don't think she's broken anything. Luckily for me, the poker struck the bedpost before my legs.'

'She shouldn't be allowed to come in here acting like she rules the roost, just 'cos she lives here with her mam,' snapped Penny.

'Ancrum doesn't care. As far as she's concerned, she's getting an extra member of staff for free,' said Jess, 'and the governors couldn't give two hoots because it's saving money!'

Penny tapped the side of her nose knowingly. 'I think they would if they found out what Ancrum's been up to, slave labour being the tip of the iceberg.'

'Ha!' said Jess. 'I don't think Bonnie sees herself as a slave.'

Penny shook her head darkly and opened her mouth to speak but her pal, Alice, nudged her into silence. 'Come on you, before you say something you can't take back.'

Penny grumbled something under her breath as she begrudgingly followed her friend out of the room.

Jess frowned at Ruby. 'What on earth did she mean by that?'

Ruby pulled a face. 'I haven't a clue.' She hesitated. 'If we do go to war, d'you reckon we'll be evacuated to a big place like Greystones? 'Cos if we are, McKinley and Bonnie'll come too, and we might end up jumping out of the frying pan into the fire.'

Jess stared at Ruby in horror. 'I was relying on this war to get us away from Greystones and the McKinleys, but if you really think we might be no better off than we are now I reckon we take our chances, do a runner and sign on the dotted line. I don't care if we end up in the WAAF, the ATS or the Wrens – anything's better than staying with that lot.' She pushed her bare feet into her plimsolls, noting as she did so that another hole had appeared, making them look more like sandals than shoes.

Ruby looked worried. 'We've not got our papers, and even if we had, I don't think we're old enough to join up.'

Jess shrugged. 'We'll have to cross that bridge when we come to it.' She took a few steps. 'Oh Rubes, my legs are throbbing something awful.'

'I'm not surprised,' said Ruby as she examined the large lumps which had formed on Jess's shins. 'You should tell Mrs Ancrum ...' She held up a hand to silence Jess who was starting to say it wasn't worth it. 'I know she couldn't give a monkey's about you personally, but it won't look good for her if you end up in hospital.'

Jess shook her head fervently. 'No chance! If they say my leg's broken, I'll be in plaster and they'll never let

28

me sign up.' Wincing as she bore weight on her legs, she began to hobble towards the door. 'I'm certain it'll get better the more I walk.'

Ruby wagged a reproving finger. 'I think you're daft, Jessica Wilson. You might end up doing more harm than good.'

Jess looked up as she heard a noise coming from the door to their dormitory. She glanced anxiously at Ruby. 'Did you hear something?'

Ruby placed a finger to her lips and stole quietly across the boarded floor. She waited by the door for a second before risking a peek into the hallway. She let out a groan before turning anxiously to Jess. 'It was Clare.' She nibbled her bottom lip nervously. 'Do you reckon she heard what we said about joining up? 'Cos if she did, you can bet your life she'll snitch on us to Bonnie.'

'Course she heard! She wasn't standing out there by accident. Bonnie will have sent her up to eavesdrop,' simmered Jess, adding, 'spying little toad.'

Ruby clenched her fists. 'One of these days I'm going to hear or see something that Clare shouldn't have done, and when I do ...'

Jess looked up sharply. 'You'll not snitch, Ruby Anderson, 'cos that'd make you as bad as Clare.' She softened a little. 'And you're a million times better than the likes of her.'

'It's not fair!' Ruby muttered. 'Why should she get away with everything? I reckon a good dose of her own medicine would do her the world of good.'

Jess raised her brow. 'Two wrongs don't make a right and besides, you don't want the other girls to think you're a tattletale.'

'I know,' said Ruby glumly, 'it's just maddening watching her get off scot-free all the time.'

Jess continued to hobble her way towards the landing. 'She'll get her come-uppance one of these days – what goes around comes around, or at least I hope it does. It's not as if Clare can stay in Greystones forever. She'll have to go to Brownhill sooner or later, and when she does she'll run into a lot of the girls she snitched on at some time or other, all of whom will have an axe to grind.'

Ruby grimaced. 'That won't be a pretty sight.'

'There you are then,' Jess said. 'She's not getting away with anything, not long-term at any rate.'

'I almost feel sorry for her,' said Ruby. Seeing the look of surprise on Jess's face, she added, 'I said *almost*.'

'Not that we'll be around to witness any of it,' said Jess, 'when we join up.'

Ruby eyed her uncertainly. 'Do you really mean it then, about joining up?'

Jess nodded. 'Too right I do. This is our ticket to a better life.'

'But how?' said Ruby. 'We're not old enough, and whilst I'm sure my dad would cover for us, he's away and won't be home for . . .' she blew her cheeks out, '. . . ever such a long time yet, and I can't see McKinley or Ancrum doing anything to help us. They'll still want the money they get paid for looking after us . . .'

'Looking after us?' repeated Jess in disbelief. 'One meal a day, if we're lucky, and no hot water to have a wash in?' As she spoke she started to tick the list off on her fingers. 'No clothes to replace the ones that don't fit you any more, or have got more holes than a sieve, no fire in the winter, no blankets on your beds, no soap if you use the old one up too soon, same for the tooth-paste, and we still have to work!' She shook her head. 'I'd like to know how much she gets paid for the sheets we wash for those posh hotels. I reckon she's onto a good little earner with us lot working for free ...' She paused. 'That's what Penny must have meant when she was talking about slave labour, because that's what we are!' As they entered the kitchen Jess let out a groan of dismay. 'Today is definitely not my lucky day,' she said, jerking her head in the direction of Clare who was whispering in Bonnie's ear, whilst Bonnie glared at Jess. 'Not only have I got that tell-tale-tit to contend with, it looks like they're serving what's left of Thurs-day's porridge.' She wrinkled her nose at the watery grey sludge in the huge saucepan, then glanced at Joanne, whose job it was to serve breakfast that morn-ing. 'Why can't they use milk?'

The younger girl raised her eyebrows. 'Same reason they don't give you butter on your toast,' she rubbed the fingers on one hand together, 'money.'

Picking up an empty bowl, Jess gave a resigned sigh as she peered inside it. 'This one's got a big crack in it ...' She went to get another but saw that Ruby had just taken the last one. 'Oh, well, no porridge for me!' She smiled hopefully at Joanne. 'Could I have toast instead?'

Bonnie, who had been deep in conversation with Clare, looked up sharply. 'What did you just say?'

'Me or your little spy?' said Jess, shooting Clare a withering glance.

'You!' snapped Bonnie. 'What makes you think you can have toast when everyone else has had porridge?'

31

Jess shot her a wry glance. 'So you did hear what I said, then?' She held up the bowl. 'This 'un's cracked, and Ruby's got the last bowl, so ...'

Bonnie tutted loudly. 'Looks fine to me!' She nodded to Joanne. 'Give her porridge, she's just making excuses.'

Glancing apologetically at Jess, Joanne scooped the porridge into the cracked bowl.

Bonnie grinned maliciously. 'Seeing as how there's plenty left, you may as well fill it!'

Jess shook her head. 'No thanks, I ...' She got no further; the porridge had seeped through the crack and was now burning her hands. With a cry of alarm, Jess dropped the bowl which promptly crashed to the floor. Hurriedly wiping the porridge off her fingers, she glared at Bonnie. 'I told you it was broken!'

Mrs Ancrum, who had been walking past the door to the dining room, came in to see what the fuss was about. 'Who did this?' she said, staring at the mixture of porridge and smashed crockery which lay at Jess's feet.

'She did it on purpose!' snapped Bonnie, pointing an accusing finger at Jess. 'She said she didn't like the porridge and asked for toast, didn't she?' She was looking at Joanne who was trying her best to keep out of things.

'Well?' said Mrs Ancrum.

Turning pink, Joanne gave Mrs Ancrum a doubtful look. 'Not exactly ...'

Bonnie folded her arms across her chest. 'You saying she didn't ask for toast?'

'Well yes,' Joanne began, 'but only because ...'

32

Bonnie, who had no intention of allowing the girl to continue, butted in. 'See?' she said with an air of triumph. She glared at Jess. 'She reckons she's better than everyone else, Mrs Ancrum, and according to what I've heard,' she glanced at Clare who was looking as though she wished the ground would swallow her whole, 'Jess and Ruby reckon they're going to join the services!'

'Join the services my eye!' scoffed the older woman. 'They're far too young!' She indicated the smashed crockery with a long, skinny forefinger then glanced at Joanne. 'Get something for her to clean this mess up.' She glared at Jess. 'Don't let me hear of you wasting food again.'

'No, Mrs Ancrum,' said Jess, but Mrs Ancrum was already halfway across the dining room, heading for the door.

Joanne hurried off, reappearing a few moments later with a mop and bucket, which she handed to Jess. 'Here you are, Jess. I'll give you a hand ...'

'No!' snapped Bonnie. She gave Jess a maniacal grin. 'I'm in charge here, so I get to say what happens.' She pointed at the porridge splattered on the floor, 'Eat it!'

Jess stared at her incredulously. 'Don't be stupid! As if I'm going to eat that!'

'Don't care,' said Bonnie, continuing to point at the porridge. 'Eat it, or I'll report you to Mr Ancrum.' Narrowing her eyes, she spoke through gritted teeth. 'He's not as forgiving as his wife. She'll cane your fingers but he'll cane the soles of your feet then make you walk around the yard.'

Folding her arms across her chest, Jess locked eyes with Bonnie. 'Tell!' Jess heard the other girls give a collective gasp.

Ruby tugged Jess's elbow. 'Jess …'

Jess shook her off. 'No, Ruby, I'm not backing down, not any more.' Much to Bonnie's surprise, Jess took a step forward so that they were standing toe to toe. Jess's eyes burned with defiance and Bonnie withered under her gaze. 'You aren't going to tell me or any other girl in here what to do, not any more, and you can go and tell Mr Ancrum what I've said, because quite frankly, I don't care!'

Seeing the approving looks of the other girls, Bonnie swept out of the room, calling over her shoulder, 'You're going to regret those words, Jessica Wilson.'

As Bonnie disappeared the dining room was filled with the buzz of excited chatter. Ruby bent down beside Jess and began scooping the porridge into the cracked bowl. 'I hope you know what you're doing, Jess …' She stopped talking and glared at Clare who was trying to leave the room unnoticed. 'Running off to tell more tales, Clare? Do you know what happens to those that spy?'

Clare looked around at the sea of unfriendly faces which had turned towards her. 'You heard what Mrs Ancrum said!' she spluttered. 'You're too young to join the services.'

'So, you admit it!'

Clare swallowed. 'I didn't admit anything …'

Ruby stood up. 'I saw you, Clare! Sneaking off to tell your little pal.'

Turning scarlet, Clare scurried out of the room.

Joanne wrung the mop out. 'How old do you have to be to sign up?'

'Eighteen,' said Jess. 'So Mrs Ancrum's right, we are too young, but the forces don't know that.'

Joanne sighed wistfully. 'I'm only thirteen, otherwise I reckon I'd give it a whirl myself,' she glanced around the hall, 'especially if I thought it'd get me out of this hellhole.'

Ruby smiled sympathetically at Joanne. 'We don't know if we'll get in yet …' She paused. 'In fact, we're jumping the gun a bit. For all we know, there mightn't even be a war!'

'There will be if we don't get a move on,' said another girl, ''cos we'll be late for church at this rate.'

Despite her brave words Jess waited with dread for Mr Ancrum to call her to his office, but it seemed he had more important things on his mind that morning. The girls went to church, where Jess and the other children gave thanks to the Lord for the food on their plates. As the words left their lips, Jess and Ruby exchanged glances with a wide grin.

When the service was over Jess craned her neck to see if she could spot George, but Father Blakely had told the boys they must hurry back to Nazareth House so that they would be in time for the Prime Minister's announcement. Pity, thought Jess, I would have liked the opportunity to say goodbye, maybe even persuade him to join us.

As they made their way back to Greystones, Jess looked up at the top windows when they passed the Durnings' house. A cold shiver ran down her spine as she saw the net curtains move gently as if caught in a breeze. Glancing back at Ruby, she jerked her head towards the house. Ruby looked up then shrugged and turned back to Jess, mouthing, 'What?'

Shaking her head, Jess whispered, 'I'll tell you later.' When they reached the back door of the orphanage Miss McKinley told the girls to head straight to the hall. As they filed into the large room with its timber-framed walls, Ruby caught hold of Jess's wrist. 'What were you on about, outside the Durnings' just now?'

'I thought I'd seen the curtain move,' explained Jess.

Ruby rolled her eyes. 'Honest to God, Jess, I thought you didn't believe in ghosts?'

Jess didn't get a chance to answer as Mrs Ancrum clapped her hands together and called for quiet while her husband twiddled the knobs on the wireless, which crackled and whined before the voice of Neville Chamberlain broke through the white noise.

'I am speaking to you from the cabinet room at 10 Downing Street. This morning the British ambassador in Berlin handed the German government a final note stating that unless we heard from them by eleven o'clock that they were prepared at once to withdraw their troops from Poland, a state of war would exist between us. I have to tell you now that no such undertaking has been received, and that consequently this country is at war with Germany.'

Scowling her disapproval, Mrs Ancrum clapped her hands to hush the children who had begun to chatter in an excited fashion. 'Quiet!'

The girls instantly fell silent and they listened to the rest of Chamberlain's speech, at the end of which Mr Ancrum turned the wireless off and nodded to his wife,

36

who straightened the bodice of her dress before addressing the room.

'I'm sorry to say this news has come as no surprise and we at Greystones have already made plans for evacuation.' She glanced around the room of children who were hanging on her every word. 'We shall be leaving for Glencoe first thing tomorrow morning.' She half smiled as she surveyed the sea of hopeful faces. 'As there isn't a building big enough to house us all, children fourteen years and older will be sent straight to Brownhill ...'

'No!' cried Jess and Ruby together.

'That's not fair!' yelled Penny.

'Quiet!' roared Mr Ancrum, pointing an angry finger at Jess. 'You're not getting any more than what you deserve, Jessica Wilson, and if I were you I'd keep my mouth shut whilst I was still able to walk.'

Turning crimson, Jess looked at Ruby. 'We can't go to Brownhill, I'm not spending the rest of my life there.'

Careful to keep an eye on Bonnie and Clare, Ruby gave a slight nod before hiding her lips behind her fingers. 'Only let's not talk about it now. Wait till we get somewhere quieter, I'm sure that Clare can lip-read.'

Jess turned to look at Clare who instantly averted her gaze.

Hurrying out of the room, the girls headed for the toilets. Ruby made sure each cubicle was empty before she started talking. 'From what I've heard, Greystones is a palace compared to Brownhill.' Tears began to form in her large brown eyes. 'I can't spend the rest of my life in the poorhouse, Jess, I just can't. Bonnie reckons once you're in you'll not get out, not alive at any rate.'

'Don't listen to Bonnie,' said Jess, but doubt flooded her thoughts. She remembered the day when Elsa, one of the younger orphans, had asked if she might be allowed to visit her sister Hattie as she hadn't seen her since she'd left Greystones some months before. Mr and Mrs Ancrum had refused, saying that Elsa would have to wait until she was old enough to go to Brownhill herself, but when a visiting governor who had overheard Elsa's request took it upon himself to override their decision. Elsa left Greystones full of smiles, but when she returned later that day, it was as though someone had stripped her soul of happiness.

'She was skin and bone,' she sobbed. 'I called her name but I don't think she could bear to look at me.'

Bonnie had nodded knowledgeably. 'She'd be better off dead than in that place, from what I hear they have to fight for their food, and your Hattie wouldn't say boo to a goose.'

'Hold your spiteful tongue!' snapped Jess. She had placed a comforting arm around Elsa's shoulders, as the younger girl began to wail. 'Don't listen to her,' she soothed, 'she doesn't know what she's talking about.'

Wiping her nose on her sleeve, Elsa lifted her head to look at Bonnie. 'I know what I saw, and my sister looked like she'd not eaten since she got there.'

Bonnie sniffed decidedly. 'She'll need to toughen up, 'cos she'll not survive the winter otherwise.'

Jess had tried to reassure Elsa that Bonnie was being spiteful, but she could see by the look in Elsa's eyes that Bonnie had probably been speaking the truth.

Now, Jess set her chin in a determined fashion. 'I'll not let them put us in Brownhill nor any other poorhouse for that matter ...' She stopped speaking as someone entered the toilets, it was Alice.

'Mrs Ancrum's looking for you, Jess, so you'd best find somewhere better than this to hide ...'

Jess shook her head. 'I'm done with keeping my head down and toeing the line.' She held her hand out to Ruby. 'Coming?'

Ruby nodded.

It didn't take them long to find Mrs Ancrum, although Jess was pleased to see the older woman looked surprised to see them. 'Probably thinks we wouldn't have the nerve to face her,' she said to Ruby out of the corner of her mouth.

Mrs Ancrum stared at them in an aloof fashion. 'I hear you plan on signing up for the services?'

Jess and Ruby shook their heads.

She shot them a withering look. 'Good, then you won't be disappointed to learn that Bonnie McKinley will be taking your papers to Brownhill before breakfast tomorrow morning,' she smiled sarcastically, 'not that it will matter to you, if you don't plan on joining up.'

Jess's mouth dropped open. 'You can't let Bonnie take our papers! She hates us.'

Tutting, Mrs Ancrum wagged a reproving finger. 'You seem to have it in for Bonnie, and I've no idea why!' She hesitated. 'She told me how you refused to clear your mess up this morning.'

'That's not true!' objected Ruby.

'Quiet!'

Mr Ancrum had been taking the wireless back to his office, but he swivelled round and walked swiftly towards them. He glared at Jess. 'You're a troublemaker, Jessica

Wilson, have been since the day you arrived. The sooner we get rid of you the better. If it was left to me I'd strip the skin off the soles of your feet,' he looked at his wife then sneered nastily, 'only my wife says it's bad sportsmanship to flog a horse before you send it to the knacker's yard.' Chuckling, he walked away with the wireless.

Jess stared at the older woman, who looked jubilant. 'Run along, girls.'

Jess waited until they were alone before speaking. 'We leave tonight.'

Ruby looked stunned. 'You heard what she said, Jess. Without our papers ...'

'Bonnie's taking them before breakfast tomorrow morning, which gives us tonight,' said Jess bluntly. 'We'll wait until everyone's asleep, then search Ancrum's office for our papers and leave.'

Since seeing Mrs Ancrum, the girls had set about the business of getting themselves ready to run away.

'We'll need enough food to tide us over for a couple of days,' said Jess as she led the way towards the kitchen. 'We won't be able to take it out from under their noses, 'cos the kitchen will be busy 'til late on, but we can make sure we stash something so that we can have it ready to hand when we leave tonight.' She spoke from the corner of her mouth as she entered the kitchen. 'Follow my lead.' She strode over to the cook and smiled pleasantly. 'Hello, Aide, would you like a hand with the dishes?'

The fat cook eyed them suspiciously. 'How come you're offering to work? You done something you shouldn't?'

Ruby smiled sweetly. 'Not at all, only we won't see you again after tomorrow so this is our way of saying thank you for all the wonderful meals you've made us over the years.' Seeing the look of incredulity on Jess's face Ruby had to stifle a giggle.

The cook shrugged. She had no idea why the girls were offering to help, but if it meant she finished sooner, it was fine by her. She looked at Jess then pointed to the basin. 'You can wash,' she handed Ruby a tea towel, 'and you can dry.' Wiping her podgy fingers on her apron, she sat down heavily on a large wooden chair next to the range. 'Make sure you do a good job.'

'We will,' Jess assured her. She winked at Ruby and whispered, 'Give her five minutes and she'll be snoring like a pig. That's when I'll nip into the pantry and get us whatever I can lay my hands on, whilst you carry on here.'

Ruby nodded. 'Be careful, Jess. I know you say they can't do anything to us, but I'd not put anything past Ancrum – if she can twist the knife she will.'

It didn't take long before the cook's snores were reverberating around the kitchen. Taking her chance, Jess disappeared into the pantry only to appear a few moments later. Grinning like the cat that got the cream, she whispered excitedly, 'Two huge chunks of cheese, half a loaf of bread and ...' She pulled back the piece of linen which she had wrapped the food in to reveal a large slice of Dundee cake. 'Pudding.'

Ruby's eyes rounded. 'Where did you—' she stopped short as the cook stirred in her sleep.

Putting a finger to her lips, Jess covered the loaf before pushing the food under the kitchen sink. 'No one's going to think of looking under there. We'll come back and get it before we leave.'

They finished the dishes and left the kitchen before the cook woke up. Jubilant that their plan appeared to be a success, their hearts dropped when Mrs Ancrum hailed them from the bottom of the staircase as they were making their way back to their dorm.

'I'd prefer to keep you two where I can see you this evening,' she said stiffly, 'so I'm giving you the task of making sure each girl is bathed before bed.'

Jess and Ruby nodded, hearts hammering in their chests. They would have agreed to just about anything if it meant the older woman didn't ask them where they had been or what they had been up to.

'Why are they giving everyone a bath?' said Ruby. 'It's not Christmas and we've not got an inspection, so ...'

Jess shook her head. 'The girls will have to get on a train to go to Glencoe. It won't look good for Ancrum if the other passengers see them looking anything other than squeaky clean.'

It was a long while later when Ruby appeared with the last two girls. She pulled Jess to one side and whispered, 'I just saw Aide leaving. She called me over and I felt certain we were for the high jump, but she only wanted to thank us for doing the dishes and she gave me this ...' she held up a scone '...'cos of the nice things I said about her food!'

Jess giggled. 'I can't believe she fell for all that drivel. She can't possibly have ever tasted her own grub.'

Ruby shrugged as she broke the scone into two halves. 'I was scared she was going to say she'd found the food under the sink and ask if I knew anything about it, but she never said a word.'

Jess gave Ruby a secretive wink before pointing to the youngest girl, whose large blonde curls hung in ringlets around her ears. 'Strip!'

The girl took her thumb out of her mouth, causing Jess to grimace. 'Blimey, Lettie, your thumb may be as clean as a whistle but it's the only part of you that is!'

Lettie giggled as she looked at her grubby hand with its pink thumb. 'The rest of me will be clean as a whistle too once I've had my bath.'

With all the children bathed, Ruby got into the bath, and relaxed as Jess poured the warm water over her head and shoulders. 'I was a bit dubious when you first suggested running away, but I really think we can do this.' She smiled as the water washed the dirt and grime from her body. 'It's going to be a new start for us, isn't it, Jess?'

Nodding, Jess began to wash her friend's hair. 'A new life, even.'

Taking the bar of soap from Jess, Ruby washed her arms and chest, before handing it back. 'For most people war is the worst thing that could've happened, but not for us.'

Jess rinsed the soap from Ruby's back. 'That's because most folk have happy lives with loving families.'

Looking over towards the closed door, Ruby lowered her voice. 'Do you really think we'll find our papers? What if Bonnie's already taken them to Brownhill?'

'Bonnie's not been here all day, and Ancrum said she'd have to take them over first thing in the morning, so I think we're safe enough.'

Ruby brightened. 'All we have to do is find them.' She smiled. 'What do you reckon they'll do when they wake up tomorrow and realise we've gone?'

Jess's tummy gave an anxious flutter. 'They'll know we've run away, which won't bother them one iota, although they won't be happy when they find out our papers have gone. They'll guess we've nicked them so we can sign on. If they want to be spiteful, they might report us as runaways, in the hope that we'll be captured and sent to Brownhill anyway.'

Ruby stood up and wrapped herself in the towel which Jess handed to her. Stepping out of the bath, she began to vigorously rub herself from head to toe. 'We'll never be able to join up if they tell on us,' she said, her voice muffled by the towel.

'We'll just have to keep our fingers crossed that they're too busy to notice the papers have gone,' said Jess as she stepped into Ruby's bath water.

'We have to take our chances,' said Ruby simply. 'We either go ahead with our plan, or spend the rest of our lives in Brownhill.'

Baths finished, the girls headed back to their dorm. Seeing Bonnie walking towards them down the corridor, Jess cast Ruby a furtive glance.

'Well, well, well,' sneered Bonnie. 'I thought you two were off to join up?'

'Sod off, Bonnie,' muttered Jess.

Laughing, Bonnie watched the two girls enter their dorm. 'She who laughs last, Jessica Wilson!'

As they climbed into their beds Jess whispered to Ruby, 'We'll see who has the last laugh.'

Later, lying in the dark, Jess gave a little start as the church clock began to chime midnight. Slipping silently out of her bed, she landed panther-like on the floor. She had half expected she would have to wake Ruby up, and was pleased to see that her friend was smiling up at her. Having gone to bed fully clothed, Jess pushed her feet into her plimsolls, and waited for Ruby to do the same, then together they stole out of the dormitory.

'Are you sure we shouldn't have used our pillows as decoys?' said Ruby as they tiptoed down the staircase.

'No. If they found them they'd know we were up to something,' said Jess with certainty, 'but if they see our beds looking like they normally do, they'll assume we've gone down for breakfast.'

Standing at the bottom of the staircase, Jess checked to see if the coast was clear then nodded to Ruby, and the pair made their way to Mrs Ancrum's office. As she grasped the door handle, Jess noticed that Ruby had crossed her fingers on both hands. Closing her eyes, Jess gave the handle a slow experimental twist, then her eyes snapped open as the door yielded to her touch. Their plan was underway.

'You get the food, I'll find our papers, two birds, one stone,' she hissed to Ruby, who nodded and headed off down the corridor.

Jess closed the office door softly behind her then paused for a moment whilst she looked around the room. The remainder of a fire burned in its grid, giving enough light for her to see her surroundings. The pictures which had previously adorned the walls had gone but the hooks remained; the shelves, once full of books, now stood empty, and the elaborately woven woollen rug which covered the floor was hidden under numerous cardboard boxes.

Bending down, Jess began to search the box closest to her. It contained a few framed certificates, and she pulled one of them out and cast her eyes over the writing. *To certify that Madeleine Ancrum has …* Jess gave a snort of contempt. 'Outstanding service indeed,' she muttered under her breath. She looked into another box and discovered that it was full of information regarding some of the girls in her dormitory. Upon closer inspection she realised the box contained birth certificates as well as other bits and pieces relating to the identity of each child. Rocking back on her heels she let out a small groan. If their papers were in amongst these boxes she'd never find them.

A thought occurred to her as she glanced at the filing cabinet. Mrs Ancrum wouldn't have put their papers with everyone else's as they weren't being evacuated to Glencoe, so it only stood to reason that their papers might still be in the filing cabinet. She stole quietly across the room and gently opened each of the drawers only to find them empty. Pursing her lips, she cast an eye around the rest of the room, but there was little left that wasn't in boxes, save for a wastepaper basket full of crumpled pieces of paper. She smiled hopefully, but after a quick inspection of the bin she found nothing but old receipts and half-written letters. Scratching her head, she continued to look around the room and accidentally kicked a piece of crumpled up paper towards the embers of the fire. Bending down, she noticed that there were two or three more pieces of paper which had escaped the wastepaper bin. She uncrumpled one and glanced at the writing. Her heart thudded. It was Ruby's birth certificate. She folded it carefully then grabbed the next one, and was not surprised to find it was a document relating to the night she was found on the doorstep of Greystones. Placing it together with Ruby's birth certificate, she rummaged through the rest of the papers which she now suspected hadn't escaped the wastepaper bin, but were stacked up ready for burning.

'All our papers,' she muttered under her breath, 'to be burned so that we would never be able to sign up.' She tucked the papers into the pocket of her dress and made her way to the door. She was just about to open it when someone on the other side pushed it inwards. Swiftly ducking behind the door, she held her breath, hoping that it was Ruby who had entered the room, but to her horror she heard Bonnie's voice.

'I can't believe you'd be so stupid!' hissed Bonnie. 'I gave you one small job, and what do you do? Lazy cat!'

'But Bonnie,' whined Clare, 'your mam said we wasn't to burn the papers.'

'I don't care what my mam said!' snapped Bonnie. 'If you'd have done what *I* told you to do in the first place I'd still be tucked up in bed. No one can prove we burned them. It's not as if they're going to come back and complain, and who cares even if they do? We'll be long gone.'

'I hope you're right …' said Clare doubtfully.

'Where are they?' said Bonnie, her voice sharp.

'I left them by the fire,' Clare said.

Jess could hear sounds of movement then the scraping of the poker as Bonnie prodded the still smouldering ashes of the fire. Bonnie cackled. 'Looks like Ancrum's done the job for us and burned them without realising what they were!'

Clare hesitated. 'Why do you hate them so much?'

'Not them, *her*,' Bonnie corrected. 'That Jess has been nothing but trouble since she arrived at Greystones.'

Much to Jess's surprise, Clare pressed on, 'I thought Jess was a baby when she arrived? How can a baby cause any trouble?'

Bonnie sighed impatiently. 'Not so much Jess, but … Promise you won't tell?'

'Cross my heart and hope to die,' Clare said fervently.

Jess listened in rapt silence as Bonnie relayed the story of the night her mother had found Jess, winding up with: 'So Ancrum accused me mam of stealing the money, but she didn't.'

There was a pause before Clare spoke again. 'I thought Jess was a foundling?' she said slowly. 'But she wasn't really, was she?'

'Her dad wouldn't give my mam any details,' Bonnie said, 'so she's no different to a foundling, not really.'

Behind the door Jess held her breath, scarcely able to believe what she was hearing. Miss McKinley was always saying how Jess had been trouble since the day she arrived at Greystones, Mr Ancrum had said those very words earlier that day, yet whenever Jess had asked the staff what they meant, not one of them had mentioned the altercation between McKinley and her father.

'What I don't understand,' said Clare slowly, 'is why your mam didn't give Jess's dad what for. I've seen her lose her temper, and I find it hard to believe she'd be afraid of an old man who needed a cane to walk.'

'Shows what you know, then, doesn't it!' said Bonnie sharply. 'Mam reckons the handle of the cane was a huge cobra's head made from solid silver, which means it'd be really heavy. One hit with that and bam … good-night sweetheart.'

'Solid silver!' repeated Clare. 'He must've been really rich if he could afford something like that.'

'Not only that, but she reckons he were a Scouser,' Bonnie told her, 'a posh one, but a Scouser nonetheless.'

'Gosh,' breathed Clare, 'your mam was brave standing up to someone like that!' She paused, then added uncertainly, 'What's a Scouser?'

'Not sure, but they don't sound pleasant,' Bonnie said. 'They're probably a bit like the Billy Boys, and we all know what a nasty bunch of so-and-sos they are!'

'If her dad's like them then she's lucky he left her behind,' Clare agreed.

Bonnie continued, 'You'd think Ancrum would applaud my mam for standing up to the evil swine, not accuse her of stealing!' She stopped suddenly. 'Did you hear something?'

Jess's eyes widened. She had been so engrossed in Bonnie's tale, she hadn't been paying proper attention. What if the noise they heard was Ruby coming to get her?

She waited in her hiding place as Bonnie tiptoed towards the door. Jess wondered what to do for the best: should she push past Bonnie and make a run for it, or keep still and hope for the best? To her surprise she heard Bonnie making a shooing noise. 'Someone must have let that stupid cat from the Horseshoe pub in.'

Jess crossed her fingers tightly. It looked as though Bonnie and Clare were going to leave the office, but this still meant they could bump into an unsuspecting Ruby. As Bonnie left the office, she closed the door behind her. Jess placed an ear to the door so that she might hear what was going on outside, but all seemed quiet. She was about to open the door and risk a peek, when a face appeared on the other side of the office window. Jess let out a small scream which she quickly muffled beneath the palm of her hand. It was Ruby. She dashed across and lifted the sash.

'Quick!' said Ruby. 'Before someone else comes along.'

Jess wriggled out of the window and hugged her friend. 'What on earth are you doing out here?'

Ruby slid her hand into Jess's and led her around the yard, using the buildings as cover from the moon which shone bright in the sky above them. 'I heard Bonnie and Clare talking when I came out of the kitchen,' she explained. 'I guessed they hadn't found you because they'd have shouted blue murder if they had, so I decided to wait until they left. Only they seemed to be having a right old natter, so I decided to come round outside instead and went back to the kitchen and when I opened the back door the cat from the Horseshoe shot past me.'

Jess grinned. 'So it was you who let him in! And there I was worrying they might bump into you by accident!'

Ruby looked smug. 'Got rid of them, though, didn't he?'

Jess nodded. 'They were gossiping about the night McKinley found me.'

Ruby frowned. 'Oh? By all accounts I didn't think there was much to tell.'

Jess relayed everything she had overheard.

Ruby was flummoxed. 'All these years and not a word!' She hesitated. 'Do you believe her? About your father, I mean?'

Jess nodded. 'What would be the point in lying? She didn't know I was listening, and when you think about it, it makes perfect sense as to why Bonnie and McKinley treat me like everything's my fault, 'cos as far as they're concerned it is.'

As they left the courtyard, Jess closed the large wrought-iron gates behind them. Holding on to the bars, she looked back at the orphanage. Cloaked under the cover of darkness it looked as dank and dismal from the outside as it did on the inside.

Ruby joined her. 'What now?'

Jess turned her back to the gates and looked down the street. 'I've been thinking about it and I reckon we take a look at the Durnings' old house.'

Ruby looked doubtful. 'Shouldn't we try and get as far away from here as possible?'

Jess shook her head. 'Why bother? They're going to Glencoe in the morning, so it's not as if we'll have to worry about any of them spotting us round here because they'll be long gone.'

'How will we get in?' said Ruby.

Jess shrugged. 'Cross that bridge when we come to it?'

Ruby giggled. 'That's your answer for everything!'

Jess linked arms with Ruby and together they walked in the direction of the house. Remembering the papers which she had rescued from the fire, Jess pulled them out of her pocket and showed them to Ruby. 'I found our papers. Clare and Bonnie were going to burn them, so it's just as well we left when we did.'

Ruby shook her head sadly. 'I can understand Bonnie, but why would Clare do something so spiteful? What's in it for her?'

'Being pals with Bonnie has its positives,' said Jess. 'She gets special treatment, like sweets and extra helpings, and every now and then she gets to stay overnight with Bonnie and her mam in their private room.' She paused. 'Talking of food, I take it you managed to get the grub?'

Ruby held up the linen which contained the goodies they had stashed earlier. 'Now all we need is some decent clothes,' she said.

'Clothes are easy,' said Jess dismissively. 'We can borrow something off someone's washing line.'

Ruby eyed her friend with interest. 'What do you mean, "borrow" someone else's clothes?'

'We'll give them back once we have a uniform,' said Jess reasonably.

'But taking other people's stuff without permission is wrong – and before you say it, I know we took food from the kitchens, but Greystones have to feed us, and we aren't going to be there for breakfast, so that makes us even.' She gave Jess a reproachful glance. 'What you're suggesting is stealing!'

Jess feigned shocked innocence. 'I said we'd give them back, so that counts as borrowing, *not* stealing!'

Ruby giggled at Jess's expression. 'I know you, Jess Wilson, and whilst you've a heart of gold, you can be a law unto yourself at times!'

'All I can say in my defence is our need is greater than theirs,' said Jess.

As they approached the abandoned house, Ruby looked back at the forbidding building which used to be their home: the large black windows, the towering chimneys, the grey slate roof and the stone walls. 'I can't believe we've really done it!'

Jess followed her line of sight. 'Feels good, doesn't it?'

Ruby nodded. 'I was so desperate to get away I never thought about where we'd stay.'

Jess slid her arm out of Ruby's and placed it around her shoulders. 'Remember, Rubes, this is only temporary until we sign up. After that we'll have a proper home, with paid jobs, the lot.' As she spoke she opened the Durnings' garden gate and together the girls followed the path around the side of the house.

Jess muttered a curse as her foot caught in a bramble. 'Careful where you tread!' she warned Ruby.

The girls eyed the back of the house. 'What now?' hissed Ruby.

Jess placed her hand on the handle of the back door and gave it an experimental twist. 'Locked!' she said with disappointment.

Ruby peered through the window, but it was no use; it was as dark inside as it was out.

Kneeling down, Jess ran her hands over the ground. 'Looks like we're going to have to be a bit resourceful.'

'What're you looking for?' asked Ruby.

'Something to break the window.'

Ruby's eyes rounded. 'You can't do that! Spending the night in an abandoned house is one thing, but breaking windows?' She shook her head. 'That's what robbers do.'

Jess frowned as she continued her search. 'Only we're not going to rob the place. And it's not our fault we can't get in.'

Ruby gave her friend a lopsided grin. 'You've a funny way of justifying your actions, Jessica Wilson. I can just see you in front of the judge.' She adopted a haughty voice: 'I'm frightfully sorry, your honour, but people really should leave their back doors unlocked if they don't want their windows broken!'

Jess stifled her giggles. 'Glad you see my point of view.' Much to Ruby's horror, she then bent down and proceeded to pick up a plant pot.

'No, Jess!' hissed Ruby. 'You can't!'

Jess placed the pot to one side and picked up something else. Grinning, she held it up for Ruby to see.

'That can't be the key!' said Ruby in disbelieving tones.

'Only one way to find out!' Jess slid the key into the lock and danced a small jig as they both heard the lock click open.

Ruby nudged her friend. 'You first.'

Jess cringed as the door scraped across the tiled floor, expecting the noise to have woken the neighbours, but all was quiet. Tiptoeing inside the room, she waited until Ruby was behind her before carefully easing the door shut. The girls stood in the darkened room and waited until their eyes had adjusted. 'I reckon we're in some kind of kitchen,' said Jess. 'Put your hands on my shoulders, Rubes – that way we won't bump into each other.' Stepping forward, she gave a stifled scream.

Ruby gripped Jess's shoulders between her hands. 'Is it the ghost?'

'No!' said Jess indignantly. 'I walked into a cobweb and it's too dark to see if I've got any spiders on me!'

Ruby let go of Jess and started wiping herself down. 'I hate spiders! I bet this place is covered in them, what with no one coming in to clean and dust.'

Jess tried to look around her as well as she could whilst not moving from the spot where she stood. 'I think I can see some sort of range. I wonder if there's any matches?'

'I hope so,' said Ruby. 'I don't fancy us blundering our way through a houseful of cobwebs ...' She fell silent as something scraped, hissed then flared.

'Found some,' said Jess. Holding the match up so that she could see more clearly, she pointed to some cupboards. 'Keep your fingers crossed.'

'No need,' said Ruby. 'There's one of those big oil lamps in the middle of the kitchen table – look.'

The flame neared Jess's fingertips, causing her to drop the match.

'Steady on!' said Ruby. 'You don't want to set the place on fire.'

Jess lit another match, removed the shade and lit the wick. Seeing the flame dance into life, she turned the wick down and quickly put the shade back over the top. She stopped in her tracks.

'What's up?' said Ruby.

'It's warm,' said Jess.

'Course it is ...' Ruby began but Jess was shaking her head.

'It was warm before I lit it.'

Ruby's jaw dropped. 'Are you sure?'

'Positive,' said Jess. She looked around the room. 'Ruby?'

'Yes?'

'You know how you said the whole house is probably covered in dust and cobwebs?'

Ruby swallowed. She didn't like the sound of Jess's voice. 'Yes?'

'Apart from the cobweb I walked into, it's not.' To prove her point, Jess wiped a finger along a sideboard and held it up for Ruby to see.

'We'd best get out of here ...' Ruby began before Jess cried out in alarm. Ruby stared in horror as someone placed a hand over her friend's mouth.

Chapter Two

'For God's sake, shut your trap before you wake the neighbours!' hissed a voice in Jess's ear.

Jess's eyes swivelled in her head as she tried to see the speaker. 'George?' she said, although her words were muffled by his hand.

'Yes,' said George. 'Promise you won't scream if I move my hand?'

Jess nodded.

George slowly took his hand away from her mouth. 'Come with me.' He disappeared into another room.

Jess and Ruby exchanged glances. 'What's he doing here?' hissed Ruby as they followed him into a small room, although in her heart she was secretly pleased to see their old friend. She didn't like to worry Jess, but she had been very concerned when George had continually failed to turn up for church over the past few weeks.

George indicated a couple of chairs. 'Take a seat.'

The girls did as they were told. Jess was next to speak. 'We've not seen you in church for ages. Did that horrible Bonnie get you in trouble with Blakely?'

He nodded. 'But that's not why I ran away from Nazareth House.'

'Then why?' said Jess, who was feeling confused. 'We didn't know we were going to war until yesterday.'

In answer George pulled his shirt over his head and turned his back to the girls. Tears instantly pricked both girls' eyes as they saw the long lacerations across his back.

'George!' squealed Ruby. 'Who did that to you?'

Pulling his shirt back over his head, he winced as he took a seat on the chair opposite. 'Father Blakely,' he said simply. 'And not because I nicked some stupid apples neither, before you ask.'

'Nobody deserves that,' said Ruby, 'not even if they've stolen a tree full of apples.'

George's smile broadened. 'Thanks, Ruby.' He looked at Jess. 'Remember how I said they give us the rod to teach us to be grateful?'

Nodding, Jess looked aghast. 'I didn't realise ...'

George shook his head. 'Father Blakely saw me giving my bread to one of the little 'uns. When he asked why I'd done it, I told him the truth – I thought Archie needed it more than me. He said I were being ungrateful and I should learn to appreciate what I'd been given.'

Jess's bottom lip trembled. 'Evil, evil man!'

'Jess!' hissed Ruby. 'You can't say that about a priest!'

'Yes, I can,' said Jess. 'I don't give a rat's behind if he's a priest, a vicar or the bleeding pope himself, hitting someone because they tried to stick up for little kiddies is evil, Ruby Anderson, plain and simple.'

Ruby opened her mouth to speak, then nodded, shamefaced. 'You're right, Jess. Just because he's a man of the cloth doesn't mean to say he's a good man.' She glanced at George. 'Are you in a lot of pain?'

George shrugged. 'I found some salt in the kitchen cupboard so I've been keeping it clean, and I reckon it's started to heal 'cos it's not as painful as it was when he first did it.' He paused. 'But never mind me, what are you two doing here?'

Jess smiled grimly. 'Ancrum was going to send us to Brownhill, so we decided to run away.'

He grinned. 'If I thought anyone was going to defy Ancrum, I'd have guessed it would be you two!'

Jess pointed towards the bundle she'd placed next to them on the sideboard. 'We've got some food if you'd like some? Have you had anything to eat?'

George winked at Ruby. 'Apples, 'cos they're free, and some bread and cheese.'

Feeling the start of a flush begin to make its way up her neck, Ruby pulled out the chunk of cake and handed it to George. 'Fancy a slice?'

George's eyes sparkled. 'Blimey! Where'd you get that from?'

'We "found" it in the kitchens,' giggled Ruby.

He raised an admiring brow then winked at Ruby, causing her to blush. 'As far as windfalls go, this beats apples hands down!'

Ruby looked embarrassed. 'I must've sounded like a righteous little twerp.'

George shook his head. 'There's nothing wrong with principles and morals for those that can afford them.'

She smiled, grateful for his forgiveness. 'You've told us why you ran away, but not when or how,' she said. 'Has anyone come looking for you?'

'They did in the beginning. I saw a couple of the lads snooping round the back garden, so I scared them off quick.'

Ruby frowned. 'How'd you scare them off?'

Jess, who was quicker off the mark than her friend, grinned. 'It was you making those awful whooping and wailing noises! You're the Durnings' ghost!'

George nodded. 'You should've seen them run! They scattered like rats before the farmer's gun.'

Jess quickly did the maths in her head. 'Just how long have you been here?'

He grimaced. 'A few weeks ...'

Ruby's jaw dropped. 'Weeks? I wondered where you'd got to.' Her eyes travelled the length of his body. 'No wonder you look so skinny!'

He shrugged. 'I had to get out there and then. I've been going down the docks and getting work, but it's hard work and poorly paid.'

Jess eyed his skinny form. 'Me and Ruby are going to join up – why don't you come with us?'

'Already been!' said George. He followed Jess's gaze as she took in his threadbare, torn trousers, tatty plim-solls, and his dirty shirt. Guessing her thoughts, he continued, 'I don't think the army are too bothered about what you look like.'

Blushing, Jess spoke hastily. 'I'm sure they're not. I ...' her voice faded.

He smiled kindly at her. 'Don't worry, I wondered what kind of reception I'd get turning up looking like a scarecrow, but they couldn't have given two figs. They were more concerned about me having no proof of identity, but I soon got round that – I told them I'd lost it in work earlier that morning.'

'And they fell for that?' Ruby asked.

'I said I'd been loading up one of the ships and me papers had come out my pocket and fallen in the sea.' He pulled a face. 'I thought they'd ask more questions, like where I was born and that, but they weren't interested. They said to go home and wait and that I should hear something in a week or so.'

'I hope it's as easy as that for us!' said Jess, who had been getting quite worried at the thought of someone examining her and Ruby's credentials, especially as she intended to alter their date of birth.

She picked up a photograph of a young boy from the sideboard. 'I don't remember seeing any kids here – this must be an old photo.' She glanced in the direction of the stairs. 'What's it like upstairs?'

'I'll show you.' He raised a finger to his lips. 'But make sure you're quiet, 'cos the people next door are in bed.'

The girls followed George up the stairs and through the first of two doors. 'Look at that bed!' hissed Ruby. She crossed the room and sat on the plush eiderdown, bouncing up and down, then beckoned Jess to join her.

Jess sat down beside her friend. 'I'll sleep like a baby in this,' she said. 'It's soft and cushy, not like the beds in the orphanage.'

'You're welcome to it,' said George, keeping his voice low. 'I sleep in the room across the hall.'

61

Getting up from the bed, the girls started to follow him out of the room, when something caught Ruby's eye. 'With you in a mo.'

Jess hesitated. 'What are you … oh, Ruby!'

Ruby had pulled the most beautiful dress Jess had ever seen out of a large oak wardrobe. She held it up against herself. 'It's a bit old-fashioned but I reckon I could do something with it.' She glanced at George. 'Me and Jess can't go to the recruitment office wearing our own clothes, because with two of us it'll be obvious we're from the orphanage.'

George looked at their identical grey pinafore dresses. 'You've got a point there.' He eyed the dress approvingly. 'I don't see the harm in you two borrowing a couple of dresses.' He stifled a yawn behind the back of his hand.

'I think we should leave the grand tour until the morning,' said Jess.

George nodded gratefully. 'I've got to be up in a few hours. I could really do with some kip before I head off down the docks.'

'Sorry, George,' said Ruby. 'I'd forgotten you have to go to work. Come on, Jess, let's leave him to get some shuteye.'

The girls bade their friend goodnight before heading back into their newly appointed bedroom.

Jess stripped down to her vest and knickers before climbing between the sheets. 'I dunno about you, Rubes, but I reckon I could sleep for a week!' She waited for a response, but all she heard were the soft snores of her friend, who had fallen asleep as soon as her head hit the pillow.

Smiling broadly, Jess pulled the eiderdown up around her ears. They may not have been out of Greystones for more than a few hours, but their future was already beginning to look a lot brighter, and within moments, she too was sound asleep.

The next morning Ruby woke up with a start. 'For goodness' sake, Jess, you mustn't stand over folk like that!' She sat up and knuckled her eyes. 'What time is it?'

'Church bell chimed ten not so long ago.'

'Ten!' squeaked Ruby, only to have Jess shush her into silence.

She pointed to the wall behind Ruby's head. 'Someone might hear us!'

Ruby quickly apologised. 'Why didn't you wake me?' She looked past Jess to the bedroom door. 'Where's George?'

'Down the docks.' Rooting in the wardrobe, Jess turned to face Ruby, a dress in each hand. 'Which one do you want?'

Ruby wrinkled her nose. 'I don't suppose you've come across a sewing box?' She got out of bed and took one of the dresses from her friend. 'I'll have to take these frills off so they don't look so fancy, as well as taking them up and in, but once I've done that I reckon they won't look half bad.'

Jess held up a small box and opened the lid so that Ruby could see inside. 'Found this whilst you were sleeping.'

'Good girl!' Ruby was beginning to smile, when the distinct noise of a lot of children being marched down the road came from outside the window. 'Oh, my Lord!' She looked at Jess expectantly. 'Do you suppose …?'

Crossing the room, Jess carefully took hold of the curtain and lifted it a fraction so that she could see outside. 'It's Ancrum and the rest of them from the orphanage.'

'Can you see McKinley or Bonnie?' Ruby asked.

Jess was studying the parade of girls when Bonnie, who was near the back, suddenly looked up at the window. Jess quickly ducked out of sight. 'I think Bonnie saw me!'

Ruby hurried over to where Jess was standing and leaned towards the window, as if she were trying to hear what was going on in the street below. Leaning back, she smiled confidently. 'They're still marching,' she told Jess. 'If Bonnie had seen you she'd have been sure to raise the alarm.'

A slow smile spread across Jess's face. But had she looked outside the window again her smile would soon have disappeared, because contrary to Ruby's belief, Bonnie had stopped marching and was staring fixedly up at their window.

'For heaven's sake, don't just stand there!' Agnes snapped at her daughter.

'I could've sworn I just seen that Jess in the upstairs window of the Durnings',' said Bonnie. Reluctantly, she started walking again.

Agnes spared a backward glance at the house before continuing. 'So what if you did? After all the trouble that child's caused, I'd have thought you'd be glad to say good riddance to bad rubbish.'

'If I never see her again in my life it'll be a day too soon,' agreed Bonnie. 'Only why should we have been the ones to get it in the neck for her running off?'

Agnes caught her daughter by the elbow and pulled her alongside. 'You know full well why you got into trouble and it had bugger all to do with her running off. It's because you couldn't blooming well help yourself, could you? You had to twist the knife by burning their papers and because of your actions Mrs Ancrum's had a whole heap of explaining to do!'

'It wasn't me!' Bonnie protested.

Her mother raised a disbelieving brow. 'Well I sure as hell didn't do it, nor did Mrs Ancrum. You were the only one who knew where the papers were, so it doesn't take a genius to work out who's responsible.'

'I swear I didn't do it, Mam,' whined Bonnie. She shot a backward glance at Clare, who was keeping her head down. A thought occurred to Bonnie. 'Who's to say she didn't set fire to her own papers?'

Agnes glared at Bonnie. 'Don't be so stupid! Why on earth would she do a thing like that?'

'To get me in trouble,' said Bonnie simply.

'So she'd see herself homeless, with no chance of a fresh start, just to get you in trouble?' said Agnes, barely holding on to her temper.

'I think she might, yes,' Bonnie insisted stubbornly.

'You're being ridiculous!' Agnes stopped in her tracks and pulled her daughter round to face her. 'Why not own up instead of making outlandish claims?'

'Because I didn't do it!' wailed Bonnie.

Shaking her head, Agnes strode ahead, muttering under her breath that Bonnie needed to grow up and own up.

Inside the Durnings', Jess had slipped into one of the dresses so that Ruby could shorten the hem. Jess held a finger to her lips. 'Did you hear that?'

Ruby, who had a mouthful of pins, gave a muffled, 'No.'

'It sounded like someone shouting,' said Jess. She very much wanted to look out of the window to see what was going on.

'Stand still, Jess!' Ruby ordered. 'You'll fall off the …' She leaned back as Jess fell off the pile of books they were using as a step.

'Sorry,' Jess said. She nipped across the room and took a peek out of the window, but all she saw was the backs of the girls as they continued to march down the street. Satisfied that they were in the clear, she piled the books back on top of each other and stood on top of them again.

'Well?' said Ruby.

Jess shrugged. 'False alarm. Thanks for doing this, Rubes. They'll not say no to us down that recruiting office when we show up looking all posh.'

'I hope not,' said Ruby, ''cos I don't know what we'll do otherwise. It's not as if we can join George down the docks.' She twirled her index finger, indicating Jess should turn around.

'You're right there …' Jess stopped short as she heard the letterbox snap shut. 'That might be his papers!'

Ruby nodded. 'I hope so, 'cos if the Germans are going to target the docks, then the sooner George gets away from them the better!' She paused as she took another pin and pushed it firmly into place. 'I wonder where they'll send him?'

'Anywhere's better than here,' said Jess, stepping down from her perch. She made her way down the stairs, returning a moment or so later with a letter in her hands. 'It's addressed to George.'

Ruby's heart quickened. 'Do you think we should take it to him?'

Jess shook her head. 'We've no idea whereabouts he'll be. Besides, we've a lot to do here. Whatever that letter says, it can wait 'til he comes home this evening.'

The girls spent the rest of the day making adjustments to their new clothes, until they were satisfied that they looked as though they were their own.

'Very nice too!' George said as he admired the girls' handiwork later that evening.

Jess looked at the letter which George was holding. 'Are you excited about leaving?'

He beamed. 'Too right I am, Sandhurst is the best in the country.' He sighed wistfully. 'Proper clothes, proper meals ...' he glanced at the ceiling above him '... although I will miss that bed.'

'You're going to be a real man!' said Jess.

'Only 'cos they don't know how old he is,' interjected Ruby, who was feeling apprehensive at the thought of George becoming a soldier.

'Doesn't matter how old he is,' said Jess, 'he'll be taught to hold a gun, and they don't give guns to kids!'

'Yeah!' agreed George. 'Stop being such a stick-in-the-mud, Ruby!'

Ruby smiled apologetically. 'I don't mean to be, and I really am pleased for you, George. I'm just worried about you.'

'Like me mam would be, if I had one.' George smiled and winked at her. 'It's nice to have someone worry about me, I've never had that before.'

'How are we going to know if you're all right?' Ruby could feel the start of a blush invade her neckline.

'I'll write to you, and you can write me back,' he said simply. He placed a hand over hers. 'We're all we've got, so we've got to look out for each other. Agreed?'

Ruby smiled. 'Agreed.'

The next morning Jess and Ruby took a deep breath as they made their way up the steps of the town hall. 'Remember to look confident,' Jess reminded her friend. 'George said we'd sail through as long as we look like we know what we're doing.'

'I just wish we could've done something with our hair,' said Ruby, pulling her slouch hat down over her ears.

Mrs Ancrum didn't approve of long hair, believing it to be prone to head lice, so once a month she would gather the girls into the hall where the cook, or whoever was available at the time, would cut their hair short, whilst inspecting them for lice. The girls knew it made them stand out from everyone else.

A man wearing a smart pinstriped suit doffed his hat as he walked ahead of them. 'Morning, ladies.'

Jess nudged Ruby in the ribs. 'I've never been called a lady in my life!' she said with a touch of pride.

'And if he reckons we look like ladies, then maybe the recruiting officer will too,' Ruby said hopefully.

The man glanced back at them over his shoulder as he continued to walk. 'Are you here for anything in particular?'

'We were hoping to sign up for one of the services,' beamed Jess, who was feeling far more confident after being referred to as a lady.

He gestured to a room off to one side of the marbled corridor. 'That's the one you want. Good luck, ladies.'

As Jess and Ruby entered the room they were surprised to find it empty save for a man in soldier's uniform sitting behind a desk. Seeing the girls, he beckoned them over.

'Good morning! Are you here to sign up?'

They nodded.

He looked expectantly at them. 'Well, come in then. I can hardly take your details when you're all the way over there, now can I?'

The girls hastily crossed the room and Jess took her papers out from her dress pocket and placed them face down on the table. She waited whilst the corporal inspected them before holding his hand out for Ruby's. Leaning back in his seat, he eyed them thoughtfully before speaking. 'According to your birth certificates you're both eighteen ...'

Both girls nodded mutely. They had spent a rather nervous ten minutes changing the date of their birth from 1923 to 1920, but neither of them thought it looked convincing. He cast his eyes back to the certificates in front of him then glanced up at Jess. 'I see you've got no parents?'

Her face dropped. 'No, does that matter?'

He held her gaze. 'It depends. Are you in any trouble?'

She shook her head. 'No,' she crossed her fingers behind her back, 'only there's not much for us around here, so we were hoping to join up so that we might make something of ourselves.'

He appeared to weigh something up in his mind before nodding thoughtfully. 'Can you make a cup of tea?'

Jess and Ruby exchanged glances. Was he asking them to make him one? Jess nodded slowly. 'Ye-es.'

He smiled. 'Good, you'll do all right in the NAAFI then.'

'What's the NAAFI?' said Ruby.

'It's where they make the tea and coffee, amongst other things.'

Jess and Ruby beamed with relief. Not only did it look as if they were being accepted into the services, but they were being given easy jobs to do.

He looked at their address and frowned as he wrote it down. 'Do you live here?'

'Course we do,' said Ruby, adding as point of proof, 'number nine, Edinburgh Road.'

He looked over their shoulders as a young man in khaki uniform entered the room. The corporal nodded. 'You should hear something within the next week or so.' As the two girls left the room the corporal beckoned the newcomer to join him. He pointed towards their retreating figures. 'See those two?'

The man nodded.

'They reckon they live at nine Edinburgh Road ...'

The man put his head on one side. 'Nine Edinburgh Road, nine …' He looked up sharply. 'A feller came in a couple of weeks ago claiming he lived there … brother, perhaps?'

'Did he now?' The corporal folded his arms across his chest. 'What did he look like?'

The man pulled a face. 'He's a docker, so filthy – he didn't look anything like those two.'

The corporal shook his head. 'What I'm wondering is why there seems to be a bunch of kids living in a house that we've been offered as a billet.'

The man cocked an eyebrow. 'Runaways?'

The corporal scraped his chair back from the desk as he got to his feet. 'Those girls may have looked posh, but did you see their shoes?'

'No, why?'

'They had more holes than a sieve.' He shook his head. 'I'm going to check this out. Make sure you let me know if anyone else comes here claiming they live at nine Edinburgh Road.'

The other man nodded and sat in the empty seat. 'Where are you going?'

The corporal held up the papers in his hands. 'To see if I'm right, 'cos if I am those girls are in for one hell of a surprise!'

Outside, Jess and Ruby waited until they had walked far enough from the building before cheering and taking hold of each other in a tight embrace. 'We're in!' beamed Jess. 'And it's something we can actually do. Oh Ruby, we've really landed on our feet, and I reckon we can thank your fancy sewing skills for that!'

Ruby made a mock curtsey. 'You're welcome.' She added, 'George'll be so pleased.'

Jess threaded her arm through Ruby's. 'I reckon you've got a soft spot for that boy.'

'Boy!' echoed Ruby. 'You've hit the nail on the head there, 'cos that's just what he is, a boy.'

'What else would you have him do?' said Jess. 'He's probably safer in the army than he is working down the docks.'

Ruby looked glum. 'I know, but what if they send him to fight in France?'

Jess stiffened. 'Then he'll be the best fighter the army have ever seen, but I doubt it'll come to that.'

Ruby looked uncertain. 'Really?'

Jess nodded authoritatively. 'We're not the only ones who'll see him as a boy; the army will too. They'll send the more experienced men over to fight.'

'I hope you're right,' said Ruby, beginning to feel a little better. 'I'd hate to think they'd send a boy into battle.'

Three days after Ruby and Jess had signed up, they walked George to the train station to see him off.

'Write as soon as you get there,' Jess instructed. 'Goodness knows where we're all going to end up so it's important that we keep in touch.'

'Wouldn't it be grand if they sent you to Sandhurst?' said George wishfully.

'We'd be sure to slip you an extra lump of sugar or two!' said Ruby.

She watched as passengers began to board the train and opened her mouth to tell George he should get on as well, but the words stuck in her throat.

George cast an eye around the platform. 'Pity we couldn't've had a few more days ...'

They turned to look at the guard who was making his way along the carriages making sure all the doors were closed.

George hastily pecked both girls on the cheek, picked up his bag and boarded the train. He pushed the window down and leaned out. 'So long, girls. I'll write as soon as I get there. Good luck with everything!'

Ruby fished a hanky out of her pocket and went to blow her nose before rushing over to George. 'I've got yours by mistake!'

He grinned down at her. 'Keep it as a reminder! I'm sure the army will have plenty of tissues. Besides, real men don't cry.' He winked cheerfully at her.

The conductor blew his whistle, startling Ruby. 'Take care of yourself!' she called out as the train began to pull away.

They waved until George was lost from view. Ruby turned to face Jess who was holding her arms out in readiness. 'Come here, hen,' she said, pulling Ruby into a tight embrace. 'He'll be fine, Rubes. He's got gumption, has George. He stood up to Father Blakely, didn't he?'

'Father Blakely's a cowardly bully,' sniffed Ruby, 'he's not a Nazi with a gun!' Her bottom lip trembled. 'And I don't reckon George can weigh more than seven stone soaking wet.'

Jess clenched her jaw as she tried to remain strong for her friend. 'He's feisty, Rubes, and that goes a long way. Besides, you don't have to be built like a brick whatchamacallit if you've a gun in your hand.'

Ruby lifted the hanky to blow her nose, then stopped. 'It smells like George.' She pushed it back into her pocket. 'Where are the lavvies?'

Jess pointed to the sign further up the platform and they headed in that direction.

'You're right about the gun thing,' Ruby acknowledged, 'and I suppose it's easier to hide behind things if you're as skinny as George.'

Jess hoped her words were true, and that George had an advantage over his comrades, because as far as they could see there was no alternative. If the Luftwaffe started bombing the Glaswegian docks, then life as a docker could be just as dangerous as being on the front line. She dabbed her eyes as Ruby emerged from the station lavatories.

Determined to change the subject, Ruby threaded her arm through Jess's. 'Let's get back and see if the postie's been.'

Jess nodded. 'That's the spirit! Onwards and upwards. Who knows what the day may bring?'

By the time the girls got back to Edinburgh Road, they had both cheered up immensely. George would be in training for several months, by which time the war could be over. Jess had crossed her fingers behind her back during this part of the conversation, because she knew that if this war was anything like the last lot it could go on for years.

Stepping inside the house, Jess checked to see whether any mail had been delivered and was disappointed to find the hallway bare. 'I suppose it was a bit much to expect our papers through so early. The man at the office did say it could take a week or so.'

'I hope not,' said Ruby, 'because the food George left won't last us that long ...' She paused. 'Did you just hear something?'

Jess shook her head. 'Like what?'

'I thought I heard the back door close.' Ruby lowered her voice. 'Didn't you lock it?'

A male voice spoke from behind Jess. 'No, she didn't lock it. I think you've got some explaining to do.'

Jess slowly turned around. The man who had spoken was a few years older than herself and dressed in a khaki uniform, and he was glaring angrily at them. She went to speak, then hesitated. He was familiar – she could've sworn she knew him from somewhere, but where?

With nothing forthcoming, he arched an eyebrow. 'Well?'

Something in Jess's mind clicked. She went over to the sideboard and picked up a framed photograph. She turned it to face him. 'Is this you?'

He nodded briefly as he eyed the boy in the photo, then stared fixedly at her. 'The question isn't who am I, but who are *you*?'

Ruby stepped forward guiltily. 'I'm Ruby and this is Jess. We're sorry for breaking in, but we didn't know anyone was living here. We'll go.'

The man looked over Ruby's shoulder. 'What about the boy?'

Jess's heart was in her mouth. How could he possibly know about George? Another thought occurred to her: if he knew about George it was because someone must have tipped him off. She glared angrily at him. 'Who told you? Was it that Bonnie? If it was ...' She got no further.

'Whoa there, slow down.' Folding his arms across his chest, he continued, 'I'm the one who's asking questions.'

Jess shrugged pettishly. 'He's gone and he won't be coming back.'

He looked down at her. 'Got his papers through, did he? I didn't realise they were taking on scruffy little toerags ...'

Jess shot him an icy glare. 'He's not a boy, nor a toe-rag. If you must know, he's gone to war, and if those men down the recruiting office thought he was a boy, why on earth did they let him sign on the dotted line?' She was pleased to see a guilty glimmer sweep the man's face.

'That's beside the point. He had no right to give this place out as his address, and neither did you,' he wagged a finger at Ruby who had made to intervene, 'and don't try and deny you've been living here, because it's plain to see you are.' Taking the photo-graph from Jess's unresisting fingers, he placed it back on the sideboard. 'Question is, why?'

Jess's first reaction had been to blame Bonnie, but now she thought about it, Bonnie couldn't possibly have known about George. In which case it was far more likely to be one of the neighbours. Resigned to the fact that they had been caught with their hand in the biscuit tin, Jess sank resignedly into one of the chairs. 'We've got nowhere else to go ...'

Ruby corrected her friend. 'Apart from Brownhill, only we don't want to live there.'

He frowned. 'Why not?'

Jess leaned back and sighed. 'You may as well know the truth.' She went on to tell him all about the orphanage, Brownhill and their escape.

'I see,' said the man. His features had softened through the course of Jess's story.

'You're not going to tell, are you?' asked Ruby anxiously.

He sat down on the chair opposite Jess's and eyed them thoughtfully over his steepled fingers. 'I should ...' Seeing Ruby clutch Jess's shoulder, he heaved a sigh. 'I said I should, but I won't, but only because I think you're better off in the services than somewhere like Brownhill.' He shrugged. 'Maybe that's why the fellers down the office accepted your pal – they probably guessed he was lying but thought he needed a break.' He laughed without mirth. 'Although I'm not sure putting yourself up for active service would be considered a break.'

'What's your name?' Jess asked.

A small smile formed on his lips and for the first time Jess noticed how handsome he was when he wasn't frowning. 'I'm Tom. This house belongs to my Auntie Edna.'

Jess leaned forward. 'You said something about the recruiting office.'

He nodded. 'One of the fellers recognised the address. You see, my auntie's turned the house over for the war effort, to use as billets or offices – whatever they want – so they knew the place was empty ... or at least they thought it was.'

Ruby looked confused. 'That can't be right. Your auntie died years back, after they carted her off to the loony bin.'

Tom burst out laughing. 'Did she indeed? I'll make sure I tell her.'

'Where is she then?' asked Jess suspiciously. 'And if she's still alive, why's all her stuff here?'

Tom's eyes danced as he looked at Jess. ''Cos she's a stubborn old goat who didn't want to leave her home!' He tutted to himself. 'Even insisted on staying after they put her in a wheelchair, but after a while things got too much and she finally agreed to come and live with us in Liverpool.'

Ruby clicked her fingers. 'The little 'uns used to say they'd seen a woman gliding past the window like a ghost – they must've seen your auntie in her wheelchair. That's why she looked like she was gliding not walking, because she was!'

He nodded with a chuckle. 'Ghosts indeed.'

Jess began to turn pink. 'I know you said you wouldn't dob us in to the recruiting office, but what are you going to tell your auntie?'

He eyed her thoughtfully. 'Any idea how long 'til your papers come through?'

They both shook their heads mutely.

He sucked his cheeks in as he contemplated his decision. 'Auntie never liked the staff at the orphanage – she reckoned they were overbearing and mean – so she'll be pleased to know her home helped some of you escape. As for the recruiting office, I'll tell them there's been a bit of a mix-up and that we've some guests who'll be staying until their papers come through.'

Jess sagged with relief. 'Oh Tom ...' she paused, 'do you mind if I call you Tom?'

The corners of his lips turned up. 'Not at all.'

She smiled thankfully. 'That's ever so kind of you, Tom.'

'It looks as though you've spruced the place up a bit.' He cocked an eyebrow. 'I told my auntie that I'd empty the house whilst I was up here, so that it'd be ready for the army.'

'We'll help, won't we, Rubes?'

He smiled. 'I could do with a hand because there's an awful lot to get through.' He cast an eye around the room. 'It's been a while since I last visited here – I'd forgotten how many things she had.'

Jess stood up and made her way into the kitchen. 'I can't offer you any tea,' she picked up the tea urn and gave it a tentative sniff, 'I think it's been here too long, but we've some lemonade if you'd like some?' She looked at Tom who was reeling with laughter. 'What?'

Gently removing the urn from Jess's hands, he placed it back on the shelf. 'That's not tea! It's my Uncle Kevin.'

Jess stared aghast at the urn. 'Please tell me you're joking?'

Ruby, too, was staring at Tom in horror. 'You mean to tell me we've been sharing a home with your dead uncle?'

Still grinning, Tom nodded. 'That's about the size of it.'

Jess giggled. 'So you want lemonade then?'

Tom nodded. 'Yes, please.'

Ruby looked at him anxiously. 'I don't want to be rude, but would you mind taking Uncle Kevin home with you? Only I don't think I'll get a wink of sleep knowing he's in the kitchen.'

Tom smiled. 'I think that might be for the best.'

Ruby felt relieved that Uncle Kevin was no longer going to be residing downstairs. 'What do you do in the army?'

'I work on the ack-acks,' he said with a touch of pride.

'What are they?' Jess asked inquisitively.

Now that they were in the kitchen where the light was better, she could see just how handsome their saviour looked with his thick brown curly hair and deep-set brown eyes. Jess immediately thought of her own hair, which was only a bit longer than his. Wishing she was wearing the hat that she'd worn to the recruitment office, she pulled the bottle of lemonade out of the cupboard.

'They're the anti-aircraft guns which we use to shoot down the Luftwaffe,' explained Tom. 'My brother works in the Motor Transport section, and my dad's an ARP warden.'

'Gosh! Sounds like it runs in the family!' said Ruby.

He nodded. 'It certainly does. My old man was in the last lot, and my grandfather served in the Boer War.'

'Golly,' said Jess. She was very impressed. Tom's family sounded like good, honourable, reliable people, and when he talked of his family's service history she noticed his chest puffed out a little. 'Where did you say you were from?'

'Liverpool ...' he looked at their blank expressions, 'it's a couple of hundred miles south of here, in England.'

Jess's cheeks reddened. 'You haven't come all this way just because of us?'

He waved a dismissive hand. 'Don't worry about it. I would've had to come up sooner or later, and I even got special leave because it's to help the war effort. I really don't mind – it's been a while since I've been up in this neck of the woods, and it's good to be back.'

Jess's blush deepened. 'I still feel guilty. All this fuss because of us ...'

He smiled reassuringly. 'Not to worry. I suppose you've done me a favour really.'

'Oh?' said Ruby.

'I've been telling my auntie we should come and empty the house for ages, but she always came up with one excuse or another as to why we should leave things be, but when they rang to say she might have squatters, she couldn't get me up here fast enough!' He waved a vague hand in the direction of the parlour. 'I'm quite surprised nobody's broken in to nick what's here. They might not be interested in the photographs, but some of the frames are silver. She's lucky it was you who broke in and not some lowlife who'd rob her blind.'

'I think the tales of ghosts have kept people at bay,' Jess said. She cast an eye around the kitchen. 'When are you planning on getting everything out?'

As he took the glass of lemonade from Jess, his fingers slid over the top of hers, causing her to blush again.

'My brother's pal is coming to give me a hand tomorrow,' Tom said. 'I don't have to be back for a few days, so there's no immediate rush.'

Jess felt her tummy flutter. 'So, you're going to be here for a little while?'

He nodded. 'Looks like it.'

Jess smiled broadly. A short time ago she had been disappointed to learn that they still hadn't received their papers, but now she found herself hoping that they wouldn't arrive until after Tom had left. That way she might get to spend some time with the handsome corporal.

Jess and Ruby were having their breakfast of blueberry jam on toast, when they heard the letterbox snap.

Jess hurriedly put her toast back on her plate, licked her fingers and made her way to the front door to pick up the envelopes.

'Well?' urged Ruby, barely able to contain her excitement. 'Is it ...?'

Jess handed Ruby her envelope. 'Got to be, 'cos we've got three, and two of them are official-looking whilst the third,' she grinned, 'looks like it's from George.'

'George's first!' said Ruby eagerly.

Jess slit the envelope open and pulled out the letter, and they read it together.

Dear Ruby and Jess,

If the NAAFI is as good as the army, you're in for a real treat. We get proper meals, warm beds and decent clothes. The chaps I'm with are a grand lot. It's kind of like being in the orphanage only no one hits you with a rod, or not so far at any rate, ha ha. We're going to be here for at least six weeks – where we'll go after that

82

who knows! It's only been a few days and I'm sure I've put on weight already. I can't wait to hear where you're going. With a bit of luck it won't be far from me.

Don't forget to write me back.

George

PS I've got Ruby's hanky if she's worried she mislaid it!

Ruby smiled. 'I'm glad he's settled in well.' She looked expectantly at the two remaining envelopes. 'Go on then, put us out of our misery!'

Jess passed Ruby's over then waited until her friend had read the contents. Ruby glanced at Jess from over the top of her letter. 'Seaforth Barracks. Open yours.'

Jess held her breath as she looked at the letter in her hands before letting it out in a rush. 'Me too!' she squealed. 'Oh Rubes, I felt sure we were going to be separated. I know Tom said the NAAFI's different, but I've been ever so worried.' Relaxing back into the kitchen chair, she took another bite out of her toast, then re-read the letter in case she'd made a mistake.

Ruby beamed. 'I reckon it's because we filled our forms in on the same day! I wonder how far Seaforth is from Sandhurst?'

Jess swallowed the piece of toast she had been chewing. 'I'll ask Tom when he comes round – he's good with geography.'

'And he's very helpful.' Ruby giggled suggestively.

'Meaning?' said Jess, not prepared to let Ruby's comment go unchecked.

'Meaning that he'd bend over backwards for a certain young lady not a million miles away from where I'm sitting!' Ruby took a sip of her tea. 'He was ready for a war when he knew he had squatters, but as soon as you batted those large green eyes at him, he was like putty in your hands … which is just as well.'

Jess rolled her eyes dismissively. 'Tom likes helping people out. It wouldn't matter what I looked like – he's a nice feller and that's all there is to it.' Seeing the wry look on her friend's face, she added, 'It runs in his family – that's why they're all in the forces.'

Ruby coughed. 'I'm sure that's true, but it doesn't change the fact that he's keen on you.' She wagged a finger at her friend. 'He doesn't look at me the same way he does you, and when I opened the front door yesterday he asked where you were before he'd even said good morning!'

Jess dropped her gaze back to the letter in her hands. She hoped her friend was right, because she was equally keen on Tom, and not just because he had come to their rescue by allowing them to stay in his aunt's house. He was also kind and considerate. He had listened to their stories about the orphanage without judgement and had applauded their bravery to leave in the dead of night and start a new life.

Ruby, who had been reading her railcard, looked up sharply. 'When do you leave?'

Jess turned her own card over. 'Friday afternoon, same as you.'

Ruby stared at her card in disbelief. 'No, it's not, I'm leaving tomorrow.' She handed the card over to Jess. 'I know Tom said we should be prepared, but they should've given me more notice than that!'

Jess looked up from the railcard. 'You're on the ten o'clock train.'

Ruby's mouth dropped open. 'I've never been on a train before, I won't know what to do. Does it go straight from Glasgow to Seaforth?'

Jess grimaced. 'I don't know. You'll have to ask someone. There's bound to be a driver, he'll know.'

Ruby thought back to the day they had seen George off. 'The driver's in a different part to the rest of us. I'll have to find out before we set off.' She eyed Jess fretfully. 'I wish we were travelling together – everything's a lot easier when there's two of you.'

'You're going to get to do everything first!' said Jess, a touch of envy in her voice. She was beginning to feel like she was missing out. 'Go on a train, see our new home, meet the other girls …' she splayed her hands wide, 'everything, and I so wanted us to do everything together!'

A loud horn sounded from outside. Leaning back on her chair, Jess glanced through the window. 'It's Tom, he's in a lorry with that pal of his.' She looked around the half-empty kitchen. It had taken a lot of work, but in the past three days they had managed to clear most of the contents from the house, taking the more valuable things to be auctioned. They had donated the rest to make money for the war effort, leaving the bigger furniture such as tables and chairs until last. 'Come on, Rubes, let's go and tell him the good news.'

Tom's face appeared around the side of the door. 'What's this I hear about good news?'

Jess told him about the letters, adding, 'So you needn't worry about us leaving before the army moves in.'

Tom rubbed his hands together enthusiastically. 'And you'll not be far away neither!'

Jess looked at him hopefully. 'You've heard of Seaforth, then?'

Tom's face split into a wide grin. ''Course I have! It's not far from where I grew up. Come to that, it's just down the road from where I'm stationed.'

Ruby pouted. 'I wish George was in Seaforth.'

Jess patted Ruby's hands from across the table. 'He can always come and visit, and we can go and see him too.'

Tom pushed his hands into his pockets. 'I'm afraid Sandhurst's a fair old distance from Seaforth.'

The driver of the lorry appeared in the doorway. 'Morning all!' He jerked his head at Tom. 'Are you going to stand here gassing all day or what?'

'Sorry, Mick, we're coming now.' Tom glanced at the boxes which they had stacked the previous day. 'Me and Mick'll start on the furniture if you girls take the last of the boxes.'

'Right you are,' Jess said. Picking up a box each, she and Ruby made their way outside to the lorry.

Ruby grinned. 'Looks like you've made Tom's day.'

Jess eyed her friend doubtfully. 'Don't you think he's a bit posh for me?'

'Not really, why? Do you?'

Jess nodded. 'He's not like us, Rubes, he comes from a proper family, *and* he's got both parents.'

'What's that got to do with anything?' said Ruby. She lifted the box over the top of the gatepost as she passed through. 'Just because you've got a family doesn't mean to say you're posh, or better than anyone else. I very much doubt Tom thinks that.'

'Well, maybe not posh, then ...' she screwed her lips in thought as she followed Ruby through the gateway. 'Perhaps I mean normal?'

Ruby pulled a face. 'Who's to say what's normal?' She studied the awkward look on her friend's face and nodded her understanding. 'You don't think you measure up.'

'Well, I don't, do I?' said Jess plainly. 'My own parents didn't want me, and not because they couldn't afford to keep me neither from the sounds of it.'

Ruby tutted. 'Well, it wasn't because of anything you'd done. You were only a baby!' She pushed her box onto the lorry and waited whilst Jess did the same. Ruby glanced up at the bedroom window and saw Tom and Mick taking the mattress off the bed. 'He doesn't view you as something nobody wants – far from it!' she said firmly.

'How can you be sure?' Jess asked.

'Because a bomb could go off when he's in the same room as you and he wouldn't bat an eye!' Ruby waved a hand in the general direction of the house. 'Surely you don't think he'd have gone through all this for George?'

Jess opened her mouth to speak, closed it, then tried again. 'He did say he was coming up to empty the house, so he's not doing this for us, not really.'

Ruby eyed her friend in mild surprise. 'He could've had this house cleared in two days – he's only dragged his feet so that he can spend time with you.'

Jess smiled. Tom had certainly taken his time over packing the boxes, always asking Jess to help him decide whether something should go for auction or be donated to the war fund. She looked at the bedroom window to where Mick was drawing Tom's attention from the girls outside back to the job in hand. Ruby followed her gaze.

'See?' Ruby insisted. 'You drive that man to distraction!' She wrinkled her nose. 'I wish I had that effect on someone!'

Jess followed Ruby up the garden path. 'Like George, you mean?'

Ruby shrugged. 'I suppose so, only I would hope that if someone really liked me they wouldn't shoot spit balls at me!'

'That's why he did it, it was his way of getting your attention,' said Jess. 'And it worked, too!'

Ruby laughed mockingly. 'So the sort of feller that's attracted to you lets you stay in his aunt's house for free, whereas mine shoots spit balls into my hair! Talk about drawing the short end of the stick.'

Jess began to giggle. 'George was a lot younger when you first met!' She nudged her friend. 'He's giving you hankies now, not spit balls.'

'By accident!' Ruby corrected.

Jess shook her head. 'Your hanky is pink with primroses on it. There's no way that boy picked yours up by accident – he did a switch so that you'd each have a keepsake. How else do you think his hanky wound up in your pocket?'

Ruby stared at her, open-mouthed. 'I must say, I did think it was a bit odd!'

'There you are then. So I'm not the only one with an admirer – not that I'm saying that's what Tom is, even if you think so.'

Ruby lowered her head so that Jess might not see the blush that crossed her cheeks. When they had lived in Greystones they had never managed to spend more than five minutes at a time talking with George, but things had been very different in the Durnings' house. They had spent their few evenings together chatting about Nazareth House, Greystones and life on the outside of these institutions, as well as their hopes and dreams for the future. Ruby had very much enjoyed her time with George and before she knew it she had developed a real fondness for him.

It took them the best part of the day to clear the house. 'Are you sure you don't mind sleeping on a mattress?' Tom asked Jess. 'I don't mind bringing one of the beds back up.'

'I do,' Mick objected.

'I'll be fine,' Jess assured him. 'It's only for a couple more days.'

Ruby emerged from the house, which she'd been giving a quick once-over to make sure they hadn't left anything behind. 'That's the lot!'

Jess eyed the contents in the back of the lorry. 'Why do you think she left it so long?'

'I think she hoped she might be able to come back one day,' said Tom. He pulled the canvas down and started strapping it into place. 'It must be hard having to admit you're no longer the person you once were.'

'Independent, was she?' said Ruby.

He nodded. 'Fiercely, that's why she stayed as long as she did.'

Mick secured the back of the lorry. 'Adios, ladies.' He winked. 'That's foreign for goodbye!' He turned to Tom. 'Come on, Tom, we need to get this stuff to the auction house before we set off, and I'd like to be back in Liverpool before it gets too dark.'

Tom waved an acknowledging hand. 'Righto.' He smiled at Jess. 'Looks like this is goodbye, but …' he lifted a hopeful eyebrow '… see you soon?'

Smiling back at him, Jess felt her tummy flip. 'That would be nice. You'll have to come to Seaforth.'

Tom climbed into the passenger side of the vehicle and wound the window down. 'Will do. I often call in to Seaforth Barracks for one thing or another.'

Jess looked at him in surprise. 'Don't they mind?'

He shook his head. 'Nah, they all know me in Seaforth.' He gave them a small wave. 'Ta-ra, girls.'

Ruby linked her arm through Jess's and together they waved him goodbye. 'Cheerio, Tom, and thanks for everything!'

He leaned out of the lorry as it pulled away. 'My pleasure! I wouldn't be much of a Scouser if I didn't help a lady in distress!'

Jess stopped waving. She stared disbelievingly as the lorry disappeared from view. 'Did he just say what I thought he said?'

Ruby nodded slowly. 'He said he was a Scouser.'

'I don't understand!' said Jess, feeling thoroughly confused. 'According to Bonnie, Scousers are like the Billy Boys, but he didn't seem like a mindless thug to me, far from it!'

Ruby scratched the top of her head. 'Perhaps Bonnie got it wrong?'

The girls fell silent as they each tried to work out whether Tom had meant some other kind of Scouser. Jess was the first to speak. 'He said it as though he was proud!'

'It certainly sounded that way,' Ruby conceded. 'On the other hand, the Billy Boys run Glasgow like they're top dog, proud of their achievements – maybe it's like that for the Scousers.'

'Bonnie didn't say my father tried to deny that he was a Scouser, so it doesn't seem as if he was ashamed,' Jess said, then added nodded darkly, 'but we've all heard the stories about the Billy Boys and how vicious they can be when it comes to getting their own way. My dad sounds just like them.'

Ruby walked up the path to the house. 'You can't believe everything Bonnie says. She can be so spiteful …'

Jess gave a mirthless laugh. 'Normally I'd agree with you, but Bonnie didn't know I was listening. If she had she'd most likely have kept shtum!'

Ruby rubbed the tip of her nose. 'Even so, it doesn't mean to say your father and Tom are connected. There's bound to be some good Scousers – Tom must be one of them.'

Jess felt her mouth turn dry. 'I've just had a horrible thought.'

Ruby looked at her anxiously. 'What?'

'They're both Scousers, and they've both come to the same part of Scotland. What if they're related?' Jess hesitated. 'For all we know, Tom's Auntie Edna could be a Scouser. Maybe that's why my father brought my mother up here, so she could give birth somewhere private, where no one would be any the wiser!' She clasped a hand to her forehead as the enormity of this hit home. 'My God, Rubes – all he had to do was cross the blooming street and leave me on the doorstep!' Jess sank down onto the stairs. 'It makes perfect sense!'

Ruby placed a comforting hand on Jess's. She opened her mouth several times to try and convince Jess that she was wrong, and that she shouldn't jump to conclusions, but the more she tried to think of reasons as to why Jess was wrong, the more she realised her friend was right, it did make perfect sense. She took her thumb and wiped the tears which trickled down Jess's cheeks. 'Do you think his auntie was in on it?'

Jess nodded miserably. 'Course she was, people like that don't see anything wrong with that sort of behaviour. Besides, you can't hide a baby. Even if she didn't know his intentions, she must've realised my mother had given birth and there were no baby to show for it.'

Ruby swallowed nervously. 'Do you think Tom knows?'

Jess shook her head with certainty. 'No, he didn't bat an eye when we said we were from the orphanage.'

'That's true, but so are a lot of other kids. You never told him about your father so he wouldn't suspect a thing!' She looked at Jess, round-eyed. 'He's going to come and see you in Seaforth!'

Jess paled. She had all but forgotten about Tom's promise to visit. What would she say to him when he appeared in the NAAFI asking for a cup of tea? Ruby voiced the same thought. Jess blew her cheeks out. 'I'll tell him I'm busy. I won't mention anything about him being a Scouser.' She heaved a sigh. 'I don't understand it, Rubes. He seemed like such a lovely feller, and he bent over backwards to make sure we were all right.' She stared into space. 'How could I have got him so wrong?'

'Just because he's in a gang doesn't mean to say he wants to be. Perhaps he's been pressured into it, and you're not the only one who got him wrong. I thought he was lovely too.' She eyed Jess thoughtfully. 'Why don't you ask him? He could tell you about your father.'

Jess shook her head. 'I don't want to find my father or have anything to do with anyone who knows him. People like that are bad news, and who knows what he might do should his unwanted daughter appear on his doorstep?' She grimaced. 'At best he'd tell me to sling me hook. At worst ...' She shuddered.

'What about your mam? For all you know she might welcome you with open arms.'

'On the other hand she might not.' Jess looked at Ruby for guidance. 'How could Tom have anything to do with monsters like that?'

Ruby heaved a sigh. Everyone knew that Brownhill was bad, which was why some of the people who left the orphanages joined the gangs – it might not be to everyone's liking but it was better than being starved to death whilst working yourself into an early grave. 'People get into gangs for all sorts of reasons, and once they're in it's hard to get out ...' She wrinkled her brow as a thought occurred to her. 'Tom's in the army.'

'So?'

'I can't see the forces taking gang members on, can you?' said Ruby.

'Perhaps they don't know. It's not something you'd put down on your application, is it? Present job, gang member ...' Jess tutted sarcastically beneath her breath.

Ruby clicked her fingers. 'He said it in front of Mick, the one who was driving the lorry, but he didn't say anything, did he? Are you sure you're right about this gang thing? It seems very odd that Tom would boast about it so openly.'

Jess looked uncertain. 'Men are different to women, they don't see anything wrong with violence. It's men what create war, Rubes, not women.'

Ruby sagged visibly. 'I still think you should ask him, hear it straight from the horse's mouth as it were. It'd be a dreadful shame if you did nothing to find your father, especially if you're wrong and he isn't part of a gang.'

Jess clutched her stomach which was doing cart-wheels. 'I think I'd rather not know.'

Ruby frowned. 'Why on earth not?'

Jess glared at Ruby. 'Because he dumped me on Christmas Eve! He didn't even knock on the door, he was just going to leave me lying in the snow. I might not like McKinley, but at least she took me in. I'd have been dead for sure if it weren't for her!'

Ruby chewed the corner of her lip. 'It was a long time ago, Jess. I'm not saying what he did was right, but everyone makes mistakes. For all you know, your mam could be wondering where you are, how you are, and Tom deserves to be given the benefit of the doubt.

It'd be grossly unfair to accuse him of something when you don't know the facts.'

'Even if I'm wrong, and they're not gang members, they could well be related. It's a bit coincidental that two men from Liverpool end up on Edinburgh Road.'

'You've got a point there.' Ruby eyed Jess shrewdly. 'What if Tom tries to get closer? He seems awfully keen on you.'

Jess opened her mouth to reply, then closed it again. 'Why do you have to make things complicated?'

Ruby raised an eyebrow. 'I'm only pointing out the obvious. Don't go blaming me because Tom's interested in you.'

Jess sighed. 'Sorry, Rubes. Like I said before, I'll tell him I'm busy, and if he persists, I'll tell him I'm not interested.'

'That's a bit daft, isn't it?' said Ruby. 'Especially when it's plain for all to see that you like him too.'

'Doesn't matter,' Jess said simply, ''cos if we are related, or if he's in a gang …'

'And those are big ifs …' Ruby interjected.

'Like I say, *if* we're related or whatever, then it's a no go.' Jess hoped that Ruby would stop being so reasonable and allow the matter to rest.

Ruby sucked her lips in then let them out with a smacking sound. 'But if you're not, you've just waved goodbye to the best thing that might ever happen to you.' She waved Jess into silence as she tried to speak. 'Just because Tom's a Scouser, and he might be related to that pitiful excuse for a father of yours, doesn't mean to say that they're closely related. For all we know, Tom could be your fourth cousin twice removed or something daft like that.'

Jess's lips moved soundlessly as she tried to work this out. She knitted her brows. 'Is that even possible?'

'I think so, but it'd mean you didn't really share the same blood ...' Ruby paused '... or at least I think it does, especially if it's down to marriage and that.' She shrugged hopelessly. 'My dad's got loads of cousins – second cousins, third cousins, some of them are removed, some not – all I know is I never see none of them, so I figure we can't be that closely related.'

'I had no idea that families could be so complicated,' said Jess. 'If I ask him will you promise to get off my back?'

'Cross my heart and all that!' Ruby grinned at Jess. 'You're doing the right thing. You have to know the truth, whether it's good or bad.'

Mick grinned at Tom. 'There's been a bit of a misunderstanding ... my arse!'

Tom avoided the other man's gaze. 'I don't know what you mean,' he said, with a half grin.

'Your misunderstanding being the beautiful Jess, that's what I mean. You were spitting feathers when they first told you your aunt's house had been taken over by squatters, but that all changed the moment you met Jess.' He waggled his eyebrows suggestively. 'And I can't say as I blame you – she's not bad, not bad at all!'

Tom gazed out of the window. As far as he was concerned, Jessica Wilson was a lot more than 'not bad' – she was downright beautiful and had a personality to match. 'I can assure you that had nothing to do with it,' he said, trying unsuccessfully to hide his smile.

Mick chuckled. 'Bet you'll be round Seaforth Barracks quicker than you can say knife once a certain young lady arrives.'

'Be rude not to,' said Tom. 'Besides, if I don't move quickly she'll get snapped up by another feller.' He glanced at Mick. 'Women like Jess aren't two a penny.' He envisaged Jess in his mind's eye. Curly blonde hair, wide green eyes and a smile that lit up the room. Put someone like her in a NAAFI full of eager young men and Tom feared he might find himself at the back of the line. No, if he was to stand a chance with Jess, he would have to get in quickly and use their pre-existing friendship to his advantage.

Jess checked the clock above the platform. She knew the likelihood of her train being on time was remote, since Ruby's train had arrived an hour late. When they had questioned the station staff as to what the hold-up was, they had been informed that nothing ran on time any more because of the war. Jess felt a pang as she pictured Ruby boarding the train.

'What if I miss my connection?' Ruby had asked anxiously, her bottom lip trembling as she spoke.

'You'll be fine!' Jess had said reassuringly. 'Just make sure you don't doze off!'

'I'm too nervous to fall asleep.' Ruby took a step back as the guard closed the door.

Jess looked up suddenly. 'Have you remembered your photo?'

Ruby patted her pocket. 'Safe and sound!'

The girls had been told they would need a passport-sized photograph so that they might enter military camps. Having never had a photograph of themselves, they had decided to make the most of the occasion by trying to do something with their hair which would make them look less boyish. Given the choice Jess would have waited until it had at least grown to shoulder length before having a photograph taken, but under the circumstances she had to do the best she could by using some hair clips which she had found to try to clip her curls into place, only to have them spring free. Ruby, who had relatively straight hair, had combed hers flat, then spent a good half-hour smiling at her reflection in the dressing-table mirror, asking Jess which smile she thought looked prettiest. 'It might be the only photo I ever have,' said Ruby. 'I want to make sure I look my best.'

'You look beautiful,' sighed Jess as another curl escaped its clip. 'Stop worrying.'

'It's all right for you with your pouty lips and doe eyes,' said Ruby, grimacing at her own reflection. 'Some of us have to work hard just to look half decent.' She glanced at Jess who was trying to push another hairclip into place. 'You always look good.'

Later that same day when Ruby was striking what she considered to be her best pose for the photographer, she was not at all happy when he told her to 'sit still and try not to smile'. Her worst fears had been confirmed when they examined the end results. 'I look like a criminal!' she said, holding the small photograph up for Jess to examine.

'You're not the only one,' Jess said, but Ruby was having none of it. She took Jess's photograph and examined the two side by side before handing Jess's back.

'Yes, I am. You look serene and mysterious – look at your eyes, they look all happy and smiley!' Ruby glanced at her own photograph before shoving it into her pocket. 'I look like I've lost a pound and there isn't a penny in sight!' She fished the photograph back out of her pocket and examined it again. 'I look miserable!'

Jess burst out laughing. 'That's 'cos you were! Honestly, Rubes, I did tell you it was a waste of time practising your smile.'

Chuckling at the memory, Jess peered up the line to see if she could see a wisp of smoke, but there was still no sign. She would have asked the guard, but the last time she had done this he had looked annoyed and snapped, 'I've already told you, she'll get here when she gets here. There is a war on, you know!'

It had only been a few days since Ruby's departure but to Jess it felt like weeks. She couldn't remember a time when she had not woken up to Ruby's smiling face and friendly voice. The first time she had woken up on her own in the Durnings' house, Jess had felt more alone than she had ever done in her life. She took a bite into an apple which she had taken from the tree in their garden. She couldn't wait to be back with Ruby and was looking forward to hearing everything her dearest friend had to say about life in the NAAFI.

She turned her thoughts to Tom. Kind, caring, not to mention tall and dark, with twinkling eyes so deep a brown they were almost black. She sighed heavily. How could someone as wonderful as Tom get themselves involved in some awful gang? She thought back to Ruby's comments about Tom's attraction to Jess, something which Jess had very much doubted, with him coming from a loving family. With hindsight his attraction to Jess made far more sense if he was running with the wrong pack. She shook her head. How could someone who appeared to have it all be silly enough to get in with the wrong crowd, whereas someone like George, who came from nothing, did everything he could to ensure a better life for himself? She felt a wave of envy flow through her. Ruby was very lucky having someone like George hold a torch for her.

She was so deep in thought that it took her a moment or so to realise that someone was calling her name. She ignored it at first, believing it to be another Jess who was being hailed. But whoever was calling out was persistent, and they were getting louder. Jess peered around and was surprised to see a girl waving at her from further down the platform. Raising a rather tentative hand, Jess waved back. As the girl drew closer Jess beamed. 'Penny! Where on earth did you spring from?'

Penny arrived, rather out of breath, by Jess's side. 'Took you long enough!'

'Be fair! I wasn't expecting to see you, or anyone from Greystones for that matter.' Jess was thoroughly relieved to see that the face was a friendly one. With that thought in her mind, she looked wildly around her. 'The McKinleys aren't here, are they?'

Penny's eyes were out on stalks. 'Golly, no! Blimey, Jess, they'd have my guts for garters if they knew I were here.'

Jess sagged with relief. 'Thank goodness for that, although, if you're not with them …' She arched a questioning eyebrow.

Looking around to make sure no one was listening, Penny pulled Jess close. 'Not here, wait 'til we …' A loud whistle startled her. Further down the line she saw a steam train with a large number of carriages pulling into the station.

Curious to learn what Penny had to say, Jess led the way along the platform until she found an empty carriage. 'This one's free. If we're lucky we'll have it all to ourselves.'

Penny followed Jess into the carriage. As luck would have it, the train had a corridor so the girls could easily see anyone approaching. 'We could be here for a while yet,' Jess explained to Penny as she took the seat nearest the window. 'Ruby's train took an age to leave.'

Penny raised her brow in surprise as she took the seat next to Jess's. 'You mean she's not with you?'

Jess shook her head. 'We were together until a few days ago,' she said as she explained everything that had happened to them since running away.

Penny clapped her hands together excitedly. 'We wondered what'd happened, of course we did, but you know what Greystones is like for rumours – you can't believe half of what you hear.'

Jess was intrigued. 'What rumours were these?'

'According to the grapevine, Ancrum had you sent off to Brownhill before the rest of us woke up, only I knew that wasn't right, 'cos I woke up just after the clock struck one, and your beds were already empty!' Grinning, she tapped the side of her nose in a knowing fashion. 'I *knew* you'd run away – it was the only thing that made sense – but I kept my mouth shut.' She winked at Jess. 'I know the best way to find out what's really going on in that place, which is why I volunteered for breakfast duty, so that I could be in the kitchen, because whenever Ancrum loses her rag or talks about anything she doesn't want anyone to hear, she stands outside the pantry, 'cos there's no obvious windows or rooms nearby where she can be overheard ...'

Jess grinned. Everyone who worked in the kitchens knew the pantry was below ground level. The only form of ventilation came from a couple of air vents situated above the top shelves. 'You clever girl! I wouldn't have thought to go in there to eavesdrop!'

Penny beamed. 'I waited 'til everyone was busy then I snuck in and hid under the air vent, behind the shelves.' She flashed her eyebrows at Jess. 'Sure as eggs are eggs it wasn't long before I heard Ancrum and McKinley arguing fit to burn. At first Ancrum accused McKinley of going behind her back and striking up her own deal with Brownhill, giving you two up at a cheaper price, but McKinley started crying, saying she would never do something like that, but then Ancrum reminded her of the night you arrived.' Penny broke off and stared at Jess; her demeanour had gone from uncontainable excitement to someone who had bad news to impart. She looked down at her hands and started to fidget.

Jess frowned. 'What's wrong?'

After a moment or so, Penny looked up at Jess. 'Ancrum said she'd caught McKinley red-handed trying to nick the money your dad had left for you – apparently it was quite a lot.'

Jess placed her hands over Penny's. 'Don't worry, Penny, I already know about the money. I overheard Bonnie telling Clare. What I don't understand is what happened to the money if McKinley didn't take it?'

Penny blew her cheeks out. 'McKinley was foolish enough to ask Ancrum what she had done with it …'

'And?' said Jess eagerly.

'And I thought Ancrum were going to explode – she was furious! Said it was none of McKinley's business what had happened to the money, and if she heard that McKinley was spreading rumours that Ancrum had taken it she'd have her sacked and out on the streets before she could blink.'

'Blimey, looks like McKinley hit a raw nerve!' said Jess bitterly. 'Only, what did she mean about McKinley giving us to Brownhill at a cheap price?'

Penny gave Jess a dark look. 'I discovered the pantry was a good place to eavesdrop by accident one day when I overheard Ancrum and her husband talking about Brownhill. Mrs Ancrum was saying how they should ask for more money …' She stared at Jess's blank expression. 'They sell us to the poorhouse, Jess, as slave labour.'

Remembering the stories of Brownhill, and how nearly all the orphans had ended up there, Jess felt her heart sink into her shoes. 'Are you sure you've got this right?'

Penny nodded. 'They hadn't a clue I was there so they talked quite freely about it being a good little earner, but they thought they should ask for more or threaten to send us somewhere else.' She held her hands up. 'Think about it, Jess, they've got a never-ending supply of girls who they can sell on to the highest bidder. Brownhill isn't the only poorhouse in Scotland, and so long as they never pass on any orphans who've got family nearby, like Ruby and Alice, the authorities will never be any the wiser. I expect it would be hard to prove the girls couldn't find work elsewhere.'

Jess was aghast. 'But they were sending me and Ruby to Brownhill, so Ancrum ...'

Penny chopped her off. 'When McKinley pointed that out, Ancrum said she wasn't really going to send Ruby, and had only said it to scare her.'

'What about me?' said Jess, hardly able to believe what she was hearing.

Penny pulled a face. 'You haven't got any family ...'

Jess stared out of the window whilst she let it sink in. 'So where does Ancrum think we are?'

'She thinks you've run away because of Bonnie, and she's holding Bonnie and McKinley personally responsible should Ruby's father come looking for his daughter.'

Jess smiled with satisfaction. 'Serves her right, although I'm surprised she didn't sack McKinley then and there!'

Penny laughed mirthlessly. 'With everything McKinley knows? The Ancrums have to be careful she doesn't go blabbing to the bobbies.'

Jess digested this, then cocked her head to one side. 'So, what's your story? How did you get here?'

'I'm fifteen, Jess, there's only one place I was going unless I plucked up the courage to leave. Knowing you'd already done it, I decided to do the same, only I was luckier than you. As you know, Alice's mam only put her in Greystones because they couldn't afford to look after her, but with war breaking out there's plenty of work to be had, so she came to Greystones to collect her. Alice asked her mam if it would be all right for me to stay with them until I'd got my posting and she said yes!'

'Bravo to Alice's mam! What did Ancrum say?'

'She couldn't have cared less. I think she had bigger fish to fry what with you and Ruby running off.'

'Good! I'm glad we've given her cause for concern, and by the sound of things she's not going to go to the bobbies because she wouldn't want us giving our version of events, so it looks like we can breathe easy and not have to look over our shoulders.' For the first time since they had left Greystones, Jess felt she could truly relax. 'So how come you're on this train?'

Penny grinned. 'I'm in the NAAFI, same as you. We must've joined up within hours of each other, that's why we're being sent to the same place!'

Jess squealed with delight. 'You're coming to Seaforth?'

Penny nodded.

'I can't wait to see the look on Ruby's face when she sees you! She'll be so pleased to hear we weren't the only ones that escaped, and that we don't have to worry about the bobbies coming after us, although she'll not be happy to hear about what the Ancrums have been up to.'

Penny's smile broadened. 'I told Alice's mam what I'd overheard,' she shook her head with a chuckle. 'Alice's mammy was mad as fire! She stormed round to the government buildings and gave them hell. Said it was a disgrace and that the whole system needs a good shake-up. She also said she'd report it to the papers unless something was done about it.'

Jess gave a small whoop of joy. 'I hope they lock the Ancrums and the McKinleys up.' She hesitated. 'Where's Alice? Didn't she join up?'

Penny shook her head. 'Her mam got her a job working in one of the factories. They offered to let me stay, but I want to get out of Scotland and start a new life.'

Jess looked out at the deserted platform and was pleased to see that the guard was placing his whistle between his lips. 'Looks like we're on the move,' she said. The guard blew his whistle and waved his flag, and Jess turned to Penny as the train set into motion. 'I always did like Alice, and her mam sounds a decent sort too.' She glanced at Penny. 'Makes you wonder how on earth people get themselves into these predicaments, doesn't it?'

Penny shrugged. 'Her dad lost his job, and her mam's wages barely covered the rent.'

Jess tutted loudly. 'My old man's a right scallywag who isn't fit to look after a dog, yet he has money to burn. Some people shouldn't be allowed to have children.'

Her mind full of Penny's revelations, Jess closed her eyes and thought of all the girls who'd passed through the door of Brownhill. If there was any justice in the world, Brownhill and Greystones would be closed and the Ancrums would be hauled before a judge. Jess listened to the sound of the wheels as they raced along the tracks. She was on her way to a new life, hundreds of miles away from Brownhill and Greystones.

Chapter Three

When Ruby had first arrived in Seaforth, she had been unsure what to expect. From what George said in his letters, people who joined up were subject to endless hours of square bashing, all kinds of inoculations, and inspections from head to toe. So she had been pleasantly surprised to learn that life in the NAAFI was very different to that of the regular servicemen and women.

'Once you've made your bed, come back to the canteen and I'll show you what's what, although it's all pretty simple really,' said Mrs Armstrong, the mature woman who was in charge of the NAAFI. 'Have you had your medical yet?'

Ruby shook her head. 'Should I have? No one mentioned it.'

Mrs Armstrong cast her eyes skyward. 'Typical,' she muttered to herself, 'just because we're not officially in the services, they seem to think we don't matter. They soon come running when they want something from the NAAFI, but when push comes to shove they consider us civilians because we can leave any time we like.' She opened the flap to the canvas tent which was serving as Ruby's new billet, and nodded a greeting to a woman who was lying on the bottom layer of a bunk bed. 'Michelle, this is Ruby – she's new to the NAAFI as well as Seaforth. Can you show her where to put her things?' She turned back to Ruby. 'If you can't remember where the canteen is, just ask Michelle, she'll show you.' She turned to leave then thought better of it. 'Apart from keeping your billet tidy, we've only got one rule here, and that's no men in the billet, no matter who they are.' She smiled fleetingly at Ruby. 'With that being said, I shall leave you in Michelle's capable hands.'

As the older woman left them to get acquainted, Michelle walked over to one of the beds. 'This is yours,' she said, patting the mattress of the bottom bunk. 'You can put your worldly possessions in here.' She opened the door to a locker situated beside the bed, then leaned against the bedpost and smiled at Ruby. 'Not very glamorous, I'm afraid,' she eyed the tent roof, 'but at least it's dry, and it hasn't blown away ... yet.'

Ruby glanced at the locker. 'I haven't got anything to put in there, save my clothes when I've changed into my overalls.'

Michelle shrugged. 'Much the same as the rest of us, then, but not to worry, you'll soon start filling it up with all sorts of things.' She sat down heavily on her own bed and watched Ruby spreading her sheets out. 'Are you from Scotland?'

Ruby looked surprised. 'Is it that obvious?'

Michelle nodded. 'It is to me, although your accent isn't as strong as some of the fellers on camp.

Sometimes I find it very hard to understand them.' She chuckled to herself. 'You'd not think we all lived in the same country!'

Ruby smiled. 'Are there many Scottish people here?'

Michelle leaned forward. 'We get folk from all over, but mostly they pass through on their way to other places. Nobody seems to stay for long.'

This worried Ruby. She had assumed that once she got billeted to a NAAFI she wouldn't have to move again. 'Surely that's just for those that are in the forces? They don't do the same with us, do they?'

'It's still early days and the forces are having to play catch-up as they train up the new recruits,' Michelle explained. 'I daresay we won't stay here for the duration. As they set up new camps they'll need experienced staff to run them, and that includes us, or it will do once you're trained up. Besides, I would rather hope we wouldn't be sleeping under canvas for too much longer.' She lay down on her bed. 'My pal Beryl's well and truly landed on her feet with a posting to somewhere up north. She reckons the RAF took over a hotel, and that's where she's staying, lucky blighter.'

Ruby glanced around her. 'I think it's quite exciting. I've never been camping before.'

'Novelty wears off after a while, and it can get pretty hairy when the wind picks up.' Michelle waited until Ruby had finished smoothing the blanket down on her bed. 'Come on, I'll show you where everything is.' She hesitated. 'When was the last time you had something to eat?'

Ruby's tummy rumbled loudly, causing them both to giggle. 'This morning,' Ruby said.

'In that case, first port of call is the canteen, where you can have a cup of tea and a sarnie as well as meet the natives, and by natives, I mean the rest of the girls!'

Considering how anxious Ruby had felt at the thought of going to Seaforth on her own, within a few days she felt as though she'd been there for weeks. She had worried everyone might be sombre, given the fact that the country was at war, but that couldn't have been further from the truth. The soldiers were full of high spirits, cracking jokes and offering to help in any way they could. If life in Sandhurst was the same as Seaforth, it was no wonder George was happy.

Now, as Ruby prepared the tea and coffee for morning break, she jumped as a voice came across the tannoy advising that all personnel should assemble in the canteen at seventeen hundred hours.

'Watch out! I like me coffee in a cup, not on the floor!' chuckled Toby, a corporal in the Motor Transport section.

'I'll never get used to that bloomin' thing,' giggled Ruby. 'You having the usual, Toby?'

He grinned. 'You know me so well! Who cooked them?'

Ruby eyed him shrewdly. 'Why?'

Toby grinned. 'Just wondering whether I need a knife or a sledgehammer.'

Ruby shook her head. 'Michelle cooked them, so you'll need a knife, although I wouldn't let the other cooks hear what you say about their rock cakes.'

'They don't scare me,' he said, his eyes quickly scanning the kitchen area. 'Besides, they'd have to catch me first because I'm off to pastures new after lunch – again.'

Ruby set the cake on a plate. 'Where are you off to, or is it all hush-hush?'

'Lincoln,' said Toby, taking the plate and placing it on his tray. 'If you like, I'll give you my new address so you can write to me. Life's pretty lonely on the road.'

Ruby was thrilled. Toby was going to be her second pen pal – though she wasn't sure if she could call George a pen pal, not when she'd known him for so long. She poured the coffee and handed it to Toby. 'Make sure you jot it down before you leave.'

'Will do.' Toby handed her the money and took the tray, calling over his shoulder, 'see you later, queen.'

Michelle, who had been spreading slices of bread with a smear of margarine, called over to Ruby. 'He's got the cheek of the devil, that one.' She jerked her head at a slab of cheese. 'Do me a favour and start slicing that.'

Ruby began to slice the cheese as thinly as she could – she had soon learned that everything had to be done sparsely so that there would be enough to go round. 'Why does he call all the girls queen?'

''Cos he's a Scouser,' said Michelle matter-of-factly. 'That's how they talk to all the women.'

Ruby stopped mid-slice and looked sharply at Michelle. 'Sorry, did you just say he was a Scouser?'

Michelle looked up from her task. 'Yes, I'm surprised you couldn't tell by his accent.' She looked at Ruby, who was looking thoroughly confused. 'What's up, love?'

Ruby shook her head. 'Nothing, I just never knew he was a Scouser.'

112

The other woman glanced at Ruby's stony expression. 'Don't you like Scousers, then?'

Ruby shrugged. 'I've only ever met one, aside from Toby that is, and he seemed nice enough, but my pal's dad's a Scouser, and he were a right swine by all accounts.'

Michelle picked up a slice of cheese and placed it on the bread. 'There's good and bad wherever you go – you can't let it tarnish your opinion.'

Ruby debated if she should ask Michelle what she knew about Scousers, then thought better of it. Michelle had spoken of Toby and Scousers as though there was nothing wrong.

She watched Michelle from the corner of her eye. She had only been sharing a tent with the other woman for a few days, but she seemed pleasant enough. Would she really approve of people like the Billy Boys? She was sure the answer had to be no, but what if she was wrong? She sliced the sandwich she was preparing in half, and decided it would be better all round if she waited until Jess's train came in later that evening so that she could ask her friend's opinion on the matter.

George eyed his reflection in the mirror. 'Where's all my beautiful curls gone?'

In reply the barber indicated the floor below the chair with his scissors. 'I told you, I don't do requests.'

'They were my best feature!' said George, looking at the floor below him. He supposed with hindsight it should have been a clue when he walked across the carpet of squaddies' hair in order to get to the barber's chair. He got up from his seat and walked out of the hut.

The next man in line swore loudly. 'He's bleeding well scalped you!'

George ran a hand over his stubbled head. 'I asked him for a Clark Gable, but he reckons he doesn't do requests.'

The man, known as Swanny to the rest of his platoon, clutched his hat to his head as he strode into the hut. 'He'll not do that to me if he knows what's good for him!'

George grinned as he heard the familiar snipping of the hair clippers, followed by an anguished cry. Seconds later Swanny reappeared, his hat pushed firmly down onto his stubbled head as a stream of profanities escaped his lips.

'I thought you said ...' George began, only to be silenced by Swanny's steely glare.

'Not one bleeding word,' Swanny replied through gritted teeth.

George being George however was unable to resist temptation. 'What'll Cassie think? Does she like coots?'

Swanny took a playful swipe at his young friend. 'At least I've got a woman,' he said with satisfaction.

'Only 'til she sees your new do ...' teased George as he dodged Swanny's outstretched arm once more.

'Says the boy who looks like a burnt match!' chuckled Swanny. He grasped George's chin in one hand. 'At least I can grow a beard. I've seen more hairs on a baby's bum than I have your chin. Just how old are you anyway?'

Jerking his head away from his friend's grasp, George kicked a stone so that it skipped along the path ahead of him. Ever since he had arrived in Sandhurst the other men had taken the mick out of him for his size and boyish looks, jesting that he looked as though he should be in primary school, not the army, but up until now, none of them had asked him outright how old he actually was. He kept his head down to hide the pinkness spreading across his cheeks. 'Eighteen ...' hearing Swanny's disbelieving cough, he quickly added, '... only just, mind you.'

'Eighteen my arse!' scoffed Swanny. Laying a heavy hand on George's shoulder, he swung him round to face him. Studying George's hairless cheeks, Swanny's own expression went from jovial to serious as the penny dropped. 'Bloody hell, George, just how old are you?'

George opened his mouth to repeat his last answer, then changed his mind. Instead he decided to skirt the issue. 'Does it matter how old I am? As long as the army accepted me then surely that's all that matters?'

Swanny pulled George to one side as a few of the squaddies made their way to the cookhouse. Roaring with laughter, the man in front pointed at George and Swanny. 'Bleeding hell, you poor sods! What with winter on its way, I bet you'll be asking Father Christmas for a full barnet.'

'Either that or a syrup!' laughed one of the men in his group.

George looked at them, confused, but in truth he was grateful for a chance to change the subject. He turned to Swanny. 'What's a barnet and a ...' he hesitated, 'I

115

know what syrup is, but I haven't a clue what he was on about.'

'Bleeding cockneys,' chuckled Swanny. 'Got a language of their own, they have. It's called rhyming slang, so a barnet stands for Barnet Fair, which rhymes with hair, and a syrup of figs rhymes with wig. Get it?'

George ran over the comments in his head, smiled and nodded. 'That's quite clever!'

'A damned sight cleverer than you pretending you're older than what you are in order to join the army,' said Swanny, folding his arms across his chest. 'As for the army accepting you, they'll turn a blind eye if they think you're desperate enough. War isn't glorious, lad, it's bleeding dangerous – people get killed.'

Shrugging, George stuffed his hands into his pockets. 'I didn't have much of a choice. It was either the army or the poorhouse.'

Swanny eyed him thoughtfully. 'What did your folks say?'

George fixed Swanny with a wooden stare. 'I haven't got any folks, nor siblings, so no cosy little family with a mammy that cooks your tea – it's just me, always has been, always will be.'

Swanny nodded slowly. 'No friends that could've taken you in?'

George glanced skywards. 'The only friends I've got are back in Nazareth House,' he hesitated, 'apart from Ruby and Jess.'

Swanny cocked an eyebrow. 'Nazareth House?'

Nodding, George told Swanny all about Nazareth House, and Father Blakely.

'If it was a home for boys, who're Ruby and Jess?' said Swanny.

'They were in Greystones,' George said, 'a home for girls. I only used to see them on a Sunday when we all went to church. They ran away and joined the NAAFI, 'cos they didn't want to end up in the poorhouse. They've been posted to Seaforth.' He hesitated. 'That's by Liverpool – have you ever heard of it?'

Swanny nodded. 'Lovely place is Seaforth, not too far from where I live.' He thought for a moment. 'Are these girls the same age as you?'

Shaking his head, George eyed Swanny beseechingly. 'Please don't say anything. I wouldn't want the girls to get into trouble on my account.'

Swanny winked at him. 'What girls?'

George breathed a sigh of relief. 'Thanks, Swanny.'

Swanny looked serious. 'They'll not come to any harm in the NAAFI, but you on the other hand ...'

George's eyes grew wide. 'Please don't say anything. If they chuck me out, I'll be on the streets, because there's no way I'm going into the poorhouse, fighting for scraps of food.' He shook his head in disgust. 'I'd rather take my chances in France than live like that.'

Taking a deep breath, Swanny repeated his earlier question. 'How old are you, lad?'

'Fifteen, just,' said George. 'I lied about the year I were born, not the date – that part was true.'

Swanny rubbed his chin thoughtfully. 'So you shouldn't be going overseas for four years, yet they'll send you in one if no one tells them the truth, and if that happens you might never see your seventeenth birthday, never mind your nineteenth.'

'Don't see why,' said George defensively. 'Being older doesn't make you bulletproof. Besides, I've been looking forward to seeing something of the world.'

Swanny shot him a dark glance. 'None of us are bullet-proof, but the older ones have more experience and a bit of nous, which gives them a better chance than you. As for seeing something of the world, that's all fine and good as long as you make it back. That's why they send men off to war, not boys.'

George, who was normally a mild-mannered, happy-go-lucky sort of chap, felt his temper beginning to rise. He pointed at his back. 'I got scars on my back from Father Blakely, who thought I deserved to be beat with a rod for sharing my food with the young 'uns.' His jaw flexed as he fixed Swanny with a determined glare. 'Father Blakely must be sixty if he's a day, but that doesn't make him a man, not in my opinion.' He waited for Swanny to object, to tell him he should respect his elders, but he didn't.

Swanny nodded. 'You're right. He's not a man, he's a coward, but that still doesn't mean you're ready to go overseas.' He laid a hand on George's shoulder. 'I promise I won't get you thrown out of the army, but I can't stand by and watch you go off as cannon fodder, which is why I'm going to have a word with Sarge.' He shook his head as George went to protest. 'He's a good sort and he's got kids of his own, and I'm pretty sure one of them's around your age. Go and get yourself something to eat in the NAAFI and wait for me there, I shan't be long.'

George wanted to protest, to forbid the older man from breaking a confidence, but George hadn't sworn him to secrecy. It had seemed pointless to do so because Swanny had already guessed him to be far younger than he was making himself out to be. Realising that he had no choice but to place his faith in Swanny, George made his way to the NAAFI. He wondered how the girls were getting along, or more to the point, how Ruby was getting on. A picture of Ruby formed in his mind, her rosy cheeks, laughing eyes and silky hair as black as ebony. He wondered how she would react if she knew someone had discovered the truth about his age, then tutted to himself – she'd be pleased, because she was worried about him joining the army under-age. He had seen the fear in her eyes when he had been telling her how excited he was to finally get out and see something of the world. Swanny's words matched Ruby's eyes: 'Cannon Fodder'. He knew war was dangerous, of course it was, and they all knew from their history lessons what had happened in the last lot, and the truth behind the wars before, only you couldn't think of that, not when you had no alternative. You had to keep your fingers crossed, pray for the best and believe it wouldn't happen to you.

He pushed the door to the NAAFI open and looked around at the various men, all minding their own business, having a quiet brew. For the first time it hit him how ridiculous it was that the army had taken him on; it was blindingly obvious when you compared him to the others that he was nowhere near as old as the rest of them. What Swanny said about the army not caring had to be true. He walked over to the lady serving tea and asked for a cup. He would wait for Swanny to come back and ask him why the army set an age limit if they had no intention of following their own rules. Another question entered his thoughts. Would the army serve him beer? They should, because they believed him old enough to drink it. Taking his tea, he sat down at the nearest table and waited for Swanny.

Ruby stood on the platform at Lime Street Station, eagerly scanning the carriages for a glimpse of Jess, but the train was so full she could barely check one compartment before another took its place. As one of the carriages whizzed by she caught sight of someone waving desperately from one of the windows. Ruby's heart leapt as she recognised Jess beaming at her.

Ruby pushed her way along the platform until she caught up with the carriage. To her surprise, a girl sitting next to Jess also started waving frantically at her. Ruby stared before exclaiming, 'Penny!'

She waited patiently whilst passengers filed out of the carriage, and when Jess and Penny finally descended the train she rushed over and enveloped them both in a firm hug. Standing back, she stared wide-eyed at Penny.

'I've a million and one questions,' she gabbled, 'first one being, where did you spring from?'

'It's a long story,' said Penny as she slid her arm through Ruby's, 'although it's safe to say, I took a leaf out of both your books!'

Ruby squealed with delight. Ever since arriving at the NAAFI, she had had time to reflect on the plight of the girls they had left behind, and had begun to wish she and Jess had told them of their plan to escape, only at the time the thought never entered their heads. Everything had moved so quickly, they barely had time to plan their own escape, never mind anyone else's. Realistically, she knew it would have been impossible to try to sneak fifteen or more girls as well as their documents out of the orphanage without being discovered. She looked at Penny hopefully. 'Did anyone else escape or was it just you?'

'Alice went back to her folks, but as far as I know that's it,' Penny said. 'Although I suppose some of the others might have legged it after I'd gone.'

Ruby slipped her free arm through Jess's. 'I'm so glad you're here. You're going to love life in the NAAFI …' Hesitating, she turned to look at Penny. 'I was so surprised to see you I didn't think to ask, but are you coming with us?'

Penny grinned and nodded. 'Turns out I signed up the same day as you.'

'Imagine if you hadn't,' Jess said to Penny, 'we'd never have known half of what was going on in Greystones.' She gave Ruby a dark look. 'Penny told me things that will make your hair curlier than mine.'

Ruby glanced fearfully at Penny. 'They aren't on to us, are they? Greystones, I mean?'

Penny shook her head. 'They know you've run away, but that's not what Jess is referring to …'

As they walked Penny told Ruby all about Ancrum's deal with Brownhill, and how she'd accused McKinley of trying to take the money which Jess's father had left her.

Ruby pursed her lips. 'Ancrum's kept it for herself, that's obvious, although I should think that would be impossible to prove.' Angry tears pricked her eyes. 'As for their arrangement with Brownhill, I don't know why we didn't click sooner, although that's probably why they never let us go anywhere – that way they could keep us in the dark.' She led the girls to the head of a line of cars.

Climbing into the back of the first taxi, Ruby leaned forward in her seat. 'Seaforth Barracks, please.'

Jess gave her an admiring smile. 'You've changed! You were a bag of nerves before boarding the train in Glasgow.'

Ruby beamed. 'You've no choice but to get on with things when you're on your own. I think it probably did me the world of good. Just wait 'til you see our billet!'

Penny's eyes grew wide with expectation. 'Is it big? Have we got our own bathroom?'

Laughing, Ruby shook her head. 'It is big, but that's because we're sleeping in a tent.' Seeing the look of disbelief on her friends' faces, she added, 'A really big tent – there's ten beds in there, and we've each got a locker, and as for a bathroom, not quite, we've got what they call the ablutions, which is a kind of hut with shower cubicles, toilets and wash basins.' She giggled at their disappointed expressions. 'It doesn't sound much, but it's ten times better than Greystones, and the girls in the NAAFI are a wonderful bunch, really friendly. So are the fellers we serve.' As these last words left her lips an image of Toby appeared in her mind. She quickly glanced at the rear-view mirror to see if the driver was paying them any attention, before speaking in hushed tones, 'Remind me to tell you about the Scousers when we're alone.' She shot a meaningful glance in the driver's direction.

Jess felt her tummy twist unpleasantly. She had no idea what news her friend had to impart regarding Scousers, but it didn't sound as if it was good.

As they drove through the streets of Liverpool, Jess and Penny stared in awe at their surroundings. 'Have you visited the city yet?' Jess asked Ruby as they came to a standstill outside an enormous building.

'Not had the chance as yet because I've been too busy learning the ropes. Besides, I wanted to wait for you to get here so that we could explore the city together.' She glanced across Jess to Penny. 'That includes you too, now.'

Penny, however, was too busy crouching down in her seat so that she might see the top of the building they were currently outside. 'Look at the size of those statues ...' She glanced at the driver. 'How on earth did they get them up there? And what are they?'

He caught her eye in his mirror. 'That's the Royal Liver Building, and those are the Liver Birds, and in answer to how they got them up there?' He chortled. 'With great difficulty, I should imagine.'

Jess stared around her. She couldn't help wondering whether her father and mother were living or working in one of the magnificent buildings. She felt a shiver run down her spine. It was odd to think that her parents could be a stone's throw away. She glanced at Ruby. 'I know you sent word to your father's ship, telling him where you were, but have you heard anything back yet?'

Ruby grinned. 'I got a letter yesterday. He was as pleased as punch to hear we'd left Greystones and joined the NAAFI.'

'Oh Rubes, I'm so glad. I was worried he might fret not knowing where you were.'

Ruby nodded. 'Me too, and even though it won't be easy keeping in touch, I'm certain we'll manage somehow.'

A short while later they pulled up outside the barracks. As they alighted from the taxi Ruby waved to the guard on the gate.

'Howard, I'd like you to meet my friends Jess and Penny.'

Smiling, Howard nodded to the girls. 'Welcome to Seaforth, ladies.' He grinned. 'Just for the record, I like my tea with milk and sugar.'

'Cheeky blighter,' giggled Ruby, then turned to Jess and Penny. 'I'll take you to the office so that you can get all the official stuff out of the way.'

As they walked, Ruby explained the use of each building. When she got level with the men's billet she decided that now was a good time to tell Jess what Michelle had said about the Scousers.

As Jess listened to her friend, she became more confused than ever. 'I just don't get it! The people of Liverpool – apart from my father – seem to be a warm, friendly, welcoming lot. Why do they put up with those awful Scousers?'

Penny stopped walking so abruptly the girls looked down to see if she had dropped something. She suppressed a giggle. 'What did you just say about Scousers?'

Jess shook her head chidingly. 'It's not a laughing matter, Penny. My dad's a Scouser, and from what we've heard they're a bit like the Billy Boys ...'

Penny clapped a hand to her tummy as she roared with laughter. Tears trickling down her cheeks, she regarded them with disbelief. 'Who on earth told you that pile of codswallop?'

Jess and Ruby exchanged slightly embarrassed glances. 'Bonnie,' Jess said hesitantly, realising how silly it sounded that she had taken Bonnie's word for it.

'And you believed her?' said Penny, her tone incredulous.

Jess shrugged. 'She didn't know I was listening so she had no reason to lie ...'

'Maybe not, but that doesn't mean to say she knows what she's talking about!' She started to reel with laughter again.

'Don't laugh!' Jess pouted.

'Yes, tell us what the joke is,' said Ruby, who was bemused as to why their friend found the matter so amusing.

Penny calmed herself. 'Do you know what a cockney is?'

Both girls shook their heads, so Penny explained that a cockney was someone who lived in London, 'and a Scouser is someone who lives in ...'

Realising why Penny had been laughing so hard, Jess finished the sentence for her. 'Liverpool.' She began to giggle uncontrollably. 'What a pair of wallies!' Her eyes grew round as a thought occurred to her. 'Thank goodness we didn't say anything to Tom! I'd have felt such a fool!'

'I did say I thought you shouldn't listen to Bonnie and that she'd probably got it wrong,' said Ruby, a touch reproachfully.

Jess placed an arm around each of her friends' shoulders. 'I know you did, Rubes, and I should've listened to you. Better late than never, eh?'

Nodding, Ruby began to giggle. 'Imagine if you'd asked him if the two of you were related!' Seeing the puzzled expression on Penny's face, Ruby went on to explain that this had been the girls' next theory.

She had expected Penny to dismiss the suggestion out of hand and was disappointed when the other girl grimaced. 'It does seem a bit odd, though, him being a Scouser and winding up on the same street as the Durnings.' She looked at Jess, who was looking wretched. 'Sorry, Jess, but it's not as if Greystones is the only orphanage in Glasgow. Maybe the two of them being related isn't as far-fetched as it sounds.'

George looked up as Swanny entered the NAAFI. He waved a hand in order to gain the older man's attention.

As Swanny approached George braced himself for bad news.

Swanny sat down in the seat opposite. 'Don't look so scared, lad. I told you I'd fix things, and I have.'

George breathed a huge sigh of relief. 'You mean they're not going to kick me out?'

Swanny levelled with George. 'You aren't the first kid that's lied about their age and you sure as hell won't be the last. Under normal circumstances they'd probably send you packing, but I had a word with

Sarge and he agrees with me.' He gave George a small nod of encouragement. 'You've got something about you. It took real gumption doing what you did to get where you are today, so he's going to pull a few strings for you.'

George leaned forward, eager to hear what had been said. 'What's he got planned for me?' He crossed his fingers beneath the table, hoping that Swanny might say he was to be sent on a secret mission where he would thwart the enemy and save the country single-handed.

'A lot of army work is filling in forms and filing paperwork, something he reckons a lad like you could do standing on your head, so once you've completed your initial training, you'll be going off to be trained up as a clerk.'

Feeling a little disappointed that he wasn't going to be given the chance to become a hero, George smiled uncertainly at Swanny. 'Isn't there anything a little more exciting I could be doing than filing paperwork? I wouldn't mind going undercover if they needed me to ...'

Swanny grinned. 'Who do you think you are? Richard Hannay?' Seeing the blank look on George's face, he explained that Richard Hannay was a character from the spy thriller *The Thirty-Nine Steps*.

George blushed. 'Perhaps I'm being a little ambitious, but I just want to feel like I'm doing something to help.'

'Keeping records is just as important as firing guns, so don't think you're not pulling your weight, because you will be.'

'Won't anyone wonder why a young chap like me's not in France?'

Swanny shrugged. 'There's a million and one reasons why some folk don't go into battle. For all they know, you could have flat feet, asthma – the list is endless – but if they've got eyes in their head, they'll guess the real reason and turn a blind eye. Like I said, you're not the only one who's joined up when they should've been at home with their mam.'

'Do the others get drafted as clerks too?' said George, who was beginning to feel more at ease with his suggested role.

Swanny shook his head. 'No, they get sent home, difference being they've got a home to go to.' He leaned forward and spoke in hushed tones. 'Folk'll guess why you've not been sent overseas, but I wouldn't go shouting about it, else you might gain yourself some unwanted attention. If people think you're boasting about being given special treatment they might not take to it too kindly, so keep shtum and think yourself lucky.' He gave George a dark look. 'Some of them lads still get sent into battle, even though folk know they're too young.'

'Why them and not me?' said George, who was beginning to see how lucky he was to have a good friend like Swanny looking out for him.

'Because they've got a rotten sergeant who couldn't give two figs for their lives,' Swanny told him. 'Some people think it makes better sense to let the young and inexperienced take the bullets, rather than the sergeants and officers, which is why I'm telling you to keep it zipped.'

'I will,' said George fervently. He shook Swanny firmly by the hand. 'Thanks, Swanny, you've been a real pal. I wish there were more out there like you.' He hesitated as a thought occurred to him. 'Have you got any kids?'

Swanny stared at George, then lowered his gaze. 'Nah, me and the missus have never been blessed with kids despite twelve years of marriage.' He looked back up. 'I guess it was never meant to be.'

George felt his cheeks grow warm, not because he was embarrassed at having asked the question, but because he felt it unfair that someone like Swanny, who would make a brilliant father, had never been blessed with children, whilst his own father, whoever he might be, had given his child away without explanation. He said as much.

Swanny gave him an embarrassed grin. 'Thanks, lad, and if you want my opinion your father was a damned fool to give you up.' He slapped both hands down on the table. 'Now let's get to the ablutions and shower all this hair off us. I don't know about you, but I'm itching like a dog with fleas!'

George followed Swanny out of the cookhouse. Was it his imagination or had his spoken thoughts brought a tear to the older man's eye? Maybe not having children had taken a greater toll on his friend than he was letting on.

He thought of Ruby and what she would say when he told her he wouldn't be going overseas. He sighed. He would have to be patient. Swanny had told him to be careful, so telling Ruby in a letter or over the telephone would be foolish. He would wait until they were face to face before giving her the news.

A week had passed since Jess and Penny's arrival at Seaforth and both girls were enjoying their new life in the NAAFI every bit as much as Ruby had expected they would.

'We should've legged it years ago!' said Penny as she placed a small amount of toothpaste on her toothbrush.

'Told you you'd like it,' said Ruby as she exited one of the toilet cubicles. 'I wish Ancrum could see us now – she'd be spitting feathers seeing how happy we all are.'

'What about Bonnie?' said Jess. 'She was determined to ruin our lives – she'd be furious if she knew we were loving life in the NAAFI.' She smiled dreamily. 'I hope I get a chance to tell her.'

Ruby was examining her reflection in the mirror above the sink as she washed her hands. 'Don't you mind cleaning the flues? Only I know you hated doing that in Greystones.'

'Nope! Because you're doing it for a reason here. I begrudged cleaning the fireplaces in Greystones because you never got a word of thanks, just criticism for taking too long, or not doing it well enough. That's one thing I'll say for Mrs Armstrong, she's always grateful for a good job done.'

Penny rinsed her toothbrush under the tap. 'True.'

Ruby walked over to Jess and pulled the back of her friend's overalls taut so that they hugged her figure. 'I could take these in for you if you like?'

Jess nodded. 'I know they said I'd grow into them, but when? I feel like I'm wearing a tent, as well as living in one.'

Penny held the door to the ablutions open. 'Best get back to it, those rock cakes won't make themselves.'

Inside the NAAFI kitchen, Ruby and Jess set about cleaning down the work surface so that Michelle could start making the cakes.

'I know we said we wished that lot from Greystones could see us now,' said Jess as she dipped her dishcloth into the soapy water, 'but I wonder what Bonnie, Ancrum and McKinley are doing right this minute?'

Ruby shrugged. 'I don't know, and what's more I don't care!'

'I do!' said Jess. 'I don't see why they should live happily ever after, not after what they've done. It's like getting away with murder.'

'I doubt Bonnie and McKinley will live happily ever after,' reasoned Ruby. 'Penny reckons they're on rocky ground with Ancrum as it is, and it sounds as though things will get a lot rougher for them now that Alice's mam has made a complaint.' She smiled wickedly. 'I couldn't think of a better Christmas present!'

Jess stopped mid-rub. 'Christmas ...' she whispered to herself. In all the years they had been in Greystones, Christmas had never been a cause for celebration. The orphanage had strong views on Christmas, the first one being that it was a holy celebration, and any child who got their hopes up that they might receive special treatment because it was Christmas Day was soon put in their place by Mrs Ancrum. 'There's no such thing as Father Christmas, so if you're waiting for him to come and give you toys you'll be waiting a long time. Grey-stones does not take part in the ridiculous affair of trees and lavish decorations. You should be grateful that you've a roof over your heads and proper beds to sleep in, unlike Jesus, who was born in a donkey's stable.'

Now, with the horrible woman's words ringing clear in her mind, Jess looked at Ruby, her face full of hope-ful anticipation. 'This is going to be our first proper Christmas, so I want it to be the best one ever. Lots of decorations, scrummy food and presents,' she waved her hands above her head, 'tinsel, mistletoe, the whole works!'

Ruby had begun weighing the tea. She poured it into the cloth bag and handed it to Penny, who had come to lend a hand. 'Fine by me!'

'Food!' said Penny, with such feeling, she caused Ruby and Jess to giggle. 'I mean real food, like we used to serve the Ancrums.' She smacked her lips. 'Sausage rolls, pork pies, bacon, black pudding and Christmas cake covered in marzipan and thick white icing sugar!'

'Too right.' Jess was beginning to salivate. 'I always thought it hypocritical that Ancrum said she didn't agree with Christmas in any way, shape or form, yet her and her husband stuffed themselves silly on Christ-mas Day.' She turned to Penny. 'This year's going to be different.' She hesitated as she remembered the beauti-fully decorated Christmas trees and the ceilings adorned with paper chains which could be seen through the windows of the houses on Edinburgh Road. 'Do you think they'd let us put a Christmas tree in our billet?'

Ruby nodded excitedly. 'I'm certain they would. Mrs Armstrong says it's important to celebrate Christmases and birthdays when there's a war on because it helps boost morale.' She hesitated. 'I wonder how much Christmas trees are.'

'We could share the expense with the other girls,' suggested Jess. 'I'm sure they'd be up for that.'

Penny grinned. 'We can cover it in beautiful glass baubles, then show it off to the rest of the camp.' Her grin broadened. 'We could have a party, maybe even invite some of the fellers round ...'

Jess coughed on a chuckle. 'You know Mrs Armstrong wouldn't agree to us having men in our billet, it was her only rule.' She put on a stern face and wagged a reproving finger, 'No men in the billet, no matter who they are.'

The girls giggled at Jess's imitation of Mrs Armstrong.

'I know that's what she said,' said Penny, 'but surely she'd make allowances for Christmas.'

Jess pictured Mrs Armstrong, a kindly but old-fashioned woman who held the firm belief that men and women were a recipe for disaster if left alone in each other's company. 'Some of them are harmless, but if you follow my advice, you'll keep your distance!' she had warned Jess and Penny when she caught some of the young corporals flirting with the girls from across the counter. 'War can have a funny effect on some folk, make them act in a carefree manner they wouldn't dream of doing otherwise. I don't want to see or hear of any shotgun weddings, or war brides, who haven't known each other more than five minutes.' She rolled her eyes at Jess who had let a giggle escape her lips. 'You may well laugh, but I was in the last lot, and it happens more often than you'd think, so smile, be polite, but keep them at arm's length ...' She had hesitated, seeing the grin forming on Penny's lips. 'And that goes for you too!'

Jess reminded Penny of Mrs Armstrong's words of warning.

'Bah humbug! Just because she doesn't like to have fun any more, I don't see why the rest of us can't.' Penny pouted sullenly. 'I was looking forward to the idea of us having our first Christmas party.'

'We still can,' Jess assured her friend, 'only without any men.'

'Pfft,' said Penny. 'Not much of a party without fellers! Who'd we dance with?'

'Each other?' suggested Ruby.

'You two don't know how to lead, and neither do I,' Penny pointed out. 'If we don't have a feller leading the way we'll end up going round in circles.' She put the coffee which Jess had handed her into the pan. 'I bet the NAAFI will hold a Christmas party, although I daresay that old windbag'll be there, keeping an eye on everyone, making sure we keep our distance.'

'Don't call her a windbag,' Ruby said reproachfully. 'She's only looking out for us.'

'Well I wish she wouldn't,' muttered Penny, 'especially if she's going to spoil all our fun.'

A male voice spoke as someone approached the counter. 'Spoiling all the fun? That'll never do!'

'Tom ...?' ventured Jess. Peering round the side of the urn, her face split into a wide grin. 'I thought I recognised that voice.' Wiping her hands on her apron, she joined him at the counter. 'I'm afraid we're not ready for service quite yet, but you're welcome to come back.'

He beamed back at her. 'It wasn't a cup of tea I was after.'

'Oh?' said Jess innocently, although she soon twigged his meaning after hearing Penny's stifled chortles. 'Oh,' she said, a little more quietly.

'Ahem!' Ruby cleared her throat in a sarcastic fashion.

'Ruby!' said Tom. 'Sorry, queen, I didn't see you there!'

Ruby gave him a wry smile. 'I know you didn't.'

'That's because he's only got eyes for a certain someone,' Penny whispered into Ruby's ear. She held a hand out to Tom. 'Hello, Tom. I'm Penny, it's nice to meet you at last.'

Shaking her by the hand, he raised an inquisitive brow. 'You've heard of me then?'

'Aye, and I can see why,' said Penny.

'Penny!' gasped Jess, embarrassed.

Tom tried to swallow his smile, but he couldn't hide the fact that he was pleased to hear he had been talked about. He gazed at Jess, his eyes glittering. 'Have you been for a gander around the city yet?'

Relieved that the subject had taken a different turn, Jess shook her head. 'We're going to, only we're trying to save up a bit of money first.'

'You don't need money. I can take you on tour, show you the sights.' He looked at her hopefully. 'If you fancy it, that is?'

An excited squeal escaped Ruby's lips. 'Sorry, just remembered something!' She grabbed Penny's arm and hastily pulled her into the kitchen area. 'C'mon, Penny, you can help me.'

Penny tutted loudly. 'I wanted to see ...' she began before being hushed into silence by Ruby.

'I thought you wanted us to see the city together?' said Jess, raising her voice so that Ruby could hear her.

'Another time!' Ruby called over her shoulder before closing the dividing door.

Turning to face Tom, Jess felt the blush deepen in her cheeks. She had planned to tell Tom that she was too busy to see him should he ask, but only because in her head she believed it to be the sensible thing to do. However, seeing him now, with such a hopeful look on his face, she hadn't the heart or the desire to turn him down. Aware that she was keeping him waiting, she tried to find something suitable to say. 'I – I ...' she faltered.

Looking slightly embarrassed, he spoke across her. 'Is that a yes, or would you rather not? I quite understand if you ...' he hesitated, '... have you got a boyfriend?'

Jess shook her head rapidly. 'No! And I'd love to see the city with you.' She smiled guiltily as a look of relief swept across his face.

'Then how about I pick you up this Saturday, if you're free, that is?'

Jess's inner thoughts told her that this would be a perfect opportunity for her to make an excuse and say she was working. Her heart, however, told her inner thoughts to go take a running jump. She nodded nervously. 'I'll be free all day.'

Tom beamed. 'Splendid! Shall I pick you up around nine?'

'Pick me up?' said Jess. 'Have you got a car?'

'It's not mine, it's my brother's. He said I could use Olly whilst he's away.'

'Olly?'

He grinned. 'It's what he called the car because it's short and round like Oliver Hardy.'

Peering around the side of the kitchen door, Penny hissed at them. 'Watch out, Iron Britches is on her way!'

Tom grinned curiously. 'Who's Iron Britches?'

Jess chuckled. 'She's our manageress, and she doesn't approve of us fraternising with the opposite sex.'

Penny appeared at Jess's elbow. 'She's got it in her head that we'll be at it like rabbits if left alone for more than a few seconds!'

Jess's jaw almost hit the floor.

Tom burst out laughing. 'Has she, by God!' he said, fighting for breath.

Not appearing to notice that she had said something out of place, Penny continued, 'I know! I wouldn't mind, but we only wanted to have a Christmas party. Fat chance of that with her on patrol.'

Tom stopped laughing abruptly. 'Christmas party, you say?'

Jess held up a warning hand before he got any further. 'We won't be having one, so don't go getting your hopes up.'

Tom's shoulders sagged. 'That's a shame ...'

Ruby's voice called out in an exaggerated fashion from the kitchen. 'They're just coming now, Mrs Armstrong ...'

Jess and Penny flapped their hands at Tom, shooing him away. 'Quick!' hissed Jess. 'Before she sees you and starts reading us the riot act!'

'Iron Britches,' laughed Tom as he opened the door to the NAAFI. He turned to face Jess. 'Don't forget, Saturday, nine o'clock, by the gate.'

Jess rolled her eyes, worried that Mrs Armstrong might hear him. 'Yes!' she hissed. 'Now go before you get me in trouble!'

As the door to the NAAFI swung behind him, Penny and Jess hurried into the kitchen. 'Come on before she asks us what we've been up to,' Penny urged beneath her breath. 'Not that I've been up to anything, of course. You, on the other hand ...'

Jess looked alarmed. 'Me? I've not done anything!'

Penny raised her eyebrows. 'Oh no, only arranged a date with the handsome Tom!'

'Date?' Ruby said excitedly. 'You lucky devil!'

'Date!' echoed Jess. 'Who said anything about a date?'

Before either of them could answer, Mrs Armstrong beckoned them over. 'Come along, girls, you've no time for idle chat. Give Michelle a hand with these rock cakes else they won't be ready for the hungry hordes when they arrive.'

'Yes, Mrs Armstrong,' the girls chorused. They waited until she was out of earshot before Jess continued.

'Who said it was a date?'

Michelle looked up from the large mixing bowl. 'Are you going on a date?'

'No!' said Jess abruptly. 'I'm just meeting a friend, that's all.'

Grinning, Penny and Ruby exchanged glances. 'A boyfriend,' giggled Ruby.

Michelle pushed the bowl towards the girls. Picking up some of the dough on a tablespoon, she placed it on a baking tray. 'Take no notice of those two,' adding with a wry smile, 'although if it's not a date, what is it?'

Jess shrugged. 'I met him in Scotland, and when he found out I was coming to Liverpool he offered to show me round, but that's all there is to it.'

Michelle raised a brow fleetingly at Penny and Ruby, something which did not go unnoticed by Jess. 'What's that look supposed to mean?'

Michelle tried to hide the smirk which was threatening to cross her lips. 'Nothing,' she said innocently, 'only I take it he's not on the same camp as us?'

'You guessed correctly,' said Penny, who thought she knew where Michelle's thoughts were headed.

Michelle eyed Jess thoughtfully. 'So, he's come out of his way to find you and ask you out on a ...' seeing the warning glance which Jess shot her, she went on '... guided tour?'

'Precisely!' said Jess, collecting some of the mixture onto her spoon. 'He's a very kind, considerate man.'

Michelle grinned. 'He is, isn't he? You'd not find many fellers going to that much trouble for a girl unless they were keen on her.'

Determined to concentrate on the job in hand, Jess carried on spooning mixture onto the baking trays. 'Like I said, he's a very kind man.' From the corner of her eye she could see Michelle, Ruby and Penny mugging furiously at each other. 'Sod off, you lot!' Holding the spoon in her hand, she flicked it in their direction. Only Penny, who had half expected some sort of retaliation for their teasing, dodged out of the way.

'Jessica Wilson!' snapped Mrs Armstrong. 'What are you doing?'

Looking up, Jess saw Mrs Armstrong standing to the side of Penny, a large dollop of cake mixture hanging from her cheek. Penny, her eyes like saucers, made a snorting noise as she tried to suppress her laughter, whilst Michelle, Ruby and Jess stood gaping at the older woman.

'I'm so sorry!' Jess gabbled. 'I didn't mean it to hit you!'

Taking a dishcloth from the sink, Mrs Armstrong wiped the mixture from her face. 'I can see I can't leave you girls alone for two minutes before you start horsing around!'

'It's my fault,' said Penny apologetically. 'I was teasing Jess, and I shouldn't have.'

Jess smiled thankfully at Penny, but Mrs Armstrong wanted answers.

'And what could you possibly have said that would warrant such a reaction?' she said, fixing Penny with a disapproving glare.

Jess looked imploringly at her friend, willing her not to mention anything to do with Tom or dates.

Without missing a beat Penny replied, 'I said it was a good job she wasn't the one making the cakes or they really would be like rocks.'

Mrs Armstrong considered this for a moment, then wagged a reproving finger at Penny and Jess. 'Well, whilst that wasn't a very kind thing to say, I don't approve of your reaction, Jessica. Please control yourself in future.'

Jess nodded quickly. 'Yes, Mrs Armstrong, sorry, Mrs Armstrong.'

Satisfied that she had brought the matter to an end, Mrs Armstrong turned to Michelle. 'I'm putting you in charge. Make sure they behave themselves.'

Michelle nodded. 'I will.'

The manager turned her attention back to the girls. 'You mustn't waste food. I daresay it won't be long before they start rationing, and every ounce will count.'

Nodding mutely, they waited until she had left the kitchen before collectively breathing out.

'Bloomin' heck,' gasped Ruby, 'I didn't know whether to laugh or cry.'

Jess stared at Penny. 'I thought we were for the high jump when you started laughing.'

'Couldn't help myself,' said Penny. 'Did you see her face?'

Nodding, Jess began to giggle. 'I couldn't do that again if I tried.'

'Talk about hitting the bullseye,' agreed Michelle.

'She was ever so good about it, though,' said Ruby, 'although she might not be happy if we don't get a move on with these cakes.'

'Whilst we've still got some of the mixture left,' giggled Penny.

Jess began to spoon the rest of the mixture onto the baking tray. She may have been determined that she shouldn't go on a date with Tom, but the thought of spending time with him filled her with anticipation and excitement. She drew a deep breath. She knew it was only sensible to ask him whether he thought there was a chance that they might be related sooner rather than later, because the more she saw of him the more she liked him. She frowned. If it had crossed her mind, then surely it had crossed Tom's? She took a tray and placed it in the oven. It was pointless to guess. There was only one way to find out for certain, so whether she liked it or not she would have to bite the bullet and ask him on Saturday – better that than set herself up for a fall.

Ruby read the letter from George out loud to Jess.

'I'm telling you, Ruby, when these fellers give you a haircut they don't mess around – a coot's got more hair than me. You want to thank your lucky stars they don't try to cut your hair in the NAAFI.

'How's Jess and Penny? I'm glad Penny got out too. I know I don't know her as well as I do you and Jess, but she always seemed a good egg to me.

'I've got some really big news, but you'll have to wait until I can get some leave before I spill the beans. The only thing I can tell you by letter, is that I owe it all to my mate Swanny. He's a real gent, with a good heart. He's

from Liverpool, and his wife Cassie has kindly offered for me to stay with her when I come to Seaforth on leave, although that won't be for quite some time yet.'

Ruby looked at Jess, who appeared to be mystified. 'I don't know what he's got to tell you, but it must be something important if he can't write it in a letter or tell you over the phone.'

'That's what I thought,' said Ruby. She quickly scanned George's letter again in the hope that she had missed something. 'What could a scrawny little feller like George do that's so exciting he can't tell us in a letter?'

'Whatever it is sounds top secret,' said Jess, pulling her overalls over her head. 'Maybe they're going to use him to spy on the enemy or something like that.' She turned to Penny who was lying in the bed opposite. 'What do you think, Penny?'

Penny's sheets rustled as she sat up. 'Not a chance. They want someone with experience to do a job like that, someone who can think on his feet and outwit the enemy. Does that sound like George to you?'

Ruby frowned. An image of George formed in her mind. Skinny, kind-hearted and rough round the edges, that's how she'd describe George. He didn't want much out of life, although he had got excited when he'd talked about going overseas.

'A feller like me wouldn't normally get a chance to see the world unless I became a sailor or something like that, and I get seasick sitting in the bath!' he had carried on enthusiastically. 'But if I'm lucky the army'll send me over to France. I could learn a trade, maybe

143

even live out there once the war's over – how grand would that be?'

Ruby's stomach lurched unpleasantly at the memory. 'When he was talking about going into the army, the only thing that got him excited was the thought of going to France.' She rolled her eyes as the words left her lips. 'It filled me with absolute dread, only I didn't want to dampen his fire, so I kept my thoughts to myself.' She nodded in a determined fashion. 'I bet they're sending him to France, and that's why he can't mention it in his letter or on the phone in case someone's listening who shouldn't be.'

Penny grimaced. 'That sounds more likely.'

Jess nodded sympathetically, adding. 'Oh, Rubes ...' as tears brimmed in her friend's eyes.

'That's why he's coming to visit after his training,' said Ruby, her voice thick with tears, ''cos he knows it's going to be the last chance he gets to see me before he goes.' She nodded solemnly. 'And I daresay they won't send him home on leave once he's there, 'cos it's too far away. It's not like he can catch a bus or a train.' Hiding her face, she spoke through her hands. 'He shouldn't be going overseas, he's just a kid ...' She looked up and eyed her friends anxiously. 'Do you think I should say something?'

Jess sat down next to Ruby. 'To who?'

Ruby shrugged. 'Whoever's in charge at his barracks. I know he might get into trouble, but better that than the alternative. I'm sure they'll stop him going if they find out he's too young.'

Jess placed her arms around Ruby as the other girl allowed silent tears to fall. 'You can't, Rubes, not if it's what he wants …' She kissed her friend on the cheek. 'I know he's too young and that he shouldn't be going, but he'll never forgive you if you stop him following his dreams.' She squeezed her tightly. 'You're just going to have to keep a stiff upper lip on this one, Ruby, for his sake as well as your own.'

Chapter Four

It was eight o'clock on the Saturday morning that Jess was due to meet Tom. Ruby was helping Penny try to tame Jess's curls as best they could so that it gave her hair more length.

'I wish I had straight hair like you and Penny,' Jess muttered as she watched another curl escape its grip.

'I think your curls are beautiful,' said Penny. 'I wish I had curly hair.'

Ruby held up a mirror to allow Jess to see the back of her hair.

Jess gasped in admiration. 'You've done an amazing job!' She twisted her head from left to right. 'I never knew my hair could look so pretty!'

'Told you!' said Ruby.

Michelle wandered into the billet. 'Golly, you're going to set a few pulses racing! Although I must say you'd look a damned sight better with a decent hair-cut. I don't know who your old hairdresser was, but their scissors couldn't have been very sharp.' She glanced at Penny and Ruby, a frown appearing, then added, 'Is there only the one hairdresser in Glasgow?'

The three girls exchanged awkward glances.

'Did I say something wrong? I didn't mean to be rude, it's just ...' Michelle began, only to be cut short by Jess.

'We never had a real hairdresser in the orphanage.' She watched Michelle as she waited for the penny to drop.

'Your hair should've grown back by now,' Michelle said, frowning. 'How long ago did you leave the orphanage?' She fell silent as she saw Ruby's worried reflection in the mirror. 'Oh crikey ...' She paused. 'How *old* are you? Or shouldn't I ask?'

Penny gave her a hesitant smile. 'We're all coming up for sixteen ...'

To their surprise, Michelle looked relieved. 'That's not too bad. For a minute there I was worried you were going to say fourteen.'

'Does that mean you won't tell?' said Jess.

Michelle shook her head. 'Nah! It's not as if you're doing anything dangerous ...' she chuckled softly '... although they could use some of Penny's rock cakes as deadly weapons.'

Overwhelmed with relief, the girls burst out laughing. They had previously discussed what they would say if anyone asked them outright about their past, and had decided they would tell the truth and hope for the best. 'Start telling lies,' Jess had warned her friends, 'and you'll have to start fabricating a whole new life for yourself, and you'll get caught out when you least expect it. After all, we don't have to say when we left the orphanage!' It hadn't occurred to any of them at the time that someone might put two and two together after seeing the length of their hair.

'I must admit I did have my doubts when I saw the dress you were going to wear to meet Tom,' Michelle said, jerking her head towards Jess's locker. 'I didn't like to say anything, but it does seem awfully old-fashioned. Was that what they made you wear in the orphanage?'

Jess looked at Michelle in astonishment. 'Golly, no, our clothes from the orphanage were horrid grey pinafores, dull as dishwater and full of holes. That dress is much better than the stuff we used to wear.'

Michelle looked confused. 'So where on earth did you get that old-fashioned frock from?'

Jess told Michelle everything. Michelle hissed between her teeth. 'I can see why you ran away. If anything, I'm surprised there wasn't a mass exodus.'

'There's not a lot the little 'uns could do,' said Jess, who had often wished she could have taken them with her, 'but we're hoping that the powers that be actually listened to Alice's mam and took her seriously, then Greystones and Brownhill might get shut down for good.'

Michelle wandered over to her locker and pulled out a pale green floral-patterned tea dress. She handed it to Jess. 'You can wear this to meet Tom if you like.'

Beaming, Jess gratefully took the dress. 'Are you sure?'

'Positive, and whilst you're out, get him to take you to Paddy's Market. You should be able to pick something up cheap enough whilst you're there.' She glanced at the old-fashioned dress which Jess had been going to wear. ''Cos you can't keep wearing that.'

Jess slipped into the frock and Ruby buttoned up the back. 'Thank you so much, Michelle, this really is awfully kind of you.'

'My pleasure,' Michelle put the hanger back in the locker, 'and seeing as you're all in the same boat, why don't we go into the city next time we have a day off and do the markets? It'll be a fun girls' day together.'

Penny's face lit up. 'What a brilliant idea. I've been wanting to go to the dances, but there's no way I'd go in my overalls, and whilst it was sweet of Alice's mam to give me one of her hand-me-downs, it's a bit frumpy for me.'

Jess gave a startled squeal as her eyes settled on her alarm clock. 'I've got to go!'

Ruby, Michelle and Penny gave their friend the once-over.

'You look beautiful, Jess,' said Ruby.

Penny smiled approvingly. 'Our Tom's a lucky boy!'

Michelle nodded her agreement. 'That frock goes well with your hair and eyes.'

Jess giggled. 'I've not got green hair!'

Michelle gave her a wry smile. 'I know that, silly! But it's a kind of auburny, golden colour, and that goes well with green.'

Jess looked earnestly at her friends. 'Do you think it's too much – the dress, the hair and everything else?' She rubbed her eyebrows which still felt sore from being plucked. 'I don't want him to think I'm trying too hard.'

Michelle tutted dismissively. 'No, I do not! You've no idea where he might take you, and I'd say you look just right for any occasion, from Lyons to Lewis's.'

Jess swallowed. 'Not somewhere too posh, I hope. I wouldn't know how to behave, or …'

Ruby caught Jess by her elbow and gently propelled her out of the tent. 'Don't you worry, Tom wouldn't do anything to make you feel uncomfortable. Now get out there, forget about everything else and enjoy yourself!'

Penny waved over Ruby's shoulder. 'Cheerio, Jess. Keep us in mind when you're shopping for dresses.'

Michelle appeared by Penny's side. 'See you later!' She breathed in sharply. 'Is that him?'

Jess turned to look and saw Tom waving to her from the driver's seat of a car. She turned back and nodded.

'He's a real bobby-dazzler!' Michelle said approvingly.

Jess waved goodbye to her friends and walked over to Tom who had got out of the car ready to greet her. She felt her heart begin to race. Michelle was right, he was a real bobby-dazzler and way out of her league. Handsome, intelligent, with a good job, he made her feel like Cinderella. Seeing him now she wondered how long it would take for him to come to his senses and realise he would be better off with someone else, someone more suitable. Her tummy fluttered. None of that would matter, of course, if she found out they were related. She banished the thought from her mind. She could hardly ask him outright – she'd have to wait for a more appropriate opportunity to present itself, whenever that might be. As she neared the vehicle, he opened the passenger door.

He eyed her with approval. 'Blimey, you look beautiful, Jess!'

Blushing, Jess slid into the passenger seat with a quiet 'thank you' as he closed the door behind her.

Compliments from men were new to her, and whilst she liked receiving them, she also felt slightly awkward and embarrassed by the attention.

Tom cranked the car into life before taking his place behind the wheel. 'Have you got to be back for anything?'

'No, I'm yours for the day.'

'Mine for the day, eh?' He grinned. 'Sounds good to me! Liverpool is a big city, you'll not see it all in a day, not even if we stayed out all night, so we'll cover what I'd call the "must sees", such as the Liver Building and St George's Hall today.' He hesitated. 'Is there anywhere in particular you'd like to go?'

Jess began to shake her head, until she remembered Michelle's advice. 'Paddy's Market?'

He grinned. 'Perfect place for a bargain! What are you after?'

'I'd like a frock for dances and going out, something that looks more my age than ...' She hesitated as she remembered where she got her previous dress from. 'Not that I'm saying there's anything wrong with your aunt's dresses, they're lovely, it's just ...'

Tom twinkled at her. 'Don't worry, queen, Auntie Edna's clobber is way too old for young women like yourself and Ruby.' He glanced at the frock she was wearing. 'That's far more suitable, where did you get it?'

Jess fingered the dress. 'Michelle – she's one of the cooks – lent it to me. It was her that told me to go to Paddy's Market.'

He nodded. 'Very wise. They sell some nice things in the market. Not as good as you'd get in Blacklers or

Lewis's, but on the other hand the kind of things they sell in the markets will be half if not a third of the price.'

Jess was intrigued. 'What are Blacklers and Lewis's?'

'They're like the markets in the sense that they sell all sorts of things under one roof, but the stuff they sell is a lot more upmarket.'

'Can we go there after we've been to Paddy's Market?' Jess asked hopefully. 'I know I won't be able to afford anything but I'm interested to see for myself.'

'Course we can. We've got all day, and what we don't get to see today we can save for next time.'

Jess felt her heart rise in her chest. Tom had said next time which meant that he was already planning on seeing her again. 'That would be wonderful, Tom, as long as you don't mind, that is I wouldn't like you to get bored.'

He feigned surprise. 'Bored? With Liverpool?'

Jess smiled shyly. 'It must be lovely to feel that way about your home town. I didn't feel that way about Glasgow, in fact I couldn't wait to leave,' she shook her head, 'too many bad memories.'

Tom pulled up a little way from a row of tables which lined the street adjacent to the one they were on. He extended his arm in a sweeping motion. 'Paddy's Market.'

Jess got out of the car before Tom had a chance to open the door for her. Having never been shopping in her life, she was very much looking forward to the experience and couldn't wait to get started. Tom offered her the crook of his elbow. 'It can get a bit crowded, and it's easy to get lost in places like this.'

As they wandered along, Jess looked at the stalls, laden with all kinds of wares. She decided she wouldn't mind getting lost in Paddy's Market.

The first clothes stall they came to, Jess picked up two of the dresses nearest to hand and held them up against herself. She looked at Tom. 'Shall I get one of these?' Before he could reply she had put the dresses down and picked up two more. 'Or one of these?'

Tom laughed. 'You're like a kid in a sweet shop.'

Jess stopped in her tracks. 'Sweet shop? They don't really have shops for sweets? I thought that was something Bonnie made up just to be spiteful.'

He gave her a sympathetic smile. 'They certainly do, although how long they'll last if rationing kicks in is anyone's guess.' He tilted his head to one side. 'I can't believe you've never been to a sweet shop.'

'Never even had sweets,' Jess admitted.

He stopped walking. 'What about at Christmas?'

Jess laughed sarcastically. 'What about Christmas? Ancrum – the woman who ran Greystones – wouldn't waste money on the likes of us.'

He shook his head in angry disapproval. 'That woman wants locking up! Everyone deserves a treat at Christmas.' He pointed down the row of stalls. 'After we've bought your dress I'll take you to one of the sweet stalls.'

Jess sighed wistfully. Tom would make someone a wonderful husband one of these days – it was a pity it wouldn't be her. She followed him to the next stall, where they were greeted by an Irish woman with rosy cheeks and a cheery demeanour. 'Hello, duck, what can I do for you?'

Jess asked the woman if she could look at a dress which was hanging up on a rail. As the woman fetched the dress Jess turned to Tom. 'I've never seen so many clothes! I can't wait to bring Ruby and Penny to Paddy's Market – they'll be spoilt for choice.'

The woman laughed heartily. 'We've everything a young lady needs.' She handed the dress to Jess who held it up against her. The older woman nodded approvingly. 'You remind me of that cartoon character, what's her name again …' She furrowed her brow in thought then clicked her fingers. 'Betty Boop! It's them big eyes and that beautiful curly hair.'

Jess blushed. 'I've always thought my hair made me look like a boy.' She eyed Tom shyly from under her lashes.

'You don't look like a feller!' Tom blurted out. 'Blimey, I'd not …' There was an awkward silence as Tom sought the right words. 'That is to say, you've got …' Scratching his head, he turned to the older woman for help.

'Curves!' said the woman, much to Jess's surprise. 'Or at least you will have when you get a decent meal or ten inside you.'

Tom's cheeks flushed pink. 'What I was trying to say is, I've never seen a feller who looks like you do.'

The woman indicated the dress with a nod of her head. 'Do you like it?'

'Oh yes,' said Tom without thinking. Then, realising that the woman had been referring to the dress he added, 'The dress! Oh yes, very nice.'

The woman was grinning fit to burst. She cocked an eyebrow at Jess, who nodded. 'Very much so, but I like all of them. Could I take a look at the blue one, please?'

'Course you can, duck.' The woman spread the dress out on the stall.

Jess was busy admiring the dress when a thought struck her. 'How much are they?'

'They're two and eight each, but if you take the two today, I can do 'em for four shillings the pair.' Adding as an afterthought, 'I'll do the same for your pals if you bring 'em to me.'

Jess looked anxiously up at Tom. 'Is that good?'

Laughing, Tom smoothed his hand over her shoulder. 'I think so, but I don't tend to buy many dresses.'

Jess giggled. 'You know what I meant!' She fished her money out and examined the coins in her hand. 'I can't afford the two, so I'll ...' She stopped short. Tom was rooting in one of his pockets. He withdrew his hand and looked at something before handing it over to the woman.

He turned to Jess. 'I insist on paying for one of them because I shouldn't have brought you somewhere so tempting.'

Jess gaped at him. 'I can't ask you to do that!'

His eyebrows climbed towards his hairline. 'I didn't hear you asking me to do anything, I offered.' He held his index finger up. 'Insisted!'

Jess handed her two shillings to the stall holder who promptly wrapped the dresses in paper and handed them over. 'There you go, duck, and don't forget to bring your pals.' Adding, with a wide smile, 'And their boyfriends if they've got any.'

Jess stopped short. She wanted to correct the woman and explain that Tom was just a friend, but the woman was already talking to another customer. Tucking the package under one arm, she smiled up at Tom. 'Thank you for buying me the dress, Tom, it really was awfully kind of you.'

'My pleasure.' He pointed to a stall further up. 'Time for sweets!'

Jess's mouth began to salivate at the thought. 'I won't know what to choose.'

Tom winked, causing a pleasurable shiver to run through Jess's body. 'I've got a sweet tooth so I'll help you to choose.'

Jess stared in wonder as they approached the jars full of colourful sweets. 'A month ago, all I had in my future was a life in the poorhouse, but look at me now.'

'You're enjoying your independence then?' Tom asked.

'I should say so!' she said. 'At Greystones, they owned everything from the clothes on your back to the food that you ate, and they made sure we knew it too, by making us give thanks to the orphanage in our morning prayers! It's wonderful to have my own clothes, knowing they're mine and no one can take them away from me!'

He waved a hand at the sweets. 'I know you want to buy your own, but I wouldn't consider myself to be much of a gent if I didn't pay for your sweets. So with your approval I shall buy us a bag of Everton Mints to share.'

Jess liked her independence but it was equally nice to have someone treat her for a change. 'You're spoiling me, Tom.'

His smile broadened. 'That's because you're worth spoiling.' Turning to the stall holder, he pointed to a jar of black and white sweets. 'I'd like two ounces of Everton Mints, please.'

He paid for them and offered the paper bag to Jess.

Jess picked out a mint and popped it into her mouth, stowing it in one cheek. She took a moment to savour the fresh minty taste before turning to Tom. 'I like sweets!'

Tom chuckled under his breath. 'Next time I'll get us a bar of chocolate to share – fruit and nut is my favourite.' He glanced around him. 'We could spend all day here, or we could take a wander around the city and stop for a spot of lunch in Lyons café – which would you prefer?'

Jess threaded her hand through his extended elbow. 'I vote we go for a wander around the city.' She tightened her grip on his arm. Tom being taller meant she had to lengthen her stride in order to keep up with him. 'Did they have places like Paddy's Market in Glasgow?'

He nodded. 'Every city has markets like Paddy's, only not as good of course because they're not in Liverpool.' He winked at her. 'I can't believe you lived just down the road from my auntie – talk about a small world.'

Jess's stomach somersaulted at the mention of his aunt. Tom had inadvertently given her the perfect opportunity to mention her father and the fact that he, too, was a Scouser, but she was enjoying herself so much she didn't want to spoil things. On the other hand, goodness knows when such an occasion might arise again. Taking a deep breath, she crossed her fingers. 'There's something I've been meaning to ask you …' She paused and glanced nervously at him. Her intention had been to ask whether he thought they might be related, but she quickly decided to approach the matter from a different angle.

Tom looked at her, a frown creasing his brow. 'Sounds ominous.'

'Seeing as how your auntie used to live down the road from the orphanage, I've been wondering if she might have heard or seen anything suspicious the night my father abandoned me.' Jess spoke quickly before she could back out.

Tom shook his head fervently. 'Not a chance! If she had, she would have been out the house before you could say knife and clobbered him with her rolling pin. She'd never have allowed someone to abandon a baby.' His eyes flashed angrily. 'Especially not on Christmas Eve.'

Jess felt a wave of relief sweep through her. She didn't know what she would have done if it turned out that Tom's aunt had been involved. Daring to ask the question she dreaded the most, her heart pounded in her chest as she voiced the thoughts in her mind. 'You're right about it being a small world, what with my father coming from Liverpool, and your auntie living in Liverpool, one or two of the girls wondered whether they might be related somehow.'

Tom stopped walking abruptly. 'I bloomin' well hope not.' He shook his head. 'They couldn't be. My auntie's Scottish born and bred; it was her husband – my grandfather's brother – who was related to the Liverpool side of the family. Apart from the Durnings, she doesn't know anyone in Liverpool.'

Jess felt as though an enormous weight had been lifted from her shoulders. 'I didn't think they could be,' she said, 'although I do wonder what made him go to that orphanage in particular, especially when he wasn't from around that area.' She gave Tom a brittle smile. 'I wish I knew what was going through his head that night.'

Tom looked at her in surprise. 'Are you saying you want to find him?'

She nodded, then shook her head. 'Not so much find him, but I would like to know why they abandoned me. I say "they" because I must have had a mother, and I want to know why she didn't want me, or if she did, why she didn't fight to keep me or ...' She looked at Tom round-eyed. 'What if she died during child-birth, like Ruby's mam? If that was the case then I could be judging this whole situation unfairly.' She nodded to herself as she continued to voice her thoughts. 'According to McKinley, my father was old, so maybe he thought he couldn't cope with a baby on his own.' She looked hopefully at Tom. 'It would explain why he had lots of money but abandoned me anyway.'

Placing his arm around her shoulders, Tom gave her a comforting squeeze. 'Why don't you come for after-noon tea one day? You could ask my auntie if she remembers anything. Even if she didn't see him, she might have heard something on the grapevine.'

'Really?' said Jess, her voice awash with relief in the hope that all was not lost. 'Do you think she'd mind?'

He shook his head. 'She'd be happy to help.'

Staring up at him, Jess wondered how she could ever have doubted him. 'I can't believe I thought you were part of a criminal gang ...'

Tom eyed her with horrified fascination. 'What on earth made you think that?' he asked, his tone filled with amusement.

'I overheard Bonnie telling Clare that Scousers were the same as the Billy Boys that run Glasgow, so when you said you were a Scouser ...'

Tom roared with laughter. 'Oh, Jess! When did you realise you'd got it wrong?'

Jess looked at her feet in embarrassment. 'Penny told us.' She rolled her eyes. 'She thought it was pretty funny too.'

He smoothed his hand over the back of her curly hair. 'Dear me, you must've thought you'd got yourself mixed up with a right bunch of ne'er-do-wells!'

She half smiled. 'I thought you must be the best of a bad bunch.' As her words caught up with her she began to giggle. 'I suppose that's why people say it's wrong to eavesdrop.'

Running his hand over the top of her shoulders, he pulled her close. 'If they'd been honest with you from the start, you wouldn't have had to rely on gossip and snippets of overheard conversations.' His brow wrinkled. 'Why didn't they tell you the truth? It's not as if they did anything wrong.' He caught her eye. 'Or did they?'

Jess told him about the money. 'I wouldn't mind, but Ancrum never told me about the money either, so she's as bad as McKinley, if not worse, because at least McKinley had an excuse for her behaviour. Being a single mother to an unborn child, it's hardly surprising she couldn't resist the temptation.'

Tom looked annoyed. 'But it was your money, Jess! Pregnant or not, McKinley had no right to take it. At least her daughter had a parent, which is more than you had – you were in more need of that money than her.' His jaw tightened. 'No wonder they didn't want you to know anything about the night your father left you – they wanted to keep the money for themselves!' He shook his head. 'I hope my auntie did see something that night; that way we can tell him what became of his daughter and his money.'

Jess looked at him doubtfully. 'You really think he'd be interested?'

'I would be,' said Tom, 'but then again I'd never have given you away in the first place.' His cheeks turned a light shade of pink. 'What your father did was wrong, but who knows? All this happened a long time ago. He might have had a change of heart or circumstance since then – for all we know he might be looking for you.'

Jess shook her head. 'I don't think so, Tom, else he'd have come back to the orphanage.'

A sudden thought crossed his mind which he voiced without thinking. 'He might be dead.' He regretted the words as soon as they left his mouth. 'I'm so sorry! I don't know why I said that ...'

Jess had felt her stomach wrench as the words left his lips, but she knew Tom hadn't meant to upset her. 'You were just being honest, Tom, there's nothing wrong with that. In fact, I prefer it! Although you do make a good point, 'cos that's something I hadn't thought of.'

Mentally kicking himself for thinking out loud, Tom pointed at a large department store which stood on the corner of two streets. 'Blacklers!'

Jess stared at the impressive building. 'What, all of it?'

Tom nodded. An impish grin tweaked the corners of his lips. 'Have you ever ridden a horse?'

Jess laughed sarcastically. 'Oh yes, they took us for pony rides, when they weren't teaching us to swim!' she said, slapping him playfully on the arm.

He shrugged in a nonchalant fashion. 'I only asked because I thought you might like to ride the one in Blacklers.'

Jess stared up at him, her eyes widening in astonishment. 'You're not telling me they've got horses in Blacklers? I know you said they had all sorts of things there, but ...'

He grinned. 'Just the one, but don't worry, I promise he won't bite, kick or try and throw you off.'

Taking Jess by the hand, he instructed her to close her eyes until he said she could open them. Jess allowed him to guide her through the doors, realising as she did so that she had the utmost faith in him. After a moment or two, she sensed him positioning himself behind her. Placing his hands over her eyes, he whispered in her ear. 'Ready?'

Feeling the warmth of his breath against her neck, Jess wished this moment could last a little longer, so she paused for a moment before nodding. 'Ready.'

He pulled his hands away. 'Jess, meet Blackie ...'

Jess burst out laughing. 'Tom Durning, you rotten swine! You never said it was a rocking horse!'

Tom winked. 'I never said it was a real horse either, I just promised it wouldn't bite or kick and he certainly won't throw you off.'

'He'd have a job.' Jess giggled. She ran a hand over the beautifully polished dappled paintwork, before running her fingers through the horse's mane. 'He's beautiful!' She gave the horse a small push and smiled as it gently rocked back and forth. 'If I were a kid I'd be on him like a shot ... oh!' She gasped as Tom scooped her into his arms and sat her side-saddle on the back of the horse. She heard several amused shoppers laugh as Tom told her to 'hold on tight'. Gently rocking the horse, Tom placed his arm around her waist, 'to make sure you don't slide off backwards', he told Jess, or at least that was his excuse. Jess wondered what it would have been like to have something like that in the orphanage. 'We never had anything as wonderful as this in Greystones,' she said, sliding down from the horse's back. She went to wipe a tear away from her cheek, only to be beaten to it by Tom.

'Did I do something wrong?' he asked earnestly. 'I thought you liked him?'

She looked up sadly. 'I loved him, Tom, he's a wonderful toy. It just reminds me of how unfair it is that some folk have everything whilst others, through no fault of their own, have nothing at all.'

He gently brushed her cheek with the back of his fingers. 'Some folk only think they've got it all because they're wealthy and can buy whatever they want, but money isn't everything.'

She frowned curiously at him. 'It is when you haven't got any, believe me – I should know.'

He smiled softly. 'Perhaps what I should have said is that money can't buy you everything …' He stopped speaking as a woman rudely interrupted from behind.

'That toy's meant for kiddies, and my Arthur wants a ride, so if you don't mind …' She shouldered her way past Tom before he had a chance to move.

'For example,' Tom said in an exaggerated voice, 'some people don't have manners, yet they don't cost a penny!'

The woman scowled angrily, causing Jess to giggle. 'You're right, Tom, money can't buy you everything.'

Tom took Jess around the rest of the department store before taking her to Lyons where they ordered tea and sandwiches.

Jess thanked the waitress as she laid a plate of cheese and onion sandwiches down in front of her. 'No one's ever served me food like that before,' she told Tom. 'I feel like the queen!'

Cocking his head to one side, Tom smiled at her from across the table. 'It's strange to think you've never gone out for lunch before.'

Jess blushed a little. 'You must think me very backward.'

The smile instantly vanished from Tom's lips. 'Not at all!' he said fervently. 'I think you're wonderful, Jess. You take everything in your stride and you're not at all bitter. I'm not sure I'd be as forgiving as you if I were in your shoes.'

'Thanks, Tom, but I think it's more a case of having to get on with things,' she said pragmatically. 'After all, wallowing in self-pity won't make me feel any better.'

Tom twinkled at her. 'You're one very special lady, Jessica Wilson, and I hope we do find your father because you deserve some answers.'

Jess finished a mouthful of sandwich. 'You've said *we* a couple of times now?'

Tom nodded. 'I'm hoping my auntie will know something, but if she doesn't it doesn't mean to say we have to stop looking.' He wiped his napkin across his lips. 'Maybe try the hospitals in Glasgow?'

Reaching out, Jess held his hand across the table. 'Thanks, Tom, that's ever such a kind offer, but you really don't have to put yourself out like this ...'

He squeezed her fingers in his. 'I'm not putting myself out for anyone. If anything, I shall rather enjoy playing detective.'

They spent the rest of the afternoon looking round Lewis's and Bon Marche, as well as some of the smaller shops. By the time they had finished it was time for supper, and at Tom's suggestion they bought fish and chips which they ate on the overhead railway as they made their way back to Seaforth.

Feeling happier than she thought she had ever been, Jess looked down at the docks as the train slowly trundled its way along the line, then up to the sun which was setting over the sea. 'It's so beautiful, Tom.'

'You like Liverpool then?' he asked, popping a chip into his mouth.

'I don't like it, I love it!' said Jess. She broke off a piece of fish and crunched the crispy batter. She held up the remaining piece. 'This has got to be the best thing I've ever eaten in my life!' Lowering her voice, she confided in Tom. 'We serve fish and chips in the NAAFI but this is much nicer, 'cos the batter's thick and crunchy.'

Tom gazed at Jess who was continuing to admire the sunset. He had met plenty of women in the army, most of them from good homes, with a moderate education, but none of them could hold a candle to Jess. She seemed oblivious of her beauty, a quality which Tom found very attractive, and nothing seemed to faze her. He had taken her to some of the grandest drapers which Liverpool had to offer, and even though she had never been anywhere like that before, you would not have guessed it to look at her. She seemed to take the whole world in her stride. He watched as the dying rays lit up Jess's face with a golden glow, giving her an almost angelic appearance. He frowned slightly as he tried to pinpoint the word which encapsulated how he saw her. The frown disappeared and was replaced with the ghost of a smile. Captivating, that's what Jess was. The more time he spent with her the more he liked her. She could be eating fish and chips, serving tea, or snatching forty winks, it didn't matter to Tom as long as he was with her.

As the train drew into Seaforth, the last station on the line, Tom took Jess's hand in his and led her off the train and down the steps. At the bottom he was pleased to see that she didn't try to take her hand out of his.

'Have you enjoyed yourself?' he asked, although he was sure he knew the answer to be yes.

'I've had a wonderful time, Tom,' said Jess, hugging her new dresses close to her chest. 'And I adore Liverpool!'

Tom gave her a satisfied smile. 'I knew you would. We'll have to go again soon, only next time I'll take you to the cinema …' He hesitated. 'Have you ever been to a cinema?'

She shook her head. 'Michelle, that's the girl whose frock I borrowed, told us all about it, and I must say it sounds thrilling! Although I can't see how it works.'

'What do you fancy watching? Romance, comedy, action or thrillers?' Hoping she would say 'romance' he crossed his fingers behind his back. Normally he'd do his best to avoid a romance – action films were more his cup of tea – but if watching a romance helped his relationship with Jess, he was all for it.

'I didn't realise there were so many choices!' she confessed. 'I'll have to have a good think and let you know.' She shivered as the cooling night air caressed her bare arms.

Seeing her discomfort, Tom swiftly removed his jacket and placed it around her shoulders. 'Next time we go to Paddy's Market we shall have to buy you a coat.'

Thanking him, she snuggled her cheek against the collar of his jacket. She closed her eyes and breathed in the scent of his aftershave. 'Not "we", Tom Durning – you've done enough for me already. Besides, I thought we were going to meet your Auntie Edna next?'

Tom pushed his hands into his pockets. 'That's right. Didn't you say you have a few hours off every afternoon?'

She nodded.

'Well in that case, why don't we go one afternoon next week? I'll see when I'm off and let you know.'

She nodded again, then clapped a hand to her mouth. She had been so caught up in her time with Tom, she had completely forgotten his brother's car. 'Tom! We left Olly by Paddy's Market!'

He grinned sheepishly. 'I know, but it was more fun on the railway, don't you think?'

'Much more!' Pulling the jacket tightly round her, Jess thought of an excuse to make their evening last a little longer. 'Why don't I come back with you? You can always drop me off before heading back.'

Tom sighed regretfully. He would very much have liked Jess to go back with him, but he knew he wouldn't have time to bring her back to Seaforth. 'I'll get a right ear bashing if I get back too late; I would otherwise.' Silently adding, 'like a shot' in the privacy of his own mind.

Disappointed, Jess nodded and handed his jacket back. 'You'll give me a call?'

'I'll be in touch as soon as I know, when I'm free' Tom said.

They both stood in awkward silence, each wishing the other to say something which would give them an excuse to carry on talking. As the silence began to get embarrassing, Jess mumbled a quick 'goodbye' and half turned towards the gate. Hearing movement behind her, she turned back in time to see Tom quickly leaning back, his lips barely grazing her cheek.

'G'night, Jess,' he murmured before walking swiftly away.

Jess stared after him. Was it her imagination or had he gone to kiss her? She bade a quick hello to the guard on the gate before hurrying off in the direction of her billet. Opening the tent flap, she hurried over to Penny and Ruby who were looking expectantly at her. She sat down on Ruby's bed and beckoned them to lean closer. 'I think he just tried to kiss me!'

Penny and Jess immediately hushed Ruby who was squealing with excitement. 'What do you mean, you "think"?' said Penny, confused. 'He either did or he didn't.'

Jess glanced around the billet to make sure no one was listening before continuing in hushed tones. 'We were chatting outside and it all got a bit awkward, like neither of us knew what to say or do next, and rather than stand there like a lemon I went to walk away ...' She went on to explain what happened next.

'I see!' said Ruby. 'So, you think he was leaning in for a kiss?'

'Yes!' said Jess. 'What do you think?'

Ruby and Penny exchanged glances. 'We were chatting earlier,' explained Ruby, 'and we both thought Tom would probably try and kiss you goodbye.'

'Looks like we were right!' said Penny excitedly. 'Or at least we would've been had you not moved.'

'Did he mention wanting to see you again?' asked Ruby eagerly.

'He's taking me to see his auntie one afternoon next week.' Jess smiled coyly. 'He asked me before we'd had our lunch.'

Ruby snapped her fingers. 'Knew it!' She turned to Penny. 'Didn't I say?'

Penny unfurled her bedsocks. 'You certainly did!'

Ruby wriggled her feet in an excited fashion. 'I knew he liked you, but he must be frightfully keen to have asked you out on another date before you'd finished the first one!' Her face fell as a thought occurred to her.

'Oh heck! I don't suppose you're any the wiser as to whether or not the two of you are related?'

Grinning, Jess relayed the conversation she'd had with Tom regarding the Christmas Eve of 1923 and how she'd decided there was no possibility that they could be related.

Ruby blew her cheeks out. 'Thank goodness for that! I'm ever so glad you agreed to go out with him, Jess. I think you two were made for each other.'

'I've got to say, I really hope you're right.' Jess slipped off Michelle's tea dress and hung it back on the hanger, looking at the other girl's bed which was empty. 'Where's Michelle?'

'Gone to the camp cinema with Mabel,' said Ruby. She eyed Jess curiously. 'What'll you do if he tries to kiss you next time?'

Jess's face fell. 'I have no idea, but I do know one thing – it's going to be awful wondering whether he's going to try or not. It was different tonight because he caught me off guard.'

'Surely that's good!' said Ruby encouragingly. ''Cos you'll be prepared next time.'

'Not good!' said Jess, who could already feel the butterflies rising in her tummy. ''Cos I'll get all nervy and anxious, and then I'll start sweating and I'll go all blotchy ...'

Ruby grimaced. 'You do all that and you won't have to worry about him trying to kiss you.'

'Better that than making a mess of things. I haven't a clue what to do.'

'I know!' said Penny. 'Why don't you pretend you're sucking a lemon.'

Ruby looked at Penny aghast. 'Lemons are horrible! The cook in Greystones used to make us suck one of them as punishment if we didn't eat her horrible grub.'

Jess pulled a reproving face. 'I hope he tastes better than a lemon.' She smiled wistfully. 'He certainly smells nicer. He gave me his jacket to wear when it got a little chilly.'

Ruby clasped her hands together. 'How romantic!'

Penny nodded. 'He'll be throwing it over puddles like that Wally bloke next.'

'Wally bloke?' Jess chuckled. 'You mean Sir Walter Raleigh?'

Penny shrugged. 'If he throws his cloak into puddles for ladies to walk over, then yes.'

Jess gathered her wash kit from her locker. She might have found Penny's comparison amusing at first, but with hindsight she felt her friend wasn't so far off the mark. Tom had practically paid for her entire day out, and had made sure she had everything she needed. Not to mention lifting her onto the rocking horse's back. She sighed dreamily as she felt the memory of his strong arms around her waist when he'd lifted her effortlessly onto the horse. She would save the story of her ride on the painted horse for the morning. Right now she wanted to have a quick wash before she climbed into bed, where she could snuggle down and dream of the wonderful, gallant Tom.

Tom struck his forehead with the palm of his hand. How could he have been so stupid? Faint heart never won fair lady – how often had he heard those words?

He hadn't wanted to appear pushy, so had kept his distance until the last minute, which had been a mistake because as soon as he decided to make his move, he had found himself puckering up to thin air, his lips clumsily brushing her cheek. He gave himself a hypothetical kick. Had Jess realised his intent when she turned back, and what on earth would he say to her when he saw her next? He hesitated. Would she still want to see him?

'Some kind of knight in shining armour you are!' Tom muttered to himself. Stuffing his hands into his pockets, he wondered what he should do for the best. He would feel a fool if he rang the NAAFI to make arrangements only to have her make excuses. On the other hand, he couldn't bear to imagine the disappointment on her face if he failed to get in touch. He sighed heavily. He would have to grin and bear it and hope Jess hadn't realised his intention.

Fists on hips, Agnes McKinley glared accusingly at her daughter. 'What the hell have you done this time?'

Still half asleep, Bonnie knuckled her eyes, then stared blearily up at her mother. 'How could I have done anything? I'm still in bed!'

'Well, you'd better get up, because Mrs Ancrum wants to see us both in her office, and she does not sound happy. In fact, she sounds livid.'

Swinging her legs out of bed, Bonnie pulled on her dressing gown and shoved her feet into her sheepskin slippers. 'Well, I haven't done anything ...' She covered a yawn with the back of her hand and tied the belt into a bow. 'What time is it anyway?'

'Nine o'clock, you should've been up over an hour ago,' said Agnes through pursed lips. 'I know you're my daughter, but you've got to start pulling your weight.' She thought for a moment then brightened a little. 'Perhaps that's what this is all about. I told you we'd all have to pitch in when we got here, but so far you've not done a stroke.' Feeling a sense of relief, she continued, 'She's probably called you in to give you a slap on the wrists and wants me to be there to make sure you start toeing the line.'

'Why can't the others do it?' said Bonnie sulkily. 'Ancrum made them do everything in the orphanage, I don't see why it's any different here.'

'For a start, it's Mrs Ancrum, and as for the rest of it, we're not the only ones here, are we? There's lots of other folk around, and they might not understand, they might think we were being unfair.'

'Who cares what they think?' said Bonnie. 'You've always said those girls should be grateful we put a roof over their heads because you don't get anything in life for free, which is why they do the laundry.' She raised her eyebrows. 'I reckon people would be more understanding than you think.'

Rapping a brief tattoo on the door to Mrs Ancrum's office, they waited until they heard 'Come in!' from the other side of the door.

When Bonnie stepped into the room, she was surprised to see Clare standing beside the window. Why on earth was the other girl in Ancrum's office? She eyed Mrs Ancrum who was staring back at her stony-faced.

When the older woman spoke, it was through pursed lips, as though she was trying very hard to control her temper. She stared icily at Bonnie. 'I want to know exactly what you've been saying to people, and don't even think about lying because I've already spoken to Clare.'

Bonnie glanced at Clare who quickly averted her attention to the floor by her feet. Bonnie wished she had had a chance to speak to Clare so that she might find out exactly what it was the other girl had been saying, but as it was clear she wasn't going to be given any such opportunity, she decided to do the only thing she could do, lie. 'I don't know what Clare's been saying, but if it's to do with Jess and Ruby's papers ...'

Mrs Ancrum's jaw tightened as she interrupted Bonnie. 'I'm not here to talk about them, although I will say this – I know damned well that it was you that destroyed their papers, and you did it out of jealousy.'

'Jealous!' spluttered Bonnie. 'Of them?' She snorted her contempt. 'Why would I be jealous of a couple of ...' She stopped speaking as the other woman's words caught up with her. 'If you've not got me here to talk about those two, then why *have* you got me here?'

Mrs Ancrum peered at Bonnie over the top of her steepled fingers. 'Because someone has been gossiping about our arrangement with Brownhill, and aside from myself and my husband your mother is the only person who knew about it ...' She feigned sarcastic surprise, 'And I mustn't forget Clare, of course, because you told her about it, didn't you, Bonnie?'

Agnes McKinley cast her eyes to the ceiling before speaking to her daughter. 'Please tell me you didn't ...'

'I only told Clare ...' protested Bonnie. 'And she swore she'd keep her gob shut, so you can blame her ...'

'You told more than Clare,' said Mrs Ancrum slowly, 'because Alice's mother knew all about it. I know this because the governors – as well as a few others – have been in touch—'

Agnes butted in quickly. 'Maybe Clare's the one who blabbed to Alice.'

Mrs Ancrum stared icily at Agnes. 'Only Clare wouldn't have been able to tell anyone had your daughter not told her in the first place, which brings me to another point. Bonnie couldn't have said anything if you hadn't told her!'

Agnes swallowed nervously. 'I swear I never said a word direct to her. She might have overheard the two of us speaking ...'

Mrs Ancrum shook her head slowly. 'Loose lips, that's what they say, and how right they are.' Standing up, she rested her fists on the surface of her desk. 'Because of you two, I'm under investigation, and so is Brownhill!'

Bonnie thrust her fists down by her sides. 'Don't blame me and Mam! We weren't the ones selling kids to Brownhill – that's what you and your rotten husband did.'

Mrs Ancrum thrust a trembling finger in the direction of the door. 'Get your things and get out!'

Bonnie gave a sneering laugh. 'You can't throw us out.'

Her face turning white with fury, Mrs Ancrum stared steely-eyed at Bonnie. 'I can do what I like.' She turned her attention to Agnes. 'You're sacked – something I should have done a long time ago.'

Agnes's mouth dropped. 'Why me?' she said quietly. 'I never told anyone, I can understand you being angry at the girls but ...'

'Because she's your daughter! You should have given her a good hiding years ago; at least that way she'd have a bit more respect.' Mrs Ancrum's eyes narrowed maliciously. 'I only kept you on to make sure you'd keep your mouth shut, but it's too late for that now.'

Agnes took half a step towards the desk. 'Please don't do this, I've nowhere to go. I promise I'll make Bonnie toe the line, she'll not say another word.' She looked earnestly at Bonnie. 'Tell her, Bonnie, tell her you're sorry, and that you promise to behave and keep quiet in future.'

Bonnie stamped her foot. 'Why am I getting the blame for all this? I didn't do anything wrong.' She pointed an accusing finger at Clare. 'She's the one that went blabbing because I swear to you, I never told another soul.' She threw her hands up in despair. 'And let's face it, if you hadn't been selling the girls to Brownhill in the first place, no one could report you for it! So I shan't say I'm sorry, and you can stuff your billet.' She cast a disapproving eye around the poky little office. 'I'll go and tell the billeting officer that you've chucked us out on the streets. They'll soon find us somewhere to live, somewhere better too I shouldn't wonder.'

'Bonnie!' shrieked Agnes. She turned to her employer in order to plead her case. 'She's in shock, she doesn't know what she's saying ...'

Mrs Ancrum opened the drawer to her desk and handed Agnes an envelope. 'Here's your papers, and wages up to date.' She gave Bonnie a sidelong glance. 'You'd best learn to control that tongue of yours before it gets you or someone else into more trouble.'

Bonnie opened her mouth to reply, but Agnes quickly ushered her daughter out of the room before she could do any more damage. 'Stay here. I'm going back in to try and change her mind. In the meantime, you'd best start learning how to say you're sorry, 'cos if you don't we're homeless, with no money. Don't kid yourself we'll be billeted somewhere else, 'cos you're too old. The only reason you came to Glencoe was because you're with me and I work ...' she drew a deep breath, 'or I hope I work, for the orphanage, so as I say, if you want to sleep in a bed tonight with a roof over your head you'd best start learning how to say you're sorry!'

Bonnie eyed her mother incredulously. 'They can't make me go back to Glasgow! I'm too young—'

'You're old enough to work,' said Agnes, who was coming to the end of her tether, 'and if you're old enough to work you're too old to be evacuated.'

'What am I meant to do for a job?' said Bonnie, who was finding her new reality a little hard to bear.

Her mother shrugged. 'Whatever you can, whether it be washing sheets or cleaning privies.'

Bonnie wrinkled her nose up in disgust. 'I'm not cleaning privies, especially not the public ones – you get all sorts in there.'

'You'll do what it takes or starve ...' said her mother, '... either that or end up in Brownhill.'

177

Bonnie swallowed hard. She had no intention of apologising to that wretched Ancrum, but on the other hand she didn't wish to spend her days cleaning up other people's … She shuddered at the thought. 'All right, tell her I'll apologise.'

Agnes smiled gratefully. 'Good girl.' She disappeared into the office only to reappear a few seconds later. Bonnie looked at her hopefully, but she could see by her mother's expression that the answer was still the same. 'She wouldn't have it,' explained Agnes, her tone hollow with disbelief. She led Bonnie back to her room. 'She says we've got an hour to get out.'

For the first time in her life, the gravity of Bonnie's actions hit home. She looked at her mother, who shrugged. 'I've got enough to get us back to Glasgow. We'll have to find a room and start looking for work. Luckily for us there's a war on, so there's plenty of work to be had.'

'It's all that blooming Jess's fault!' muttered Bonnie. 'I wish you'd never opened the door that night.'

Agnes rounded on her daughter. 'You're the one who couldn't keep your mouth shut! What did you say to her? Did you brag that you knew more than she did?'

Bonnie stamped her foot petulantly. 'No, I bleedin' well didn't! I told you in there,' she pointed towards the office, 'the only person I told is Clare. If you want to blame anyone, blame her, she's the one that tattle-taled, although I can't think why. What's in it for her? That's what I'd like to know.'

Agnes folded her arms across her chest. 'Ancrum probably suspected it had something to do with you so she must have told Clare to tell the truth or risk the consequences.'

'Well, she's lying!' snapped Bonnie. 'And what consequences?'

Agnes strode ahead of her daughter down the corridor and thrust the door to their room open with the palm of her hand. 'If Clare ends up in Brownhill she'll have to face all those girls you got her to spy on. Even Clare's not stupid enough to think they'd forgive and forget. Ancrum probably cut her a deal, saying she'd keep her out of Brownhill as long as Clare told her who was responsible for telling Alice.' She shook her head. 'And all this because you don't like Jessica Wilson.' She threw their suitcase onto the bed and opened the top drawer of the chest which stood next to the window. 'What I don't understand is why you've always had it in for her.'

Bonnie opened the door to their shared wardrobe and began taking her dresses down from their hangers. 'Because of you!' She stared at her mother. 'You've always told me how Jess nearly got you the sack, and how beastly her father was to you, and how you wish he'd taken her to a different orphanage.'

Agnes placed a hand to her forehead as she sank onto the bed. 'None of that has anything to do with Jess directly.' She covered her face in order to hide her tears. 'I should have kept my mouth shut.'

Bonnie put an arm around her mother's shoulders. 'Don't cry, Mam, they're not worth it.'

If Bonnie thought she loathed Jess before, it was nothing compared to the sheer hatred she felt towards her now. As far as Bonnie was concerned, Jess was responsible for everything, and she would not rest until she had made her pay for all the hurt and upset she had caused the McKinleys.

Jess finished scrubbing the counter. 'I've got to go, Tom'll be waiting for me.'

'Good luck, Jess!' Ruby said as she hurried over to Jess and hugged her briefly. 'I hope it all goes well and his auntie gives you some answers.'

Penny called out from the far side of the kitchen where she was preparing the tea for their lunchtime break. 'I'll be keeping my fingers crossed.'

Jess slipped off her overalls. 'See you in a couple of hours.'

Outside she was pleased to see that Tom was already waiting for her. Smiling, he waved a greeting then made his way round to the passenger side of the car. Jess felt a rush of excitement as she walked towards him. Since their trip to Liverpool last week all she could think about was Tom, how much she liked him and when she would see him again. As promised, he had telephoned the morning after their trip to make arrangements to take her to see his family that Wednesday afternoon, and as far as Jess was concerned it couldn't come soon enough. The only thing that put a dampener on their anticipated rendezvous was the thought of meeting his aunt and what, if anything, she might have to say regarding the night of Jess's birth.

Sliding into the passenger seat, she waited for Tom to take his place behind the wheel. 'Have you been waiting long?'

He checked the road was clear before pulling out. 'I got here two minutes before you appeared.' He gave her a dazzling smile. 'How are you feeling?'

She blew her cheeks out. 'A bit nervous. Half of me hopes your auntie's a mine of information, the other half wonders whether it'd be better to leave sleeping dogs lie because I could be opening a real can of worms.'

Tom drummed his fingers against the steering wheel. 'Sounds to me like you're caught between a rock and a hard place.'

'That's what it feels like. I only want to hear good news, but that's not how it works.' She turned to face him. 'You've heard the expression, be careful what you wish for?'

He frowned. 'I have, but I've never really understood it. Surely you'd only wish for something you really want?'

'If I wish to find my dad, it's because I want him to welcome me with open arms, tell me it was all a horrible mistake and he rues the day he gave me away, before whisking me off to meet my mother, and we'll all live happily ever after in a cottage by the sea.' She arched an eyebrow. 'Only I'm not naïve enough to think that will be the reality. It's far more likely that neither of my parents will welcome me into their lives. I might even have siblings who will resent me for turning up ...'

Tom gave a low whistle. 'Flippin' heck, I can see what you mean about being careful what you wish for.' He slowed the car down as they approached a set of traffic lights. 'Only if you don't try to find him you'll never know what could have been.' He hesitated. 'What about the woman that found you? Could she have been making it up? For all we know your father might have been full of remorse the day he left you at Greystones. He might have insisted she give you the money and given her a letter explaining his actions.'

Jess looked doubtful. 'I wouldn't trust McKinley as far as I could throw her, but I do believe her when she said he went to hit her, because there was no need for her to make it up. She could've said she found me with the money tucked into my blankets, no one would have been any the wiser, or had reason to doubt her, but she didn't, and I reckon that's because he scared the wits out of her and she was angry with Ancrum for calling her a liar.'

Tom turned on the windscreen wipers as rain speckled the window. 'I've been thinking about that. Do you really believe a young woman – as she would have been at the time – like McKinley would be frightened of an old man?'

'No, but I do believe she'd be frightened of a vicious old man who had no qualms about beating her with his cane.' Jess glanced at the road ahead. 'Don't forget, she was pregnant with Bonnie at the time, so she was hardly in a position to fight back, and from what Bonnie said, he threatened to hit McKinley with the handle of the cane, which sounds bad enough, but when you hear it was in the shape of a cobra's head and was made of solid silver ...'

Tom raised his eyebrows. 'I see!' He leaned his elbow against the window. 'Sounds like the actions of someone who's desperate.'

'Or a thug who thinks nothing of threatening to hit a woman,' Jess said simply. 'I know McKinley, and she's got a vicious tongue on her. There's not a doubt in my mind that she would've given him an earful for giving the orphanage another mouth to feed.' She shrugged. 'Maybe that's what made him so angry.'

Tom turned up a side road. 'I don't know whether my auntie will know anything, but whatever she has to say, good or bad, I want you to know I'm with you all the way, so don't think you're doing this on your own – you're not. We're in this together.'

Smiling shyly, Jess bit back her tears. She knew Penny and Ruby were there for her, but when it came to confronting an old man with a violent temper, she'd far rather have someone like Tom by her side. 'Thanks, Tom. I must admit I wouldn't relish the thought of meeting him on my own and I'd be reluctant to take the girls with me in case he got nasty.'

'That's why I'll be coming with you,' he said as he took another turning up a street lined with terraced houses and pulled up outside one of them. 'Here we are!'

Jess looked at the house in surprise. She had always assumed that Tom lived in a house like the one on Edinburgh Road. She eyed the blue-painted door with its brass knocker, and was starting to wonder what answers lay behind the threshold when it opened and a pleasant-looking woman, who Jess guessed to be in her early fifties, waved to them briefly before walking forward and opening Jess's door. She held out a hand to help Jess from the car. 'Hello, Jess, I'm Sylvie Durning, Tom's mam.'

Jess smiled back. 'It's lovely to meet you, Mrs Durning. Thank you for inviting me round.'

Sylvie waved a carefree hand. 'It's our pleasure, chuck, we've been quite eager to meet you. Tom's father sends his apologies, but he's had to go out, something to do with the ARP.' She glanced at Tom. 'Our Tom's not stopped talking about you since he came back from Glasgow ...'

Jess giggled as Tom gave an indignant, 'Mam!'

Sylvie slid her arm through Jess's and pulled her close so that she could continue to talk without being overheard by Tom. 'We think it's rather sweet. He's had a real spring in his step since meeting you.' She indicated a white-haired old lady who was fast asleep by the fire in her wheelchair. 'That's Great-Aunt Edna, she's the one you want to talk to.'

Tom had told Jess that his aunt was really his great-aunt, but she was much older than Jess had anticipated and she couldn't help but wonder whether the woman would be able to remember what day of the week it was, let alone something that had taken place nigh on sixteen years ago.

Tom must have seen the uncertainty on Jess's face as he swiftly assured her that even though his aunt was old, she had a brilliant memory. 'She might not be able to tell you what she had for lunch,' he admitted, 'but you ask her what she was doing when the Great War broke out, and she can tell you where she was, what she was doing and who she was with.'

He took Jess's coat and hung it up with his own on a hook on the back of the kitchen door. 'I've told me mam and me auntie that you used to live in the orphanage,

184

but I thought I'd leave it to you to tell the rest of your story.'

The old woman yawned loudly and looked up. 'Is it time for supper?'

Tom spoke in a loud voice. 'Not yet, Auntie.' He bent down so that she could see him clearly. Aunt Edna's face lit up upon seeing her great-nephew. 'Tom dear, how lovely to see you.'

He smiled. 'I've brought a friend of mine to meet you.' He beckoned Jess to join him. 'This is Jess, she's from Glasgow same as you.'

The woman's eyes positively sparkled when she heard that Jess was from Glasgow. Beckoning Jess to come closer, she took her hand in a firm grip. 'Oh, I do miss my home. Are you going to take me back?'

Jess shook her head apologetically. 'I'm afraid I don't live there any more. I've moved to Liverpool the same as you.'

'Jess used to live in Greystones ...' Tom began, but he got no further before his aunt voiced her opinions on the orphanage.

'Poor little blighter!' she said fervently. 'Rotten place for a kiddie to end up.' She smiled warmly at Jess. 'It's much nicer here.' She glanced around her before adding, 'Where's our Sylvie? I need the little girls' room.'

Stepping forward, Sylvie leaned down beside Edna. 'I'll take you.' She glanced at Tom. 'Get the door for us, there's a good lad, and pop the kettle on whilst you're about it.'

Tom gestured to one of the armchairs by the fire. 'Make yourself at home, Jess, I shan't be long.' He disappeared into the kitchen.

Jess sat down and took in her surroundings. The house seemed a lot bigger on the inside; the two downstairs rooms had been made into one large one, with the introduction of an archway. Jess guessed this had been done to accommodate Tom's aunt, because there was a bed at the far side of the room. The rest of the space was taken up with a blue and white melamine kitchen table and Jess was sitting in one of two easy chairs which flanked the fireplace. It was cosier and more homely than the house in Edinburgh Road. The walls were hidden behind multiple photographs and pictures. Jess smiled. The photograph of Tom which she had first seen in Edinburgh Road now stood on the mantelpiece.

'What do you think?' Tom called from the kitchen.

'You've a lovely house, Tom, you're very lucky.'

Tom glanced around the room. 'It's not much, but it's home, and it's far easier to keep an eye on Auntie. She doesn't have to walk more than a few paces here, so it's a lot safer for her.'

Tom carried through a tin tea tray laden with cups, saucers and a plate of mixed biscuits. Hearing the back door open, he hurried over to help his mother push the wheelchair over the small step which separated the house from the yard. Expressing her thanks, Tom's mother settled Edna beside Jess. 'I'll leave you two to have a chat whilst I help our Tom with the rest of the tea things.' She moved the biscuits onto a small brass table next to the older woman's chair. 'Help yourselves.'

Aunt Edna smiled up at Jess. 'My niece tells me you've come to talk about Greystones?'

Jess smiled awkwardly. 'Sort of. You see, I'm looking for my father. He left me on the steps of the orphanage on the Christmas Eve of 1923, and I was wondering if you might have remembered seeing anything?' Seeing the doubtful look on the old lady's face, she added, 'I realise it was a long time ago.'

Aunt Edna took a bourbon cream from the plate then waited until Sylvie had placed a cup of tea beside her elbow before dunking the biscuit into the liquid. 'You're right, it was a long time ago, but I can say with certainty that I never saw someone abandoning a baby outside the orphanage. I'd have had their guts for garters.' She cradled Jess's smooth hand in her own weathered one. 'Sorry.'

'That's what I said,' came Tom's muffled response. His mouth half full of a Garibaldi biscuit, he added, 'Not that it helps you much.'

Tom's mother frowned at her son. 'Thomas! Don't speak with your mouth full!' She smiled sweetly at Jess as she strained the tea into the cup. 'Milk and sugar?'

'Milk but no sugar for me, please,' Jess said, sagging back into her chair. She knew it had been a long shot coming to see his aunt, but it still didn't make the news any easier to take.

Seeing the disappointment etched on Jess's face, Edna leaned forward. 'I'm sorry I couldn't be of any more help to you,' she soothed, 'but I reckon you're probably better off without him. I mean, who abandons their own child on Christmas Eve?'

Jess pulled a brave face. 'That was my reaction at first, but then all sorts of different scenarios started popping into my head. We know my father had money, so I began to wonder whether my mam might've died whilst she gave birth to me.'

Aunt Edna and Sylvie exchanged knowing glances. 'Or he could've got the wrong woman pregnant?' Sylvie suggested cautiously.

'That's another possibility,' conceded Jess, 'only if that's the case, then who was my mother, and did she have any say in the matter? Because I can't see any woman letting a man like that take their baby away without a struggle, not unless they were just as scared of him as McKinley was, and if so, what on earth were they doing lying down with someone like that in the first place?'

Aunt Edna frowned, causing her face to become a sea of wrinkles. 'Who's this McKinley person?'

'She was the woman who took me in that night ...' Jess went on to tell them everything she knew about the night she had been abandoned at Greystones.

Sylvie's cheeks bloomed scarlet. 'If everything that McKinley woman said is true, then your mother might not have had a choice. He sounds like the sort of man who doesn't take no for an answer.'

Jess's mouth hung open. 'You think he might have raped her?'

Aunt Edna held up a hand. 'This is the problem with making assumptions. I'm not sure I'd believe everything that McKinley woman told you. They're a right bunch of so-and-sos that run that orphanage.' She cocked her head to one side. 'If he was as old as you say, he might well have been married. He wouldn't be the first man to get his mistress pregnant.'

'Quite likely,' said Tom. 'From what Jess knows, he sounds old enough to be someone's grandfather.'

'Grey hair, with mutton chops,' said Jess promptly, adding as an afterthought, 'and he had a walking cane with a silver cobra's head as the handle ...' She paused. Aunt Edna had looked up sharply.

'What's that about a cane?' she said, her tone suddenly serious.

'That's what he threatened to hit McKinley with. It was black, with a solid silver cobra's head as the handle ...' Jess stared at the old woman, who was looking haunted. 'Did you see him?'

Aunt Edna dropped her gaze. 'It rings a bell, but I couldn't tell you for certain that it was him.'

Tom frowned. 'Do you think you might have seen him dumping Jess ...' He stopped speaking because his aunt was shaking her head vigorously.

'No!' she said quickly. 'But I do remember seeing a man like that in the hospital where I used to work.' She looked at Jess, before turning her attention to the dancing flames of the fire. 'Only the memory plays tricks, and I must have seen hundreds of older men with canes in my time.'

Jess was leaning forward eagerly. 'What hospital? Where?'

Tom's mother passed Jess a cup of tea. 'Aunt Edna was a matron at the Royal Hospital in Glasgow.' She looked at the bowed white head then placed a comforting hand on her aunt's shoulder. 'Don't worry yourself, Auntie, no one expects you to remember every detail.'

The older woman looked up at Jess, her eyes full of sorrow. 'That's as maybe, but there's something about that cane that rings a bell.' She heaved a sigh. 'Even so, there's not a lot I can say that'd be of any help to you, because I very much doubt his details will have been recorded, not unless he gave them to us, and I can't see he'd have done that, not if his plan was to leave you on the steps of the orphanage.' She stared into the fire, still deep in thought.

'Do you remember anything about my mother?' asked Jess, hoping against hope that she would say yes.

Aunt Edna remained still for a moment or two as though she were mulling something over, then she looked up and shook her head. 'Too long ago,' she eyed Jess darkly. 'If you take my advice, you'll leave sleeping dogs lie.'

Jess felt her heart sink. It was obvious the woman had remembered something, but what? 'Perhaps if I tried the hospital where you used to work …?'

The old woman cut her short with a deep sigh. 'All this happened nigh on sixteen years ago!' she said irritably, waving her hands in an exasperated manner. 'Do you really think these people give us their real names?' Her voice became shrill. 'For goodness' sake, child …' Seeing the shocked faces of those around her, she immediately apologised for her outburst. 'I'm sorry for raising my voice, I just think it's best if you forget about looking for your folks. After all, those that don't want to be found, won't be.'

Sylvie cleared her throat. 'Aunt's brought a lot of children into the world, not all of whom went home with their parents.'

'I didn't mean to upset you,' said Jess quickly. 'And you're right, my father didn't want to be found, otherwise he'd have left his details.' She had no desire to see the older woman in any more distress so she quickly changed the subject. 'Do you miss Glasgow an awful lot?'

A visible wave of relief crossed Aunt Edna's face. 'Like you wouldn't believe. Liverpool's a wonderful city, but it'll never be home.'

'It must be difficult moving away from somewhere you love,' said Jess. 'It wasn't like that for me, I was running away to a better life.' Hastily, she added, 'Not that there's anything wrong with Glasgow, of course – not that we got to see any of it.'

Aunt Edna sucked her teeth. 'We all knew that Ancrum woman was up to no good.'

Remembering Penny's words, Jess told the other woman about the Ancrums' deal with Brownhill.

'I knew they were up to something,' the older woman tutted loudly. 'It was obvious, but knowing something's no good without proof.'

Jess glanced at the clock on the mantelpiece. 'Gosh! I'd better be making tracks!' She got up hastily from her seat and held out a hand to Tom's mother. 'Thanks for the tea and biscuits.'

Sylvie took a napkin and wrapped up a couple of custard creams. 'Take some with you, or else our Tom'll eat the lot.'

Jess pocketed the biscuits. 'I shall save them for later!' She turned to Edna. 'And thanks for talking to me. I always knew it was a long shot, but I think I shall take your advice and let sleeping dogs lie.'

Sylvie went with them to the door and glanced at the grey clouds gathering in the sky. 'You'll have to visit again, Jess. Only come for your tea next time.'

'I will,' Jess called over her shoulder as she got into the car.

With the rain beginning to lash down, Sylvie quickly closed the door, then turned to face her aunt and raised an inquisitive eyebrow. 'What on earth was all that about?'

The smile vanished from Edna's lips. 'Don't know what you're on about,' she said guardedly.

'Oh yes, you do! I'm not still wet behind the ears like those young 'uns. You're hiding something.'

The old woman glanced at the rain-blurred window. 'Why won't people leave things be!' she snapped. 'No good can come from raking up the past.'

'The child wants answers, and there's nowt wrong with that,' said Sylvie levelly. 'You've always said you wondered what happened to the babies you brought into this world,' she began putting the empty cups onto the tray, 'and you were quite happy to help until you heard who her father was. She was right, you definitely remembered him, so was he violent? Part of a gang?' Her eyes bored into the top of the old woman's head. 'Don't think you can get away with ignoring me, because I'm not so easily fobbed off as the children.'

Aunt Edna rubbed her face in her hands before patting the chair which Jess had previously occupied. 'Sit down.'

Sylvie leaned forward, eager to hear what her aunt had to say.

Edna eyed her plainly. 'I told her the truth, I don't know who her father was, nor her mother, and I very much suspect that they never gave their real names, but I do remember a man like she described – nasty piece of work he was, vicious and controlling, I felt sorry for the girl, she was too young to know what was going on.' She shuddered. 'Disgusting. He should be …' Falling into silence, she shook her head.

'So why not tell Jess?' said Sylvie, miffed.

When Edna spoke next, her voice was barely above a whisper. 'Because it was fifteen years ago, and even though I'm fairly sure, I can't be certain, and I'm not about to upset the apple cart by saying things which might've got muddled in my mind over time. It's easy to string two instances together when they happened so long ago, and Jess wasn't the only baby born that night. I don't want to go putting two and two together only to come up with five – that won't help anybody, least of all Jess.'

Sylvie looked confused. 'She already knows her father was a beast of a man, what else could you possibly tell her?'

Aunt Edna studied Sylvie sombrely. 'The first thing they teach you in my line of work, is to not ask questions. Our job was to make sure the babies were delivered safely, and that's where it ends. It does no good to concern yourself with matters beyond your control.' She rolled her eyes. 'Goodness knows I parroted it enough to the nurses and midwives that worked under me.'

Sylvie shrugged. 'I still don't understand.'

Edna drew a deep breath. 'I remember someone like him hanging around demanding to know how long she'd be giving birth, and insisting we hurry things up.'

Sylvie stared at her aunt in horrified disbelief. 'My God, the man's a monster! Jess is better off without him.' She nodded uncertainly. 'Although ...'

Aunt Edna nodded. 'It all happened such a long time ago, and I could've got him confused with someone else.' She held her hands up. 'I'm almost certain I'm right, but that's not enough. I have to be absolutely sure.'

'Couldn't you telephone the hospital,' suggested Sylvie, 'make a few enquiries? Once you explain who you are, I'm sure they'd speak to you ...'

Edna laughed mockingly. 'If they wouldn't tell us then, what makes you think they'll tell us now?' She shook her head. 'If the parents don't want to be found, then believe you me, they won't be.'

'Maybe one of the nurses who worked with you will remember something?' said Sylvie, eager to learn the truth.

Edna shrugged. 'They won't know any more than me.' She nodded slowly to herself as memories came flooding back. 'There was one nurse, she was like a dog with a bone because she didn't approve ...' She fell silent.

'You mean she wanted to do the right thing?' said Sylvie quietly.

Edna's head whipped up. 'You sound just like her, and I'll say to you as I said to her, who're we to say what's right?'

'Every child deserves two parents ...' Sylvie began defensively, only to be cut short.

'That want them, yes! But these didn't, and even if they did, how's a young chit of a girl meant to cope?

194

Especially when the father's old enough to be their grandpa?'

Sylvie stared at her aunt wide-eyed. 'I thought they were exaggerating. Was he really that old?'

Edna nodded. 'That's if I've got the right man, of course.'

Leaning over, Sylvie placed a reassuring hand over her aunt's. 'I can see why you kept quiet.'

Edna smiled gratefully. 'I've spent a lifetime turning a blind eye, and it's not been easy. If I could help that girl find her folks I would, but the truth of the matter is I could be sending her on a wild goose chase with only heartache at the end.'

Oblivious of the drama unfolding inside the terraced house, Tom pulled away from the kerb. 'Well, I'm not sure any of that was of much use to you.'

Jess shrugged. 'She tried her best.' She turned her attention to the rain-soaked pavements. She had seen the look on Edna's face when she had described her father, and there was no doubt in Jess's mind that the old woman remembered far more than she was letting on. 'I love the rain, especially when you're tucked up in bed, listening to it drumming on the roof.'

'I prefer snow,' said Tom, '"cos you get to go sledging and have snowball fights.'

Jess grinned. 'We used to have snowball fights at Greystones, until one of the staff found us and put an end to it, of course, but I've never been sledging. Is it fun?'

Tom nodded. 'Lots. I'll take you in the winter, providing I'm still here, of course.'

She twisted in her seat. 'You're leaving?'

He shrugged. 'They're bound to start moving us around at some point.'

Jess tried to imagine life without Tom, then immediately dismissed the thought from her mind before it took hold. Since she'd left Greystones, Tom had become a big part of her life and her feelings towards him grew stronger every time they met. Life without him was something she'd rather not contemplate.

Tom drew the car up beside the gate to the barracks. 'How about I take you to the cinema this Saturday?'

Jess nodded. 'Sounds grand to me.' Remembering the last time she and Tom had said goodbye, she decided it would be better if she got out of the car quickly to prevent any awkward misunderstandings. She leaned through the open door. 'What time on Saturday?'

Tom shrugged. 'Will you be free after five?'

She nodded. 'I'll meet you by the gate.' She shut the door. 'Cheerio, Tom.' She waved until he was out of sight before making a beeline for the NAAFI. She had so much to tell the girls and couldn't wait to hear their opinions.

She hurried into the kitchen and spoke hastily to Ruby and Penny, trying to relay as much of her afternoon as she could before Mrs Armstrong caught them chatting.

'So what do you think?' she asked them. 'I think Aunt Edna knows much more than she's letting on.'

Ruby looked doubtful. 'She must have seen hundreds of babies being born in her time. Judging by what you've told us, it sounds as though she was quite used to parents giving their babies away for one reason or another. If you want my opinion she's trying to protect you.'

Jess frowned. 'Protect me?'

Penny nodded. 'I agree with Ruby. She doesn't want you to go digging up the past, in case you get covered in dirt.'

Jess felt rather disappointed by her friends' response. Personally, Jess thought there was a lot more to it than Edna had let on, although when she thought about it, Tom had also seemed quite happy to put the matter to rest.

Mrs Armstrong entered the kitchen. 'Come along, ladies.'

Jess, Ruby and Penny immediately set about their duties. As Jess got the bread from the store cupboard, she couldn't help but feel deflated, as though everything was over before it had begun. She sighed heavily. How was she meant to look for her father on her own? She knew Tom had offered to help but he was as clueless as her. She placed the loaf on the table and went to fetch the margarine. The image of the woman's face when Jess had described her father played over and over in her mind. She shook her head. She was positive she wasn't imagining things; Tom's aunt had been happy to help Jess until she heard a description of her father. There was more to this than met the eye and Jess was determined to get to the bottom of it.

October 1939

Ruby looked up from the letter she was reading. 'George's pal Swanny has gone to Europe.'

Jess looked up from ironing her overalls. 'How do you know? Surely the censor didn't leave it in?'

Ruby showed Jess the letter.

Dear Ruby,

I'm glad to hear you're enjoying life in Seaforth and I can't wait to see you and Jess again. The only downside is my old pal Swanny's left for pastures new, so I've lost my partner in crime as it were. I must admit, I'm a tad jealous because he's living my dream, lucky devil ...

She looked up at Jess. 'It was George's dream to go to France, so I'm guessing that's what he means.'

Jess pulled a face. 'Maybe you're right, but so what if he has? As long as George doesn't go with him ...'

Ruby sank back down onto her bed. 'Only we all thought George's news was that he was going to France, but if that was the case he would have told me in the same manner, don't you think?'

Jess mulled this over before agreeing. 'I do, so why the long face?'

Ruby shrugged. 'If he's not going to France, then what?'

'Perhaps he's moving to Seaforth Barracks?' Jess suggested, but Ruby quickly dismissed this.

'I can't see why he couldn't tell us that in a letter.'

Jess turned her overalls round and started on the other side. 'I can't say as I'd know,' she grinned, ''cos George doesn't write to me as often as he does to you.'

Ruby blushed. 'I don't know about that ...'

'I do,' said Jess. 'He seems to write to you every other day. All I get is a quick note,' she gave a little giggle, 'mainly asking me if you're okay.'

The blush deepened in Ruby's cheeks. 'Perhaps we have more in common.'

Jess raised her brows. 'Maybe, but then again he's always been sweet on you.'

Ruby turned the letter over in her hands and looked at the bottom of the last page which he always signed off in the same fashion: *Affectionately yours, George.* She glanced up at Jess who was grinning at her. 'He means affectionately, in a brotherly fashion.'

Jess returned her attention to her ironing. 'Really? I know I've never had a brother, but Michelle has, and she says her brother never signs off like that.'

Ruby ran her finger over the words. She hoped Jess was right, because even though she hadn't seen George for over a month, she couldn't wait to see him again, and she very much hoped he felt the same way.

December 1939
Totally unsuspecting about what awaited her, Mrs Armstrong opened the doors to the NAAFI ready for service, to find herself face to face with a larger-than-life snowman, complete with tunic, trousers and tin hat, greeting her a 'good morning'.

Having heard the piercing scream, Jess and the other girls came rushing out to see what was going on, only to witness the older woman subjecting Tom to the dressing-down of a lifetime as he desperately tried to apologise.

The girls stood in stunned silence until Mrs Armstrong disappeared across the yard, before bursting into laughter.

'I wish she'd seen the funny side,' said Tom, as he began to hastily dismantle the mountain of snow.

'Her nerves are on tenterhooks because the ovens keep cutting out,' Jess said, wiping the tears of laughter from her eyes. 'She's not a bad old stick really.'

Tom wrinkled his nose sullenly. 'Humbug!' He looked at Jess who was helping him to get rid of the snowman. 'Well, it's true! I'm surprised she hasn't tried to ban Christmas altogether on account of not wishing for everyone to be merry and jolly in fear of a population explosion!'

Jess snorted with laughter, but Penny had overheard Tom's comments and nodded her agreement. 'Old Iron Britches is colder than that 'un,' she indicated the last ball of snow which Tom was rolling to one side. 'I hope she gets posted somewhere else. This was meant to be a real celebration, our first Christmas away from Greystones, only I can't see it being much fun with her around.'

'She can't follow us everywhere we go,' Tom said reasonably.

Jess arched an eyebrow. 'Have you somewhere in mind?'

'It'd be grand to go to sledging in one of the parks. We could even organise a snowball fight, army versus RAF, and after that we could go to the NAAFI for ...' his voice trailed off, '... are you working Christmas Day?'

Jess nodded. 'We're taking it in shifts.'

Penny clasped Jess's elbow and beckoned Tom to lean in. 'If we take the last shift, we can stay on after hours. You know what Armstrong's like for wanting to shoot off as soon as that shift's over ...'

Tom was grinning. 'Surely you're not suggesting we have a party?'

Beaming, Penny nodded. 'Too right I am! What the old bat doesn't know won't harm her, and I can't see anyone snitching on us.'

'Sounds grand to me,' said Tom. 'When will you know which shift you're taking?'

'Armstrong's telling us at the end of work today,' said Jess, 'so I should be able to tell you when we go out later.'

As she got ready to go out later that evening, Jess reflected how much she and her friends had changed in their first few months at Seaforth. They had had their first proper haircuts, styling their hair to frame their faces, and the other change had come in the form of make-up, something they had all found to be transforming, especially lipstick.

'You look completely different,' Ruby said as she admired Jess's appearance in the mirror, 'like a movie star.'

'You've got lashes as long as a giraffe!' said Penny as she carefully coated Jess's lashes with a touch of mascara.

Jess stared uncertainly at her reflection. 'You don't think it's too much?'

'You're going to the cinema then dancing at the Grafton – if that isn't something worth dressing up for, I don't know what is!' said Ruby.

'You don't think I look like a ...' she hesitated '... a tart?'

The girls roared with laughter. 'You? A tart?' echoed Ruby. 'Anyone who thinks that needs their head examined. I've never known anyone less ...' she furrowed her brow as she tried to come up with the right word, '... wanton?'

When Jess met Tom later that evening, she worried that he might look at her with disapproval, but as soon as she saw him she knew he very much approved.

Pushing his tie into place he offered her his arm, revelling in the fact that everyone around knew that they were together. He hadn't let go until they boarded the tram bound for the Coliseum Picture House on City Road.

'Golly, you look a real picture, Jess!' he said as Jess took a seat by the window.

She smiled shyly. 'Not too much then?'

He shook his head silently. 'Some girls look like they shovel it on with a trowel.' He smiled as a laugh escaped Jess's lips. 'Not you, though.'

'Mrs Armstrong spoke to us earlier. She says we're doing the morning shift on Christmas Day, much to Penny's disappointment.' She studied him curiously. 'Why are you looking so pleased?'

'I was rather hoping that you might come to ours for your Christmas dinner?'

Jess nodded. She felt as though her heart was going to burst. 'I'd love to, Tom.'

Tom wanted to jump for joy. Not only had she said yes, but she'd said she'd love to. Their evening had only just begun, but he was already on cloud nine.

Later that evening as he guided her around the dance floor of the Grafton, Tom wondered whether now was the time to try to kiss Jess again. After all, the whole evening had been a success – surely a kiss would be the perfect end to the perfect evening? He envisaged the last time he had tried to kiss her goodbye, then grimaced. On reflection, perhaps it would be better to leave things whilst the going was good.

Chapter Five

Ruby and Jess alighted from the overhead railway at Pier Head Station and descended the steps to the pavement below. 'I can't wait to see George,' said Ruby, her eyes sparkling with excited anticipation. 'I've been tying myself in knots trying to work out what his big secret could be, apart from the haircut. Do you think he'll look any different?'

Jess flashed an approving eye over her own appearance before doing the same to Ruby. 'I reckon so. We look different, so George definitely will.'

Ruby slipped her arm through Jess's. 'What if he's grown a moustache, or a beard?'

Jess snorted. Careful not to be overheard, she lowered her voice. 'He's only just turned fifteen! I'd be amazed if he'd managed to sprout a single hair, let alone a face full of them.'

'I keep forgetting he's younger than us,' Ruby agreed quietly. 'I hope he's filled out a bit, and that those awful marks on his back have healed.'

Jess shuddered as she remembered the lashes which had scarred their friend's back. 'They were starting to heal over before he left for Sandhurst, so I should imagine they'll be nowt but scars now. It's been …' her lips moved silently as she did the maths, 'just over three months since we saw him last, so his wounds should be nothing but a distant memory.'

Ruby's jaw stiffened. 'Dunno about distant, I should imagine you'd not forget getting thrashed like that in a hurry.'

'Perhaps I put that badly,' said Jess. 'What I meant was he won't be reminded every time he leans back in a chair, like when he was in Edinburgh Road.' She indicated a tram which was heading towards them. 'This one's ours.'

The girls waited until the passengers had alighted before boarding the tram bound for Lime Street Station. They gave the clippie their fare and took a seat on one of the varnished wooden benches on the top deck. The bell rang and the tram continued on its route.

Jess looked down at the people below as they tried to pick their way along the pavements without getting their feet wet. It had been snowing heavily the night before, but the volume of people and traffic ensured the snow was quickly turning to slush. She turned to face Ruby. 'Is he still going to be staying with Swanny's wife?'

'Cassie? I believe so, George and Swanny are such good pals. She said it would be nice for George to stay with her for Christmas, especially with Swanny being away.' Ruby's cheeks paled slightly and she glanced hopefully at Jess. 'Whatever George's secret is, it can't be anything to do with him going overseas. I've been giving it some thought, and I reckon if he was going to go, he'd have gone over with Swanny and the rest of them back in October.'

Jess smiled. 'Very true, and as I can't think of anything worse than going to the front line, I can only assume that it's good news.'

'Whatever it is has something to do with Swanny,' said Ruby thoughtfully, 'because that's what George said in his letter.'

Jess frowned. 'Did he mention whether Swanny was a sergeant or an officer?'

Ruby had been pondering on what could possibly be worse than heading over seas, but now she came out of her trance. 'Nope, which is why I'm so confused. He doesn't have any more authority than George.'

Jess pushed the bell as she rose from her seat. 'Nearly missed our stop!'

Ruby followed her gaze to the glass-domed railway station. 'Too busy nattering!'

An elderly gentleman who was sitting across the way from them gave them a reprimanding glare. 'Loose lips! You should know better than to gossip in public.'

Jess rolled her eyes in an exasperated fashion. 'If you can work out what our pal's up to off the back of our conversation then you're doing better than us. In fact, be our guest and spill the beans, because we'd love to know.'

He wagged a reproving finger. 'You never know what the enemy might find useful!'

Ruby opened her mouth to make a suitable retort but Jess had already taken her hand and was leading her down the steps to the lower deck. 'He might be a nosey old sod, but he's right, Rubes, we shouldn't have been talking as freely as we were – not that I was going to admit that in front of him, mind you.'

'He shouldn't have been eavesdropping. It's rude!' said Ruby defensively.

'I'll be sure to say that if we ever come across a German spy,' chuckled Jess. She waved her finger in an admonitory fashion. 'I don't care if you are a spy, it's still rude to eavesdrop!' She started suddenly as Ruby let out a piercing squeal.

'George!' She let go of Jess's hand and rushed over to where George stood, his arms open wide to receive her. They held each other in a warm embrace. Tears of joy brimming in her eyes, she whispered, 'I can't believe you're actually here!'

George picked her up and whirled her around before setting her back down. 'Wild horses couldn't stop me!' Standing back, his eyes travelled from the top of her hair to the tips of her toes. 'You've grown, Ruby Anderson!'

Blushing, Ruby admired his khaki uniform, most of which George actually filled. 'I'm not the only one! You look completely different.'

George gazed proudly at her. 'It's amazing what food and exercise can do for a feller!'

She nodded. 'It certainly is.'

George looked past Ruby to where Jess was standing and beckoned her to join them. 'I see you've brought the cavalry!'

Jess enveloped him in a welcoming embrace. 'You know us, like peas in a pod.' She nodded approvingly. 'You certainly look a lot better than the last time we saw you.' Standing back, she placed her hands around his middle. 'Can't feel any ribs, so army grub is obviously agreeing with you.'

Ruby sniffed haughtily. 'I doubt it, it'll be the NAAFI that's put flesh on his bones. Am I right, George?'

He placed a tentative friendly arm around her shoulders and smiled broadly when she didn't shrug him off. 'Spot on!'

Revelling in his embrace, it took a moment or two before Ruby remembered the conversation they had just been having on the tram. Ducking out from under his arm, she stood in front of him so that they were face to face. 'I can't wait a moment longer. Put me out of my misery and tell me what the big secret is.'

Puffing his chest out, George beamed at them. 'Guess who's going to France?'

The colour instantly drained from Ruby's cheeks. She gripped Jess's wrist. 'No!' she gasped.

'Not me!' George said with a triumphant air.

Ruby whooped with joy before slapping him across the bicep. 'Don't do that! It's been my biggest fear ever since you announced you had a secret.'

He tousled her hair playfully before placing his arm back around her shoulders. 'Sorry! I didn't mean to scare you.'

Jess furrowed her brow. 'Hang on, what's so secret about that? Surely you could've told us over the phone?'

He looked at her aghast. 'And run the risk that someone might overhear our conversation and grass me up for being underage? No fear! It's not just me that would've got it in the neck, but Swanny too, because he was the one who fixed things so that I could work as a clerk until the war is over or I reach the right age, whichever comes first.'

Ruby slid her arm around his waist. 'I see now why you couldn't say anything.' She smiled up at him and noticed how his cheekbones, once prominent through lack of nutrition, were now much fuller. His eyes sparkled as he looked down at her. 'I've just realised something. You're taller than me!'

George chuckled. 'Must be all them lovely meals they serve in the NAAFI.'

'Only the best!' Ruby agreed. Relieved that George would be remaining in this country, her thoughts turned to Swanny. 'You'll have to give me Swanny's details so that I can write and thank him personally.'

George nodded. 'That man's been like a father to me, or how I imagine a father should be.' He squeezed Ruby's shoulder. 'I've told Swanny all about you and Jess. I reckon he'd be chuffed to receive a letter.'

Ruby beamed. 'I can't wait to thank him for saving …' she had been about to say 'my boyfriend', but as this wasn't the case she merely said, 'your skin.'

Feeling a little left out, Jess piped up. 'How long are you here for?'

George grinned broadly. 'I was due leave after my initial training, but I managed to wangle it so that I could stay for Christmas.'

Ruby looked up at him, her eyes shining with excitement. 'Really?'

He took his index finger and chucked her under the chin. 'Really, and I reckon we start our time together with a spot of lunch. Can you recommend anywhere good?'

'Why don't we go to Coopers Café on Church Street …' Jess suggested, but Ruby interrupted her.

'Nope, this is a special occasion and a celebration to boot, so I say we go to Blacklers.'

'Posh!' said Jess. She smiled as she watched the two of them continue towards the city centre, Ruby chattering away in an excited fashion about Liverpool and all the things it had to offer. Jess noticed that when Ruby slid her arm through George's she held on to him firmly as though she was never going to let him go. It filled Jess with happiness to see two of her oldest friends so bliss-ful in each other's company. She looked up at the sky dark with snow clouds and called out to the two of them, 'We'd best get a move on before we end up like that snowman Tom made outside the entrance to the NAAFI!'

Jess took the seat opposite Ruby's in Blacklers. A smile curved her lips as she watched George gazing at Ruby the same way Tom looked at her. Seeing how Ruby's eyes shone when she looked at George, Jess wondered if she looked like that when she gazed into Tom's eyes. Watching them, she realised how lucky she was that Tom was stationed so close to Seaforth, meaning she was able to see him most days. She frowned suddenly as a thought occurred to her. 'Where are you going to be stationed?'

George looked downcast. 'London.'

'London?' echoed Ruby. 'But that's as bad as Sand-hurst. Couldn't they have sent you somewhere a bit closer?'

He leaned forward in a secretive fashion and shielded his lips with his hands, then mouthed the words 'war office'.

Ruby's eyes grew wide. 'Gosh! That sounds very important.'

He shrugged. 'I'll just be helping file records, paperwork, that kind of thing, nothing of real importance – that'll be left to the bigwigs.' He looked at Jess. 'What is it your feller does again?'

Jess opened her mouth to say that she wouldn't call Tom 'her feller' but Ruby got in there first.

'If you listen to Jess you'll hear nothing but explanations for why she and Tom aren't an item, but if you see the way they look at each other you'll realise it's only a matter of time.'

'He runs an ack-ack battery and we're taking things slowly,' Jess said.

George grinned at Jess who was slowly turning pink. 'I look forward to meeting him.' He started to turn to Ruby when another thought entered his mind. 'Are you going to do anything for your birthday this year, Jess? It'll be your first one away from the orphanage, and we could make it a double celebration, what with it being Christmas Eve.'

Ruby wriggled her eyebrows in a suggestive manner. 'She's going out with Tom – he's taking her to a dance in the Grafton.' Her eyes flickered from Jess to George. 'The Grafton's a ballroom.'

'You could always join us,' said Jess.

'And play gooseberry? No thanks ...' Ruby began before being interrupted by her friend.

'Bit like what I'm doing now? Besides, how can you be playing gooseberry if there's two of you?' said Jess, a faint smile appearing on her lips.

George chuckled at Ruby's shocked expression. He turned apologetically to Jess. 'Sorry, hen, I got so wrapped up in catching up with Ruby, I didn't realise we were leaving you out.'

Ruby's cheeks bloomed with guilty embarrassment. 'I'm so sorry, Jess. I didn't mean to exclude you, only I was so relieved to hear that George wasn't being posted overseas ...' she looked at George sheepishly, '... and it's been such a long time.'

George gently rubbed the back of Ruby's shoulder with his fingertips. 'I was just as much to blame.' He turned to Jess. 'Give me a kick if I do it again.'

Jess's smirk had fully formed. 'It'd take a darn sight more than a kick to tear you away from our Ruby.'

Laughing, he turned his attention back to Ruby. 'Why don't we do as Jess suggests and join them at the Grafton?'

Red to her hairline, Ruby nodded fervently. 'I'm game if you are. You'll love the Grafton. I bet it looks amazing at Christmas with all the sparkly decorations.'

'Then it's settled.' George leaned back so that the waitress could place their food on the table. 'What've you both got planned for Christmas Day?'

'I'm going to Tom's.' Jess told him. She tapped Ruby's arm. 'Stop laughing!'

Ruby apologised and turned to George. 'Why'd you ask?'

'Cassie's invited you for Christmas dinner. I did say I thought it might be a bit much, but she says the house has been so quiet since Swanny left, and she'd be grateful to have it full of cheer.'

Ruby looked awkward. 'It's not that I don't want to, but it wouldn't feel right to leave Penny out. Michelle – she's another pal of ours – is going home, so Penny would be all alone.'

He shook his head with a chuckle. 'The invitation includes Penny, you silly sausage.'

Ruby sagged in relief. 'In that case I think it sounds like a grand idea, and I know Penny would love to come.'

Ruby had missed George more than she thought possible since he'd left for Sandhurst. Having him here with her now, she knew she didn't want to spend a minute away from his side. She took a bite out of her sandwich, stowed it in the corner of her mouth and savoured the taste. 'This is going to be a Christmas to remember.'

It was Christmas Eve – and Jess's birthday – and the girls, including Penny, were getting ready to go to the Grafton.

'I feel like a princess!' said Ruby as she donned the red dress that she'd bought from Paddy's Market earlier in the week. She puckered up and gently brushed her lips with the tip of the soft red lipstick lent by one of the other girls in their billet. Smacking her lips together, she examined her reflection. 'How I wish that miserable Clare and Bonnie could see us now!'

'One thing's for certain,' said Jess as she gently pulled the toe of her stocking open. 'Neither of them will be going anywhere near as grand as the Grafton, and they won't be wearing nice dresses like ours neither.'

Penny, who had bought a dress identical to Ruby's only in blue, brushed her skirt down. 'I don't think they'd recognise us any more. We've changed heaps since Greystones. I think we look like grown-ups, don't you?' She glanced at Jess who was now pulling a stocking up one leg.

Jess nodded fervently. 'I should say so. I never wore stockings in Greystones, nor make-up, and ...' she hesitated as she looked down at her bosom, '... it's amazing what a decent bit of grub can do for a girl's figure!'

Placing her hands on her hips, Ruby did a twirl. 'I never had hips before I came here.'

Jess was wearing an emerald-green dress with a belted waist. She slipped her feet into her green peep-toe court shoes and stood up. 'What do you think?' she said as she turned her foot from side to side. 'I bought them at the jumble sale.'

Penny and Ruby studied the shoes. Ruby's eyes flicked up to meet Jess's as she nodded approvingly. 'They're beautiful, Jess, but have you tried walking in them yet?'

In answer Jess took a tentative step forward, wobbled slightly, then brought the other foot to meet the first. She grinned at her friends. 'It feels odd, like you're walking on the ball of your foot, whilst trying to balance on two sticks.'

Ruby gave the shoes an admiring glance. 'They look lovely, but I think I'd be flat on my face if I wore them.' She glanced at Penny then Jess. 'Tell you what, why don't we walk you arm-in-arm to the taxi? That way you can have a bit of a practice before we get to the Grafton.'

Jess nodded, took another step, wobbled, then waited for her friends to catch up to her. 'I think that would be a jolly good idea.'

Penny grinned suggestively. 'It'll give you a good excuse to hold on tight to Tom.'

Jess began to giggle. 'Trust you!' Although she thought Penny was right – it really would be the perfect excuse, and one she was sure Tom wouldn't object to.

Ruby glanced at the clock which stood on top of the tortoise stove. 'Come on, Cinders, time to get you to the ball!'

Jess frowned. 'Why do I have to be Cinders?'

Ruby grinned. 'Because it's your job to clean the flues, and you're the only one of us wearing heels, and even though they aren't glass slippers, you're walking as if they were!'

A short taxi ride later the girls arrived at the Grafton. As Ruby had predicted, it had been decked from its rafters to the dance floor in the most beautiful decorations. The girls marvelled at the fairy lights which twinkled on the Christmas tree and the shiny tinsel which sparkled against the coloured glass baubles.

Jess stared in amazement at the Christmas tree. 'Golly!' she breathed. 'Cinderella's come to the ball!'

'It truly is spectacular,' agreed Ruby. Her line of sight was interrupted by someone waving furiously at her from the bar. She grinned. 'It's George and he's with

Tom and ...' she gave a small gasp, 'that must be Cassie!' She pointed to a tall woman with dark brown hair which she wore in a bob.

'Oh good!' said Penny, waving at the group. 'I didn't fancy being on my own all night!'

Jess tightened her grip on their arms. 'I know I'm a lot steadier than when I first started out this evening, but can you walk me to the bar? I don't want to trip over my feet in front of all these people.' She glanced in particular at a group of women, all of whom wore heels higher than her own.

Penny and Ruby nodded. 'All together, girls,' Ruby said.

Having arrived safely at the bar, Penny moved to stand next to Cassie and introduced herself, whilst Ruby went to say hello to George.

Tom smiled at Jess and gingerly pecked her cheek. 'Happy birthday, Jess. You look fabulous!' He paused. 'Is it me, or are you taller?' Without waiting for a reply, he glanced down at her feet. 'Very impressive! Can you walk in them?'

Jess nodded casually. 'Oh, yes.'

'Good! Because I can't wait to get on that dance floor.' He paused. 'Would you like a drink?'

'That would be lovely.'

He waved a hand to gain the barmaid's attention. 'I'm having a beer. Would you like one?'

'No, thanks, I'll stick to squash,' said Jess, who was finding it hard enough to stand on her own two feet without being drunk as well.

'It's not to everyone's taste, and I suppose you are a little young ...'

216

Jess shot him an icy glare. She knew he wouldn't deliberately try to belittle her, but she had felt very grown up until he made the last remark. She thought about changing her mind, just to show him that she was more grown up than he thought, but to do so would be a childish reaction. Oblivious of the upset he had caused, Tom handed her a glass of squash and indicated a vacant table. 'Let's grab that one before someone else gets it.' He strode off in the direction of the table.

Jess very much wanted to sit down because her feet were already aching; on the other hand, she was eager not to fall over. She looked appealingly in Ruby's direction, but her friend was deep in conversation with George. Spying Penny chatting to Cassie a little further along the bar, Jess coughed loudly to gain her attention and was grateful when the two women quickly came to her aid. 'Sorry!' Penny hissed out of the side of her mouth. 'I've filled Cassie in on your predicament.'

Cassie grinned broadly as she threaded her arm through Jess's. 'Don't worry, chuck, we've all been there,' she said as they escorted Jess to the table.

Jess smiled gratefully at Cassie. 'Pleased to meet you at last, and I promise I'm not normally this precarious!'

Cassie giggled. 'Makes you wonder how on earth Cinderella coped, doesn't it?'

'Put it this way, they'd be picking shards out of my feet for weeks to come if these were made of glass.' Jess lifted her feet off the floor.

Tom smiled uncertainly at the women. Was it his imagination, or was Jess not keen to be on her own with him? He dismissed the thought. He was being silly. Jess wouldn't have agreed to meet him at the Grafton if she didn't like him. Standing up, he held out a hand. 'Care to dance?'

Jess looked nervously at Penny and Cassie who both gave her a small nod of encouragement.

'Just remember to take it slow,' said Jess. 'I'm still new to all of this, and I haven't mastered all the moves yet!'

Tom grinned and a glint appeared in his eye. 'Don't worry, you'll be fine. I'm sure it'll come back to you once the music starts.'

By the end of the night Jess felt as though her feet were going to drop off, but she had enjoyed herself so much she wished the music would never end, especially when it came to the slower dances, and she could rest her cheek against Tom's chest and relax into his arms.

It was the last dance of the evening and the floor was filled with couples. She glanced at George and Ruby who held each other close as they made their way slowly around the floor, and at Penny who was dancing with Cassie. She looked up at Tom, whose eyes shone as he met her gaze.

'This has been the best birthday ever!' she sighed happily. 'I know the girls were only joking when they called me Cinders earlier this evening, but that's exactly how I feel now that I've left that horrible orphanage behind me.'

He smiled slowly, his teeth glinting in the light. 'If you're Cinderella does that make me your Prince Charming?'

She rubbed his back with the flat of her hand. 'I suppose it does.' She smiled up at him, and her heart skipped a beat. It was as though they had been transported back to the night when they had their 'near miss of a kiss', as the other girls now referred to it. The same awkward silence, not knowing where to look or ...

'This is the best Christmas Eve ever!' Penny's voice cut between them like an axe, causing them both to jump.

Jess felt as though someone had woken her up from a trance. 'What? Oh yes, yes, it is.' Part of her wished that Penny had not disturbed their moment, but the other half was thankful that her first kiss had not been on a packed dance floor full of prying eyes.

Penny looked from Jess to Tom. 'Oh, I say! Did I interrupt something?'

Jess had not taken her eyes away from Tom's, but now she looked at Penny, just as the band stopped playing and the lights came on. Blinking under the brightness, she shaded her eyes with one hand. 'Oh drat, is it really time to go?'

Tom pulled a grim smile. 'Afraid so, queen. C'mon, I'll walk you out.'

Outside the venue Jess could hear friends bidding each other 'a Merry Christmas' or 'all the best' as they went on their separate ways. Ruby and George stood with the door to a taxi cab open. 'There's enough room for all of us!' called George merrily.

Tom looked hopefully at Jess. 'It doesn't have to end yet. We could go for a walk then catch a taxi later?'

Jess winced as she shifted her weight. She very much wanted to go off with Tom, to spend some quiet time walking the streets of Liverpool alone with him, but her feet were on fire. Rather than admit her fashion faux pas, she gave an exaggerated yawn. 'I've had a wonderful evening, but just like Cinderella, I'm afraid I'd better be getting back.'

Disappointed, he pushed his hands into his pockets. 'I understand. Are you still up for dinner tomorrow?'

She nodded eagerly. 'You bet I am. Four o'clock by the gate?'

'I'll be there.' He looked around at George, Ruby, Penny and Cassie who were watching with interest, and waved a goodbye. 'I fancy a bit of a walk, so I'll say goodnight and I'll see you all tomorrow.'

As he walked away from the cab, Tom reflected on the evening. He had had a wonderful time dancing with Jess and whenever he looked at her, she was positively glowing with happiness, yet as soon as he tried to get her on her own, she backed away. It couldn't have been his imagination, because he had only tried twice and both times he had received the same reaction. The first time he had found himself sitting alone at a table, until Penny and Cassie had walked over, arm-in-arm with Jess, and just now, when he had suggested a quiet walk, she had turned him down. It would have been such a romantic way to end their evening … He hesitated. Maybe that was it? Maybe Jess wasn't interested in him romantically, or maybe she was worried what would happen if they were left alone? He remembered the time he had gone to kiss her goodbye, then grimaced. They had had a similar experience when Penny came over during the last dance. He chastised himself inwardly. Jess was a nice respectable girl, it was only natural that she would want to take things slowly, and he knew from what she had told him that she had never had a boyfriend before. If he rushed her, he could end up scaring her off altogether and he liked her far too much for that to happen. He shook his head. He didn't just like Jess, it was far more than that. If he scared her off, he would be losing the woman he had already foolishly fallen in love with, and that was something he couldn't bear to live with.

Jess, Penny and Ruby were the last to get dropped off at their barracks. Piling happily but quietly out of the cab, they wished the driver a merry Christmas before hushing each other, and quietly walking towards the billet. Penny, however, had a different idea. 'My bladder doesn't like this cold weather. Do either of you need the loo?'

Jess and Ruby both nodded. 'I didn't think my poor feet could make it to the lavvy in the Grafton,' confessed Jess, 'and I could hardly ask Tom to take me!'

Ruby and Penny fell into muffled laughter. 'You should've made your excuses and given me a holler!' said Penny. 'I'd've given you a piggyback if need be.'

'Oh yes, very ladylike,' giggled Jess. 'I think Tom would've thought we'd lost our marbles if we started piggybacking each other to the loos!'

'Talking of Tom,' Penny intervened, 'did I really not interrupt anything? Because it looked like I did!'

Jess shrugged. 'I'm not sure. It felt the same as it did the night of the "near miss of a kiss", the two of us gazing at each other, not knowing what to say.'

'Talking!' Penny exclaimed, her tone full of disbelief. 'I very much doubt you were thinking of having a quick chat when you were gazing into those deep brown eyes.'

Jess took a playful swipe at her pal before diving into one of the empty cubicles. There was a moment's pause before she spoke next. 'I was looking at him thinking how handsome he was.'

Ruby's voice came from the cubicle next to hers. 'I should imagine he was thinking the same thing, only not the handsome part.'

'So why didn't he make a move?' said Jess, before flushing the toilet.

When she came out, she saw Penny grimacing. 'Because I interrupted you.' She clapped a hand to her forehead. 'I *knew* I'd interrupted something! Next time tell me to shove off.'

Jess looked shocked. 'I'm not doing that! I'd look as if I were desperate.'

Ruby emerged from the cubicle. 'She's right, it would make her look desperate.'

'Well, tomorrow's another day,' said Penny plainly, 'and with a new day come new opportunities.'

'Maybe even mistletoe!' Ruby said, wriggling her eyebrows suggestively.

Jess raised her brow. 'Is that what you were looking for when you were dancing with George this evening?'

'We didn't need mistletoe!' said Ruby to both her friends' surprise.

'You never!' gushed Penny.

'You kept that quiet!' Jess added.

Ruby grinned sheepishly. 'It was only a quick peck, during the last dance.' Her cheeks glowing, she continued, 'He told me how much he was going to miss me when he leaves for London, then asked if I'd be his girlfriend.' The blush deepened. 'I said yes, and that's when it happened.'

Jess clapped her hands together. 'I always said he was keen on you, only you were convinced he didn't like you 'cos of all them spit balls he shot at the back of your head, but I knew it meant the opposite and I was right!'

Ruby ran her fingers through her hair at the memory, then laughed at the look of utter disgust on Penny's face. 'He spat balls of paper at you, to show he liked you?'

Jess shook her head. 'No, he did that to get her attention ...' she nudged Ruby with her elbow '... and it worked.'

'It certainly did.' Ruby sighed happily before adding, 'you should be grateful you were older when you and Tom met, it's a lot less messy.'

'Any feller that spits balls of paper at me'll feel the back of my hand!' said Penny.

'Don't worry, I should imagine that's only the sort of thing little boys do,' Jess assured her pal. 'When they're older they get your attention by asking you to dance, or holding a door open for you.'

Penny looked distant as though she had just remembered something really important. 'What about giving you the last of his wine gums?'

'S'pose so,' Jess began, before the penny dropped. 'Hold on a mo ...'

A dreamy smile was crossing Penny's lips. 'Donald Aberforth!' She looked at her friends through faraway eyes. 'I wondered why he asked me what I was doing for New Year's Eve. I assumed he wanted to know if the NAAFI was open, but ...'

Jess held up a hand. 'Whoa there! Just who is Donald Aberforth and why haven't we heard of him until now?'

Penny snapped out of her trance and gave her friends an embarrassed grin. 'Because I didn't think anything of it, until now.' Aware that she hadn't answered the question, she continued, 'He's only been at Seaforth a few days. He was the one who helped me out when the tea urn threatened to tip over.' She paused for a moment whilst her friends recalled the occasion.

'I remember you saying some feller had helped you get it upright before you lost the lot, but you never said any more than that,' said Ruby, trying to place the man.

Penny shrugged. 'That's because I didn't give it much thought, but the more I think about it the more I realise he's been hanging around the NAAFI more than the others, and he always comes over to say hello when I come in.'

Jess grinned. 'And he gave you the last of his wine gums!'

'Better than a spit ball!' laughed Penny.

'I'm with you on that,' Ruby agreed, 'although I feel I should add that George has grown up a lot since then.'

'So where is he, this Donald?' said Jess, looking around her as though expecting him to materialise at any moment.

'He's gone to stay with his sister in Birkenhead.' Penny shrugged as the other girls looked at her with blank expressions. 'I don't know where it is either, but apparently it's not too far from Liverpool. He said he'd be back for New Year's Eve, though, so I'm guessing that's why he asked me what I was up to.'

'Did you tell him you were off to the Grafton?' said Ruby excitedly.

Penny thought about this for a few seconds. 'Yes, I did, because I remember him saying that he loved to go dancing ...' She faded into silence, then, 'Do you think he was hinting that he'd like to join me?'

Ruby and Penny exchanged glances. 'I reckon so!' said Ruby. 'Although if he were a real man, he should've taken the bull by the horns – pardon the expression – and asked you outright.'

'That's not fair,' said Jess a shade defensively. 'The poor feller's only been here a few days. I bet he doesn't even know if you've got a boyfriend ...' Seeing the look on her friend's face, she continued, 'You mean to tell me he's asked?'

Penny nodded mutely.

'Honestly, Penny!' said Jess in an exasperated tone. 'How could you not have realised he was keen on you?' She began ticking the list off on her fingers. 'He came to your rescue with the tea urn, gave you the last of his sweets, asked if you had a boyfriend, and asked you what you're doing for New Year's Eve!'

'Well, when you put it like that it sounds obvious,' Penny agreed. 'I wonder if he'll go to the Grafton anyway?'

Ruby clapped her hands together excitedly. 'I hope so!'

'Me too!' said Jess. 'I want to know what he looks like.'

Penny beamed. 'I could have a boyfriend to start the New Year!' She looked pointedly at Jess. 'And if Prince Charming plucks up the courage, so might you, Cinders!'

'It certainly would make saying goodbye easier.' Jess smiled. 'As things stand, I don't know whether he's trying to kiss me or struggling to make conversation.'

Ruby held the door to the ablutions open whilst Jess and Penny trooped through. 'Believe me, Jess, he's trying to kiss you. First chance you get to be alone, and it'll be a done deal.'

Jess's heart gave a flutter. Now that was something she was very much looking forward to, albeit a little apprehensively.

Lying in bed, Jess listened to the gentle snores and sighs around her. Today was her first Christmas free from Greystones and its archaic rules and regulations. She winced as she realised that had Bonnie had her way, she would now be in Brownhill. A shiver ran down her spine as she tried to imagine what Christmas was like for those poor souls in the poorhouse. She pictured Elsa's sister Hattie, her bones protruding through her skin, her hair matted to her face, waking up on Christmas morning probably wishing she was … A tear ran down her cheek and vanished into her pillowcase. She crossed her fingers beneath her sheets, praying that something would have been done about Brownhill by now.

Sitting up on one elbow, she peered around her. Why were they all asleep? Had they forgotten what day it was? She got out of bed, slipped on her dressing gown and padded over to the gloriously warm tortoise stove. She stifled a giggle. No wonder everyone was sleeping – it wasn't yet five o'clock. Wondering whether the snow was any thicker now than it had been the day before, she took a quick peek through the tent flap and gasped as the cold air hit her. More snow had fallen during the night, and there were no footprints or car tracks to be seen. She smiled. Jess thought snow always looked its best when it was still fresh and untouched. Tiptoeing across the room, she picked up a bauble which had fallen off the tree and hung it back on one of the branches. Standing back, she admired the tree, festooned with the girls' homemade decorations, paper chains and tinsel. The NAAFI girls' Christmas tree had been much admired. Sighing happily, Jess climbed back into her bed and pulled the blankets up around her ears. She closed her eyes and tried to go back to sleep, but it was no use, she was far too excited.

She looked across to Penny in the opposite bunk, the sheets rising and falling as she breathed softly in her sleep. With money being tight, the girls in their billet had suggested buying a small gift of no more than sixpence and handing it to the person in the bunk above or below their own, as the case may be. This was ideal for Jess and Ruby as it meant that they would be buying for each other. Jess had been with Ruby when she had bought the red frock from Paddy's Market, so she'd waited until Ruby was busy at another stall before asking the woman if she could find a piece of ribbon to match Ruby's dress. She knew Penny and Michelle had unwittingly bought each other the exact same scented soap, only with Michelle being away, they had already exchanged but not opened their presents.

Jess cast her thoughts ahead to the evening she would be spending with Tom and his family. She knew that when she visited this time, his father would be present, which pleased Jess because she had often wondered what Mr Durning was like. This reminded her of her own father. She had already made her mind up that she would not pursue Tom's aunt for answers which the old woman might genuinely not be able to give. After talking things through with the girls, she had come to the conclusion that sixteen years is a long time for anyone, and whilst Tom might feel that his aunt had a better memory regarding her past than the present, it only stood to reason that memory gets worse over time, not better. She pictured the older woman's face, how it had flinched when she'd heard the description of Jess's father, then corrected herself – it wasn't his description which had jolted Edna's memory, but that of his cane. Jess tutted to herself. All this because of a cane? She could understand McKinley being certain as to what the cane looked like, seeing as she'd had a close-up view, but could Aunt Edna really be certain of the handle, when in all probability it would have been hidden from view in the man's grasp?

Jess's thoughts turned to Tom. He had been there, yet he hadn't mentioned a thing on the car journey home, save to say he was sorry that his aunt had been unable to help. If anyone knew his aunt it was him, so if she had been covering something up Tom would know. Turning over in her bed, Jess tried to get more comfortable. Tom was as eager as she was to find her father. If he'd thought there was something he could do to help, there wasn't a doubt in Jess's mind that he'd do it. What was it he'd said again? She smiled. That was right, he'd said they'd find her father together. If Jess could rely on anyone it was Tom. Ruby's voice broke the silence.

'Merry Christmas!'

Startled, Jess held her hand to her chest and glanced up into Ruby's face. 'It'll be my last Christmas if you do that again!'

'Sorry, chuck,' said Ruby. Sliding off her bed, she sat down on the end of Jess's. 'I could hear you tossing and turning so I knew you were awake.' She hesitated. 'What was causing you to be so restless?'

'Christmas dinner at Tom's,' said Jess. 'I know you and Penny think I'm being silly about his auntie ...' Hearing Ruby's groan she fell quiet.

'Please tell me you're not thinking of broaching the subject again?' said Ruby. 'Not on Christmas Day?'

'Don't worry,' Jess assured her. 'I've been having a think and I reckon you're right. It all happened too long ago, and it was more his cane she remembered – she didn't react until I mentioned it.'

'In that case I think it's very sensible to lay the matter to rest. As far as his auntie's concerned, that is. I'm not suggesting you stop looking for your parents, just try a different route.'

Jess shrugged. 'I don't know where else to start looking.'

'Yes, you do,' said Ruby simply. 'There can't be that many hospitals in Glasgow, and the rules might be different now to when you were born. Sixteen years is a long time.'

Jess brightened. 'You're right, and their information is probably going to be a lot more reliable than Tom's auntie's memory.'

'Precisely!' said Ruby. 'Now for goodness' sake cheer up, it's Christmas Day!' She fished out a small package from her nightgown pocket and handed it to Jess. 'Merry Christmas, Jess.'

Smiling, Jess pulled Ruby's present out from under her pillow and handed it over. 'And a Merry Christmas to you too, Rubes.'

They each undid the other's parcel and Jess was pleased when she saw Ruby give a small gasp of pleasure. 'Oh Jess, it's beautiful!'

Jess looked down at the bag of sweets. 'Everton Mints, my favourite!'

Penny stirred in the bunk opposite Jess's. 'Merry Christmas, girls!' She yawned sleepily. 'What time is it?'

'Too early to get up,' said Jess, 'but not too early for presents.'

Christmas morning in the NAAFI soon passed and it wasn't long before the girls were cleaning down ready for the next shift, when one of the girls from the cookhouse peered around the corner of the kitchen door. 'Are you lot ready?'

Penny grinned. 'Oh, we're ready all right.' She threw her dishcloth into the sink and called out to the rest of the kitchen staff. 'Come on, girls, we've the pride of the NAAFI to uphold!'

In the spirit of Christmas, the girls from the NAAFI had arranged to have a snowball fight against the kitchen staff of the cookhouse. The melee left Jess, Penny and Ruby exhausted from laughing and wet through from either being hit by snowballs or falling over trying to throw them. The conclusion had been a draw, and everyone retired to their billets to dry off before going about the rest of their day.

Jess looked through the tent flap and waved at Tom who was sitting in the car outside the gates waiting for her, then turned to say goodbye to Ruby and Penny. 'Give my love to George, and tell him I'll see him tomorrow.' She gave each girl a peck on the cheek before hurrying outside.

Tom hopped out of the car and opened the passenger door. 'Merry Christmas, Cinders! I hope you're hungry, Mam's gone all out.'

'Merry Christmas, Tom, and yes, I'm starving!' She told him about the snowball fight.

'I'm game if they're up for another one tomorrow?' Tom said eagerly. 'I'll be on your team, of course.'

She laughed. 'I should hope so too! And it's already been arranged for after dinner as long as the snow doesn't melt overnight.' She looked at the pavements which were still covered in a thick layer of snow. 'I must admit, I did wonder whether Olly would make it.'

He tapped the steering wheel. 'Like a tank is our Olly, get through anything.'

Jess enjoyed the short trip from the barracks to Tom's family home. Liverpool looked very different covered in snow. 'It looks like one of those snow globes,' she said to Tom as they passed the Liver Building. When Tom drew up outside his parents' house, Jess noticed the parlour room curtain drop as though someone had been peeking through.

Leaning forward, Tom took something out of his pocket and handed it to her. 'Merry Christmas, Jess.'

Carefully, she removed the tissue paper and looked at the blue beaded necklace which lay in the wrappings. She held it over her fingers. 'It's beautiful, Tom,' she breathed.

Smiling, Tom gestured for her to turn so that he could put it on for her. 'I'm glad you like it. I know we said we wouldn't bother, but I couldn't resist.'

Blushing, Jess admired her neckline before opening her handbag. 'I remember you saying it was your favourite,' she said, handing Tom a small chocolate bar of fruit and nut, and watching his face light up.

Inside the house, Aunt Edna called 'They're here!' over her shoulder to Sylvie, who was in the kitchen making the final preparations.

Wiping her hands on her pinny, Sylvie rushed over to look through the window, waving at Tom and Jess who waved back. 'Shall I you push back by the fire, Auntie?'

Aunt Edna shrugged. 'I'd rather not be here at all, as well you know. I don't understand why she had to come! Christmas Day should be for families, and she isn't part of ours.'

Sylvie took hold of the handles of the wheelchair and pushed her aunt through to the other side of the room. 'Not yet she's not, but our Tom seems real keen on her, so much so it wouldn't surprise me if there were wedding bells in the near future.' She glanced down at her aunt who had rested her forehead in her weathered hand. 'Stop worrying yourself that Jess is going to start asking awkward questions. You put that matter to rest the last time she was here, so for goodness' sake take that grumpy look off your face and smile! That poor child's never had a proper Christmas before, and I don't want her to think a family Christmas is full of miserable faces and arguments.'

'Why not?' chortled Tom's father from behind his newspaper. 'That's what most family Christmases are like!'

Sylvie had quite forgotten her husband was in the room. She waved a tea towel in order to gain his attention. 'And for heaven's sake button your trousers, we've got guests!'

Taking a deep breath, her husband did as his wife instructed.

Aunt Edna kept her head lowered, grateful that her niece and nephew were concentrating on each other, else they might see the pink blush which was creeping its way up her deeply wrinkled cheeks.

Ever since Jess's visit, Edna had relived the Christmas Eve of 1923 over and over, until there was no doubt in her mind that the swine of a man was indeed Jess's father, but that wasn't what worried her. She closed her eyes. Why had Jess come into her life now after all these years? Was it to punish her? She'd certainly been plagued with nightmares over the years, the worst part being that she couldn't share her secret with anyone. She heard the front door open. If she could have one wish right now it would be for Tom and Jess to have never met. At least that way she would have carried on living in blissful ignorance, instead of being tormented by her guilty secret. She heard a chorus of seasonal greetings being exchanged and the stamping of feet as Tom and Jess knocked the snow from their shoes.

Sylvie entered the room first, followed closely by Tom and Jess.

Tom leaned down and gently kissed his aunt's soft cheek. 'Merry Christmas, Auntie!' He stood back and gestured for Jess to come over.

Jess smiled warmly at his aunt, who glared icily back. The smile instantly left Jess's lips. She glanced at Tom to see if he had noticed, but he was busy saying hello to his father. Deciding that Aunt Edna must have had a falling-out with Tom's parents, Jess went over to Tom to be introduced to his father, who hastily folded his newspaper and stood up to greet her.

'Merry Christmas, Miss Wilson,' he said warmly, smiling at her.

Jess smiled back. 'Merry Christmas, Mr Durning, and please call me Jess. It's very kind of you and your wife to invite me to dinner. I do hope I'm not intruding.' Tom's mother shot Edna a stern look – which did not go unnoticed by Jess – before turning a far more pleasant and friendly face to Jess.

'Course not!' said Mr Durning he sat back down in his chair. 'More the merrier, isn't that right?'

Jess watched Aunt Edna with interest wondering what the old woman's response would be. Looking up, Aunt Edna gave her nephew a fleeting smile. 'That's right.'

Jess glanced at Tom to see if he had noticed the tension, but he was busy hanging up their coats. She hadn't a clue what his family's disagreement could have been about, but as she had parted on good terms the last time she visited, she assumed it was nothing to do with her. She would just have to hope that the old woman's mood brightened during the course of the evening.

Sylvie cut through her thoughts. 'If you'd like to sit next to Tom, Jess,' she gestured towards the table, 'I'll make a start.' She stopped short after seeing Jess's necklace. 'Oh Tom, it looks even more beautiful on!'

The evening passed pleasantly, although Aunt Edna offered little conversation, only answering with a brief 'yes' or 'no' when asked a direct question. Knowing that she missed her home in Glasgow, Jess supposed that Christmas might not be a happy time for the older woman, having lost her husband as well as her home, this time of year probably emphasised those losses.

It was after a delicious serving of bread and butter pudding that Tom decided to break the news that he would be leaving Liverpool. 'We shall be leaving for London on the first of January.'

Sylvie, who had been collecting the empty bowls, stopped short. 'Oh, Tom, no!' She sank back into the seat next to her husband. 'Can't they send someone else?'

'It won't just be me, Mam, there's a lot of us going.' Seeing the tears form in his mother's eyes, he got up from his seat. 'Come on, Mam, how about I give you a hand in the kitchen?'

Seeing his wife's distress, Mr Durning excused himself from the table, placed his arm around her shoulders and went with her and Tom into the kitchen. 'There, there, Sylvie ... he soothed.'

Jess stared after them. She very much wanted to follow, to ask the same questions his mother was undoubtedly asking, but she knew this was a time for family. She glanced over to his aunt, who called out to Tom as he disappeared through the kitchen door, 'Close the door, Tom, there's a good lad, I'm sure there's a draught.'

Jess's brow shot upwards. She liked his parents very much and had no desire to hear his aunt's grievances towards them, especially not after Tom's sudden announcement. Jess eyed him imploringly, wishing he would look at her and ignore his aunt's request, but, holding the gravy boat in one hand, he pulled the door to without so much as a backward glance.

Jess smiled at the older woman. If I steer the conversation away from his parents, she thought, Aunt Edna won't be able to bad-mouth them in front of me. She picked a safe subject. 'I wonder if it'll snow again tonight?'

Ignoring the question, Aunt Edna spoke her thoughts. 'They'll be sending him to London because they know that's where the bombing will start,' she said in a leaden tone. 'He'll be put into all sorts of dangerous situations, and he'll have a lot more on his mind than the likes of us.'

Jess stared aghast at the old woman. How could she be so callous when talking of her great-nephew? 'We don't know that for certain ...' she began but his aunt cut her short without apology.

'I can see that our Tom is keen on you, Jessica, and that's why I'm appealing to you, woman to woman, if you like him as much as he appears to like you, then you'll back off and let him concentrate on his job. He needs to be focused in his line of work, not worrying about you whilst he's away.' She decided to play her ace. 'If you care for him, you'll let him go.'

Jess stared in shock at the older woman, tears threatening to spill. Where on earth had all this come from? Tom's announcement had come as a surprise to everyone, yet Edna seemed to have given Tom and Jess's relationship some thought. Why was she picking on everyone today? It was at this moment the penny dropped. It wasn't his parents Edna had a problem with, it was Jess. She opened her mouth to tell her that she and Tom were only friends, and that she would never do anything to hurt him, but the kitchen door opened before she had a chance to speak.

Tom stood in the doorway. He looked at the two women sitting in stony silence and immediately jumped to the wrong conclusion.

'Cheer up! We all knew I'd probably be leaving Liverpool sooner or later, but I could be back before you know it. That's the beauty of ack-ack batteries being mobile – you get to travel all over.' He gave them both a reassuring smile, hoping that this would lighten the mood.

Edna stared at Jess. She knew she had no right to scare the girl off and that Tom would be furious if he knew what she'd said, not to mention how her niece would react. She watched Jess blinking back tears and that's when the truth hit. Jess was in love with Tom.

She looked at her great-nephew, who was gazing at Jess with loving eyes. What had she done? Determined to put things right, she asked Tom to fetch his mother, hoping that he would leave her alone with Jess, giving her the opportunity to take back her words. Only instead of leaving the room Tom called his mother, who came in and helped Edna out of the room.

A wave of relief swept over Jess. Blinking back tears, she smiled at Tom. 'You'll be back before we know it.' Not wishing to see his aunt again, she looked at the clock which stood on the mantel. 'Would it be all right for you to take me back to the barracks, Tom? Only I'm quite tired and I've a full shift tomorrow.'

Tom nodded. 'I'll fetch our coats.'

Sylvie, who had left her aunt to take care of her business, came around the table and took Jess in a warm embrace. 'Thanks for coming, Jess, it's been lovely to see you. You'll have to come and have your dinner again one evening – doesn't matter if Tom's not here, you're always welcome in our house.'

Thank you. It's been wonderful, and your bread and butter pudding was simply delicious!' Jess turned to Tom's father. 'Goodbye, Mr Durning, it was lovely to meet you at last.' Her eyes flicked towards the back yard. 'Will you say goodbye to Aunt Edna for me, please?'

Sylvie nodded, and Jess thought she saw a glimpse of disapproval cross her face. 'Of course.'

Eager to leave, Jess hastened to the car, which Tom had already started. He wiped the condensation off the inside of the windscreen as Jess wound down the window and waved to his parents who were standing on the doorstep. 'Goodbye, and if I don't see you before, all the best for the New Year.'

The wheels slipped as they tried to gain traction on the snow, and for a moment Jess thought she might have to get out and push, but with Tom's expertise the little car soon set off.

Tom smiled guiltily at her. 'Sorry I didn't tell you about my leaving, only I wanted to tell you all together.'

Jess nodded. 'You did the right thing, Tom.' She wondered whether she should tell him what his aunt had said, then thought better of it. The last thing she wanted to do was cause any trouble. She cast him a sideways glance. 'Your auntie seemed a bit quiet tonight.'

A small furrow creased his brow. 'She did seem quieter than usual, now that you mention it, although she's always a bit miserable around Christmas time. She misses my great-uncle more at Christmas than any other time of year, which is understandable.' He gave Jess a cheeky grin. 'She also says it's going to be her last Christmas, and has done for at least the past six years.'

Jess gave this some thought. If his aunt was normally miserable around Christmas, then maybe she was taking her bad mood out on Jess? She peered at the road ahead, although it was quite difficult to see anything in the blackout. Misery loves company, Jess thought to herself. The old woman felt miserable and she was trying to make Jess feel the same. She stopped. Not just her, but by the looks of it Tom's mother as well. She drew a deep breath. She felt better knowing that it hadn't been just her in the firing line. Relaxing, she decided to dismiss his aunt's opinions and enjoy the rest of the journey home.

Tom drew Olly to a halt outside the barracks and gave the guard on the gate a wave of acknowledgement. He turned to Jess. 'Here we are.'

Leaning across the seat, she pecked him on the cheek. 'Thanks for inviting me over, Tom, I really enjoyed myself. This has been a wonderful Christmas, one I'll never forget.'

Tom grinned. 'My pleasure, Cinders!'

Jess looked at the guard who was watching them with great interest. Blushing, she got out of the car and waved Tom goodbye. 'I can't see this lot melting overnight. See you tomorrow for the snowball fight?'

He wound down his window, calling out as he put the car into gear, 'Wouldn't miss it for the world!'

Jess entered the barracks and headed straight over to Ruby and Penny in their tent as they were just finishing a game of charades with some of the other girls.

Ruby smiled as Jess approached. 'Two minutes.' She turned back to face the other girls, just as someone squealed.

'Over the rainbow! Am I right?'

The woman doing the charade nodded and everyone gave a round of applause.

'Can we take a quick break?' said Ruby, eager to hear whether her best friend had finally had her first kiss.

The ginger-headed cook, who was captain of their team, nodded. 'Ten minutes. I could do with wettin' me whistle, me throat's that parched from laughing.'

Ruby turned excitedly to Jess. 'So? Did he kiss you?'

'Nope,' said Jess, unbuttoning her coat. She wasn't about to admit she'd chickened out of giving him the opportunity. 'How'd it go with Cassie?'

'We've had a wonderful time, haven't we, Penny?' said Ruby. 'She's a genius in the kitchen – she made a Dundee cake, like the one we got when we left Greystones, only hers wasn't dry, and she'd made mince pies and sausage rolls.' Ruby gently patted her tummy. 'I thought I was going to burst, and I'm surprised George didn't. I swear that boy's got hollow legs.'

Jess hung her coat on the wooden clothes hanger. 'Sounds like you had a wonderful time.'

Ruby nodded enthusiastically. 'She's invited us for New Year's Day lunch. I said yes, and I've accepted an invitation on your and Tom's behalf – I hope that's okay?' She saw the doubtful look cross Jess's face. 'What's up? You can come, can't you?'

'I can,' Jess said as she sat on the bed and began to remove her shoes, 'but Tom's leaving for London on New Year's Day, so I'm afraid he won't be able to, although that should please his miserable old goat of an aunt.'

Ruby groaned. 'Please don't tell me you tried to interrogate her, not after all we said?'

'No, I didn't,' Jess said reproachfully. 'She was frosty from the moment we arrived, but things got worse after Tom made his announcement.' She explained what Aunt Edna had said to her.

'Did you tell Tom?' Ruby asked.

Jess shook her head. 'I didn't want to cause trouble or upset anyone, so I kept quiet about that part. I did mention her being distant, in case he could shed any light on the matter.'

'Distant!' echoed Ruby. 'She certainly wasn't distant when it came to warning you to stay away!' She furrowed her brow. 'You say she was off with you as soon as you entered the room, and you think she'd had a go at his mam as well?'

Jess nodded. 'I'd say they'd definitely had words before we arrived, I reckon his mam had told his aunt to hold her tongue, and she did, for most of the evening at any rate.'

Ruby shook her head. 'Sorry, Jess, but I find it hard to believe that she'd act in such a manner over her husband – he's been gone for years. I think this has something to do with your last visit, although I can't imagine what.'

Jess frowned. 'She's had a lot of time to think since I saw her last. Maybe she remembered something bad?'

'That's hardly your fault,' Penny said defensively. 'She'd be wrong to take that out on you.'

Ruby nodded decidedly. 'I think you've hit the nail on the head, Jess. I reckon she's had time to sit and stew over whatever it is and she's decided her life was easier when you weren't in it and she wants it back the way it was.' She shuffled forward on her bed so that she might speak without being overheard. 'Think about it. It doesn't matter whether Tom's with you or not – you could argue just as well that your refusal to become his belle could distract him from his job.'

'Exactly!' said Jess, a little loudly, causing some of the others to glance in their direction. Lowering her voice, she continued, 'What could she have remembered which would cause such a bitter reaction?'

Ruby mulled it over for a moment. 'Maybe she feels guilty over your father's actions. I know she had nothing to do with it, but it must be hard watching families get torn apart, knowing you're powerless to do anything about it.' She glanced at Jess. 'She probably never banked on having one of those kiddies turn up in her home some sixteen years later.'

Jess looked miserable. 'I was looking forward to seeing Tom tomorrow, but now I don't know how I feel. Part of me thinks I should tell him what his aunt said, but the other part of me thinks I should just leave well alone.' She glanced at her friends. 'What do you think?'

'I'd tell,' said Penny promptly. 'What that woman did was wrong, plain and simple, and Tom has a right to know what she gets up to behind his back.'

'I'm not keen on Jess telling Tom,' said Ruby severely. 'Blood's thicker than water, and it'd make things awkward next time you call round.'

Jess heaved an exasperated sigh. 'Looks like I've got no choice but to keep quiet, although I don't like the idea of keeping secrets from Tom.'

Penny shook her head in annoyance. 'She had no right to go poking her nose in and stirring up trouble. She might be old but I think she knew exactly what she was doing.' She looked sternly at Jess. 'I hope you ignore the mean old biddy – that'd soon put her in her place.'

'Let's not forget, Tom and I are only friends,' Jess reminded them.

'Well, I hope he asks you to be his belle,' said Ruby. 'And I hope you say yes.'

The ginger-headed cook called over to them. 'Are we counting you in?'

Penny started to shake her head but Jess stood up. 'This is our first real Christmas and I don't intend to let some old biddy spoil it.'

Ruby nodded firmly. 'That's the spirit! Go on, Jess, you haven't had a turn yet.'

Jess pulled a piece of paper out of the hat. Until today she hadn't given much thought to Tom asking her to be his girlfriend as she thought he was out of her league, but if he did, her answer would be yes, yes and yes again!

Having left Glencoe with their tails between their legs, Bonnie and her mother had had no choice but to move back to Glasgow and rent a room in one of the tenement housing blocks. In Bonnie's opinion, this was worse than Brownhill and Greystones put together, because of the dreadful living conditions and close proximity to their neighbours.

'For goodness' sake, stop whining, Bonnie!' Agnes hissed from the corner of her mouth. 'You might not like our new home, you might not like our new home, but it's better than living on the streets, we need jobs in order to pay the rent …'

'They should be paying *us* to live here,' said Bonnie with disgust. 'Those girls in Greystones don't know how lucky they were.'

Agnes rolled her eyes. 'You need to wake up, my girl, because if we don't get jobs soon and we can't pay rent, then we might have to go knocking on Brown-hill's door.'

Bonnie snorted her contempt. 'You said there was plenty of work to be had.'

'There is!' Agnes insisted. 'Only you keep turning them down – well, not this time!'

This conversation had taken place some months earlier. Now, Bonnie scowled at her mother over the top of the washbasin she was scrubbing. 'Some Christmas Day this is! If you think I'm going to be doing this in 1940, you're wrong. I don't care what you say, I'm going to join up.'

Agnes McKinley rolled her eyes. 'You seem to think that life in the services will be easy, sitting on your backside all day watching the world go by. It'll be anything but. You'll be expected to share a billet with lots of other girls, a bit like the dorms in Grey-stones, and they'll make you do square-bashing – that's where they get you to march round and round before you've even had breakfast, not to mention running on the spot, star jumps ...' She glanced at her daughter's ample bottom. 'You'd not last more than five minutes, only you'd have to stay, 'cos once you're in, you're in.' She hesitated, almost dreading to suggest her proposed alternative. 'Why don't you join the NAAFI? It's a lot easier ...' She got no further. Bonnie spun round, waving her brush at her mother.

'Like some kind of skivvy? I'd rather die than do that. They only give the NAAFI jobs to those who're too thick to do anything decent!'

Agnes glanced from the brush in her daughter's hand to the sink she had just been scrubbing. 'What do you call cleaning lavvies?'

Bonnie chucked her brush into the bucket, causing the soapy water to spill over the sides. 'I'm only doing this until I find something better, and you know full well I'm not trained up to do anything else. That's why I want to join the ATS – they'll train me to do something important.' She sniffed haughtily. 'I don't call making cups of tea important,' she cast her mother a look of disdain, 'though it might be good enough for you.'

Agnes wagged her finger reprovingly. 'You're a snob, Bonnie McKinley, thinking you're better than everyone else, but you're no different to the rest of us.'

'You were always telling me I was better than the orphans, so if I'm a snob you've only yourself to blame,' Bonnie replied levelly.

Agnes folded her arms. 'I only wanted to do what was best for you. If it wasn't for me you would have ended up in that orphanage, or one similar, because you'd not have had anyone to look after you.'

'My dad would've looked after me, probably taken me somewhere a lot better than Glasgow an' all,' Bonnie said sulkily.

Agnes's jaw twitched. 'Your father decided to stay in America rather than come home and be a dad, so don't you dare stand there and lecture me on what a kind, caring father he is, because you couldn't be more wrong.'

'Ran away from you more like,' muttered Bonnie, although her words did not go unheard.

'You really are an ungrateful little beast!' Agnes seethed. 'I've tried my hardest to make a good life for you, put up with all the filthy looks and snide comments, even begged that miserable Ancrum to keep me on just so that I could put a roof over your head.'

'How'd you even get pregnant if you weren't married?' Bonnie asked nastily.

Agnes threw her scrubbing brush at Bonnie, who ducked out of the way just in time. 'Because I was a gullible fool who fell for a line as old as the hills, *not* because I was a bad or wanton woman. I was infatuated with your father and I was idiotic enough to believe he felt the same way about me. I never planned on getting pregnant ...' She fell silent.

Bonnie spoke through pursed lips. 'So, I was a mistake?'

Agnes hung her head in shame, before giving her daughter an apologetic look. 'I didn't mean it like that.'

Bonnie shrugged her indifference. 'Then you shouldn't have said it.'

'I never regretted having you, not for one minute!' Agnes said, tears brimming. She walked towards her daughter.

'Well, I regret having you as a mother!' snapped Bonnie. 'Although that'll all change when I get out of this ...' she glanced around the toilets '... cesspit.'

Agnes frowned. 'What on earth do you mean?'

'Once I get out of here I'm never coming back.'

'You can't mean you'll never see me again ...' said Agnes, tears now running freely down her cheeks.

Bonnie's jaw stiffened, then relaxed. She knew she was wrong to say such dreadful things to her mother, but she had needed to vent her anger on someone and with her father nowhere to be seen, her poor mother had bared the brunt of her wrath. She glanced at her mother through tear wet lashes. 'Of course I'll see you again, just not in this place. I want a fresh start, far away from here.'

Venturing forward, Agnes gingerly took Bonnie in her arms, and was relieved when her daughter didn't attempt to pull away. 'Then a fresh start you shall have, and I'll do whatever I can to help you get where you want.'

It was Boxing Day and the snow from the previous day still lay thick on the ground. Jess peeked through the door to the NAAFI kitchen. 'I hope Tom'll be able to make it. According to some of the lads there's some pretty big drifts on the roads.'

A snowball whizzed through the air and smashed against the door frame. 'What the ...' She stepped back hurriedly as another one hurtled past. Peering cautiously round the side of the door, she saw Tom grinning at her as he ducked behind one of the snow defences they had made in their fight the previous day. Grinning, she scooped up some of the snow, pressed it into a firm ball and hurled it back, just as another one came her way. Closing the door, she burst into a fit of giggles as the snow thudded against the wood. She turned to face Penny and Ruby. 'Looks like he didn't have any trouble getting here!'

Ruby hastily shoved her feet into her wellington boots, then got her coat, hat, scarf and gloves from the staff room. 'He's a jolly good aim, I'm glad he's on our side.'

The other girls quickly donned their outdoor winter clothing and were about to open the kitchen door when Jess shook her head with a grin. 'I've had an idea. I'm going to go out the main entrance. When you hear an owl call, open the door just a tad so that he thinks we're coming out, and meanwhile I'll steal around the back and creep up on him from behind.'

Giggling like a bunch of schoolgirls, they put their plan into action. Jess pushed the main door open a fraction and peered cautiously around to make sure Tom couldn't see her. Seeing the coast was clear, she stealthily made her way to the wall of snow. She could see Tom's posterior protruding from behind the wall, and smothered a giggle behind her hand, quickly ducking out of sight in case he turned around. Gathering as much snow as she could, she formed it into a firm ball which she placed on the ground, then she cupped her hands around her mouth and blew between her thumbs. Tutting under her breath she reflected it would have been a good idea to see if she could actually make a noise like an owl before choosing that as her signal. She peeped above the bank of snow and tried to hoot like an owl.

From inside the kitchen Ruby turned to Penny. 'What the hell was that?'

Penny stifled a giggle. 'It was either Jess doing a very poor impression of an owl, or someone's trodden on a cat.'

Outside Jess watched the kitchen door open a fraction. She saw Tom straighten up slightly, then threw her ball at him with a cry of triumph as it broke over his back. The girls came charging out from the kitchen, gathering snow as they went, and pretty soon it was a free-for-all, with Tom as the main target. Hearing the shouts, calls and laughter coming from outside, the girls from the cookhouse appeared and it wasn't long before the air was filled with snowballs.

Jess hurried over to Tom and the others who were making repairs to the NAAFI's snow defence. 'How's it going?'

Ducking down as a barrage of snowballs flew over their heads, Tom picked up some of the broken snow and patted it down on top of the wall. 'I'm not sure. How do you know whether you're winning or not?'

Jess grinned. 'The losers are the first side who gives up because they're too cold, wet or plain exhausted.'

He nodded thoughtfully. 'If we want to win this battle we need to get organised, get anyone who's not got a good throwing arm or a sharp aim to start making the snowballs so the rest of us can concentrate on pelting them.'

Jess looked impressed. 'Bit like a factory line? Clever boy!'

An hour later, red with effort and wet through, the cookhouse surrendered, much to the delight of the NAAFI girls. Jess looked at Tom who was starting to resemble a snowman. 'I think you'd best get back to your billet and have a change of clothes!'

Pulling off his gloves, he wrung them out in front of her. 'I reckon you're right.' He glanced around the former battleground. 'I've not had that much fun since I was a nipper!'

Jess's eyes met his and she felt herself melting under his gaze. He had the kindest, warmest eyes she had ever seen, and when he looked at her they twinkled with affection. Aware that she was staring, Jess turned her gaze to her sodden clothes. 'I'd best get into the shower, although I expect there's already a queue forming, and if I don't hurry I'll have dried out before it's my turn.'

He nodded, went to turn away then hesitated. 'I'm not going to have any free time between now and New Year's Eve. Would you like to come to the Grafton with me?'

'Yes!' The word was out of her mouth before she had time to think.

He grinned. 'Pick you up around six?'

She gestured towards Ruby and Penny who were heading for their billet. 'I promised the girls we'd go together, but I could meet you there for six?'

He nodded. 'I'll look forward to it.'

Penny peered at her reflection in the mirror. 'Do I pass muster?'

'You most certainly do,' said Ruby. 'That Donald's a lucky boy.'

Penny beamed. 'He's lovely. I was pleased as punch when he finally plucked up the courage to ask me to be his date.'

Jess took her court shoes from the locker and slipped her feet into them, then stood up and grinned at her friends. 'Cinders is ready for the ball!'

Penny frowned. 'I've been thinking about this, and if you're Cinders who the heck are we? The Ugly Sisters?'

Jess snorted with laughter. 'Blame Ruby, she was the one who started it!'

'Only because you were walking like you were wearing glass slippers ...' said Ruby.

'Carry on like this and we'll all be late for the ball!' said Penny, pushing her arms into the sleeves of her coat.

Jess strode ahead of her friends. 'At least I don't look like I'm walking on stilts any more!'

Ruby rolled her eyes. 'I'm not surprised – you've been practically living in those heels since Boxing Day.'

Jess gave her a smug smile. 'Practice makes perfect!'

Life on an army base meant the roads were kept clear of snow, so getting to the Grafton didn't prove to be a problem. Jess pointed at some of the houses as the taxi drove past.

'Don't they look cosy?' she said, indicating one house in particular which was still covered in snow. Through the window they could see a fire burning brightly in the grate lighting the room in a soft orange glow, a Christmas tree lavishly decorated with tinsel and baubles stood to one side and on top of the mantle there was a neat row of Christmas cards. 'When I get married, I'm going to have a house just like that,' she said wistfully. 'I'll pin stockings on the fireplace and I'll …'

'Stockings?' repeated Penny uncertainly. 'Why would you do that?'

'Not mine, silly,' giggled Jess. 'I meant the ones you give to children.'

Ruby gave her friend a look of surprised admiration. 'You've thought that far ahead?'

Jess nodded. 'I've always known I'd like to have children. What about you?'

Ruby looked perplexed. 'I don't know. I suppose I'd have to think about it because of what happened to my mum.'

Jess patted Ruby's hand encouragingly. 'You know what they say, lightning doesn't strike in the same place twice,' she gently nudged Ruby with her elbow, 'and I reckon you'd make a brilliant mother.'

Penny stared out of the window. 'Well, I'm never having kids. It was bad enough having to live with that lot in Greystones.' She shook her head. 'I'd rather have a puppy.'

'Honestly, Penny,' giggled Jess, 'I think you'd feel different if they were *your* kids, although I'll agree with you on the puppy part, because I'd like to have pets.'

Ruby thought back to the small terraced house which had sparked the conversation. 'You're going to need a bigger house then.'

Jess pointed to Tom and George who were waiting for them on the pavement outside the Grafton. 'They're here.'

Getting out of the taxi, Penny peered around anxiously for Donald and was delighted when she saw him stepping down from a tram. She headed towards him, calling over her shoulder as she went. 'Back in a mo.'

Taking Jess by the hand, Tom stood back to admire her. 'Looking beautiful as always, Cinders.'

Ruby stifled a giggle behind them. 'Don't call her that. When me and Penny are around, people will think we're her ugly sisters!'

George placed his arm around Ruby's waist. 'Impossible!'

'Charmer,' blushed Ruby.

Penny caught up with them just as they were going through the doors. 'Donald, I'd like you to meet Jess, Tom, George and Ruby.'

Jess noticed that when Donald shook each of their hands in turn, he appeared rather shy. Evidently Ruby had spotted the same thing, because she commented on it when Donald took Penny for a turn around the floor.

'I'm not surprised we didn't notice him before,' she said. 'He really keeps himself to himself. No wonder it took him so long to ask Penny out on a date – he seems painfully shy.'

Jess nodded. 'He seems nice enough, but I always assumed Penny would go for a more confident type of man, someone who could match her outgoing personality.'

Ruby took a sip of her lemonade before answering. 'I think she'll overpower him ...' She waited until Jess's laughter had subsided before continuing. 'You know what I mean. She's a bit of a character is our Penny – she needs a man, not a shrinking violet.'

'Do you think that's why he took her straight onto the dance floor, because he's too nervous to sit and talk with us?' said Jess.

Ruby nodded. 'It took him a while to get the guts to talk to Penny.'

Jess nodded at George. 'Not like you, eh, George? You know how to grab a woman's attention, pelt her with paper balls 'til she gives in.'

George beamed proudly. 'Worked, though, didn't it?'

Ruby pulled a face. 'I don't know about that ...'

Leaning over, George kissed her full on the lips, causing Ruby to give an embarrassed squeal. 'George!'

He waggled his eyebrows mischievously whilst giving her a large wink. 'And you said my methods don't work!'

'All right, you've proved your point,' said Ruby, 'but we're getting off track.'

Tom had kept quiet, but now he spoke up. 'I think it's up to Penny who she dates.'

Jess pulled a guilty face. 'Oh dear, were we sounding like a couple of fishwives?'

He stood up. 'More like two friends who care about their bezzie, but even good friends should know when they need to take a step back.' He held his hand out to Jess. 'Come along, Cinders, I want a dance before you turn into a pumpkin!'

Jess rolled her eyes. 'It's the coach that turns into a pumpkin!' As Tom guided her with ease around the dance floor, she couldn't help wondering whether she should tell him about his aunt's stark warning for her to stay away from him, especially as he obviously had strong views when it came to not interfering in other people's relationships. This led her to wonder whether his aunt might have told him what she'd said to Jess. She shook her head. Tom would have said something straight away if he knew what his aunt had done. You're being paranoid, Jessica Wilson, she told herself. That's what living with secrets does to someone. Laying her head against his chest, she relaxed against him.

Feeling as though hardly any time had passed since she first went onto the dance floor, Jess was surprised when the band stopped playing and the conductor called for silence.

'Ladies and gentlemen!' He waited until he had everyone's attention before continuing. 'I'd like you to join me in counting down to the New Year in ...' he looked at his watch and paused for a moment '... ten ... nine ...'

Tom glanced at the ceiling above him. In a few hours' time he would be leaving for pastures new, and he might not see Jess again for a very long time, if ever. He had spoken to his parents about his future in the army and with Jess. His father's advice had been simple.

'You'll never know how she feels unless you summon up the courage to ask her. Don't waste your time waiting for the right moment, because trust me, son, you'll be waiting a long time. Sometimes it's better to jump in feet first and see where you land.'

Tom had listened to his father, then his mother, who said that most women wanted a man to take charge.

'I've spoken to the ladies in my WI meetings ...'

'Oh, Mam!' Tom had objected, only to have his mother wave him into silence.

'Don't be silly, Tom, they're only trying to help.' She cleared her throat. 'As I was saying, I've spoken to the women in my WI and we all agree that whilst most women want their independence, and to be shown respect by a man, at the end of the day we all want someone to put their arms around us and tell us everything's going to be all right.'

Now, Tom looked to Jess whose eyes danced with excitement as she joined in the count. Everyone cheered when they reached zero, and the band played the opening chords of 'Auld Lang Syne'. Tom took a deep breath. His heart pounded in his chest as though it were trying to escape, bearing in mind his parents' advice, Tom knew that now was the right time. Turning Jess to face him, he looked up before stepping her to one side, then he gestured to something above her head. Looking up Jess saw a sprig of mistletoe. Her heart rising in her chest, she looked back, wondering if this was going to be another one of their awkward moments, but Tom wasn't taking any chances. Before she knew it, he was gently brushing his lips against hers, kissing her softly. Jess risked a peek and saw that he was gazing down at her. Wishing that this moment would last forever, she gazed back before closing her eyes and allowing herself to relax into the kiss. Kissing was nothing like she had imagined it to be. His lips were firm and yet he was so gentle; she quivered as she felt him tighten his embrace. Standing in this beautiful, magical setting, with everyone dressed up, Jess felt like a real-life Cinderella, and with Tom, the most handsome man in Liverpool, choosing to kiss her above everyone else, she thought he really had to be her Prince Charming.

Pulling away, Tom smiled down at her. 'So now that I've kissed you, does that make you my princess?'

Jess gave a blissful sigh. 'I suppose it must do.'

He cocked an eyebrow. 'And my girlfriend?'

'If you'd like me to be.'

His arms tightened around her waist and he leaned down so that their noses touched. 'I would like that very much, Jessica Wilson.' As the song finished the room erupted in cheers, not that Jess noticed, for she was being kissed for the second time, by the man she loved most in the world.

Chapter Six

October 1940

While there had been no bombings or attacks on Britain, Jess, Penny and Ruby had believed along with the rest of the nation that the Phoney War was proving to be just that, and that Britain was exempt from hostilities. All that had come to an end, however, when the Luftwaffe had shown its might, bombing London and just about every other major city in the country including Liverpool.

George had written to Ruby around this time to let her know that Swanny had failed to return after the evacuation of France and was now officially reported as missing in action, since he had not been seen by his regiment since the Battle of Dunkirk.

I've spoken to Cassie, and as you can imagine, she doesn't know which way to turn, because until she hears something official, she's fearing the worst. I've tried to reassure her that he's probably hunkered down somewhere, or even been captured, but even I'm beginning to have my doubts. It's no secret that Swanny saved my skin, and I will be forever indebted to him. I know you and Cassie got on well when I came home for Christmas, and I was hoping that you might consider moving in with her for a bit just to keep her company. It won't do her any good to sit and dwell.

George's letter had coincided with a new posting for Jess, Ruby and Penny. 'You're to go to Normanton Barracks in Derby,' Mrs Armstrong had informed them. Ruby had waited until she finished giving them the details before explaining her predicament. 'Normally, I'd do anything to stay with my pals, Mrs Armstrong, but I think Cassie needs me more than they do right now.'

Mrs Armstrong had listened to Ruby before giving her consent. 'Very well, my dear, you may keep your position in Seaforth. I'll set up a travel pass for you so that you might stay with your friend.'

After some careful consideration Jess and Penny decided to take the posting in Normanton. The parting had been tearful, but as Ruby had said, she could hardly leave Cassie on her own, and she didn't expect Jess and Penny to stay at Seaforth when Jess could be based much closer to Tom, who had moved from London to Chilwell Barracks in Nottingham.

'I'll miss you both terribly, but Swanny saved George's life – I feel I owe it to Cassie – and it's not as if we'll never see each other again.' Ruby sniffed as she stood on the station platform.

'And if anything changes you can hop on the first train and come to Normanton,' Penny assured her.

With her emotions getting the better of her, Jess didn't trust herself to speak. She placed her arms around Ruby's neck and hugged her tight, before pecking her on the cheek. Her lips trembled as she spoke. 'It's going to be like losing my right arm ...'

Blinking back her own tears, Ruby nodded. 'That's exactly how I feel. We've been together all our lives, but we knew we'd have to part sooner or later.'

Jess nodded, then hearing the guard blow his whistle, she and Penny dashed onto the train. Wagging an admonitory finger the guard slammed their door shut just as the train began to pull away. Leaning out of the window Jess and Penny waved until Ruby was lost from sight.

At first their new life in Normanton had seemed a little daunting because the barracks were enormous compared to Seaforth, but after a few weeks the girls had settled in, feeling as at home in Normanton as they had in Seaforth.

Jess and Penny had just started their morning break when the young girl responsible for distributing the mail handed them each a letter.

Seeing Tom's familiar writing, Jess smiled. She glanced meaningfully at Penny's letter.

'Alice,' Penny said in answer.

Jess slit her envelope open and removed the contents.

Darling Jess,

So pleased that you're in Normanton. I have missed you so much since leaving Liverpool. Have you any idea how long you'll be staying? I'm going to be in Chilwell for a few months yet. Give me a call when you've settled in properly and we'll arrange to meet. I've not been to Derby even though it's only half an

hour or so away, but I hear it's very nice. Anyway,
must dash. Look forward to speaking to you soon, ring
me as soon as you can.
*   All my love as always,*
*   Tom xxxx*

Jess looked up from reading her letter, a wide smiling spreading across her face. 'Tom's going to come to Derby …' She remembered Alice's letter. 'Did Alice say much?'

Penny beamed. 'She's joined the WAAF and is based in Leeds. She's asked if there's a possibility to meet up.'

'Very impressive!' said Jess. 'I bet she's changed heaps.' She glanced at the clock which hung above the door to the NAAFI. 'Shan't be a mo.'

She walked over to the telephone, picked up the receiver and spoke to the operator. 'Chilwell Barracks, please.' She waited patiently until a man's voice came down the phone.

'Hello, can I speak to Corporal Tom Durning?'

She heard the man turn away from the receiver and address the room in general before turning back a moment or so later. 'He's on his way.'

A few seconds later, Tom's voice came down the receiver; he sounded as though he had been running. 'Hello?'

'Tom!'

'Hello, Jess!' said Tom, the smile evident in his voice. 'Did you get my letter?'

'Just this minute, and I think it's a marvellous idea. When were you thinking of coming over?'

'How about this Saturday?' said Tom. 'We could catch a movie, go for a stroll through the town, whatever you fancy.'

Jess beamed. She loved spending time with Tom and had missed him dreadfully since they'd parted at New Year, and even though they wrote to each other often, and telephoned at least once a week, it wasn't the same as seeing each other.

'I'd like that very much,' she said. 'How about you come to my NAAFI for ten and we go from there?'

'Will do!' There was a slight pause before he added, 'Can't wait to see you.'

Hearing the affection in his voice, Jess replied, 'Nor I you.'

Jess waited eagerly by the gate. Tom wasn't due to arrive for ten minutes yet, but she couldn't wait to see him, and even though she knew 'a watched pot never boils' she couldn't help herself. When Olly trundled into view, she felt her heart leap with joy as she went to meet him. He opened the door, got out and picked Jess up before swinging her round then setting her down again.

'It's so good to see you,' he enthused before leaning in to kiss her.

Jess heard a chortle escape the guard's lips, but she couldn't have cared less. She had been looking forward to this moment ever since she had spoken to Tom last.

Pulling back from their embrace, Tom twinkled down at her.

'Good to see you too,' said Jess. 'Where would you like to go first?'

Still keeping her in his arms he gave her a gentle squeeze. 'With you? Anywhere.'

She patted him lightly on the chest. 'Charmer!'

He shrugged. 'Well, if I am it's your fault, 'cos that's the effect you have on me.'

Standing on tiptoe Jess leaned up to kiss him lightly on the lips. 'Come on, Casanova, where's it to be?'

Tom shrugged. 'I'll leave it up to you to decide.'

'How about we go for a walk down the canal then have lunch at one of the cafés? In the afternoon we could go to Markeaton Park, before a trip to the cinema, then dinner in the Dolphin.'

Tom looked at her with admiration. 'I like a woman who knows her mind.'

Extricating herself from his embrace, Jess walked round to the passenger side of the car. Tom might have thought she'd made her mind up on the spot, but in fact she'd been planning this day since they had arranged to meet.

As Jess had suggested, they started with a walk down the canal towpath where they fed the ducks with some bread which Jess had brought from the NAAFI canteen. After that they had lunched in what Jess described as a cheap but cheerful café down by the cathedral before heading to Markeaton Park. Once a recreation ground, the park had been taken over by the forces and was now being used as a training ground, with the hall housing the soldiers. Every Saturday afternoon an open-air dance was held on the two lawns in front of the hall. With the sun beating down, Jess felt as though she really were a princess at some grand party being held by a lord, as Tom, her very own Prince Charming, guided her effortlessly. After the dance they headed for the Regal Cinema on East Street, where they watched Laurel and Hardy in the comedy *Saps at*

Sea. A film which they particularly enjoyed when the cross-eyed janitor mixed up the water and gas taps, with the inevitable hilarious results.

With the day coming to an end, the pair entered Ye Olde Dolphin Inne on Queen Street, not far from where they had lunched. With the sun fading, the chill of the evening began to set in. Seeing the fire roaring in the hearth beside the bar, Jess strode towards it, her hands held up to receive the warmth.

Tom walked over to the bar, then half turned to face Jess. 'I'm guessing you'd rather have a cup of tea than a cold drink?'

Jess nodded. 'Anything warm'll do.'

Tom looked hopefully at the barmaid. 'I don't suppose you do tea?'

Seeing Jess warming herself by the fire, she called over, 'I've got cocoa if you'd like some?' Jess's eyes lit up with approval and the barmaid continued, 'We don't normally serve it, but if you hang on a mo I'll check with my dad.' She made to turn away then hesitated. 'Are you having anything to eat?'

Tom nodded. So she passed him a couple of menus before disappearing into the back. Tom handed one to Jess. Turning his back to the fire, he examined the menu. 'I'll have the sausage casserole with gooseberry crumble and custard for afters,' he said promptly.

Jess scanned her menu. 'Liver and onions with mash for me. How do you know you'll have room for afters?'

Tom looked surprised. 'Doesn't everyone have room for afters?'

Jess giggled, then gave an 'ooh' as the barmaid returned with two steaming cups of cocoa. 'My dad said to charge the same as we would for lemonade.'

Jess cradled the hot mug in her hands. 'Thank you!'

The barmaid smiled. 'Are you ready to order?'

In answer Tom gave her their order before selecting a table close to the fire. He glanced around the bar, his eyes resting on the low beamed ceiling. He looked at Jess with approval. 'Do you come here often?'

Jess shook her head. 'I would, but it's expensive eating out, especially when we work in the NAAFI.'

Tom considered this. 'I suppose it is daft to eat out when you get food cheaper back on camp, but it's nice to spoil yourself once in a while.'

Jess gave him a shrewd smile. 'Only you're the one doing the spoiling, as usual.' She wagged a reproving finger. 'You really should let me pay my way, Tom.'

He pulled his mouth down into a disapproving grimace. 'Sorry, Jess, but I'm a bit old-fashioned in that respect. A gentleman never allows a lady to pay.'

Jess sipped her cocoa, which warmed her from the inside out. She eyed Tom curiously through her thick lashes. 'Have you told your mam and dad about us?'

'Of course I have. Mam was cock-a-hoop, she really likes you. So does Dad.'

'I like them too.' Jess stared into her mug of cocoa before looking up. 'How's your auntie?'

Tom shrugged. 'As well as can be expected for someone her age.' He leaned back as the barmaid placed their meals on to the table. Tom breathed in the aroma of sausage and onions. 'Proper grub, that,' he said before tucking into his dinner.

Taking a forkful of mashed potato, Jess waited to see if he would mention his aunt again, but it seemed she was the furthest thing from his mind. Instead he talked of life in Chilwell Barracks and how the NAAFI there was nowhere near as good as the one in Seaforth. Jess studied him carefully for signs of discontent, but Tom seemed perfectly happy to eat his dinner and make small talk.

When he dropped her off at Normanton much later that evening, he made arrangements to meet up as soon as they could. Waving him goodbye, Jess came to the conclusion that Tom was none the wiser to his auntie's warnings all those months ago. If his parents knew of their blossoming relationship it seemed only logical that his auntie must also know. That being the case, Jess wondered what the old lady's response had been on hearing the news. Had she voiced her discontent or was she hatching a plan to split them up further down the line? She mulled this over before another thought entered her mind. Perhaps Auntie Edna had decided to let things lie? Turning in the direction of her billet, Jess decided that it was pointless stewing over the thoughts of another person, especially one who had acted so irrationally, and she resolved to put the matter behind her.

Penny and Donald's relationship hadn't lasted more than a few weeks into the New Year, with Penny deciding that she needed someone a little more outgoing. 'I'm more used to the lads from Nazareth House,' she told Jess as they entered the café in the recreation park.

'You mean gobby little blighters?' Jess laughed.

Penny nodded. 'Someone who's up for a laugh like Tom and George. Donald was a little too reserved for me.'

A shiver ran down Jess's back as they passed the Messerschmitt which was being paraded around the country in a bid to raise funds for the war effort, after being shot down somewhere in the south of England. 'I know it's war and that's what happens, but I can't help feeling like we're celebrating killing someone's son, or brother, or husband.'

Penny slid her arm through Jess's. 'You just have to keep in mind that we never started this, and *he* was coming over here to bomb our cities and shoot down our boys.'

They sat down at their favourite table close to the window where they could people-watch. 'When are you seeing Tom next?' said Penny in a bid to change the subject to a more palatable one.

Jess smiled. 'During the Christmas holidays. He can't come to me, but I said we could both …' she shook her head as Penny opened her mouth to say she didn't want to play gooseberry '… go to him.' She wagged a reproving finger. 'It won't be until the day after Boxing Day, but even so I'm not leaving you on your tod over Christmas.'

Penny smiled gratefully. 'That's a lovely idea, but I rang Alice this morning and she asked if I'd like to go and see her on Boxing Day.'

The waitress came over to take their order. 'Hello, girls, are you having the usual?'

Jess nodded. 'Pot of tea and two iced buns, please, Avril.'

As the waitress went to get their order, Jess got back to their conversation. 'I knew she'd written suggesting you meet up, but I didn't realise you'd been in touch with her. It'll be lovely for the two of you to see each other after all this time. How is she?'

Penny leaned back as the waitress placed the tray on the table and began distributing cups and saucers. 'She sounded really happy on the phone. She's working as a radio operator. She asked after you and Ruby ...' She paused. 'I've just remembered, we received a letter from Ruby this morning. Hang on a mo ...' As she spoke she pulled the letter from her handbag and handed it to Jess, who scanned the letter before reading some of it aloud.

'I've spoken to George and he's coming home to spend Christmas with me and Cassie, so that'll be nice. We've still no word on Swanny, but we're trying our best to keep positive, after all, no news is good news.'

She shook her head darkly. 'I appreciate Ruby's trying to remain positive, but it doesn't look good, does it? It's been months now.'

Penny grimaced. 'Cassie's such a lovely woman, it seems such a shame that she and Swanny never had kids. She really mothered us when we went there for Christmas dinner, fussing whether we had enough to eat and drink, and making sure we were happy. You ever worry about shooting the enemy down again, just you think of poor old Cassie and her Swanny.'

Jess nodded grimly. 'I hope they find him safe and well soon.'

Penny gently blew on the surface of her tea. 'Have you and Tom arranged anything for Christmas or are you going to do that nearer the time?'

'Tom said he'd book one of the B&Bs in town,' said Jess.

Penny raised her brow tauntingly. 'You're staying over?'

Jess gave her a wry smile. 'Yes, I am, Penny, but only because it's easier and it means we'll get to spend a couple of days together.'

Penny winked. 'You just make sure he behaves himself!'

'Tom wouldn't dream of behaving in an ungentle-manly manner.'

Penny smiled. 'I'm only teasing. He's a good man is Tom, you're lucky to have him.'

Jess nodded thoughtfully. 'I know I am. I can't believe I ever considered listening to his aunt's words of warning.'

'Are you ever going to tell him about that?' Penny asked.

Jess shook her head. 'I've no intention of stirring the pot. Although if she ever brings the matter up again, I'll tell her straight – it's none of her business who Tom's with.'

27 December 1940

Jess looked anxiously out of the carriage window as the train slowed down. The platform was crowded with a sea of umbrellas, and she was worried she might not spot Tom, or worse still that he might not have been able to make it and she would find herself stranded, all alone in a town she didn't know. Her heart leapt as she spotted Tom waving madly at her from under a large black umbrella. Smiling, she picked up the small suitcase which she had borrowed from one of the girls in the NAAFI, and hastened to the carriage door. As the train drew to a halt she steadied herself against the carriage wall. The conductor opened the door, and Jess was pleased to see Tom's handsome face, his hand held out ready to help her down.

Smiling fit to burst, he took her in his arms and, much to her embarrassment, he kissed her in front of everyone. Breaking away, he grinned. 'Hello, princess!'

Blushing from to ear to ear, Jess tapped his arm playfully. 'Honestly, Tom, everyone's staring!'

'Let them stare!' Picking her suitcase up in one hand he took her arm with the other whilst keeping the umbrella in the middle. 'Good God, Jess! What've you got in here – the NAAFI sink?'

She giggled. 'I didn't know what to bring, so I thought I'd bring everything!' She glanced at the suitcase. 'It's amazing how much stuff you can squeeze in when you really need to.'

Unable to resist, he leaned over and pecked her on the cheek. 'It's so good to see you.'

She smiled up at him. 'You too! Penny sends her love, as does Ruby.'

He walked past a line of cars. 'The B&B's not far from the station.'

Jess glanced at him from the corner of her eye. 'How's everyone at home?'

He shrugged. 'Doing all right. Did you hear about the Christmas blitz?'

She nodded. 'I spoke to Ruby the day after the first night of bombing. She said it was frightening, but not as bad as Manchester had it. I tried to persuade her to come to us, but she said she'd rather stay put. It looks as though it's all over now, though, thank goodness.'

Tom grimaced. 'I doubt that's the last we've seen of them.'

Jess looked up sharply, an anxious frown furrowing her brow. 'Do you think they'll go back to Liverpool?'

He nodded curtly. 'It's a port, Jess, it's supplying the rest of Britain with food and the like, so they'll want to disrupt that if they can.' He gave her a reassuring smile. 'Cassie lives quite far from the docks so she shouldn't be in too much danger.'

'But Ruby takes the overhead railway to Seaforth, and that's right next to the docks.'

He shrugged. 'Perhaps she should take the tram.'

'I don't see there's much difference ...' She entwined her fingers in his. 'Take each day as it comes, that's all we can do. Did you have a good Christmas?'

He smiled down at her. 'Not as good as last year.' He cast an eye over the puddles on the pavements. 'It's never as good at Christmas if it doesn't snow. Last Christmas was brilliant,' he twinkled down at her, 'and not just because of the snow.' He stopped outside an old stone house. 'This is it!' He headed up the steps and rapped a brief tattoo on the brass knocker.

After a few seconds a woman in her late fifties appeared. She had bright eyes and her hair was set in curlers under a headscarf. She smiled warmly at them. 'Can I help you?'

Smiling back, Tom held out a hand. 'Are you Mrs Canon?' She nodded, so he continued, 'I'm Tom Durning, I booked a room for my friend Jessica Wilson.'

Still holding his hand in hers, the woman raised an inquiring eyebrow. 'Single room, wasn't it?'

Tom gave her a wry smile. 'That's right. I'm based in Chilwell Barracks.'

A look of relief swept across Mrs Canon's face. She stepped to one side so that they might enter and indicated a room to her left. 'If you'd like to take a seat in the living area, Mr Durning ...' She grimaced at the umbrella which was dripping all over the floor. 'You can leave your umbrella in the stand, I'll just see Miss Wilson to her room.'

The woman led Jess up to a neat little room with a cast-iron bed and a chest of drawers. 'I understand you're here for two nights, is that correct?'

Jess nodded. 'That's right.' She placed her suitcase on top of the chest of drawers. 'Would you like me to pay now?'

'No need, you can pay the day you leave.' She glanced down the stairs. 'Your friend's a handsome chap. Have you known each other long?'

Jess tried to swallow her smile. 'Yes, although we were stationed at opposite ends of the country for quite a while.'

Mrs Canon shook her head sympathetically. 'All because that nasty Hitler wants everything for himself.' She patted Jess's hand. 'Breakfast will be served between seven and nine.'

Jess followed her hostess down the stairs, and Mrs Canon indicated the parlour where Tom was sitting. 'I shall see you in the morning. Enjoy your evening.'

Tom got up from his chair. 'All good?'

Jess nodded. 'Perfect.'

'Splendid! Let's go grab a bite to eat and then I'll take you for a walk around town. I thought we could go into the city centre tomorrow, see the castle, the market square, have lunch out somewhere, and maybe do a bit of sightseeing.'

As they stepped out onto the pavement, Tom unfolded the umbrella and Jess threaded her arm through his. 'Got any gossip?'

He chuckled softly. 'Not about anyone you'd know.' He indicated a café with a bay-fronted window and a small sign hanging above the door which read 'The Cup and Saucer'. A bell rang as they entered and they were greeted by a young girl, whom Jess guessed to be no more than twelve. She smiled brightly and guided them over to an empty table.

She handed them each a menu before taking their coats and Tom's umbrella and placing them on the stand by the counter.

Jess examined the menu. 'It all looks lovely. I've been eating like a horse this Christmas. I'm glad George was with Ruby, but it doesn't stop me worrying about her.'

Tom took her hand in his. 'That's because you feel responsible for her. I wonder why that is? I know she's your best pal, but you seem to have taken the mother role.' He smiled. 'Do you think that's because you've got a strong maternal instinct?'

Jess shrugged. 'I've always felt sorrier for Ruby than myself, because she should have had a perfect life. Her parents really wanted a baby but it went wrong, and through no one's fault, Ruby had to be put in Grey-stones. She deserves so much better.'

He frowned. 'So do you.'

She pulled a face. 'My folks didn't want me, so I obviously wasn't planned.'

'Have you dismissed the idea of your mother dying in childbirth, same as Ruby's?'

She shook her head. 'Only I don't see the point in surmising, it gets you nowhere. Far better to forget and move on.'

He squeezed her fingers in his. 'I was speaking to Auntie Edna the other day when your name came up. She asked after you, wanting to know whether I'd spoken to you lately and how you were doing, and whether we'd any plans to meet up. I think she realises you've had a bad time and doesn't like to think of you being on your own. She really cares about you ...' He looked at Jess, who was doing her best to avoid his gaze. 'What's up?'

Whilst Jess didn't want to upset Tom or get his aunt in trouble, she could hardly sit by and hear him sing her praises whilst the old woman had done her best to scare Jess off. She took a deep breath, 'When I was at yours on Christmas Day last year ...' She paused; the waitress had arrived and was looking at them expect-antly. Jess glanced back at the menu. 'I'll have sausage, chips and beans, please, oh, and a pot of tea for two?' She looked at Tom, who nodded.

He smiled briefly at the waitress. 'I'll have the pie and mash with extra bread and butter, please.'

The waitress noted the order, took the menus and headed round the far side of the counter.

Tom turned his attention back to Jess, eyeing her shrewdly. 'You were saying?'

Jess continued. 'I didn't like to say anything before, because I didn't want to upset the apple cart or cause any trouble, and I'm only mentioning it now because I don't think your auntie likes me. Either that or it's something to do with my father, but ...' She fell silent as she tried to find the right words, but Tom was leaning forward.

'She said something to you whilst I was with me mam in the kitchen, didn't she?'

Jess eyed him curiously. 'You knew?'

He shook his head. 'Not at the time, I didn't, or at least, not for sure, but the atmosphere had changed when I came back into the room, and I assumed it was because I'd just broken the news that I would be leaving, so I didn't think much more of it, and you never mentioned it.' He cocked an eyebrow. 'What did she say exactly?'

Her cheeks flushing with embarrassment, Jess relayed the conversation, finishing just as the waitress placed the tea tray on their table. Tom waited until she had emptied it before responding.

'I knew there was more to this than meets the eye. Mam's been acting funny every time I mention your name, and even though Auntie does ask after you, it's almost in a fretful way, as though she's worried you might have said something, and I'm not surprised

276

either, not after her saying something like that to you!' He shook his head. 'This has got nothing to do with me moving far away, or about her missing my uncle at Christmas.'

Jess pulled an awkward face. 'Do you think it has anything to do with my father? Only after I gave her that description ...'

Tom interrupted without apology. 'She clammed up.' He nodded thoughtfully. 'I noticed that too.'

Jess stared at him. 'You did?'

He looked guilty. 'Yes, only I didn't know why, because I believe her when she says she didn't know his name nor your mam's.' He shrugged. 'It's almost as though there's something she's ...'

This time Jess interrupted him. '... not telling me.'

He nodded. 'Only what could she not be telling you? You only want to know two bits of information, both of which we're sure she hasn't got the answer to.'

Jess waited patiently as the waitress placed their meals on the table. 'That's just it, I can't think of anything else. I already know my mother was young, and that he was a nasty individual – what else could there be that's causing her to clam up?'

He sliced into the pie and steam poured out. 'Damned if I know!' He looked at her quizzically. 'What made you ignore her words?' He took a forkful of pie and blew on it gently. 'By agreeing to be my girlfriend, I mean.'

Jess smiled shyly. 'I knew she had nothing against me per se, and I wondered whether she had only told me to stay away because she couldn't face any more awkward meals around the family table.' She carefully sliced her sausage. 'In short, I think she feels guilty, because she knows more than she's letting on.'

Tom finished chewing his mouthful then grinned at her. 'Regular Miss Marple, aren't you?'

She giggled. 'I don't know about that. If I was, I'd have solved the mystery by now!'

'Question is, what do we do next?'

Jess's eyes grew round. 'You're not going to tell her I told you, are you?'

Tom shook his head. 'No, that would just make things ten times worse, and we'll lose any hope of her spilling the beans. We've got to be careful, take the softly, softly approach.'

Jess sipped her tea then placed the cup back on the saucer. 'I've waited nigh on seventeen years; it's not going to harm me to wait a while longer.'

He grinned. 'Leave it with me, and I'll see what I can come up with. In the meantime, I suggest we carry on as we have been.' He tilted his head to one side as he mulled things over. 'You never know, the anxiety caused by wondering what we're talking about, and whether you've told me what she's said, may drive her into letting the cat out of the bag.'

Jess eyed him dubiously. 'Do you really think so? I don't like the thought of her tying herself in knots over this.'

He stroked the back of her hand. 'Then she shouldn't have said anything, or rather, she should have told you everything she knew! That way she wouldn't have to carry the burden of guilt on her shoulders.'

'I know,' said Jess, 'but I can't help feeling sorry for her. It can't be easy having me turn up on her doorstep asking all sorts of questions.'

He indicated her plate of half-eaten food with the tip of his knife. 'No sense in letting your meal get cold. Let's agree to see what happens, yes?'

Jess nodded mutely.

Her two-day visit flew by and before she knew it they were saying goodbye on the station platform. 'I've had a wonderful time, Tom. Nottingham is such a beautiful city, I wish we could have had more time together to explore properly.'

Holding her in a loose embrace, he eyed her with affection. 'Hopefully my next posting will be a bit closer, and we can see each other more often.'

'All aboard!'

Wrapping her in his arms, Tom kissed her goodbye, then brushed her hair back from her face. 'Don't forget to ring when you get back, and give my best to Penny and Ruby when you see them next.'

Jess nodded. 'I will.' Standing on her tiptoes, she kissed him again, then blinking back the tears she picked up her suitcase and made her way towards the waiting train. The guard was walking up the line of carriages shutting doors as he passed. Hastily climbing aboard, Jess waited for the guard to close the door before pushing the window down. She leaned out. 'Look after yourself.'

The sound of the guard's whistle drowned out Tom's reply, and the train's wheels squealed as they fought to gain traction on the slippery tracks. Jess waved until Tom was lost from sight. Sighing heavily, she entered the carriage, smiled at two WAAFs who had already claimed the window seats, then stowed her suitcase on the rack and made herself comfortable. She wondered how Penny's short holiday had gone with Alice, and what it must have been like, going back to somewhere which held such bad memories. Settling back into her seat she smiled wistfully. She wouldn't go back to Glasgow for all the tea in China. She muffled a yawn behind the back of her hand. Tom had tried to cram in as many things as he could into their weekend together, and whilst she had appreciated all he had done for her, it had left her feeling worn out. Closing her eyes, she listened to the sound of the wheels on the track, and it wasn't long before the gentle sway of the carriage had rocked her to sleep.

Penny waved at Jess, who had just finished her lunchtime shift. 'Wotcher! I've just got back. Are you just starting break?'

Jess nodded. 'Fancy a cuppa?'

'Do I ever! I've not had anything since this morning. There was no buffet cart on the train, and you daren't risk more than a quick trip to the lavvy at most of the stations before the blooming guard blows his whistle ready for the off!' She followed Jess back into the NAAFI kitchen. 'Did you enjoy your time with Tom?'

Jess could hear the grin in her friend's voice. 'Yes, I did, and as usual Tom was the perfect gentleman. How were things with Alice?'

Penny was positively bursting with excitement as she sat down. 'She's changed heaps, and she's as happy as Larry, although that's not why I'm smiling like the cat that got the cream.'

Jess arched an inquisitive brow. 'Oh?'

Penny drummed her heels against the floor. 'Alice has seen Bonnie.'

Jess's jaw dropped. 'What? Where? Did she speak to her?'

Penny nodded enthusiastically. 'They bumped into each other outside the recruiting office. Alice said Bonnie nearly dropped on the spot when they made eye contact. She even tried to walk off as though she hadn't recognised her, but Alice wasn't going to allow her to get away so easily. She wanted to know all the gossip on Greystones for a start, and seeing as how Bonnie was back in Glasgow instead of being tucked up safe and sound in Glencoe she figured there was a lot to be had.'

Jess placed two cups of tea on the table and took the seat opposite Penny's. 'Tell all.'

Penny grinned. 'Bonnie said she had come back from Glencoe because a friend of her mother's had arranged for her to join the WAAF and work in the War Office, under the Official Secrets Act, and because of that she could say no more.'

Jess looked incredulous. 'She can't be telling the truth ...' Penny stopped her friend mid-sentence.

'Course she's not! Alice said she looked like she'd been dragged through a hedge backwards, not all smart and clean like when she was in Greystones.'

A thought occurred to Jess. 'Did Bonnie ask about us?'

Penny shook her head. 'Alice said she couldn't get away quick enough, another point of proof that she was lying, because had she been telling the truth she would have been crowing from the rooftops.'

Jess breathed a sigh of relief. 'Thank goodness for that. I don't fancy the idea of seeing Bonnie, not even after all this time.'

Penny's eyes widened. 'Me neither. It was all right for Alice because she never ran away, but I still think Bonnie would revel at the chance to twist the knife if she could.'

'Me too,' said Jess. 'Bonnie was always smartly turned out in Greystones, she made a point of showing off her pretty frocks and ribbons in her hair. But from what Alice says it sounds as though those days are long gone, probably because of what Alice's mam said to the authorities.' Jess sat back in her seat. If Bonnie had fallen on hard times because Jess and Ruby had run away, there wasn't a doubt in Jess's mind the other girl would set out to take her revenge given the first opportunity. She would just have to keep everything crossed that their paths would never cross.

5 May 1941

Ruby had just finished her shift and was waiting for the train to arrive at Seaforth Station. For the past four nights the Luftwaffe had been relentless in their attack on Liverpool. A lot of the shops she had once frequented with her friends had been burned to the ground or reduced to rubble, and night-time travel had become a dangerous lottery. On the third night alone, Central Station, Lime Street Station, the overhead railway and the Exchange Station had all suffered bomb damage in some way or another. Ruby had considered travelling by tram or bus, but a lot of people thought these to be the most dangerous, because you didn't just have to worry about the vehicle you were in getting hit, but also the surrounding buildings.

Ruby had relentlessly tried to persuade Cassie to leave Liverpool, but Cassie had refused.

'He's coming home, Ruby, I can feel it in my heart, and I want to be here when he arrives.' She had placed a hand on Ruby's shoulder and eyed her beseechingly. 'It's my choice to stay here, but I don't want you travelling back and forth – it's too dangerous. Please stay in the barracks, you're a lot safer there.'

Ruby shook her head determinedly. 'I promised George I'd stay with you and that's what I intend to do.'

'George is a lovely feller and I know he means well, but I'm sure he wouldn't want you to risk your life because of me.' Cassie eyed Ruby thoughtfully. 'Have you told him you're still in Liverpool?'

Ruby's cheeks reddened. She had spoken with George the day after the first bombing, and he had told her that she and Cassie should leave Liverpool at the earliest opportunity, but she hadn't the nerve to tell him they hadn't heeded his advice. She tried to reason with Cassie. 'He thinks you should go and stay with your grandmother in Anglesey. You said yourself that she could do with the help on the farm – won't you reconsider?'

Cassie smiled sympathetically. 'I'm sorry, Ruby, but if there's even the slightest chance that Swanny's on his way home, then I'm going to be here for him when he arrives.'

As Ruby wasn't prepared to leave Cassie on her own to face the might of the Luftwaffe, she had taken the decision to stay with her, much to Cassie's dismay.

'I appreciate George not wanting me to be alone, but it's different now. Please move back to the barracks, Ruby, I promise I won't tell George.'

Ruby shook her head. 'Sorry, but if you stay, then so do I.' She gave Cassie a reassuring smile. 'Don't worry about me. I'll lessen the odds by taking a different route home every night.'

Ruby had done this and so far she had been lucky every time, but even she was beginning to think her luck must run out sooner or later.

Seeing the train further up the track, she quickly scanned the sky – so far everything appeared calm. She sighed. It wasn't far from Seaforth to Liverpool, and if the Germans did decide to do another raid, she'd be down the shelter in Smithdown Road before the air-raid siren had a chance to wail its warning.

She boarded the train and glanced out of the window. Looking around, she noticed a lot of the other passengers were doing the same thing. A man in khaki uniform winked at her. 'Keeping an eye out for Jerry?'

She nodded. 'I work in the NAAFI in Seaforth Barracks, but I'm staying with a friend in Liverpool. We call this "running the gauntlet", because that's what it feels like.'

He looked at her inquisitively as the train jerked into motion. 'My pal's girlfriend works in Seaforth NAAFI.

You might know her, although I can't remember her name. I've never been good with names.'

Ruby smiled. 'I don't suppose you know what she looks like?'

He shook his head. 'Never met her.' He turned to look out of the window as the air raid alarm broke the quiet. 'Oh bugger. Looks like they're on their way.' He leaned forward, his hand outstretched. 'I'm ...' Before he could finish his sentence a massive explosion came from further up the line, and the train came to an earth-shuddering halt, flinging Ruby from her seat. Smoke, dust and the smell of melting metal filled the air. Ruby tried to cry for help, but something heavy was lying across her chest, crushing her to the floor of the carriage. She felt around with her hands, but the floor was wet and sticky. Fear gripped her. She didn't know what went into the engine to make it run, but she did know that oil was part of it, and if it was oil she was touching then the whole train could go up at any second. She could see flames through the windows of the carriage. They might be far away at the moment, but she knew from hearing about the SS *Malakand* the day before how easily fire could spread and how hard it was to extinguish. She tried to push the weight off her; in the darkness she thought it felt like one of the seats from the carriage, but it was hard to tell. She could hear someone groaning as they tried to speak.

A man's voice called out – it was the same man she had been speaking to moments before the bomb had hit. 'Hello? Can you hear me? Is everyone all right?'

Ruby listened out for a response but the carriage was silent. Realising that she hadn't said anything, she winced as she tried to take a breath. 'Hello? It's me, the girl from Seaforth NAAFI.'

When he spoke she could hear the relief in his voice. 'Thank God for that. Can you move, love? Only my legs are pinned down, or at least I think they are – it's hard to tell what's what.'

Using all her strength, Ruby heaved the object, which did turn out to be a seat, up just enough to let her wiggle out from under it. Once clear she took a moment or so to catch her breath; her ribs ached terribly from the weight of the seat. Kneeling down, she called out blindly. 'Where are you?'

'Over here!' His voice came from somewhere behind her.

Turning slowly, Ruby fumbled her way on her hands and knees across the carriage floor. 'Are you still stuck?'

There was a grunt followed by a sharp intake of breath, as though the man were in a lot of pain. 'Can't move an inch!'

Ruby stopped abruptly; his voice was right next to her. Gingerly, she felt around her, then gasped as her fingers touched a large pool of oil next to the man. She spoke hastily. 'The carriages further up are on fire, and I think there's been an oil leak in our carriage. I'm afraid you're right in the middle of it – we've got to get you out before the fire reaches us.'

There was a brief rasping noise followed by a hiss as the man struck a match. 'No!' cried Ruby, and she desperately tried to blow the match out, but he was shielding the flame with his hand.

'It's not oil, love, I'd be able to smell it if it was ...'

Ruby looked at the hand holding the match. It was covered in blood. Her fingers shaking, she took the match and lowered it; her stomach turned and she clutched her throat. It wasn't oil she had felt. The man's leg had been almost severed, and he was losing a lot of blood. Determined to stay strong, she took a deep breath. 'Everything's going to be fine.' Taking her stockings off, she instructed the man to light another match. 'I'm afraid this is going to hurt ...'

He cried out as she tied a tourniquet around the upper part of his thigh. Another voice hailed them from outside the coach. 'Is anyone in there?'

'Yes!' Ruby yelled, her voice full of relief that help had arrived. 'We need a stretcher.' She looked into the man's eyes as he placed a bloodstained hand on hers.

'Thanks for staying with me, love, but you'd best get on your way. It's not safe here ...'

Ruby attempted to wipe the blood, dirt and sweat from the back of his hand. 'I'm not going anywhere.' She smiled at him. 'I'm Ruby ...'

He managed a weak smile. ''m Swanny ...' But the loss of blood was too great and with the knowledge that help was on its way, he got no further. His eyes closed as his head slid back against her knee.

Ruby raced towards Smithdown Road. The doctor from the hospital had warned her that the outlook wasn't positive.

'He's lost a lot of blood – he's lucky you got him out when you did.'

Ruby looked at him earnestly. 'Will he be all right? I know you can't save his leg, but will he make it?'

The doctor drew a deep breath. 'Only time will tell …' He hesitated. 'Do you two know each other?'

Ruby nodded uncertainly. 'We've only just met, but I believe he's my friend's husband …'

The doctor laid a hand on her shoulder. 'In normal circumstances I'd tell you to go and get her as quickly as you can,' he glanced out of the window, 'but not when there's an air raid … oi! Where do you think you're going?'

His words had fallen on deaf ears. Ruby was racing down the corridor. She knew it was stupid for her to go back outside, but she had no choice, she had to get Cassie.

Ruby's feet barely touched the ground as she turned onto Beaumont Street, determined to get to Cassie as quickly as she could. She cried out when an air warden caught hold of her as she tried to race by.

'Get inside the shelter, you stupid girl!' he bellowed, dragging her down the steps into an air-raid shelter.

'You don't understand!' Ruby protested as she struggled to break free. 'I've got to get my friend in Smithdown Road, her husband's been taken to the Royal Southern.'

She watched the exchange of apprehensive glances between some of the people in the shelter. 'What?'

An elderly man cleared his throat. 'Smithdown Road's been hit, queen, you'd best hope your friend's down a shelter …' his voice trailed off.

Ruby shook her head. 'You've got it wrong, you must have …'

She looked beseechingly at the warden but he remained firm. 'Sorry, queen, I'm afraid he's right. I can't let you go.' He tried to reassure her. 'I'm sure your pal will be safe down a shelter somewhere, same as you.' He looked at the curtain which flapped gently as yet another bomb hit the ground somewhere in the distance. 'Best hope you've got now is that Jerry goes back to where he came from real quick.'

A silent tear traced its way through the blood and dirt on Ruby's cheeks. The warden looked at her quizzically. 'Where did you come from?'

The shelter fell silent as Ruby relived the moment the train was bombed. When she had finished she looked at the warden. 'So you see, I can't be certain it's the same Swanny, but it's got to be, don't you think?'

Taking her hand in his, he gave her fingers a reassuring squeeze. 'You've done all you can; there's only one person who can give you that answer. I'm afraid you're going to have to be patient.'

Ruby sat down on the bench nearest the door. The woman next to her offered her a cup of tea from her flask. 'It'll make you feel better.'

Ruby took a sip from the cup and winced. The tea was far sweeter than she was used to. Seeing her expression, the woman smiled kindly. 'They reckon sweet tea's good for shock, so I save me rations for times like these.'

Thanking the woman, Ruby cradled the cup, which was comfortingly warm in her hands. She stared into the surface of the tea. If only she had been more insistent that Cassie go to her grandmother's then everything would have been fine. Her heart sank as she pictured Swanny lying in the carriage. His left leg had been trapped by part of the collapsed roof, but his right leg had been almost completely severed just above the knee. It had taken them nearly twenty minutes to fully free him, and he had remained unconscious the whole time. She glanced towards the steps of the shelter, where a small cloud of dust lifted an inch or so as another bomb thudded in the distance. She knew it would be stupid to try to leave, but the thought of Cassie sitting in her house waiting for someone who would never arrive was more than Ruby could stand. She took another sip of the tea. She would have to trust that her friend had gone down the shelter as soon as the alarm was raised.

It was hours later when the all clear sounded. Ruby dashed out onto the street and pounded her way along the pavement. As she approached Smithdown Road she could see that the rumours were true. Cassie's flat above the shop had gone, and there was no sign of Cassie. Ruby began yelling Cassie's name at the top of her voice. She knew it was dangerous to go near a collapsed building but she didn't care – if Cassie was inside she had to get her out as quickly as possible. She had begun throwing bricks to one side, when a voice called her from behind. Ruby turned and saw Cassie hurrying towards her.

'Cassie!' Ruby quickly stumbled across the rubble towards her friend.

Cassie stared open-mouthed at Ruby whose face was still smeared with blood and dirt. 'You weren't in there, were you?' she said, looking at the remains of the flat.

Ruby hastily explained how she had been on the train when the bombs dropped, and about the man she'd met who was called Swanny.

Cassie's face paled. Tears streamed down her cheeks as she began to run, before realising she didn't know where she was running to. 'Which hospital is he in?' she shouted.

'He's at the Royal Southern ...'

Nodding, Cassie gripped Ruby's hand and together they raced off.

As they entered the hospital Ruby led the way to the room where Swanny had been taken, only to find his bed empty. Fearing the worst, she hurried back into the corridor and caught the attention of one of the nurses rushing past.

'Excuse me!'

'Yes?'

Ruby pointed at the ward. 'The man I came in with earlier, the one from the train, where is he?'

The nurse shrugged. 'You'll have to be more specific ...'

Walking towards her, Ruby lowered her voice. 'The man whose leg was badly severed ...'

The nurse gave a grim nod of recognition. 'He's in theatre.'

Cassie appeared by Ruby's shoulder. 'I don't suppose you noticed whether he had a tattoo between the forefinger and thumb of his left hand?'

The nurse began to shake her head then changed her mind. 'Yes, now I come to think of it, he did – it looked like a swan.'

Cassie gripped Ruby's hand tightly in her own. 'It's him, it's my Swanny.'

Ruby looked at the nurse in earnest. 'This is his wife. Is there somewhere we can wait for him?'

The nurse nodded. 'Come with me.'

It was much later that afternoon when the matron came to see them. She explained that Swanny had lost a considerable amount of blood and they had been unable to save his leg, but he was stable and in recovery, and Cassie could see him for a minute or two.

Ruby went to sit back down but Cassie insisted Ruby go with her. 'He'll want to say thank you.'

They entered the ward to see Swanny lying in the bed nearest to them. A slow smile spread across his face as he focused on Cassie. 'My darling girl!'

Tears trickled down Cassie's cheeks as she took his hand in hers. 'I thought I'd lost you.'

He shook his head then winced. 'I fought my way out of France to get back to you, so you'll not get rid of me that easily.' He turned his attention to Ruby. 'Are you the young girl that got me out the carriage?'

Ruby smiled. 'I told them where you were.' She hesitated. 'Do you remember what we were talking about before the bomb?'

He frowned as he tried to remember then shook his head. 'Sorry, did we ...' He raised a finger. 'Hang on a mo. You're the one who works in the NAAFI in Seaforth, am I right?'

In answer Ruby grinned.

He pointed at Cassie. 'That's how you knew where to find me.' He turned his finger to Ruby. 'You're our George's girl – tell me I'm wrong!'

Smiling, Ruby put up her hands. 'Guilty as charged.'

He tried to sit up but Cassie wagged a reproving finger and gently pushed him back with the tips of her fingers. 'I think that's enough excitement for one day.'

Jerking his head towards Cassie, he chuckled. 'Aye up, the boss has spoken.' He turned to Ruby. 'How's our George?'

'He's safe and well, thanks to you.'

He tried to look nonchalant. 'Dunno about that.'

'Well I do,' Ruby insisted. 'That silly sod would've been overseas by now if it weren't for you ...'

He held up a hand to quieten her. 'And I'd be dead in the back of a train carriage if it weren't for you, so I reckon that makes us even.'

Cassie gave Ruby a shrewd glance. 'He's right, you know.' She turned back to Swanny. 'George insisted Ruby stay with me in Liverpool. I told him there was no need, but he wouldn't have any of it, said he was indebted to you, and he'd not see me on my own.'

Swanny grinned. 'I always said he was a good lad, a real diamond in the rough, and I was right.' He looked back at his wife. 'What I don't understand is why you're still in Liverpool?'

'Because she wouldn't listen to me or George and insisted on waiting for you to come home,' Ruby said sternly.

He clapped a hand to his forehead. 'Cassie Swan! It comes to something when a mere chit of a girl has more sense than a woman grown!'

'I told you he'd not want you to stay,' said Ruby righteously.

Cassie grimaced apologetically. 'I promise we'll go to Anglesey as soon as you're fit.'

He went to speak then stopped and looked down at where his leg used to be, and his cheery expression faded. 'They aren't going to want me back, are they? Not like this.'

Leaning forward Cassie placed her hand against his cheek. 'You're still my Swanny, nothing will ever change that.'

He gave her a grim little smile. 'I'm not much good to anyone else, though.'

Wiping away his tears, Cassie straightened up. 'I know you, Eric Swan, you'll find some way of getting about, just like that Douglas Bader.'

He gave her a wry smile. 'You mean I'm a stubborn old sod?'

Cassie nodded. 'If you want to put it that way, then yes.'

He looked down at the sheets. 'I might not be able to go marching off to war, but I don't see why I wouldn't be able to do a lot of other things.'

Ruby grinned. 'I can see why George thought you'd make a great dad.' She blushed to the roots of her hair as the words left her lips.

Swanny chuckled. 'Don't worry, queen, George told me how he felt before we parted ways.'

The door to the ward opened and Matron cast them a reproving look. 'I said a minute or two, not half an hour!'

Swanny tapped them both playfully on the backs of their hands. 'Naughty girls! Off you go!'

Giggling, Ruby left the room, muttering an apology to Matron as she went, but Swanny asked for a moment more with Cassie.

'I can tell you one thing I'm still able to do.' He beckoned her to come closer and as she leaned down, he murmured, 'I'm still able to kiss my wife.'

July 1941

Jess and Penny had been beside themselves with worry after Ruby's telephone call to let them know about Swanny and the awful bombing of the train, but try though they might, she had refused to leave Liverpool until Swanny was well enough to go with Cassie to live on her grandmother's farm in Anglesey.

Now Hitler had finally turned his attention to Russia, though the bombing of Britain was to continue for a while yet. Swanny and Cassie had left for Anglesey at last, leaving Ruby free to ask for a transfer, but with nothing pending, Penny had suggested they swap NAAFIs.

'Are you sure you don't mind?' Ruby had said, her voice awash with relief.

'Not at all. They say a break's as good as a rest – besides, I miss the folk in Seaforth, and I think you'd benefit from a bit of time in Normanton. It'll be good to see you again, albeit briefly, 'cos you'll most likely be getting on the train I'll be getting off.'

This conversation had taken place several weeks earlier and, as Penny had predicted, she and Ruby had only had a chance for a quick hello and goodbye before Ruby had to board the train.

Now, with Liverpool far behind her, she scanned the platform with a keen eye and finally spotted Jess, who was waving frantically. Waving back, Ruby made her way through the crowd to where Jess stood, her arms wide open.

'Oh, Rubes, I haven't half missed you,' Jess said, squeezing her.

'And I you,' Ruby replied, her voice husky from being hugged so tightly. Leaning back, she touched Jess's locks. 'Your hair! It's so long and curly!'

Jess stared at Ruby. The Blitz had aged her friend, and lines of worry were etched across her forehead. Jess forced a smile. 'You're looking well.'

Ruby tucked her arm through the crook of Jess's elbow. 'Liar!' she laughed. She gave Jess a sidelong glance. 'Even Toby noticed how much I'd changed – not that he said it to my face, but you could see it in his eyes.'

'Who's Toby?' said Jess as she led the way out of the station.

'I met him when I first went to Seaforth. He didn't stay long because he's a driver in the MT – you know what they're like, always racing off to one place or another. He came back to Seaforth just after the Blitz ...' She cast her friend a dark look. 'It was horrendous, Jess, I've never seen nowt like it. I'm amazed there's anything left of the city,' she sighed sadly, 'you'd not recognise the place.'

Jess shuddered. 'We've been glued to the wireless, papers, cinema and news coming in from outside the camp. We knew it was bad, but it can't be the same as seeing it first-hand. We all think you're a blooming heroine after what you did for Swanny.' She held her hand up to signal an approaching bus. 'They should give you a medal.'

Ruby's cheeks bloomed. 'I couldn't leave him there; I only did what anyone would have done.'

Jess boarded the bus and paid their fares, despite Ruby's insistence she pay her own way, then sat in the nearest seat. 'It's going to be just like old times having you here, only we're not in a tent but a rather nice cottage just outside the village, and the camp is a lot bigger than Seaforth.' She hesitated. 'I've just thought of something – do you know how to ride a bicycle?'

Ruby shook her head. 'You know I don't.'

Jess shrugged. 'I didn't, but I do now. Two of the girls who left to join the WAAF couldn't take their bicycles with them so they said me and Penny could have them.' She chuckled as she recalled their first attempts to ride their new machines. 'Penny fell off that many times she looked like she'd been through a mangle, and I wasn't much better. It took us a few days of practice, but we got the hang of it in the end.' She grinned at Ruby. 'I could teach you if you like?'

Ruby nodded. 'I'd love to learn. It'd be good to have something new for me to focus on.'

Jess gave her a friend a grim smile. 'What did George say when you told him about Swanny?'

Ruby examined her fingernails. 'That I was damned silly for staying there, but he was grateful I had, and that he'd never forgive me if I did it again.'

'I can't say as I blame him. You were incredibly lucky under the circumstances ...' Seeing the tears glisten in Ruby's eyes, Jess fell silent.

'You needn't tell me,' Ruby said. 'I saw things that night that no one should see ... Did you hear about the maternity ward in the Royal Southern?'

Jess gave a small nod. 'We all did. It makes me sick to my stomach.'

Silent tears trickled down Ruby's cheeks. 'I tried not to look but I couldn't help myself.' Her bottom lip trembled. 'There were cots, Jess, half buried under the rubble.'

Shaking her head, Jess held Ruby in her arms. 'Don't, Rubes, there's no point in torturing yourself.' Leaning back, she wiped the tears from her own cheeks. 'You need to try and forget about the Blitz and focus on the here and now. It's the only way to cope, keep moving forward.'

Ruby nodded. 'That's what I'll be doing when I learn to ride the bicycle.'

Jess rolled her eyes. 'If you're anything like me and Penny, you'll spend most of your time on the ground with the bike on top of you!'

Ruby smiled at Jess. 'Penny was right – a change is as good as a rest, and this was just what the doctor ordered!'

October 1941
Jess trotted into the kitchen of their shared cottage, waving a fistful of letters at Ruby. 'I think the postie must have had these in the bottom of his sack, because I've got three from Tom, you've got two from George, and there's one from Penny and another from Michelle.'

Ruby held her hands out in readiness. 'I'm going to read George's first, he always brightens my day.'

Jess handed them over, then sat down and slit the first one from Tom open.

Darling Jess,
Well, here I am in ****** training the girls how to operate the machinery! Some of the fellers thought it was a real hoot at first and that the women wouldn't last

five minutes, but I'm pleased to say the girls soon showed those old blighters that they were stuck in the past. Although I must admit a mixed battery has taken quite a bit of getting used to, as you tend to live in each other's pockets. There's a couple of girls from Glasgow joined up, and seeing as I'm the only one who can understand what they say, I think it's just as well they came to me.

I've had a word with my sergeant and he's agreed to give me the time off over Christmas, so if the offer still stands, I should be able to join you at Cassie's farm.

A wide smile spread across Jess's cheeks as she read the last part. By way of a thank you, Jess, Tom, Ruby, George and Penny had all been invited to spend Christmas with Cassie and Swanny at her grandmother's farm. She corrected herself – Cassie's farm. Cassie's grandmother, or as Cassie called her, her nain, had announced the work was too much for a woman her age and that she would prefer to live in the small bungalow on the edge of the property, leaving Cassie and Swanny to run the farm.

Jess glanced at Ruby over the top of her letter. 'Tom's coming to Cassie's for Christmas. Has George said anything ...' She stopped. Ruby's eyes were brimming with tears. 'Oh, Rubes! What's happened?'

Ruby handed the letter over wordlessly. Jess scanned it then clapped a hand to her mouth. She stared at Ruby in bemusement. 'I don't understand. I thought he wouldn't have to go overseas for a long time yet?'

299

A tear fell down Ruby's cheek. She pointed at the letter. 'Read the rest.'

Jess carried on reading.

Someone grassed me up, so they know how old I am, and they said I was close enough in age to go. Sarge reckons they did it to punish me for lying in the first place. I'm so sorry, Ruby, but I'm afraid I shan't be able to make it for Christmas ...

'Close enough in age? He's not even seventeen.' Jess shook her head angrily. 'Who on earth would do such a spiteful thing?'

Ruby clutched a hand to her stomach. 'I feel sick.'

Jess rubbed a hand over her friend's shoulders. 'I'm not surprised. At least George is older now ...' She shut up as Ruby shot her a withering glance.

'Like he said all them years back, being older doesn't make you bulletproof.' She held up a hand as Jess tried to explain. 'Please don't, Jess, because there's nothing you can say to make this better.'

Jess nodded grimly. 'I know, but I don't know what else to do, and I want to make you feel better.'

Smiling, Ruby held Jess's hand in hers. 'You being here makes me feel better.' She leaned her head against Jess's shoulder. 'Open Penny's letter, that'll cheer me up.'

Jess slit Penny's envelope and began to read aloud the letter within.

'Dear Jess and Ruby,
'Guess what? I've finally found the man of my dreams, and it turns out he's a friend of Ruby's, called Toby.'

Ruby sat up to look at the letter. 'That's the feller I was on about before. He's lovely, is Toby.' She smiled. 'He's outgoing so will make a good match for Penny.'

Jess continued to read.

'I know we've not been together long, but I feel like I've known him for ages and he feels the same way, so I've rung Cassie and asked if it's all right for him to join us at the farm ...'

'Blimey!' said Ruby. 'Our Penny doesn't hang about, does she?'

Jess giggled. 'I hope this Toby can keep up with her.'

Ruby nodded. 'He's a proper Scouser, full of fun and laughter, a real go-getter. I can see why the two of them have hit it off. He'll keep our Penny on her toes.'

Bonnie turned to the girl next to her. 'When I joined the ATS I thought I'd be working in an office somewhere,' she said sulkily, 'not plane-spottin' down some dirty great hole waiting for a plane to drop bombs on me!' She glanced at the corporal who waved a greeting as he passed by.

'There's nothing wrong with working on the ack-acks,' the other woman said defensively.

Bonnie smirked to herself as she remembered the day she had put two and two together.

She had been standing in line as they queued for their lunch, when one of the WAAFs brought the handsome corporal a letter. 'Sorry, Tom, they've given me your mail again by accident!'

'Thanks, Sal.' He took the envelope and slit it open. 'I reckon the only answer is for you to get married – at least that way you'll have a different surname to mine.'

'Tell Billy, not me!' she said with a chuckle before leaving him to it.

Tom read the letter with interest before hastily tucking it into his trouser pocket. 'Sorry, Milly,' he said to the woman serving the food, 'I'll have corned beef hash with chips, please.'

Bonnie had thought no more of the incident until she left the cookhouse for the ablutions a short while later. As the door to the cookhouse closed, she noticed a piece of paper lying on the ground and bent down to pick it up, glancing at the writing.

Dear Tom …

She nodded slowly. Someone was writing to the corporal who ran her battery, his girlfriend, most likely. She glanced to the signature at the bottom of the page: *lots of love, Jess.*

Bonnie looked around to see if anyone had noticed her picking the letter up, but as far as she could see she was all alone. She shrugged. Surely it wouldn't harm for her to have a quick read – she was going to the lavvy, after all. Folding it in half, she headed for the ablutions. Once inside she smoothed the paper out and began to read.

I've heard from Ruby, and you won't believe what happened to her during the Blitz …

Frowning, Bonnie glanced at the signature at the bottom of the letter then back to the bit about Ruby. She tutted under her breath. She was being silly. There was no way it could be the same Jess and Ruby from

Greystones – it would be far too coincidental. Even if it was them, how would they know Corporal Durning? The last time she had seen either girl, or at least she was almost certain she had seen Jess, was in the old … Bonnie looked up sharply. It had to be! She hurriedly read the rest of the letter which told of Ruby's bravery in Seaforth when she saved a man called Swanny, who'd got George his job at the War Office.

She read the rest, then quickly refolded the letter and pushed it into her pocket before leaving the ablutions without bothering to wash her hands. She ran to the NAAFI and rang the number of the public house where her mother was working as a barmaid. As soon as her mother came on the phone, Bonnie asked whether she knew the name of the boy who had been talking to Jessica Wilson when they had been making their way to church. Her mother was perplexed – she couldn't see what the boy had to do with anything – but such was Bonnie's insistence, Agnes thought hard before replying.

'I wouldn't lay my life on it, but I'm fairly sure his name was George Miller. I remember because he was the same one who ran away from Father Blakely. Why?'

'No reason,' lied Bonnie. 'See you, Mam.' And she clicked the receiver down without waiting for her mother's response, because she knew her mother would start asking questions, and Bonnie would have to admit she had read someone else's private letter.

Bonnie recalled the day she had reprimanded Jess and Ruby for talking to George and how rude he had been to her. Her jaw stiffened. The thought that the despicable sprog was working for the War Office was more than she could stand. Not only that, but she had told that dreadful Alice girl that she also worked for the War Office, something which George would be able to deny should their paths ever cross. She stared back down at the letter. How could a tiresome little oik like George Miller be working in such an important place whilst she spent her days looking through a pair of glorified binoculars? A thought crossed her mind. She had referred to George as a sprog, because that's how she saw him. She didn't know how old George was, but she guessed he couldn't be any older than her or Jess, which must have meant he'd joined up underage. A slow, malicious grin formed on her lips. She would report the lot of them! Then they'd all get chucked out for lying about their age when they first joined up. She pictured their faces as they were hauled before the authorities, stripped of their uniforms – if you could call a NAAFI girl's overalls a uniform – and sent packing. Oh, how she wished she could be a fly on the wall when that day came!

Back in his billet Tom had looked under his bed, in his locker, checked the pockets of every pair of trousers, jacket and shirt that he owned, then checked his locker again. He had spent the last ten minutes searching for Jess's letter, but it was nowhere to be seen. Sighing heavily, he headed back outside; he would have to retrace his steps to the last place he remembered having it. He walked the relatively short distance to the cookhouse, scouring the ground as he went, but there was still no sign of the damned thing. He checked by the fences, under the hedges and even asked the girls in the cookhouse if anything had been handed in.

Tutting to himself for being so negligent, he decided someone must have discovered it and thrown it in the bin – either that or a gust of wind must have picked it up and blown it away. It was a good job he had read it first, or he would have had to confess to Jess that he had been less than careful with her letter.

Chapter Seven

23 December 1941

Jess looked up the road to see if she could see Swanny, but there wasn't a soul in sight, unless you counted the people who had twitched their curtains aside as the girls climbed off the bus in the small Welsh village of Llanfachraeth.

Squealing, Ruby nudged Jess frantically as she pointed to a pony and trap trotting down a side road, the driver of which was waving merrily at them.

Swanny pulled the pony to a halt and smiled down at the girls. 'Well,' he indicated the pony with one hand, 'what do you think?'

'I think he's marvellous!' said Ruby, who was patting the pony's neck. 'Is he yours?'

Swanny nodded. 'We've got a few horses, but Munch is the only pony.'

'Why'd you call him Munch?' said Jess, stroking the pony's velvety muzzle.

He grinned. 'Cassie said he reminded her of one of those Munchkins in *The Wizard of Oz*, 'cos he's so much smaller than the carthorses.'

'Well, I think he's adorable!' cooed Ruby.

'That's what Penny said ...' Swanny began.

Jess interrupted excitedly. 'She's here?'

He nodded. 'She and Toby arrived first thing this morning.'

'Excellent,' Jess said as she came around the side of the cart. 'I can't wait to meet him, although if some interfering do-gooder had their way, we might none of us be here.'

Swanny's face clouded over. 'George told me about that and I think it's ridiculous. Someone's obviously got far too much time on their hands if they can start checking the age of everyone who joined up since the war began.' He shook his head. 'I'd have thought the army had better things to do with their time.'

Ruby placed a comforting hand on his arm. 'Let's hope that what goes around comes around, and they get their just deserts.'

He waited until the girls were sitting either side of him on the seat before clicking his tongue and instructing the pony to 'walk on'. 'They don't realise the trouble they cause, these interfering busybodies,' he muttered. 'Luckily for you and Jess, the NAAFI were happy enough to turn a blind eye, but if anything ever happens to our George ...' He fell silent, his face like thunder.

Ruby glanced at Jess, who smiled. After leaving the forces Swanny had made it his business to take on a fatherly role as far as George was concerned, even going so far as to say that if George were any younger, he and Cassie would have gone down the adoption route.

As Munch trotted along the quaint country lane, Jess admired a long, low stone cottage with small, deep-set windows. Having only ever lived in cities, she was used to seeing grand buildings, or row upon row of terraced houses, but Anglesey was like a breath of fresh air. When they'd crossed the Menai Bridge, Ruby had pointed at a small white cottage which stood in the middle of the straits.

'Surely no one lives in that? It's in the middle of the sea!' she had exclaimed.

The man driving the bus had laughed. 'They certainly do, that's what they call Whitebait Island.'

'How on earth do they get there?' said Ruby, straining her neck to look back at the house.

'Boat,' the driver replied simply.

Now, as they trotted along the narrow lane, Jess breathed in the sea air. It seemed a lot fresher here than it had done in Seaforth. 'You're ever so lucky living here,' she said absent-mindedly.

Grinning, Swanny tapped his wooden leg with his fist. 'Not sure I'd agree with you entirely on that one ...'

'Swanny!' Jess began apologetically. 'Me and my big mouth, I wasn't thinking!'

'Not to worry. I know you didn't mean anything by it, and let's face it, I could've lost a lot more than my leg,' he laughed without mirth, 'although if I'd thought I was going to get injured anywhere I would have assumed it would be on the battlefields.'

Ruby pulled a face. 'That's what worries me about George being ...' she waved her hands in the air '... wherever he is. I know it was dangerous in London, what with all the bombing, but it must be much worse overseas.'

Swanny stared at the road ahead. 'Cassie's done us a nice bit of scouse for tea.'

Jess looked at Ruby, who was nodding slowly; they both recognised a change of subject when they heard it. 'I like scouse, it's my favourite.'

They spent the rest of the journey talking about anything but the war. George told the girls all about the farm, the cows, hens, horses and sheep which he looked after, and it wasn't too long before Munch was trotting through the farm gate which Swanny had left open. He directed the pony to a small row of stables which stood adjacent to the farm cottage.

Waiting for Ruby to get down from the trap, Swanny asked Jess when Tom would be arriving.

'Later on today,' said Jess. She looked around the stables, hoping to see some of the other animals Swanny had mentioned, but they all appeared to be empty. 'He said not to worry about picking him up because he's got a friend stationed in RAF Valley, and they've offered to bring him to the farm.' She watched Swanny descend from the trap far more easily than she had anticipated he would, before pulling out a crutch from underneath the bench they had been sitting on.

Cassie appeared in a doorway in the side of the cottage. 'Hello, girls! I don't suppose any of you saw Penny and Toby on your travels?'

Swanny shook his head. 'Not a dickie bird. Should we have?'

'Not sure. They said they were going to go for a stroll,' Cassie came over to help Swanny unhook

Munch from his traces, 'but they didn't say which way they were going. I hope they don't get lost.' She briefly hugged Jess and Ruby, before helping her husband to untack the pony. 'Did you have a good journey?'

'Yes,' said Ruby. 'Munch was the best part. I must say, Cassie, I really envy you living in such a beautiful part of the country. Is all this yours?'

Cassie nodded. 'I grew up on this farm, my nain and taid brought me here when my mam died.' Seeing the look of sympathy on the girls' faces, she continued, 'I was too little to remember what she was like. My father couldn't cope, so Nain and Taid took me in.'

'Do you ever see your father?' said Ruby, who had not seen her own father since running away from Greystones, although he wrote as often as he could.

Cassie helped Swanny, his crutch under his arm, to wheel the cart over to the side of the stable. 'No, he moved to Australia a few years after Mam died to make a new start. He's doing quite well by all accounts; he writes but I've not seen him in years.'

Taking Munch by his bridle, Swanny started to lead the pony away, calling over his shoulder to Cassie, 'You take the girls inside and get them by the fire and I'll turn Munch out.'

'I think he's surprised himself with how well he's coping with his wooden leg,' Cassie said as she watched her husband, using his crutch for support and leading the pony towards the paddock.

Ruby nodded fervently. 'He's certainly surprised me. I envisaged all sorts of awful scenarios, but apart from a stiff gait and his crutch, you'd not know anything was wrong.'

Cassie smiled proudly. 'He's been determined to get back to the way he was before the accident, so he does everything on the farm – and I mean everything, from milking the cows to ploughing the fields. He's a real marvel.' She turned to go inside. 'Come on in so I can show you around. Swanny's done a lot of work to the inside of the house – my nain rather let the place go after Taid died.'

Jess followed Cassie and Ruby, making sure she heeded Cassie's instruction to 'mind her head' as they passed through the low-slung door into the kitchen. Once inside she stared open-mouthed around the large room.

'It's beautiful, Cassie!' she said, looking at the substantial range which stood in the chimney breast. Her gaze travelled admiringly around the room. On the wall furthest away from them stood a broad Welsh dresser next to a white Belfast sink, but pride of place was given to the large oak table which was positioned in the middle of the room, surrounded by a mishmash of chairs and stools. Jess pointed to the pans hanging by hooks from the beam above the range. 'They're like the ones we use in the NAAFI.'

The door behind them opened abruptly, startling the women. 'Hello, princess.' Turning, they saw Tom beaming broadly at them. He nodded a greeting. 'Ruby, Cassie.'

Dropping her borrowed suitcase on the red-tiled floor Jess ran over to Tom and wrapped her arms around him. 'Tom! I thought you weren't arriving until later this afternoon.'

He gave her a swift peck on the lips. 'I decided to travel up last night so that I could spend a bit of time with my pal in RAF Valley,' he winked conspiratorially, 'and maybe pick up a prezzie or two en route.'

Their first Christmas as friends Tom had made her a necklace out of blue beads, and last year he had bought her some scented soap. She was intrigued to know what he had done this year and was eager to show him the handkerchief she had embroidered with his initials in red and blue cotton.

Cassie jerked her head in the direction of the stairs. 'Come on, Tom, you may as well come up, as you and Toby are sharing the room opposite the girls.'

Jess and Ruby were as impressed with their room as they had been with the rest of the farm. The wooden furniture was old but sturdy, and the three beds reminded Jess of the tale of Goldilocks and the three bears. She said as much to Ruby, who laughed.

'I know what you mean.' She smoothed the patchwork quilt which covered her mattress. 'These quilts are beautifully made. I wonder if her grandma made them.'

'You mean her nain?' corrected Jess. She had to kneel on the floor to look out of the window, which was set low in the wall. She could see Penny and Toby, who had entered the farmyard and were now talking to Swanny.

She called over her shoulder to Ruby. 'Penny and Toby have come back, are you coming to say hello?'

'Of course,' said Ruby, who had been putting her clothes away in the top drawer of the dresser.

Jess went onto the landing and knocked on Tom's door. 'Are you ready?'

In answer Tom appeared in the doorway, only instead of wearing his uniform, which, now she came to think of it, was the only thing she had ever seen him in, he was wearing a pair of fawn coloured corduroy slacks, a matching waistcoat and a checked shirt. 'Blimey, you look like the lord of the manor in that get-up!' said Jess, impressed with his appearance.

Tom gave her a broad smile. 'Glad you approve!'

Ruby appeared behind Jess. 'Tom! You look so different without your cap and uniform, I hardly recognised you.'

Tom adjusted his waistcoat. 'I've always thought I looked better in my uniform.'

Jess smiled up at him, thinking about her gift to him and how well the colours would match his shirt. 'I think you look very smart in both.' Turning, she headed down the stairs.

They piled into the kitchen, and Jess immediately enveloped Penny in a warm embrace before holding a hand out to Toby.

'Hello, Toby, I'm Jess.'

He pumped her hand enthusiastically. 'Good God, what're you doing here?'

Jess gave him a rather confused look. 'Sorry?'

Toby grinned. 'We met a few months ago, don't you remember?'

Jess shook her head a little uncertainly. 'Sorry, I don't think so.'

He shrugged. 'Not to worry, it was only briefly. I forget which station it was – I wasn't there long.'

Jess smiled kindly. 'Sorry, Toby, you've got me mixed up with someone else.'

He cast a scrutinising eye over her form, then shrugged. 'Sorry, you see so many people in our line of work, I must have mistaken you for someone else.'

Tom came forward and held out his hand. 'Hello, Toby, I'm Tom. Penny tells us you're a driver?'

'I certainly am. One of the best jobs in the forces in my opinion,' Toby boasted, "cos you get to travel all over and meet lots of different people – that's how I met Penny here.' He gave her a cheeky wink. 'Luckily for me she wasn't cooking that day, otherwise I might have thought twice.'

Penny gave him a playful swipe. 'Cheeky blighter, there's nowt wrong with my cooking.'

He grinned. 'Not if you've got a strong stomach.'

Penny rolled her eyes. 'I only got the sugar and salt mixed up once …'

'I thought them fairy cakes were lovely. Salty, but lovely.'

'Told you,' Ruby muttered to Jess, 'those two are a match made in heaven.'

'I see what you mean,' Jess agreed. Slipping her fingers through Tom's, she gestured out the window to the farm-yard. 'Do you fancy going for a walk around the farm?'

Tom nodded and looked at Swanny. 'I don't suppose you've any spare wellies we could borrow?'

Swanny looked pointedly at his wooden leg before bursting into laughter. 'Only joshing. Course we do, come with me.'

Tom clapped a hand to his forehead as he followed Swanny into the parlour. 'Trust me!'

'Don't worry about it,' said Jess as she joined them, 'I've already told him how lucky he is to be here.'

Swanny pointed to where there were boots and wellingtons lined up in various sizes. 'Have a good root and see if you can find something to fit you.'

Jess and Tom began searching through the boots, and after a few false starts they came out with a stout pair of boots for Tom, and a pair of mid-calf wellingtons for Jess.

Once they were wrapped up in coats and scarves, they headed outside towards the corner paddock where Swanny said they might find the workhorses.

She took Tom's hand in hers. 'Have you spoken to your mam and dad lately?'

Tom nodded. 'Mam was sad that we were spending Christmas with Swanny and Cassie, instead of going home.'

'Oh dear, was she dreadfully upset?'

Tom shrugged. 'I suppose I knew she'd be disappointed, but I didn't fancy spending Christmas Day with Auntie Edna, knowing what she'd said to you.'

Jess shook her head. 'You mustn't let her keep you from your family, Tom.'

He squeezed her hand. 'She's not. I consider you to be a big part of my family.'

She smiled up at him. 'Do you think it'd be better to tell your auntie that you know what she said, to clear the air?'

He rubbed a hand across his chin. 'Possibly, but not at Christmas, it wouldn't be fair to Mam and Dad.'

Jess looked up as large flakes of snow began to fall. 'I bet this place looks even more beautiful in the snow,' she said as they walked along the fence line.

Tom murmured an agreement. 'We're lucky to have friends like Cassie and Swanny. Most people I know are spending Christmas in their billets.'

Jess withdrew her arm from his and leaned against the top rail of the fence, as the larger of the two skewbald horses looked up curiously. Slowly it ambled over to her and tried to nuzzle her hand.

'He's after food,' Tom said knowledgeably. 'Our milkman's got a horse like this 'un, and that's what he does when he's after treats.'

Jess looked around her, but there was nothing but grass. Ripping some up, she held it out in her fist, until Tom told her to lay her fingers flat.

He held his hand out palm side up by way of demonstration. 'If you hold your hand like this they can't bite you by accident.'

Jess did as he instructed and the horse gently snuffled the grass from her outstretched palm, causing her to gasp with delight. 'He's so gentle, Tom,' she said, pulling up more grass.

'They certainly are,' he agreed.

Jess continued to feed the horse until it wandered away to join the others. Leaning back against the fence, she admired the cottage. 'I've never really thought about what I want to do when the war's over, but being here, I wouldn't mind trying my hand at farming, or something similar.'

Tom placed his arm around her shoulders. 'I always assumed you'd work in a café, bit like you do now.'

She looked up at him. 'What about you?'

Tom rubbed his chin thoughtfully. 'I've not really thought about it.' He jerked his head in the direction of the cottage. 'I can understand why you think it might be nice to run a farm, though, especially somewhere as peaceful and idyllic as this,' he hesitated. 'What did you make of Toby?'

'He's a better match than Donald ever was, and he's certainly not shy. Why, what did you make of him?'

Tom shrugged. 'He's quite forward, and he wasn't the least bit embarrassed when he realised he'd mistaken you for someone else.'

Jess nodded. 'Just the sort of chap for Penny.' She straightened up. 'Come on, let's head back to the warm.'

They arrived back in the kitchen to find Cassie doling the scouse onto an array of different plates. She looked up as they entered. 'Aha! Well timed.'

The first few days at the farm flew by, and before they knew it, they were celebrating Jess's birthday on Christmas Eve by attending a carol service in the tiny little stone church at the end of the lane which led to the farm. As the service came to an end, the choir surprised Jess by singing 'Happy Birthday' to her in both Welsh and English. Walking through the thick snow back to the farm, she cuddled up to Tom who wrapped his arms around her.

He kissed the top of her head. 'Happy?'

She nodded. 'Very.'

Entering the farm kitchen, everyone began removing coats, wellies, hats, scarves and mittens before making a beeline towards the fire in the parlour.

Cassie called through from the kitchen. 'Anyone for cocoa?'

A chorus of 'yes, please' came from the parlour.

With all chairs taken, Jess sat on Tom's knee. Leaning her head against his chest, she watched the flames dance merrily in the hearth. She took the proffered mug of cocoa when Cassie brought it through some ten minutes or so later and gently sipped the contents as Tom stroked the top of her hair in an absent-minded fashion.

Jess wished the moment could last forever, but it wasn't too long before the girls were making their way to bed and suggesting Jess do the same. She placed her empty mug on the table and kissed Tom goodnight before heading up the stairs. It seemed as though she had barely closed her eyes before Ruby was gently shaking her awake and wishing her a Merry Christmas.

In order to get the chores finished as quickly as possible, Jess offered to take hay to the horses' field. Once she was there she broke the film of ice which had formed on the surface of the trough so that they might get to the water beneath.

Ruby had stayed in the kitchen to help Cassie prepare the breakfast, and Penny and Toby fed the chickens whilst Tom helped Swanny see to the cattle.

The snow which had started to fall during the previous night was now lying thick on the ground, and the sunlight sparkled off it, making it look as though the whole place was covered in a dusting of diamonds.

With the animals fed, watered and milked, the workers returned to the smell of bacon and sausages being fried in the kitchen.

Jess's nostrils flared as she shook the snow from her boots. 'We fry a lot of bacon in the NAAFI, but it never smells as good as this.'

Cassie beamed. 'That's because you've been outside in the freezing cold. Food always smells and tastes better after a hard morning's work on the farm.'

Toby rubbed his stomach hungrily. 'Like them crumpets you did yesterday, hot and buttery – that's what I call proper grub!' He eyed her hopefully. 'Are you going to do some more of them after we've done seeing to the animals later on?'

Penny rolled her eyes. 'Honestly, Toby, you've not had your breakfast, and you're already thinking about what you're going to eat tonight.'

Cassie tipped the bacon out onto a plate which she placed in the middle of the table, along with mushrooms, black pudding, sausages, toast and fried mashed potato left over from the night before. 'Tuck in!'

Swanny, Tom and Toby took their places at the table before the girls had a chance to decide where they wanted to sit.

'Blimey, I bet you're not this eager when it comes to doing the dishes!' smiled Cassie, as the men began to fill their plates.

When breakfast was over, the girls began the job of clearing the table and doing the dishes whilst the men went into the parlour for a game of cards.

'I wonder what Bonnie and McKinley are doing right now?' mused Jess as she took a plate from Ruby and began to wipe it dry.

Ruby wiped her forehead with the back of her hand. 'If we're to believe Bonnie, she's rubbing shoulders with the bigwigs in the War Office, so I daresay she'll be dining out on caviar and foie gras, whatever that is.'

Tom came back into the kitchen to look for a box of matches to use in their game of cribbage. 'Who's this?'

Ruby giggled. 'Honestly! I think you men are worse than women when it comes to gossip!'

'We're talking about Bonnie from Greystones,' said Jess. 'Alice bumped into her when she was joining up and Bonnie spun her a yarn about how she was working on secret business in the War Office.'

Tom picked up a piece of fried mashed potato which someone had missed and popped it into his mouth. 'We've got a Bonnie in our battery.'

Jess shrugged her indifference. 'Well, it won't be our Bonnie, because she's *far* too important to work in a battery.'

Ruby looked quizzically at Penny who was returning the condiments to the pantry. 'Did Alice say if Bonnie had mentioned her mother?'

Penny shook her head. 'Nope, Alice said Bonnie wasn't in the mood to chat. In fact, she couldn't wait to get away from her.'

'That's 'cos she was telling porkies and was worried Alice would catch her out if she kept talking,' said Jess knowingly.

'Well,' said Penny as she brought over some more cutlery, 'whatever the McKinleys are doing it won't affect us.'

Tom's head snapped up. 'Did you say McKinley?'

Penny nodded. 'That's right.' She registered the look on Tom's face. 'It can't be ...'

Tom nodded slowly. 'The girl in my battery is called Bonnie McKinley.'

'No!' chorused Jess, Ruby and Penny.

He nodded. 'I'm sure I mentioned I was training a couple of girls from Glasgow in my last letter ...'

Jess's mouth hung open. 'You did, I just never imagined it would be anyone we knew.'

Penny stifled a giggle. 'War Office my eye! You wait 'til I tell Alice – she'll have a real hoot.'

Jess eyed Tom with intrigue. 'How do you get on with her?'

'She's not been with us long, but she's already proving to be very bossy. She likes to take charge of the other girls and tell them what to do, even though she's no authority to do so.' He shrugged. 'She's ruffled a few feathers, but she's been told over and over she has to work as part of a team, and if she doesn't she'll have to go back to basic training and start again.'

Jess shook her head. 'That's her to a T. She used to be the same with us.'

Ruby emptied the water out of the sink. 'Has she started hitting people with pokers yet?'

Tom looked shocked. 'What?'

'That's what she did to me, in order to get me up one morning,' said Jess plainly. 'She made out that she was aiming to hit the bedpost and had cracked me across the shins by accident, but she knew full well what she was doing.'

Tom shook his head. 'If she starts any of that in the ATS she'll soon get the heave-ho.'

Jess gathered the cutlery from the draining board in her tea towel. 'Well, whatever Bonnie does, it's nothing to do with us any more, and I for one am not going to waste my time talking about her or her mam,' she smiled up at Tom, 'especially not when I've not even had my prezzie yet!'

Taking the hint, Tom disappeared momentarily before reappearing with an oblong package which he handed to Jess, who carefully untied the string and pulled the paper off. She marvelled at the photo frame which Tom had decorated with seashells, all of which, he informed her, he had gathered from the beach by the RAF base in Valley.

'I thought we could have someone take our photograph and you could keep it in this,' he said.

'You never cease to surprise me, Tom. It's beautiful,' breathed Jess as she gently ran her finger over the shells.

She pulled his gift from her skirt pocket and handed it to him. 'I'm afraid mine's nowhere near as grand.'

Tom pulled the handkerchief from its wrapping and fingered the stitching. He looked up, a broad smile etched across his face. 'It's perfect, and your embroidery is so neat.' He held it up against his checked shirt. 'And it matches.'

Jess beamed. 'I'm so glad you like it.'

They headed to join the others in the parlour. It didn't matter to her if beastly Bonnie was in Tom's battery, because there was nothing the other girl could do to spoil Jess's life, not any more.

March 1942
Tom looked up from his food as his sergeant strutted towards him. 'Sarge?'

322

The sergeant sat down on the chair opposite Tom's and passed the paperwork over.

Tom examined the papers briefly then looked up. 'Doesn't surprise me. I know a few people who've had their age questioned recently. I'm surprised they've decided to take her out of the process, though – according to this she's only a month away from being eighteen.' He passed the papers back.

The sergeant shrugged. 'It was her own silly fault. She should've kept it buttoned – if she had I daresay they wouldn't have looked at her twice.'

Tom gave him a confused look. 'Surely she wasn't stupid enough to tell them she'd signed up before she was eighteen.'

The sergeant shook his head. 'She didn't grass herself up, she's not that daft, but she blew the whistle on an old pal of hers, gawd only knows why, but you know what women can be like!'

Tom nodded in a discerning manner. Having worked with several groups of women, he knew some of them could be catty, bitchy and downright vindictive if things weren't going their way, and he'd heard first-hand from Jess and Ruby how spiteful Bonnie could be.

The sergeant continued. 'Of course, the authorities wanted to know how she had so much information, and she was daft enough to admit she'd known him all her life. Well, it doesn't take a genius to put two and two together, so they did a bit of digging and sure as eggs is eggs, discovered that she was also underage.' He tutted under his breath. 'Silly mare.'

Tom shrugged. 'You said "him". Is it anyone we know?'

The sergeant placed the papers on the table. 'Nah, it was some feller she knew from Glasgow.' He shrugged in a disinterested fashion. 'He probably turned her down – you know what they say, hell hath no fury ...' He wrinkled his nose in distaste. 'I reckon it's probably a good job they found out what she was like. We can't have troublemakers working in a battery – goodness only knows what she'd do if she fell out with one of the girls!' He looked up at Tom. 'Better to get rid now, before she causes trouble in the ranks.'

Tom nodded slowly. Could it be a coincidence? He shook his head dismissively. It had to be; Bonnie hadn't a clue that George was in the army. He thrummed his fingers against the melamine tabletop.

The sergeant stood up. 'You'll be getting a new recruit in a day or so.'

Tom nodded and watched the other man walk away. He was certain he had never mentioned Jess, Ruby or George to anyone, least of all Bonnie – he hardly knew the girl – on the other hand, she *had* grassed someone up. He glanced up at the sergeant who was just about to exit the cookhouse. 'Wait!' The sergeant held the door ajar with his foot as he waited for Tom to catch up. 'Has she left yet?'

The sergeant looked in the direction of the WAAFs' billet. 'I wouldn't have thought so. She's been demoted to kitchen staff in the cookhouse, so technically she's not going anywhere.'

Thanking him, Tom headed for the WAAFs' billet. He was about to knock on the door when he caught sight of Bonnie heading for the ablutions. He called out to her.

Bonnie turned, her eyes narrowing as she focused on Tom. 'What?' she snapped irritably.

Tom jogged over. 'I've just spoken to Sarge, and he told me you're ... remustering?'

Bonnie shot him a withering glance. 'And?'

Tom's eyes narrowed. She might not be in his battery any more but she was still lower than him in rank. Folding his arms he glared stiffly at her. 'And I want to know why.'

She stared back at him levelly. If Tom knew she'd been demoted there wasn't a doubt in her mind that he knew why, so he must have suspicions that it was she who had blown the whistle on George, not that she was about to admit it. She decided to play him at his own game. 'Because I don't turn eighteen for another three weeks, which is ridiculous if you ask me.'

Tom stared at her. She was trying to portray innocence, but he could see the malicious glint in her eye. If he allowed her to, she would toy with him like a cat with a mouse, so he decided to cut to the chase. 'Why did you grass George up?'

She feigned innocent surprise. 'Who's George ...?'

Tom cut her off before she could insult his intelligence any further. 'You know damned well who George is, and I'd wager it was you who tried to get Jess and Ruby into trouble as well.'

Bored with her games, she glared at him with disapproval. 'So what if I did? I didn't do anything wrong. It's not as if I lied about his age – he did that.'

Tom stared at her in disbelief. 'So did you!'

Bonnie stared at him open-mouthed as she tried to come up with a suitable retort. With nothing springing to mind, she placed her hand on the door to the ablutions, ready to walk off, but Tom was too quick for her. He darted between her and the door. 'Come on! Tell me what's really going on here. You didn't grass him up because he was underage, so what made you do such a spiteful thing?'

Bonnie pouted sullenly. 'Wasn't being spiteful, I done it for his own good.' She gave this a moment's contemplation before adding, 'If you ask me, I done him a favour. At least he's out the army now,'

'A favour?' echoed Tom. 'You do know they've sent him to fight on the front and he's only seventeen?'

Bonnie gaped at him. 'Don't be ridiculous,' she stammered, completely forgetting that she was talking to someone who was her superior. 'They wouldn't send him to fight, he's too young, they'll have sent him ...'

His jaw flinched as an angry flush swept his features. 'Home?' spat Tom. His face was only a few inches from hers and Bonnie could see the fury in his eyes. 'You know damn well he hasn't got a home to go to, but that's not why they've chosen to send him overseas. They've done that because they don't like being lied to!'

Bonnie's throat had gone dry. People were beginning to stare. She hadn't meant for George to be sent overseas. She'd thought the army would expel him – Ruby and Jess, too, come to that. How on earth was she meant to know they would choose a different tack? She said as much to Tom who flung his hands up in exasperation.

'I knew you'd grassed them up as well, and whilst I can understand you dobbing Jess and Ruby in, I can't fathom why you'd do the same to George.'

Bonnie stamped her foot angrily. 'Because he was mean to me, called me names!'

Tom stared at her, scarcely able to believe his ears. 'How old were you when he did this?'

She sniffed haughtily and gave a half-shrug. 'I dunno, eleven, twelve?'

'He was just a kid …' said Tom, the words leaving his lips in a whisper. He locked eyes with hers. 'You sent some feller off to face the enemy's guns 'cos of something he said when he was a kid?'

Bonnie shook her head fervently. 'Not just that, it was him who was hiding them in that old house on Edinburgh Road …' Her voice trailed off as realisation dawned; she clapped a hand to her forehead. 'What right have you to judge me? You knew all along that they were underage, you must've done, because they were writing to you, and that's when I realised that it *was* the old house they hid in on Edinburgh Road.' She pursed her lips. 'Don't try telling me it's a coincidence, because I've still got that letter.'

Tom frowned. What on earth was she on about? He'd not had a letter from George, and the last one he'd had from Jess … his eyes narrowed. 'You stole my letter!'

She shook her head. 'No, I didn't, I found it outside the cookhouse. I only read it because I wanted to give it back to the correct recipient …' She stopped speaking as Tom's hand slammed on the door frame to the ablutions.

'You had to read the whole letter in order to do that, did you?' His lip curled.

Swallowing, Bonnie's eyes darted in the direction of the Sergeants' Mess. She licked her lips. 'I'll tell, I've still got the letter …'

327

Tom followed the direction of her gaze. He wondered how much trouble he would be in if they discovered that he had hidden two girls in his aunt's house and kept quiet about their joining up underage. He reasoned it wouldn't be too big a deal, until he remembered George. Now that was a different kettle of fish, not that he was about to admit it to Bonnie. He looked at her. Her face was clouded with uncertainty, so he decided to call her bluff. 'I never met George, so he has nothing to do with me, and whilst I admit I did allow the girls to stay in my auntie's house, that's where it ends.' He eyed her coolly. 'I have no idea what the joining age is for the NAAFI, although I'd wager it's not the same as the forces.' Feeling as though he was on more solid ground, he continued, 'That's why the NAAFI never reprimanded them, so despite your interference, they're still there.'

Bonnie's face fell when she heard that nothing had happened to the girls. 'That's not fair. Why am I the one being punished? They're nigh on the same age as me!'

Tom lowered his arm, adjusted the cuff and gave her an icy glare. 'Because they joined up underage, nothing else, but you ...' his jaw flexed '... you went out of your way to blow the whistle on them, and for no other reason than jealousy!' He wagged his finger under her nose. 'The army don't tolerate that kind of behaviour; you can't take someone into battle who is sneaky and untrustworthy.' He turned to leave then changed his mind. 'If anything happens to that boy, you'll have his blood on your hands for the rest of your life.' Turning on his heel he left before his temper got the better of him.

Bonnie burst into tears as he left. 'Wait! Please!'

He wanted to ignore her pleas and get as far away from her as possible, but he recalled the look on her face when she'd heard that George had been sent overseas. She had appeared genuinely shocked, and no matter how stupid her reasons, he believed her intention had not been to send George into battle. Sighing, he shoved his hands in his pockets and waited for her to catch up.

'I'm sorry,' she said between sobs, 'I'd never do that to any of them. I just wanted them to know how it felt to be excluded.'

Tom furrowed his brow in incomprehension. 'They already know – they were orphans, don't forget. At least you had a mother.'

Bonnie wiped the tears from her cheeks. 'I know that, and I do realise I was lucky compared to them, but that doesn't mean to say I was happy. They all had each other, whereas I was always the odd one out. I knew they didn't like me and there weren't any more staff with kids what lived in Greystones, so I couldn't tell anyone else how I felt.' She placed her hand on Tom's elbow as he shook his head in frustration. 'I know it's silly, but I was a kid, we all were, only I blamed them for my situation. I was jealous, you were right, but please believe me when I say I never thought for one moment that they would send George overseas. Had I known that I'd never have opened my stupid mouth.'

Tom glared defiantly at her, before his expression softened slightly. 'Only it's not me that you need to apologise to.'

Bonnie hung her head in shame, tearstains streaking her cheeks. 'I know, but I don't know how to get in touch with George and I daresay he wouldn't speak to me even if I did.' Sniffing loudly, she looked at Tom appealingly. 'Could you tell him for me?' She hesitated before adding, 'And Jess and Ruby, of course.'

Tom stared at her as he weighed up his options. 'I'm going to telephone Jess's NAAFI now, so that I can tell her what's happened.' He flushed, because he knew he would have to admit to Jess that he had been careless with her letter, something she would doubtless not appreciate. He glanced at Bonnie. 'Why don't you come with me and tell her yourself?'

Bonnie shook her head. 'If I'm going to say anything to Jess, it'll be face to face. I at least owe her that much.'

Leaving Bonnie behind, Tom headed into the NAAFI, picked up the receiver and dialled the Normanton number. He waited for the woman who had answered the telephone to fetch Jess and after a few moments he heard her voice come down the receiver.

'Hello, Tom! This is a nice surprise! How's tricks?' said Jess, her tone light-hearted.

Tom swallowed, then explained about misplacing the letter and the events that had unfolded as a result of him losing it.

There was a long silence before Jess eventually spoke slowly.

'I appreciate that Bonnie's sorry she opened her big mouth, but I'm afraid it's a case of too little too late.

330

George is at the front, and no amount of apologising will bring him back.'

'I know,' Tom leaned his arm against the wall, 'and it's my fault for not taking better care of your letter. It must have fallen out of my pocket.'

'Hardly your fault Bonnie picked it up and decided to use it as a weapon,' Jess said. 'If anyone else had found your letter, even if they'd read it, they'd have given it you back, not used it to score points ...'

Tom made to interrupt, but Jess continued, 'No, Tom. I understand that Bonnie's sorry now, but she should never have been so spiteful. It sounds like she tried to blame me, Ruby and George for her own miserable existence, but I wasn't the one whacking people with a poker, nor telling them to eat porridge off the floor, so even if she did feel that no one liked her, it was hardly surprising.'

'That's as maybe,' said Tom, 'but she was only a kid at the time ...' He got no further.

'Are you standing up for her?' Jess continued without waiting for a response, 'After everything she's done, you're actually making excuses for her and taking her side. How could you? Especially when George is in danger.'

Tom's mouth hung open. That wasn't what he was saying at all, he'd merely been trying to explain that Bonnie was bitterly sorry for her childish actions. 'I never said that!' he spluttered. 'I know it's Bonnie's fault, of course it is, I'm just saying ...'

'Well, don't,' snapped Jess. There was an audible pause followed by the sound of Jess sighing. 'Sorry, Tom, I didn't mean to shout, it's just so frustrating to hear this over the phone with no means of confronting Bonnie. I daresay if I'd had the chance to speak to her in the same way you have I might feel differently.' Although I very much doubt it, she added in the privacy of her own mind.

Tom breathed a sigh of relief. 'I've been a bit unfair, Jess, because truth be known I tore a couple of strips off Bonnie before I cooled down.'

He could hear her smiling as she replied. 'I wish I'd been there to see her face.'

Tom's cheeks flushed. In truth he felt guilty about his angry response – he was pretty sure he'd frightened Bonnie, and his mother had always taught him that a woman should never be in fear of a man.

'Whilst I've got you on the phone, I may as well tell you about my new billet,' said Jess, unaware of Tom's secret shame.

'Oh?' he said, hope rising in his voice. 'Any closer to me?'

'Afraid not. It's somewhere down south ...' he heard her call over her shoulder to Ruby before turning back to the receiver. 'Bath, ever heard of it?'

Tom grinned. 'Cheeky! I'll have you know I bathe regularly.'

'Oh, ha ha,' said Jess, her tone heavy with sarcasm. 'I meant the city!'

'I was only pulling your leg, of course I've heard of it. What sort of site is it? RAF, ATS ...'

'It's a barrage balloon site,' said Jess excitedly, 'so very different to what we're used to.'

'We?' said Tom.

'Yes, myself, Ruby and Penny, who doesn't like being on her own in Seaforth so asked if she could tag along and they said yes,' said Jess. 'We'll be going in the next month or so, and according to one of the girls in our NAAFI we'll be moving from site to site once we're down that neck of the woods. She said it's something to do with the war moving things up a gear, whatever that means.'

'It just means things are progressing at quite a speed so everything else is constantly changing to keep up.' He twisted the phone cord around his index finger. 'You'll be further away from me than ever down there.'

'You can always come and visit,' said Jess pleasantly. 'I can show you round. Toby told Penny there's some ancient Roman baths, and an abbey to visit.'

'I shall look forward to it,' said Tom, trying not to sound too glum. The sound of the operator calling the conversation to an end came down the line, and they both reluctantly said their goodbyes. Hearing the receiver click down on Jess's end of the line, Tom did the same, reflecting as he did so that it would be a long time before he saw her again, and it was lucky for him that she hadn't held him even partly responsible for Bonnie finding the letter, even if he did so himself. Still, it was a lesson learned, and a mistake he would make sure he never made again.

November 1942
Since leaving Normanton the girls had served on a variety of stations, which, as Penny pointed out, was

nice for them as they had only ever served in army NAAFIs up until that point.

'Not that it makes a tremendous difference whether it's RAF, WAAF or ATS,' said Ruby as the lorry bumped its way down the lane strewn with potholes. 'Can't you slow down?' she yelled, as her bottom left the wooden seat only to be reunited with a thud.

'He can't hear you!' bawled Jess. 'Do what me and Penny do, push your bottom down and hold on tight.'

'You'd think it wouldn't hurt so much with all my padding,' muttered Ruby.

Jess and Penny exchanged glances. Ever since George's posting abroad their friend had found comfort in food and had already outgrown several overalls. 'I can't help myself,' she had confided in them when they were getting ready to go to a dance one evening. 'I get all twitchy and anxious if I've not got anything to do, and the first thing that comes to hand is food, especially in our line of work!'

'You're worried about George,' soothed Jess, 'it's hardly surprising under the circumstances.' She shook her head. 'If I could get my hands on that Bonnie ...'

Ruby, who had been breathing in while Penny struggled to close her zip, blew out noisily as Penny announced she was 'done'. 'I'll never forgive Bonnie for speaking out. Everything was fine until she opened her big gob.' She stared at her reflection in the mirror, then pulled a face. 'If I don't do something about my weight, he'll not recognise me when he comes home.'

Jess's tummy fluttered. Ruby had remained resolute that George would come home one day and wouldn't fall victim to the Germans, but Jess and Penny had found it hard to ignore the cold hard truth. They already knew four or five girls, if not more, who had lost their boyfriends during the course of the war, and even though they hoped and prayed that George would be an exception to the rule, they knew that he was young and inexperienced compared to a lot of his comrades. Not that they would ever share their doubts and fears with Ruby, of course – far from it. In front of their friend they oozed positive thoughts, even when they had found her sitting at the bottom of her bed, a telegram in her hands.

Spying the telegram, Jess's heart skipped a beat. She glanced briefly at Penny to see if she too had seen it, before addressing Ruby. Sitting down beside her friend she placed an arm around her shoulders. 'What've you got there, Rubes?' She glanced down at the telegram and saw that there were two large teardrops slowly soaking into the paper.

Ruby had sniffed and wiped her eyes with the back of her sleeve. 'I don't know, I'm too afraid to open it.'

Penny sank down in front of Ruby and placed her hands over her friend's. 'Do you want me or Jess to take a look?'

Ruby shook her head as another tear dropped onto the telegram. 'At this moment, George is still alive, because I've not been told any different,' she lifted the telegram an inch or so from her knee, 'but if we open this and it tells me otherwise, then I won't be able to pretend any more, and my life will change forever, so if you don't mind, I'd rather hold on to this moment for just a little longer.'

They had waited a while before Ruby had eventually opened the telegram. To their collective relief, it had been from Swanny and Cassie, but none of them had forgotten that awful moment when they thought the worst.

Now, with the lorry pulling to a halt outside the gate to the balloon site, Jess leaned out the back and peered into the blackness that surrounded them.

'What can you see?' asked Ruby, craning her neck.

'Sweet Fanny Adams,' said Jess. 'It's as black as a witch's hat out there.'

Ruby pouted. She had been looking forward to seeing the balloons up close again.

'Where are we again?' yawned Penny.

'Yeovil,' chorused Jess and Ruby.

'Although I'll forgive you for forgetting,' said Jess. 'We hardly have time to get used to one place before they're moving us on to the next.'

'I prefer it like this, though,' said Ruby. 'It makes life more exciting, and we've got to visit a lot of different places.'

'True, although I can't see much of this one at the moment,' said Penny, who had left her seat and was peering through the flap which hung from the top of the lorry.

The driver appeared suddenly, startling them.

'My heart!' wheezed Ruby. 'What are you trying to do, kill us?'

He looked affronted. 'Sorry, I was only coming to say you can get out now.'

Jess smiled at him as she climbed out of the lorry. 'Take no notice, we're all a bit tired.'

He pointed to a row of houses. 'You're in the middle one.'

Ruby looked up at him, half expecting him to say he was only joking. She spoke cautiously. 'You've got to be kidding! There's no way we're getting a house all to ourselves.' She craned her neck to see if she could see into the back. 'Go on, I bet there's a tent in the garden.'

He held his hands up in mock surrender. 'No joke, it's all yours. There's only going to be the three of you in there. The WAAFs were the last lot to use it.'

Penny glanced at her friends before making her way towards the house. 'First come, first served,' she called as she opened the front door and climbed the steps two at a time.

'Bugger!' cried Ruby as Jess tore past her. She turned to the corporal who was eyeing them with interest. 'We've had some pretty rotten billets lately, so rather than argue over the beds, some of which you wouldn't lay a dog on, we've used the "first come, first served" approach.' She shrugged indifferently. 'Oh well, looks like I've got the leftovers this time.'

She bade the driver goodnight and headed up the stairs where she found Jess and Penny sitting on what looked to be comfortable beds. 'Best ones yet!' said Jess. 'So don't worry, you've not missed out.'

Ruby plonked her bag onto one of the last two remaining beds. 'I guess this one is mine.' She yawned, causing Jess and Penny to do the same. They all giggled.

'Bed!' said Jess. 'We can worry about unpacking in the morning.'

24 December 1942

Jess's eyes snapped open as Ruby's voice called up the stairs. 'Happy birthday, Jess! Get yourself up and at 'em because the boys should be here soon, and I daresay you'll want to look your best for Tom.'

'Coming!' Jess called back. She swung her legs out of bed, and winced as her toes hit the cold floorboards. 'Blimey, have you seen any brass monkeys searching in the snow out there?'

Penny, who had come in to get an extra pair of socks, giggled. 'A lot more snow fell during the night, but Toby said they should be here in an hour or so.'

'An hour!' Jess opened the top drawer of the dresser and pulled out the scarf she was knitting as Tom's Christmas present. 'I'll have to get this done before he arrives.' She frowned at Penny. 'I thought they weren't coming until after lunch.'

Penny nodded. 'They left early because of the snow. Toby didn't fancy getting stuck on the tight lanes, you know how narrow some of them are. If the snow starts to drift he'll never get through.'

Jess pulled on the woolly socks that Penny had given her as an early birthday present and nodded at the jug of water which stood on top of the washstand. 'How's the water?'

Penny smiled. 'I haven't long been up, so it should still be warm.' She was halfway out of the room when she remembered something. 'Shall I tell Rubes to put some toast on?'

'Yes, please, two slices, no butter and ...'

'A dab of Marmite,' Penny finished as she went downstairs.

Jess padded over to the washbasin and wrung her flannel in the warm water, before gently smoothing it over her face and neck. She caught her reflection in the round shaving mirror which the girls had found in one of the sideboard drawers. She placed the flannel to one side and gathered her hair up to see what it would look like in a bun, before letting it fall loose around her shoulders. She smiled at her reflection. She was unrecognisable from the orphan who had run away from Greystones some three years earlier. Her face had filled out, and her hair, once boyish and short, fell over her shoulders in a cascade of glossy curls.

She glanced at the clock – ten minutes had already passed since Ruby called out, so she had best get a move on if she wanted to be ready before the boys arrived. She hastily got dressed in her slacks and a thick jumper, both of which she had got from the market in Bath, then, knitting in hand, she headed down the stairs. She entered the kitchen just as Ruby was placing her tea and toast on the table. She looked expectantly at Jess. 'And how's the birthday girl this morning?'

Jess grimaced. 'A bit rushed, considering I've got to finish Tom's scarf a lot quicker than I intended.' She grinned as Ruby placed a slim package on the table.

'Happy birthday, chuck,' said Ruby, kissing Jess briefly on the cheek.

Jess carefully opened the paper – it was always handy to keep the paper wrappings from presents as it was in such short supply – and pulled out a green beret which she placed over her curls. 'Thanks, Rubes, it's beautiful, and just what I need to help tame my curly

339

mop, and it'll go beautifully with the scarf you got me for Christmas last year!'

Ruby smiled. 'Glad you like it. I know you aren't keen on the wind blowing your hair into your face, so I thought this would be ideal.'

Jess carefully put the beret back into its wrappings and placed it on the sideboard, before returning to the kitchen table. 'It's more the "I've been pulled through a hedge backwards" look I'm not so keen on!'

Ruby tutted as she sat down next to Jess. 'Give over, you always look good. Even on a windy day your hair looks all sultry and glamorous – it's the rest of us that end up looking like pom-poms!'

Jess bit down into her toast. 'Have you heard from George?'

Ruby got up and brushed the crumbs off her hands before picking up an envelope from the sideboard, which she handed to Jess. 'It came this morning.'

Jess pulled out a picture of George, standing next to a group of men, all smiling. She examined the picture more closely and sighed. She hadn't seen George since Liverpool some two years earlier, yet judging by the image in this picture it looked more like ten.

She glanced up at Ruby. 'I'd stop worrying about George being a boy in battle,' she turned the picture round to face her friend, 'because he doesn't look like a boy in this picture.'

Ruby took the photo and nodded as she traced a finger over the outline of her beau. 'I know, and it sickens me to wonder what he might have been through to age him so.'

Jess proceeded to read the letter.

My Darling Ruby,

Can't say where I am for obvious reasons, but it's not as cold here as it is back home, or so I'm told. I wish I could be with you all for Christmas, it's probably the time of year I miss you the most. All the fun, the decorations, the dancing, not to mention the food! It's all right over here, and everyone tries to make the best of a bad situation, but they're right when they say that home is where the heart is. We've had some pretty strange things to eat since we've been here, and I think it's true to say that there's not a living thing on God's earth that isn't up for grabs as far as these chaps are concerned. Sarge has encouraged us to try and avoid eating off camp as he doesn't want us all coming down with the trots, although in the case of one of the chaps in our camp it was more like the gallops.

I've placed a photograph inside the envelope of me and some of the boys. I know you can't tell by the photo because it's in black and white, but I've got quite a good tan, something I've never had before, and I think I look a lot better for it.

I hope this business will be over soon, so that I can come home to you, and we can have ourselves a proper Christmas!

All my love, now and forever.

Yours affectionately as ever,

George xxxx

Jess looked up from the letter and smiled at Ruby. 'He seems happy enough, but I can't imagine where he is.'

Ruby shrugged. 'At first I couldn't either, but when I showed the letter to Penny she said she reckons he could be in Africa.'

'Africa!' said Jess, clearly impressed. 'He really is getting to travel the world.'

Ruby nodded. 'That's what makes this whole nightmare bearable, the thought that he's getting to follow his dreams, which is fine by me as long as he comes back safe and sound.'

'I must admit, I've been really worried about him because I was picturing the George we used to know, but *that* George,' Jess nodded at the picture in Ruby's fingers, 'isn't the one we used to know. *That* George has seen a bit of the world and lived a little, and you combine that with the George we used to know, the one who wasn't afraid to stand up to Father Blakely, and you've got a man who knows what's what.' She finished her breakfast and headed over to the sink with her plate. 'I'll do these quickly then carry on with Tom's scarf.' She dipped the plate into the hot water and used the dishcloth to wipe away the crumbs and Marmite, then held it out to Ruby who began to wipe it dry.

'He'll love that scarf,' said Ruby. 'It goes with that checked shirt of his. In fact, you've got quite a theme going there, one that could stand you in good stead for years, with matching gloves, hats, jumpers ...'

Jess pulled a face. 'I don't know about jumpers, or gloves come to that, although mittens mightn't be out of the question.' She picked up her knitting and pushed the empty needle into the first loop. 'Mrs Armstrong only taught me how to cast on and cast off, but I reckon as long as I'm only doing a scarf it should be simple. I should imagine jumpers with sleeves and such are a much more complicated affair.'

Ruby grinned. 'You could always knit him a woollen waistcoat – I bet that'd be a lot easier without the arms.'

Jess's brow rose slightly. 'One thing at a time, Ruby Anderson. I've not had the seal of approval for this yet.'

Ruby rolled her eyes. 'Tom'll love it because you made it.' She glanced around the kitchen. 'Are you stopping in here?'

Jess nodded. 'Why?'

'I thought I'd have a sweep and mop up before they arrive. Penny had to go to work for a few hours, so she won't be back until after lunch. I did offer to go instead of her but she said she'd rather be doing something than sitting around waiting.'

Jess grinned. 'Has she still got the collywobbles over Toby's "proposal"?'

Ruby giggled. 'I reckon so, she couldn't stop fidgeting this morning. She dropped the bread and butter when she got them out the pantry earlier.'

Jess started a new row. 'Do you think he's going to propose, or do you think he meant something else?'

'Goodness knows,' said Ruby as she wrung the mop out into the bucket, 'although I did tell Penny I didn't think it very romantic for a feller to prewarn his beloved of his intentions.'

'Me too,' agreed Jess, 'which is why I reckon he was talking about something else. You don't tell a girl you've got a proposal to run by them if you're thinking of asking for her hand, or at least that's not how

Michelle's fiancé popped the question. He took her down the canal and got down on one knee.' She sighed wistfully. 'Midsummer's eve – so romantic!'

Ruby grimaced. 'Does Toby strike you as the romantic kind?'

Jess burst out laughing. 'Gosh, no! He's more likely to hide the ring under a whoopee cushion!'

It was a short while later when Jess finally cast off and held up Tom's scarf for Ruby's approval.

'Lovely!' confirmed Ruby. 'Now all you've got to do is wrap it up.'

Jess looked outside the window. 'Is that them?'

Ruby joined her, then nodded. 'Oh heck, they're even earlier than I imagined.' She pointed at Tom's scarf. 'You'd better hide that quickly before ...' As she spoke there was a brief knocking on the door before it opened.

Toby's face peered at them from around the door. 'Coo-ee! Can we come in?'

Jess rushed over to the sideboard and stuffed Tom's scarf behind the large mantel clock, hoping that would be sufficient to hide it from view, just as Toby and Tom entered the parlour. Tom walked over to her and took her hands. 'Happy birthday, love.'

Jess's eyes darted towards the sideboard just in time to see the last piece of scarf slip down the back. She breathed a sigh of relief as Tom took her in his arms and kissed her. He stood back, eyeing her quizzically. 'Everything all right?'

She nodded. 'Perfect!'

Later that evening after everyone had gone to bed, Jess stole downstairs, and lying on her stomach she groped around under the sideboard to see if she could catch hold of the scarf. She smiled as her fingertips located a soft piece of wool, which she carefully began to pull towards her, trying not to snag it on anything. She hoped there was not too much dirt on it as she would never have enough time to get it washed and dried before morning. She frowned. It seemed as though it was caught on something. Pulling gently, she was relieved to see that the scarf came out intact, but just like a fisherman's hook it had something caught on the end. She felt about in the dark and decided it must be some kind of book. She smiled hopefully. Perhaps it was a cookbook filled with old recipes for jam, chutneys and any number of tasty treats hidden among the pages. She opened the book and tried to peer inside, but it was far too dark to make out the contents. She folded the scarf neatly, then tucked the book under her arm and stole quietly upstairs and into the room she shared with Penny and Ruby. She padded across the floor and climbed into bed, stowing the scarf beneath her pillow along with the book. She grinned. For the first time in her life she could imagine what it must be like to be a child on Christmas Eve. Lying in bed with the mysterious book left by someone in the past, for her to find in the future, she couldn't wait to see what secrets lay within its pages come Christmas morning. With that in mind, she slowly drifted into a deep and happy sleep.

'Merry Christmas!'

Jess stared bleary-eyed at Ruby who was entering the room carrying a jug of water. She had been in the middle of a wonderful dream where she made the best pastries and pies in the entire NAAFI and they were about to give her an award for her efforts. Everyone, including Penny and Ruby, had been amazed at how she had become such an ingenious cook overnight, and ... she remembered the book. Fumbling beneath her pillow she pulled it out.

'What've you got there?' asked Ruby, pouring fresh water into the ewer.

'I found it last night when I went to retrieve Tom's scarf from under the sideboard.' Jess began to flick through the pages. 'Oh bother!'

'What?' said Ruby who had come over for a look.

'I thought it was going to be filled with marvellous recipes by some old woman who had written all her family's secrets down and hidden them away for safe-keeping only for me to discover them years later. Instead it's some scrapbook by ...' she frowned as she flicked through the pages '... dunno who it belongs to, I can't see a name anywhere.'

Ruby took the book from Jess and flicked from page to page. 'No recipes in here! Just a load of photographs and clippings.' She looked down at the page she was on. 'Recent clippings too, so whoever it belongs to hasn't long lost it.'

'Never mind,' said Jess. She took the book from Ruby and put it down on the bed beside her, then got up to take her turn at the basin. 'We'll just have to start a cookbook of our own.'

'What a great idea!' Ruby said enthusiastically, beginning to get dressed. 'I've often had the girls in the WAAF asking how we manage to make delicious cakes without using sugar, 'cos their mams want to know, or

346

how we make the pies so filling.' She gave Jess a look of approval. 'I reckon it would be really popular, we could even sell it.'

Penny, who was lying in her bed listening to the conversation, sat up on one elbow. 'I could do a puddings page!'

'We want to sell it,' giggled Ruby, 'not have folk ask us for compensation!'

'Oh, ha ha!' said Penny sarcastically. 'I'll have you know *some* people like my rock cakes.'

Ruby eyed her sympathetically. 'I don't know what you do to your rock cakes, but they come out so hard it's like cement is one of the ingredients, and I know you don't put anything different in than the rest of us.'

Penny shrugged. 'I've never been keen on cooking, and Mrs Armstrong said that's why my cakes never rise, and my pastry has a soggy bottom, because it knows my heart's not in it.'

Jess dabbed her face dry with the rough hand towel. 'I don't think flour, sugar and eggs can know how you're feeling, Penny, so it has to be something else.'

Penny climbed out of her bed and headed for the basin. 'Toby said he'd send me for cookery lessons as my Christmas present. Armstrong won't be happy if she finds out, she'll see it as a smear on her teaching.'

Jess raised an expectant brow. 'That reminds me, did he ever explain his proposal?'

Penny rolled her eyes. 'That was it! That he'd send me for cooking lessons.' She shook her head. 'I honestly don't think he thinks before he speaks sometimes.'

'So not for your hand in marriage?' Ruby verified.

'Golly, no!' said Penny with a sigh of relief. 'I like him an' all that, but even though we've been together for sixteen months, we've only seen each other on a handful of occasions – hardly a good grounding for marriage.'

Jess shrugged. 'I've not seen Tom more than a handful of times since we first met, but I know for certain he's the man for me.'

Ruby nodded. 'Same with George. I'd say yes tomorrow if he asked.'

Penny pulled a face. 'Do you really think you can know someone well enough to say yes if you've not seen them much?'

'If your heart says yes, then that's all that counts,' said Ruby decidedly. 'Besides, you must write to each other at least twice a week, and you telephone regularly. Just because you don't see each other in the flesh, doesn't mean to say you don't know him properly.'

Penny considered this, then nodded slowly. 'I suppose you're right, we do talk a lot over the phone.' She smiled. 'I know his favourite colour, and that he supports Everton, and that his favourite meal is scouse.'

Tom's voice called up the stairs. 'Are you girls coming down?'

'Be with you in a mo,' replied Jess.

The girls quickly dressed then hurried down the stairs to find Tom scraping off the burnt bits of toast over the sink. 'I'll have this slice seeing as it's my fault it's overdone, but there's more under the grill for those who want it.'

Ushering him to one side, Jess took the toast from his unresisting fingers and threw it into the bin. 'I know you fellers'll eat anything, but there's no need for you to be eating charcoal on Christmas Day! I'd hate for your mother to think I couldn't feed you properly.'

Grinning, he took a seat by the table. 'My mam knows I'm not fussy when it comes to food, as long as it comes in large quantities.'

Ruby carried a pan over to the stove and set it to boil. 'Well, for breakfast we've got porridge and toast, so you'll not starve.'

'Sounds heavenly!' said Toby. 'Will you be making any of it, Penny?'

Penny shot him a withering look. 'No, I won't, so you needn't worry about going hungry!'

Tom raised an eyebrow at Toby. 'Cookery classes not go down well, then?'

Penny intervened before Toby could reply. 'They're a lovely idea, and I shall make the most of them. I just thought I'd get in first before Toby made any jokes about my porridge.'

Toby grinned. 'Last time Penny made porridge, it stuck to me chops! I reckon she could sell it as denture glue, what tastes like porridge.'

Ruby stifled a giggle. 'Poor Penny.'

Tom slid his arm lovingly around Jess's waist as she placed a mug of tea down in front of him. 'This one doesn't need cookery lessons, that's for certain.' He looked at the others. 'Seeing as Penny already knows what her present is, does that mean we can open ours?'

Jess gave a squeal of delight. 'I'll go and get yours, I left it upstairs.'

Tom held her by the elbow. 'Before you do …' He held out a small package which Jess dutifully unwrapped.

She took a short breath. 'Oh, Tom! It's beautiful!' She held on the palm of her hand the thinnest silver chain on the end of which hung a small turquoise pendant.

Tom beamed as he placed it round her neck. 'It's your birthstone.'

Jess admired the blue stone which hung around her neck. 'It's so thoughtful, Tom. Did you make it yourself?'

He smiled sheepishly. 'Not this time, although I did carve the wooden box, I gave you yesterday …'

Jess's mouth dropped open. 'The jewellery box!'

He nodded. 'The one you said you hadn't got much jewellery to keep inside it 'cos you wear my first present all the time …'

Jess beamed at him. 'I have now!' Standing on tip-toes, she kissed his cheek, before rushing off upstairs, to return a few minutes later with his scarf wrapped in tissue paper. 'I made this for you.'

Tom took the gift from her hands and pulled out the scarf, which he admired greatly before winding it around his neck. He nodded to the book in her hands. 'What's that?'

She looked down at the book. 'I found it last night, and I thought I'd bring it down so that we could all take a look, see if we could find out who it belonged to.' She looked at the back of the book. 'I can't see a name, so maybe the photos will give us a clue.'

She placed it on the table, then stirred the porridge as Penny gave Toby the socks which she had knitted for him. 'Merry Christmas, Toby, although if you carry on making digs at my cooking I'll give you a thick ear next year!'

Toby laughed. 'I won't be able to take the mick once you've started those lessons.'

Jess sat down at the table and began to flick through the first few pages. She glanced at the various cuttings, then looked up at Tom who was accepting a bowlful of porridge from Ruby. 'I reckon whoever it is has to be in the WAAF, because these girls are all in WAAF uniform.' She turned the page so that he could see the cuttings.

Tom nodded, a spoonful of porridge poised before his lips. 'A driver too, if that cutting is anything to go by.'

She looked at the cutting in question and nodded her agreement. It was referring to a record number of passes in the Pwllheli Motor Transport division. She turned the page and gave a short squeal of excitement. 'It's a clipping about this place!' She ran her finger down the column. 'It's talking about a woman who broke her leg on one of the winches ...'

Toby's spoon clattered into his bowl. 'That's the woman I came to replace!' Getting up from his seat, he came around the table and leaned over Jess's shoulder. 'Whoever this belongs to must've been here the same time as me, although it was a while ago now.'

Jess shifted to a more comfortable position in her seat. 'Do you recognise anyone in these photographs?' She continued to look through the book, then she stopped short. 'Is it me, or does the woman in this photograph ...' She peered closer. 'Crikey.'

Toby looked at the photograph which had caught Jess's attention. He prodded it with his finger.

'I knew I'd seen you before!' he said with triumph. 'Only that's not you ...'

The others came around to see what all the fuss was about. Tom blew a deep whistle. 'I'd never have believed it.'

Ruby looked at Toby. 'No wonder you thought you'd already met Jess.'

Jess stared down at the photograph. The woman looked identical to Jess in every way, except the photograph was in black and white. She addressed Toby. 'Can you remember what colour her hair was?'

Nodding, he swallowed a mouthful of porridge before speaking. 'Same as yours, and I think her eyes were green too.'

Jess felt an icy chill sweep her body. 'Can you remember her name?'

'I only saw her for a short while. I dropped them off to see the balloons, I couldn't have spoken to her for more than five minutes.' He gave her an apologetic smile. 'Sorry I can't be of more help.'

Taking the book from Toby, Jess scrutinised every page but found nothing, until Penny came up with the bright idea of looking at the underneath of each photograph. 'Sometimes people write their names on the back.'

Jess carefully removed the photograph of the woman who resembled herself with a tall blonde woman and looked at the back. 'It says "girls on their hols".' She turned back to the front page and was about to start methodically looking through the book when Ruby's sharp eyes detected some faint writing in the bottom corner. She leaned in.

'It says *If found please return to ACW Lucy Jones.*'

Toby snapped his fingers. 'That's her! The one I came to replace – Lucy Jones! It must be her scrapbook.'

'Where is she now?' Jess asked.

Toby shook his head. 'Not a clue. I wasn't here for long and I've not seen her since ...' He rubbed his chin thoughtfully. 'The other girls told me where they were going next, though – it had something to do with a brewery as I recall.'

Penny laughed. 'Don't be daft! They don't have breweries in the WAAF.'

He waved her into silence as he continued to rack his brains. 'It sounded like a brewery, or something to do with a pale ale or beer.' He stared at Jess. 'Harrowbeer! That's where they've gone!'

Jess snapped the book shut. 'How far is it from here?'

Tom shrugged. 'Never heard of it. We can look it up on the map, though.' He got up from his seat. 'Shan't be a mo.'

Ruby sat next to Jess and placed an arm around her shoulders. 'How d'you feel?'

Jess continued to stare at the photograph. 'Like someone's walked over my grave.' She gave Ruby a look filled with hope and apprehension. 'Do you think we might be related? Cousins or something?'

Ruby looked from Jess to the photograph and back again. 'You certainly look very alike, although it's hard to see her properly with her WAAF cap on, and of course you can't see her hair properly ...'

Toby sat down at the table. 'Take it from me, they're like two peas in a pod. If I were to guess I'd say you were sisters, but that can't be right.'

Jess felt her stomach lurch unpleasantly and she was grateful when Tom returned with the map in hand. He spread it out on the table and they all looked for Harrowbeer.

'Got it!' Penny cried out after a few minutes of fruitless searching.

Tom placed one finger on Harrowbeer, and another on Yeovil. 'She's not that far away.'

'Are you going to go and find her?' asked Penny, eager for answers behind the mysterious girl in the photograph.

Jess looked at her aghast. 'And say what exactly?'

Tom pulled a face. 'I don't think you'd need to say anything at all. I should imagine she'll have a few questions of her own when she claps eyes on you.'

Jess held her head in her hands. 'I can't go wading into someone else's life just because she looks a bit like me.'

Tom raised his brow. 'Come on, Jess, it's more than a bit.'

'All right, very much like me, but what if ...' Her gut wrenched at the thought which had just entered her head, rendering her temporarily speechless. She looked at Tom through tear-brimmed eyes then tried again. 'What if she's living with my parents, none the wiser that I even exist? Maybe they already had one baby and didn't want another one.'

Toby spoke quietly. 'You mean she really might be your sister?'

Jess shrugged miserably. 'I don't know, Toby, because I'm an orphan, but ...' She pointed at the photograph wordlessly. 'It's not fair for me to go bursting into someone else's life.'

'If she's your sister then she has every right to know!' said Ruby, taking a seat next to Jess's. 'You'd want to know if it was you.'

Tom took a deep breath. 'There is someone we can ask.' His eyes flicked up to meet Jess's. 'We always did think my Auntie Edna was keeping something from us – maybe this is the answer.'

Jess nodded. 'It makes sense when you think about it. She probably felt guilty knowing that my parents already had a child.'

Tom put his arm around her and pulled her close so that her head rested against his chest. 'That's why she didn't want us anywhere near each other, she didn't like lying to you.' He put a hand to his forehead. 'I can see why she didn't say anything. It would be a horrible thing to tell someone, especially when you've no proof.'

Toby pushed his chair back from the table. 'I'll ask around in the MT section, someone's bound to know where Lucy is. When I find her I could ask her a few questions without raising suspicion – I can even say I found her scrapbook.' He held up a finger. 'Now I come to think of it, she's a Scouser same as me.' He cast Jess a look of sympathy. 'So were her pals.'

Jess shook her head slowly as the enormity of the situation sank in. 'I've got to see her for myself, but first,' she broke off and turned to Tom, 'can I come with you to see your auntie?'

'Of course you can!' Tom said quickly. 'Hellfire, Jess, you're the very reason why I'll be going, and we're taking this photograph with us.'

Jess put her hand on his. 'Your auntie's old, Tom, she might find it easier to talk to you alone.'

He twinkled down at her. 'I told you from the beginning, we're in this together, so stop worrying about other people and start concentrating on yourself for a change. Besides, I think you deserve to hear what she has to say first-hand.' He stood up and collected his winter coat from behind the door. 'Come on, princess, let's go for a walk in the snow. It'll do you good to get out in the fresh air, clear your head.'

Jess smiled. Tom always knew the right thing to say or do to make her feel better. She donned her winter jacket and wellies. 'Just think, if I hadn't found that book, I might never have known!'

'Where did you find it?' said Tom curiously.

Jess relayed the tale of how she'd had to hide his scarf when he had arrived earlier than expected.

Penny's eyes grew wide. 'If that isn't fate then I don't know what is.'

Toby pulled a face. 'It certainly is one heck of a coincidence.'

'Uncanny,' Jess agreed. She stepped out into the crisp snow and called back to Tom. 'You'll need your hat – it's freezing out here!'

She stood for a moment and admired the serenity before her. The airfield was barely visible under the thick blanket of snow which sparkled in the morning sun. As of yet, no one had ventured out, so it was still fresh and untouched. She smiled back at Tom who was pulling his hat down over his ears. 'Isn't it beautiful?'

He nodded. 'Idyllic. You'd not think there was a war on when it's as quiet and peaceful as this.'

She placed her hand through the crook of his elbow. 'The girl in the photograph,' she hazarded, 'it still might be a coincidence, don't you think?'

Tom looked doubtful. 'I would find it harder to believe that you weren't related.'

She followed him through the gate which he had managed to pull open enough for them to pass through. 'As soon as I saw that photograph, it was almost as though she were calling out to me, willing me to look for her.'

He squeezed her arm. 'And we will, together.'

She looked up at the underside of his chiselled chin, and the small curls which hugged the nape of his neck. Apart from Ruby, and now Penny, she had never had anyone look out for her before, although it was more a case of them looking out for each other. Tom, on the other hand, was very much in charge. He had made it plain that he would take care of her and he had remained true to his word. He hadn't missed a beat when it came to helping her find out the truth surrounding the night of her birth. She felt confident that no matter what the future held it would be a lot better with Tom by her side.

'You do think I'm doing the right thing, don't you, Tom?'

He put his arm around her shoulders and pulled her close, kissing the top of her head. 'I thought I brought you out for a walk in order to clear your head and take your mind off things?' He stopped walking and turned her to face him. 'You can think up different scenarios, ponder over the whys and wherefores and contemplate until you're blue in the face, but it won't make one iota of difference, nor, I might add, will it make you feel any better, so try and put it out of your mind until you've had a chance to talk to Auntie Edna. She's the only one who can answer your questions, or at least I hope she can.' He looked around them. 'Let's make a snowman, like we did when you were in Seaforth. That will help take your mind off things.'

Hugging him tightly, Jess laid her head against his chest. 'I don't know what I'd do without you, Tom Durning.'

Tom kissed the top of her head again. He was pleased he could be of help to Jess. He hated seeing her in distress, and if finding the mysterious woman in the photograph would make her happy, then he would move heaven and earth in order to do so.

Chapter Eight

March 1943

Jess looked up through the windscreen at the familiar row of terraced houses. It felt like years instead of months had passed since the discovery of the scrapbook. Tom had been on manoeuvres which had taken him all over the southern part of England, and getting leave had proved difficult. Toby had managed to find out where Lucy Jones was stationed but had agreed he wouldn't ring her until Tom and Jess had spoken to Aunt Edna.

Tom looked across at Jess, who was a bag of nerves. 'You've not done anything wrong,' he reminded her, 'you're simply asking for the truth.'

She smiled back at him. 'Then why do I feel so guilty?'

Leaning over, he chucked her under the chin. 'Because you're a kind, caring woman who doesn't want to make others feel uncomfortable, even when it comes at the expense of her own happiness.'

The front door opened and Tom's mother beckoned them inside, calling, 'Don't just sit there, come on in!'

Jess and Tom exchanged glances. 'Best foot forward and all that,' Tom said as he exited the car.

Jess's heart was in her mouth as she entered the small terraced house. She smiled briefly at Sylvie who stood in the parlour, her arms open wide ready to receive her son. Taking him in a firm embrace, she looked over his shoulder at Jess and the smile dissolved. A frown formed on her brow. 'Is everything all right?'

She leaned back from Tom, her eyes searching his face for answers. He looked past his mother. 'Where's Auntie Edna?'

Sylvie cocked her head in the direction of the back yard. 'In the lavvy, why?'

Before he could answer they were interrupted by a yell from outside. Sylvie excused herself. 'Coming, Auntie!'

She returned with Edna a few minutes later. She settled the old woman in front of the fire before turning to Tom and Jess. 'Cup of tea?'

'Not just yet, Mam,' Tom said as he pulled two of the ladder-backed chairs away from the table and placed them in front of his great-aunt. He sat in one and gestured for Jess to take the other.

Aunt Edna looked from one to the other, her face grey with fearful anticipation. Her gaze finally settled on Jess, and seeming to come to a conclusion, she nodded slowly. 'You know, don't you?' The words left her lips in barely a whisper.

Jess felt the hairs on the back of her head stand on end. 'So it's true? She – she's my sister?'

Shamefaced, the old woman nodded. 'How did you find out?'

Hardly able to believe what she was hearing, Jess looked at Tom. 'Have you got it?'

Nodding, Tom pulled the photograph out from his jacket pocket and handed it to his aunt. 'We found this in a scrapbook.'

Taking it in her hands, Edna looked at it briefly before asking for her spectacles, which her niece dutifully handed to her. She held them up and nodded, then handed them back to Sylvie. A tear dripped off the end of her nose, landing in her lap. She looked up at Jess, her eyes brimming with tears. 'I'm so sorry,' was all she could manage before burying her face in her hands.

Jess sank down to her knees and placed her arms around the older woman. 'Don't worry, we don't blame you.'

Sylvie gestured towards the photograph. 'May I?'

Aunt Edna handed her the photograph in answer.

Sylvie examined the photograph briefly before handing it back to Tom. She gave her aunt a disappointed but sympathetic look. 'So that's why you've been like a cat on a hot tin roof whenever Jess's name is mentioned.'

Aunt Edna nodded solemnly.

Sitting back down, Jess smiled encouragingly at her. 'I think it's time you unload yourself from the guilt you've been carrying around all these years, don't you?'

Edna heaved a sigh. She had been dreading this day would come, but now it had, she felt a sense of relief that she could finally unburden herself of her secrets. 'I was speaking the truth when I said I didn't know who your parents were.'

Jess nodded. 'You just couldn't tell me that I have a sister.' She drew a deep breath, bracing herself for the answers to come. 'Did they bring her with them – to the hospital, I mean?'

Edna frowned. 'What do you mean?'

Jess shrugged. 'I'm guessing you knew about my sister because they brought her with them when my mum was giving birth to me?'

Edna stared at Jess in confusion, then after a moment or two the older woman's mouth dropped open. 'Oh, Jessica sweetheart, you don't understand. She's not just your sister, she's your twin!'

Jess stared at Aunt Edna in disbelief. 'You're wrong,' she mumbled, 'you must be ...' She looked imploringly at the older woman but Edna remained resolute.

'I'm so sorry, Jess,' Edna murmured. 'I wasn't sure at first but the more I thought about it the more I was certain that I was right.' She glanced at Tom's breast pocket. 'And that photo proves it.'

Silent tears made their way down Jess's cheeks. Taking the handkerchief which Jess had given him as a Christmas present, Tom handed it to her. She dabbed her cheeks and looked at Edna for answers.

Sitting back in her wheelchair, Edna gazed into the fire as she relived the night of 24 December 1923. 'When they arrived at the hospital your father made it clear he wanted the birth to be a quick one. He didn't seem to care that babies come when they're ready, he wanted it over as quickly as possible. Your mother was only young,' she watched the flames which danced before her, 'how young I wouldn't like to say, but too young to be with a man his age.' She sighed. 'Your sister was born first.' She turned to face Jess. 'We were told to hand her over to a couple in the waiting room. Ours was not to question why, so we did as we were told.' At this point in the story she eyed Jess sincerely, imploring her to believe her next words. 'I thought they were waiting for you to be born, and that they'd leave as soon as you'd been brought to them.' Tears trickled down her cheeks once more as she continued to speak. 'I was flabbergasted when I learned they'd left without you.'

Sylvie sank heavily into the armchair behind Jess. 'They split up twins?'

Edna nodded, sobbing with the weight of the truth. 'I don't know why they did it, Jess, I swear I'd have said something if I'd known.'

Tears coursing down her cheeks, Jess nodded. 'I believe you.' She got up from her seat and placed her arms around Edna, and the two women held each other in a tight embrace.

Taking the handkerchief which Sylvie passed her, Jess handed it to Aunt Edna before turning to Tom. 'Who on earth would deliberately split up twins and why?'

Tom looked helplessly at her. 'I don't know but I will do everything I can to help you find out.' He turned to his aunt. 'Why didn't you say something sooner?'

The elderly woman looked at Tom, her eyes sparkling with tears. 'What was I meant to say, Tom? That I knew twins had been born in the hospital that night but I couldn't say for absolute certain that Jess was one of them? Even if I had, I couldn't tell Jess where her sister was or even if she was still alive. What good would that have done?

'None,' said Tom levelly, 'but you had no right to try and keep me and Jess apart.'

She dropped her head. 'I know, and I'm sorry, only I couldn't stand seeing Jess, suspecting something that I couldn't possibly tell her.' Her eyes flicked up to meet Jess's. 'I thought it would be easier if I never had to face you again, and for that, I am truly sorry.' She glanced at Tom. 'Please say you can forgive a foolish old woman?'

Tom opened his mouth huffily then shut it again. 'Of course I forgive you.'

She gazed at Jess hopefully.

Jess smiled. 'I understand it was difficult for you and you couldn't see a way out, and I can't imagine what it must have been like carrying around the guilt with you all this time. Of course I forgive you.'

Edna smiled thankfully. 'So, what next?'

Tom patted the photograph in his pocket. 'We shall telephone Toby to let him know he can ring Lucy – she's the one who owns the scrapbook. If she confirms Jess's sister is still in Harrowbeer then that will be our next port of call. First thing tomorrow morning.'

'I wish you both luck,' said Edna firmly. 'I hope you get the answers you're looking for, Jess, and if I can help, then just ask.'

Jess gently squeezed Edna's fingers. 'We will, and please don't blame yourself for this. You weren't the one playing silly beggars with other people's lives.'

Aunt Edna eyed Jess cautiously. 'Be careful where your journey takes you, Jessica dear. That man was a force to contend with. I remember what you said about that woman from the orphanage who had a run-in with him when he abandoned you. I believe her when she says he went to hit her with that horrible cane of his, and I'm afraid to say that even though he'll be older now than he was then, it wouldn't surprise me if he still stooped to violence should he feel cornered. After all, a man who'd treat his own children in such a manner has little conscience.'

Tom clasped Jess's hand. 'Don't you worry, Auntie, I'll be with her every step of the way. If he wants to get violent, he'll have to answer to me first!'

Penny and Ruby jiggled with nervous anticipation as they waited for Toby to come off the phone.

'Well?' said Penny as he replaced the receiver. 'What did she say?'

He sat down next to them. 'She remembers me and was really pleased that I'd found her scrapbook. I told her I recognised the photo of her friends and asked after them. She said they were still in Harrowbeer and that she'd be going to see them herself in a few weeks. I'm afraid I told her a little white lie by saying that a couple of pals of mine were heading that way tomorrow and suggested they could leave it with one of her pals, only I couldn't remember their names.' He shrugged. 'She said that would be fine and gave me their names – I've written them down so that I don't forget.'

He pushed the paper towards the girls. Penny and Ruby looked briefly before shaking their heads. 'Never heard of them.'

Ruby eyed the phone which was being used by a WAAF. 'When will you tell Jess and Tom?'

'As soon as they get back.'

*

365

It was much later that evening when Tom pulled Olly onto the parking area in front of the house.

Ruby, Penny and Toby appeared in the front garden before Jess had time to get out of the car.

Ruby was the first to speak. 'What happened? The suspense is killing us!'

'Let's go inside and put the kettle on,' said Jess. 'I'll tell you all as soon as I've sat down.'

As the kettle came to the boil Jess finished her story.

Ruby wiped the tears from her cheeks. 'No wonder she didn't want to tell you … .' Adding in almost a whisper. 'Twins!'

Penny shook her head. 'I hope I never meet your father, because I can't guarantee I won't give him a good slap across his chops.'

Toby whistled between his teeth. 'I wonder if your sister knows the truth?'

Jess nodded a little uncertainly. 'I'd assume so, although I suppose we'll not know until we meet her. It's not something I'd thought of.'

'She's nineteen years old. I'm sure they'll have told her by now – it's not as if she's a kid,' Tom said reasonably. 'You never know, she might even be searching for you.'

Jess brightened. 'I hadn't thought of that!'

'There you go, she might be really pleased to see you, especially if she's been searching for a long time.'

Jess settled back into her seat. No matter how bad things got, Tom always made everything better.

It was the morning of their trip to Harrowbeer and Jess was in the kitchen making porridge. She smiled at Tom as he came down the stairs. 'Couldn't sleep?'

Yawning, he shook his head. 'All I could think of was what we would say when we meet her for the first time.'

Jess's stomach fluttered in anticipation. 'Me too. It didn't help that I had a dream that she told me she wasn't born in Glasgow and that I'd got the wrong woman.'

Tom winced as the kitchen chair he was pulling out scraped noisily across the tiled floor. 'It never occurred to me that it might be the wrong twin.' He screwed his face up in thought. 'That would be far too much of a coincidence, surely to goodness?'

Jess nodded. 'Just my nerves getting the better of me.'

Ruby was the next to enter the kitchen. 'It's barely six o'clock!'

'Sorry,' said Jess with a guilty grimace, 'did we wake you?'

Ruby shook her head in a disgruntled fashion. 'No, I've been awake on and off for ages. I'm that nervous about today, I wish I was coming with you.'

Jess tapped the wooden spoon against the side of the saucepan and placed it in one of the empty bowls. 'I'll let you know what happens as soon as I know anything myself,' she assured her friend. She glanced at Tom from under her lashes. 'I hope you know how much I appreciate all the juggling you've been doing so that you can be with me, because I do, very much so.'

Tom put his mug back on the table. 'I know you do, princess, but believe me, wild horses couldn't keep me away.'

Jess looked at Ruby. 'Are you going back to bed for a bit, or stopping down here for some porridge?'

'I'll get washed and dressed then come back down for breakfast.' Ruby nodded at the kettle. 'Can I use some of that for washing?'

Jess nodded and poured some into a jug, then handed it to her friend. 'Careful, it's hot.'

She watched as Ruby disappeared up the wooden staircase. 'I've known that girl all my life, and I can't think of anyone who could come close to replacing her. I hope she doesn't worry that I'll forget about her if this woman does turn out to be my twin, because she couldn't be further from the truth.'

Tom sat back as Jess placed a bowl of porridge down in front of him. 'Not our Ruby,' he said with conviction, 'she knows you'd never do that to her.'

Taking some toast from under the grill, Jess dabbed it with Marmite before joining him at the table. 'Good! She means the world to me, does our Ruby. We've been through thick and thin together.'

Tom blew onto a hot spoonful of porridge. 'I was talking to Toby last night and he said Penny and Ruby are both worried for you.'

Jess gave a small smile. She knew her friends would be as anxious as she was for everything to go smoothly and that they would find it incredibly difficult not to be with her when she faced one of the biggest moments of her life, but as she'd said to Ruby when they'd gone to bed the night before, 'It would be too overwhelming for the poor girl if we all turned up at once.'

Ruby and Penny had reluctantly agreed. 'I would say make sure Tom takes care of you,' Ruby had said, 'only I know he will. He's very protective over you.'

She watched him now as he scraped his spoon round the bottom of his bowl. Most men would have run for the hills had they found out she was an orphan with a vicious father, but Tom wasn't put off by her past in the slightest. He had taken Jess's side when he suspected his aunt might be holding secrets from them, even driven her all the way to Liverpool just so that she could uncover the truth. She took a bite out of her toast. He was her knight in shining armour, someone who watched over her and looked after her. She smiled as she remembered how he had once quipped that if she was Cinderella that must make him her Prince Charming. He had been joking at the time, but the more Jess thought about it the more she realised it was a pretty good way to describe him. Just like Prince Charming with Cinderella, he was helping her to find something, only instead of a glass slipper it was her sister, and he had travelled the length and breadth of the country in order to make sure that she found her happy ever after. She nodded. It may have been said in jest, but then again, so was many a true word.

Pulling up in front of the gate at Harrowbeer base, Jess sat quietly as the guard spoke to Tom. Barely looking at Jess, he waved them through and she watched the gate close behind them in the rear-view mirror. She smiled nervously at Tom. 'That was the easy part.'

He parked the car and looked around. 'The place looks deserted.' He indicated a man in pilot's uniform. 'I'll see if he knows anything.' He hopped out of the car and jogged round to let Jess out, only she was already shutting her door. He held out a hand which Jess gladly took.

As they walked towards the man he turned to face them, and Jess knew instantly that he must be a friend of her sister's, by the way he was staring at Jess.

Tom cleared his throat. 'I wonder if you could help us ...' He told the pilot the names of the girls they were after.

The man gave a short, mirthless laugh, then, when they failed to laugh with him, he continued to stare at them in disbelief. 'Is this some kind of joke?'

Tom shook his head, but Jess was already speaking. 'You know her, don't you?'

The man nodded slowly. 'You could say that, we dated for quite a while.' He frowned at her. 'Sorry if I appear rude, but just who are you?'

Jess swallowed before answering. 'My name's Jessica Wilson, and I really need to speak to her before I talk to anyone else.'

The man held out a hand. 'I'm Pete Robinson.' He shook Jess's hand then eyed her quizzically. 'I'd wager she isn't expecting you?'

Jess stared back, round-eyed. 'I should say not.'

He nodded thoughtfully. 'She doesn't know who you are, does she?'

Jess shook her head. 'That's why I really need to speak to her before speaking to anyone else.'

Pete nodded his comprehension. 'In that case, we'd better get you out of here, because you're certainly going to cause a lot of heads to turn, not to mention tongues to wag.' He turned his attention to Tom. 'Her boyfriend, Lenny, has taken her down to Batten Bay – they've not long gone. Do you know the way?'

Tom shrugged. 'It'll be on the map. Is it far?'

Pete nodded. 'Take you well over an hour, or it would if you were going by bus like they did, but I can see you've got a car so you should get there a bit quicker.'

They thanked him for his help and climbed back into the car. As they passed through the gate, Jess saw the look on the guard's face when he locked eyes with her and she turned to Tom. 'Did you see that?'

Tom nodded. 'He looked like Pete did when he first clapped eyes on you.' He raised his brow. 'I must say, I'm rather intrigued to see her for myself.'

Jess settled into her seat. 'From what Pete says, we've got at least an hour before we get there. I hope she's not already on her way back.'

'Not a chance,' said Tom decisively. 'You heard what he said, they've taken the bus, so unless they fancy a long walk home ...'

She breathed easily once more. She very much wanted to meet her sister, but at the same time she was growing increasingly nervous. What if the other girl didn't want to know? Jess could hardly blame her if that was the case. After all, what had Jess to offer her? She voiced her thoughts to Tom who dismissed them.

'I'd be very surprised if she wasn't at least a little bit curious,' he said reasonably, 'it's only human nature.'

Jess mulled this over. She supposed he was right. After all, she was eager to find her family so why should her sister be any different?

She looked at the high hedgerows as they drove by, and wondered what sort of life the other woman had lived compared to her own. She pulled out the photograph and examined the image. She looked happy enough. She tried to imagine what the other girl's family life might have been like. Did she have any other siblings? Had she lived in a cottage or a house? By the sea or somewhere like Liverpool? Had her parents told her she had a sister or that she was adopted? Had they even told her she was adopted? If they hadn't then this whole thing was going to come as a frightful shock, and Jess's presence could cause a rift in her family ... She looked at Tom, who was concentrating on the winding roads. Should she tell him to forget everything and head back to Yeovil? After all, what was the sense in carrying on just to blow someone else's world wide open and possibly ruin their lives? She opened her mouth to tell him to turn back when she remembered Pete. She sighed heavily. She couldn't tell Tom to turn back now. Pete would be bound to say something to the other girl, which would only leave her with questions, and when her pal Lucy turned up and asked about her scrapbook ... She shook her head. She had come too far.

'Penny for them?' Tom's voice cut across her thoughts.

'Believe me, you don't want to know,' she said.

He shrugged. 'Try me.'

'I was thinking this might not be such a good idea after all, but then I realised we've come too far, we've started the ball rolling and it's too late to stop it.'

Tom pulled the car to one side. 'You don't have to do anything you don't want to.'

372

Her bottom lip trembled as she looked at him. 'It would be unfair to back out now. Pete's seen me, and he's bound to ask her whether she met me, and then there's her pal Lucy ...'

Tom smoothed her cheek with the tips of his fingers. 'I'll stand by you no matter what your decision. Remember, we're in this together.'

She smiled weakly at him. 'Just as you've been right from the start. It's good to know I can depend on you.'

He smiled. 'Always.'

She smiled back. In Greystones they were always told to thank the Lord for everything they had – something which none of the orphans wanted to do as they weren't thankful for being in the orphanage – but when it came to Tom, Jess very much gave thanks that she had found him.

It felt like hours before they eventually reached Batten Bay. Tom pulled into a lay-by along the sea front. Jess got out of the car and stared at the mass of barbed wire. Her shoulders fell. 'Why on earth did he tell us to come down here? No one in their right minds would want to spend the day looking at barbed wire. Do you think he gave us the right place?'

Tom shrugged. He had to admit it did seem a strange place to take someone on a date, but they had both heard Pete, and he had been very clear in his instruction. Tom looked around them. Across the road from where they stood there was a small café, but there was hardly anyone in it. He glanced at the many shops which lined the street, but most of them were closed. He turned back to Jess.

'He must have meant somewhere else – either that or there must be another Batten Bay?'

Jess shook her head as she peered up and down the beach. 'I can't see that. They must be round here somewhere …' She hesitated. 'Maybe we should go to the other side of the sea front? Or maybe they didn't realise what it was like until they got here.' She slid her arm through his. 'Perhaps they decided to go somewhere else?'

Tom looked at the barbed wire. 'Wouldn't surprise me, although I can't think why they'd want to come here in the first place.' He jerked his head in the direction of the car. 'Come on, princess, we'll go back to the airbase and wait for them there.'

Nodding, Jess got back into the car and waited for Tom to join her. He cranked the engine into life, put the handle into the boot and sat down behind the driver's wheel. He was looking over his shoulder to reverse when Jess placed a hand on his knee. 'Stop!'

Turning back, Tom looked at Jess, who was staring at a couple carefully picking their way through the fencing. At first he thought she was curious to see how they were managing to get through, but as he continued to look he realised it was far more than that. His jaw dropped. 'Blimey!'

Jess looked at him. 'Together?'

He nodded. 'Together!'

They got out of the car and Jess waited for Tom to join her before walking slowly towards the couple. As they neared them, Jess cleared her throat.

'Excuse me.' Once the words were out, Jess froze as the woman she believed to be her sister turned to face her. Whilst she had been prepared to see an identical version of herself, it was still unnerving, and it was a moment or two before she realised she was holding her breath.

Tom, too, found himself staring at the other woman, who was staring open-mouthed at Jess. He looked at her partner, who was also staring at Jess. Realising that someone had to break the ice, Tom was the first to speak. 'I think we ought to explain.'

The woman broke eye contact with Jess and looked at her partner. 'Am I dreaming again?'

He shook his head. 'If you are, then I'm in it too.' He turned to Tom. 'If you wouldn't mind.'

Several passers-by had stopped to stare. Jess pointed to the café across the road. 'Maybe somewhere a little more private?'

Crossing the road, they entered the café. Tom walked past the solo diner to a table at the back away from prying eyes. As they sat down the waitress walked over. She handed out the menus, then glanced around her potential customers. She opened her mouth to speak, then pointed at the girls. 'How lovely, twins!'

There followed an awkward silence, broken by Tom clearing his throat. 'We'll let you know when we're ready to order.'

Pulling a face, the waitress muttered that it was no skin off her nose and walked away.

The girl leaned forward and addressed Jess. 'If this is some kind of practical joke I don't find it very funny!'

Shaking her head fervently, Jess spoke quickly. 'I swear it's neither a dream nor a practical joke. I can understand it must be very confusing, because that's exactly how I felt when I saw your photograph.'

The girl furrowed her brow. 'What photograph?'

Jess drew a deep breath. 'The one I found in your pal's scrapbook – I believe her name's Lucy Jones?' She paused whilst the other girl nodded, then continued, 'I think it'd be better if I started at the beginning. I'm Jessica Wilson, and I was born in Glasgow on the twenty-fourth of December 1923. From what we can gather your name is Dana Quinn, and you were born on the same night in Glasgow – is that right?'

Dana nodded silently, tilting her head to one side as she studied Jess's face. 'You'll have to excuse me, only this is rather a lot to take in. I want to ask the obvious, but it's clear we're not only sisters but twins. The only thing I don't understand is how come you never came to live with me ...' She glanced down at her lap. 'Or did our mam keep you?'

Jess's eyes rounded with horror. 'No! Not at all! Our father left me on the steps of an orphanage.' She hesitated. 'You knew that you were adopted, then?'

Dana nodded. 'Although I only recently found out.' She held her hands up, then looked at Lenny. 'There's so much to explain.'

Lenny smiled and placed his hand over hers. 'One story at a time, cariad.' He caught the waitress's attention. 'I'd like tea for four, please,' he cocked a brow at the others, 'is that all right with everyone?' He waited for their consent before giving Jess an encouraging nod. 'Go ahead.'

Jess explained how she spent the first fifteen years of her life believing she was a foundling only to find out the day before she ran away that the staff at Greystones had met her father and knew where he hailed from. She went on to explain how she and Ruby had stayed at Tom's auntie's house and how she had been the matron in charge at the hospital the night she and Dana were born.

They all paused for a moment whilst the waitress distributed two pots of tea and four cups.

Once she had gone, Dana stared at Lenny. Tears pricking her eyes, she turned back to Jess. 'So you've been alone all this time, not knowing anything?'

Jess started to nod then changed her mind. 'I've had good friends with me the whole way.' She smiled at Tom. 'Tom's been my guiding star throughout everything. He's helped me to think straight, which wasn't always easy, especially when I saw your photograph.'

Dana gingerly reached out and took Jess's hand in hers. 'I'm glad you've had pals to help you through, and if it's any consolation Mam and Dad couldn't have known about you – there's no way they'd have split us up. You see, my mam and dad wanted kids more than anything in the world, and when they found out they couldn't have any they thought all was lost ...' She took a deep breath and wiped away her tears before continuing. 'Until a doctor offered them the opportunity to be parents of a new-born. Mam said they jumped at the chance before the doctor could change his mind.' She smiled grimly. 'There's not many people who would give up their baby to travellers ...'

It was at this point that Jess interrupted. 'Travellers?'

Dana nodded. 'I know a lot of people think badly of travellers, but they couldn't be more wrong when it

377

comes to my parents. They're the most loving, hard-working, loyal people you could ever wish to meet, although not everyone thinks that way, including one of the nurses who was reluctant to hand me over, as well as some grumpy old man ...' She clapped her hand to her mouth as her mother's words came back to her. 'I bet that was him!' She looked earnestly at Jess. 'Mam said there was an old man who disapproved of their taking me; she said he was foul-tempered and he kept muttering under his breath whilst they were waiting for me. Once I was in Mam's arms she said he got up and stormed out of the room. She assumed that he was something to do with the hospital, but from what you've said he might have been our father.' She tightened her grip of Jess's hand. 'I swear to you, Jess, my mam and dad would never have left you behind, and if she'd known he was our father she'd have given him what for!'

Tears seeped silently down Jess's cheeks. 'I'm so pleased you've said that, because I did think they might have rejected me the same as my mam and dad.' She spoke thickly through her tears, 'I thought I must have been the bad penny, not as pretty, or crying too much.'

Tom placed an arm around Jess's shoulders. 'Oh, my darling girl, why didn't you tell me that's what you thought?'

Jess shook her head. 'I didn't want to look like I was wallowing in self-pity.'

Dana squeezed Jess's hand tightly. 'You've every right to feel sorry for yourself, Jess.' She pushed her sister's hair back from her face. 'You deserved better in life. My mam and dad thought they'd deprived me of a good childhood, believing that I could have had better had I gone to another family – little did they know that had they left me be, I would have ended up in an orphanage.'

Jess nodded and her bottom lip quivered as she spoke. 'I'm glad they took you in. At least one of us had a decent childhood.'

Nodding, Dana did her best to hold back her tears. 'I wish Dad was still here. He'd have loved to have met you, and I could prove to him that he and Mam were right in taking me in.' She smiled at the memories. 'They gave me a wonderful childhood, surrounding me in love and allowing me to do the thing I loved the most, working with horses.'

Jess placed her other hand on top of Dana's. 'You say you wish your father was still here – does that mean you've lost him?'

Sniffing back the tears, Dana spoke softly. 'It was only a few months ago. I hadn't a clue anything was wrong until they called me into the office and said I was to go straight to Ireland as a matter of urgency ...' She took a deep breath before continuing. 'Like you, it's better if I start from the beginning ...'

Dana explained to Jess how her parents had moved from Scotland after her father had been cast out by the rest of the Quinn family for taking her in. 'I wasn't of traveller descent, you see, so they made Dad choose – me or them.' She smiled softly. 'He chose me.' She told her sister how they had settled in Liverpool where they stayed until the daylight bombing raids in 1940. 'We used to make our living by looking after the carters' horses,' Dana explained. 'When the bombing first started we moved to the countryside overnight, coming back to the city first thing in the morning, which worked fine until the daylight raids. After that, Dad decided it would be best for us to go back to Ireland, only I felt it was my duty to stay and fight for my country, which is how I wound up joining the WAAF. I hadn't a clue that I wasn't a Quinn until I visited my parents in Ireland – that's when they told me the truth.'

Jess shook her head sadly. 'So you lost your father and found out you were adopted all in one go?'

Her eyes sparkling with tears, Dana smiled feebly at Jess. 'I've gained a sister, though … and,' she held her hand up to show Jess, 'a fiancé.'

Jess beamed with happiness. 'The chap we spoke to, his name was Pete, said Lenny was your boyfriend.'

Dana smiled shyly. 'That's because Pete doesn't know yet – in fact, you're the first to hear the good news!'

Jess looked puzzled as an earlier thought entered her mind. 'When we first met, you asked Lenny if you were dreaming again. What did you mean by that?'

Dana nodded knowingly. 'To cut a long story short, Pete and I had a thing going until his Spitfire crashed over the English Channel.' She shrugged simply. 'Months went by, and with no evidence to the contrary we assumed him lost to the sea.' She glanced lovingly at Lenny. 'Me and Lenny have known each other since I first joined the WAAF, and when he came to Harrowbeer, we became an item, only to have Pete show up a few hours ago!'

Jess's eyes grew wide with surprise. 'And then we show up! Talk about having your fair share of surprises! Well, I reckon it's time things started going right for you,' she glanced at the ring on Dana's finger, 'and that's as good a start as any.' She smiled shyly. 'And I'm rather hoping my sudden appearance is too?'

Dana nodded fervently. 'I'll say it is! Just you wait 'til Mam hears she's got two daughters! She'll be cock-a-hoop.'

Jess smiled uncertainly. 'Do you really think so? Are you sure she won't feel as though I'm trying to take you away? She might be worried after losing your father ...' She got no further before Dana cut across her.

'Not a chance. Mam's always been "the more the merrier" type of person, and I know from what she's said that she always wanted a big family,' she giggled as she shot Lenny a sidelong glance, 'with lots of grandchildren.'

Lenny pulled an approving face. 'Fine by me.'

Jess eyed Dana fondly. 'Your mother sounds like a wonderful woman.'

'*Our* mother,' corrected Dana, 'and she is. You'll love her, and I know she'll feel the same way about you.' She smiled at Lenny. 'For the first time in a long while I feel like I'm the luckiest girl alive. I'm engaged to the man I love and I've gained a sister all in one day. I'm beginning to wonder what'll happen next.'

Jess spoke the thought uppermost in her mind. 'I know I've said our father seems a bit of a beast, but by all accounts our birth mam was only young,' her cheeks turned pink, 'very young, in fact, and that's why I want to find her, because she might not have had a say in what happened to us, and if that's the case I think she deserves to know what happened to her babies.' Her heart hammering in her chest, she continued, 'What do you say? Are you in?'

Dana glanced at Lenny, then turned back, nodding. 'You bet I am! Me and Lenny said we'd search for me birth mam after the war's over, and me bezzies said they'd like to help too.'

Jess grinned. 'I may not be a Scouser, but I do know that your bezzie is your best pal.'

'Yes, I don't know where I'd be without Lucy and Patty,' Dana said.

'Lucy Jones!' said Jess. 'She's the girl whose scrapbook I found.'

Dana looked curious. 'Where did you find it?'

'Behind the sideboard in our house in Yeovil,' said Jess. 'I was trying to hide Tom's Christmas present down the back, and when I went to retrieve it, I pulled out Lucy's scrapbook.'

Dana shook her head slowly. 'Well I'll be! Patty's mam would say that was fate.'

'I reckon I'd agree with her.' Jess looked into the teapot, which was empty. 'We've so much to catch up on. Shall we order some lunch?'

They all agreed that this would be a splendid idea, and spent the rest of the afternoon swapping stories and exchanging information in the seafront café. In fact, it was growing dark when Tom got up from his seat in order to stretch his legs. 'I think my bottom's gone numb,' he said, much to the amusement of the others.

Lenny also got to his feet with a slight grunt. 'My foot went to sleep ten minutes ago.' He stamped his foot on the floor. 'I've got pins and needles now.'

The girls followed suit and were surprised to find that they were just as stiff as the boys. A gasp escaped Jess's lips as she glanced at the clock above the counter. 'We've been here for hours!'

Tom grimaced. 'I'm afraid we're going to have to think about heading back.'

Jess looked out the window at the car before looking hopefully at Tom. 'Have we time to give them a lift back to Harrowbeer?'

Tom nodded. 'Of course we have, because I rather suspect they've already missed the last bus?'

The waitress, who was wiping down behind the counter, called out over her shoulder that the last bus had indeed already gone.

'Then that settles it,' Jess said. She slid her arm through Dana's and started to walk towards the door. 'I feel like I've known you for years.'

Dana squeezed Jess's arm. 'I feel the same way.' She gave a small shrug. 'Maybe it's because we're twins – some people think twins have a special kind of link.'

'I've heard that,' said Dana with interest. 'I think I read it in an article in one of the women's magazines, it was about how some twins know what each other is thinking.'

They climbed into the back seat of the car and looked at Tom and Lenny who were smiling at them.

'What?' said Jess to Tom.

'You're like two peas in a pod.' Tom grinned as he retrieved the crank handle from the boot.

Jess turned to Dana. 'I wonder what our birth mam will say when we turn up on her doorstep?'

'After all these years?' said Dana. 'I should imagine we'll come as quite the shock, if we find her, that is.'

Before Tom took his place behind the wheel he handed something to Jess, who gave a cry of alarm. 'Tom! I nearly forgot!' She passed the scrapbook to Dana. 'Toby told Lucy that we'd give you her scrapbook to look after.'

Dana took the book and began perusing the pages, occasionally pointing at a photograph and explaining to Jess who was who. The two girls nattered contentedly all the way back to Harrowbeer, where Dana asked if Jess and Tom had time to come and meet her friends.

Tom shook his head sadly. 'Sorry, but we'll be pushing it if we do, and I promised to have Cinders back before midnight!'

'Oi!' said Jess with a giggle. 'I thought I was your princess!'

'How could I forget?'

Jess got out of the car and waited for Dana to do the same before taking her in a warm embrace. 'We've got to meet up again, and the sooner the better.'

'Golly, yes,' agreed Dana. 'We've still got lots to catch up on, as well as making plans for the future.' She looked at the ring which encircled her finger. 'I hope you'll agree to be one of my bridesmaids?'

Jess nodded enthusiastically. 'I'd be delighted! I ummed and ahed about how today would go for the longest time, but I never dreamt it would turn out this well ...' She broke off as a woman hailed Dana.

Dana grinned at Jess. 'It's Patty! One of my pals that I told you about.'

Patty strode towards them. 'I think Pete's still suffering from his French escapades because …' She pointed at Jess then Dana. 'There's two of you! Blimey, so Pete wasn't exaggerating after all.'

Giggling, Dana threaded her arm through Jess's. 'Patty, meet Jess, my twin sister.'

Patty gawped at them for a moment before finding her voice. 'I don't understand! Who?'

Tom cleared his throat. 'Sorry, ladies, but we really are going to have to dash.'

Dana kissed Jess briefly on the cheek. 'Ta-ra, chuck, make sure you telephone Harrowbeer to let me know you got back safely.' She turned to Tom. 'Take good care of her, won't you?'

'Goes without saying,' said Tom with a wink.

He held the passenger door open for Jess, who wound down the window as she took her seat and then leaned out of her window to wave goodbye to Dana, Lenny and a rather stunned-looking Patty.

As soon as they were out of sight, Jess turned to Tom. 'I can't thank you enough for today. I don't think I'd have had the courage to face her alone, and I'm so glad I had you by my side.'

He grinned. 'Where else would I be?'

Having just gone through one of the most emotional days of her life, Jess smiled brightly before bursting into tears.

Tom pulled the car to one side. He reached across and cupped the side of her face in the palm of his hand. 'My poor, sweet princess, you've been through an awful lot these past few months. I expect all this has come as a huge relief.'

Looking up at him, Jess kissed the palm of his hand. 'Why me, Tom? Why settle for the chaff when you could've had the wheat? I know any number of girls who would be delighted to have you on their arm, and they don't come with half the problems I do, so why not one of them?'

Leaning forward, he kissed her gently before pulling back. 'Please stop putting yourself down, because I wouldn't have you any other way. You may see them as problems, but I see them as the things that have shaped you, and made you the woman you are today.' He kissed her softly on the lips. 'The same woman I fell in love with back when I first laid eyes on you in Edinburgh Road.'

Jess blushed in the darkness. 'I don't know what I've done to deserve you, Tom Durning.'

He smoothed her cheek with the back of his fingers. 'I'm the lucky one. I'll never forget the day I went to my auntie's house, ready to give some squatters their marching orders.' He shook his head with a chuckle. 'Never in a million years did I expect I'd meet the woman of my dreams.'

As he stroked the side of her face, Jess caught his wrist in her hand and pulled his fingers to her lips. She kissed his knuckles. 'I remember it well. You promised to look out for me and you kept that promise, helping me every step of the way and making sure you were never far from my side.'

Tom gazed into her eyes. 'I can't think of anywhere I'd rather be.' Cupping her face in his hands, he kissed her slowly.

Jess relaxed into the warmth and safety of his loving touch. Her life might have started out as something from the Brothers Grimm, but thanks to Tom it had soon turned into a fairy tale. She said as much, adding, 'You really did turn out to be my Prince Charming.'

'I'd like to think so.'

She smiled in the darkness. 'I've a long road ahead of me, Tom, and it might be a bit of a bumpy ride.'

'We've a long road ahead of us,' he corrected. 'Do you trust me to give you your happy ever after?'

Jess nodded. 'As long as you're with me I think that's pretty much guaranteed.'

As Tom beamed back, the moonlight glinted in his eyes. 'Always,' he murmured before taking her in his arms and kissing her softly.

KATIE FLYNN

A MOTHER'S JOY
Liverpool, 1939

Olivia Campbell appears to have the perfect life. However, behind closed doors she lives in constant fear of her abusive father, and has no support from her mother.

Longing for love and affection, she begins a relationship with Ted, a young lad who works in her father's factory. But her family disapprove of the relationship and forbid them from seeing each other.

When war comes to Liverpool, Olivia seizes the opportunity to leave behind her unhappy life and join the WAAF. There she meets fellow trainee Maude, and the two embrace their newly found independence. Soon Olivia meets the handsome Ralph, and all thoughts of Ted are brushed aside. Until he returns to her life with some shocking news that turns her world upside down . . .

AVAILABLE SPRING 2021
PRE-ORDER NOW

arrow books

READ IT NOW

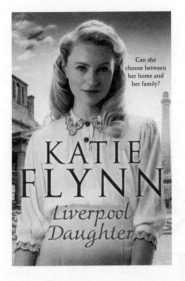

'Home is where the heart is, and my heart belongs to Liverpool.
We wouldn't dream of leavin' our beloved city . . .'

August 1940

As the Luftwaffe swarm over Liverpool, Shane Quinn
decides to move his family back to the safety of Ireland.
But his only child, the beautiful Dana, would rather stay
and serve her country than flee to a foreign land.

Determined to make it on her own, she joins the WAAF
with newfound pals Patty and Lucy. There's plenty of
excitement to be had on a RAF station, even a chance or
two at love . . .

But the stark reality of war begins to take its toll and the
three girls soon discover they need their friendship more
than ever. And when shocking news arrives from Ireland,
Dana will realise the true importance of family.

AVAILABLE IN PAPERBACK AND EBOOK

arrow books

KATIE FLYNN

If you want to continue to hear from the
Flynn family, and to receive the latest news about
new Katie Flynn books and competitions,
sign up to the Katie Flynn newsletter.

Join today by visiting
www.penguin.co.uk/katieflynnnewsletter